He heard a rumble, felt a blast of warm air from the tunnel mouth, smelled its familiar odour of dust and metal.

The train was coming.

About bloody time.

The mass of people on the platform prepared itself for the impending squeeze onto the tube, ready to fill every available gap.

Hyde saw lights in the tunnel, heard the rumbling grow louder.

Soon be home now.

The train burst from the tunnel like some oversized, jet-propelled worm, the blast filling the station.

Hyde thought about Maggie and smiled.

He was still smiling when he threw himself in front of the train.

STOLEN ANGELS

SHAUN HUTSON

WARNER BOOKS

A *Warner* Book

First published in Great Britain in 1996 by
Little, Brown and Company
This edition published by Warner Books in 1997

A CIP catalogue record for this book is
available from the British Library

ISBN 0 7515 0125 5

Typeset in Palatino by M Rules
Printed and bound in Great Britain by
Clays Ltd, St Ives plc

Warner Books
A Division of
Little, Brown and Company (UK)
Brettenham House
Lancaster Place
London WC2E 7EN

Children begin by loving their parents. After a time they judge them. Rarely, if ever, do they forgive them.

Oscar Wilde

Acknowledgements

What follows, is, as usual, a list of people, places or things which have been used, abused or welcomed, before, during or after the writing of this novel. People who have helped in some way, places which have been invaluable (for various reasons) and 'things' that have smoothed the way and sometimes just a furrowed brow. Yes, I know I'm rambling. Here's the list:

Very special thanks to my Manager, Gary Farrow, especially for his cheerful messages, gloating over my sleepless nights and general piss-taking. What are friends for? By the way, it's your turn for lunch . . .

Many thanks to my publishers and everyone connected with them especially to Barbara Boote and to my ever ready, ever fired up sales team. If there were seven of them I'd call them magnificent. There *aren't* so I'll make do with superb . . .

Thank you to Cathy Cremer (who died so elegantly, even if it wasn't in Harrods . . .), to Jo Bolsom, Dee Bhundie, Zena, Karen Crane, Malcolm Dome, Jerry Ewing, Phil Alexander, Graham Rogers, James Whale, Gordon Hopps, Neil Leaver, 'Maxim' magazine, Merck Mercuriadis, Sanctuary Music and Iron Maiden. Special thanks, too, to Sarah Cousar, Simon Wady, John Martin and Graham Joyce.

Thanks, as ever, to Mr Wally Grove, a wonderful living

embodiment of all that is politically *in*correct. Take care, mate.

Thanks also to Ian Austin, human dustbin and 'trucker'. To Martin 'Gooner' Phillips, to Jez, Terri, Rebecca and Rachel.

For those who guard my money another special thank you. To Jack Taylor and Tom Sharpe at the Clydesdale Bank. To Damian and Christina Pulle, Amin Saleh and Lewis Bloch.

Thanks to UCI, the Point 10 in Milton Keynes where I seem to spend most of my bloody time these days . . . Thanks also to Duncan Stripp, the Barry Norman of the phone lines (well, *my* phone lines anyway . . .).

Indirect thanks to Metallica, Megadeth, Trent Reznor, Lard, Clannad, Queensryche, Sam Peckinpah and Martin Scorsese.

Many thanks too are due to the Adelphi Hotel in Liverpool, the Holiday Inn, Mayfair, The Athaeneum in London, The Rihga Royal in New York, The Hotel Imperial in Vienna and the Elbow Beach Hotel in Bermuda.

Special thanks to Hailey Owen at Platinum Services, organiser supreme, talker *extraordinaire*.

Thanks to Yamaha Drums, Zildjian Cymbals, Promark sticks and Remo heads. To Chas. Foote's in London and Chappells in Milton Keynes.

Thanks also to Fraser's in The Strand.

Extra special thanks to all the doctors, nurses, midwives and other staff at Milton Keynes Hospital and Westfield Road surgery in Bletchley who helped in any way, shape or form before, during and after the birth of our beautiful daughter. We are indebted to you all.

Many thanks to Liverpool Football Club, a constant source of pride, pleasure and occasional sore throats. To all in the Bob Paisley suite, especially Sheila, Jenny and Joan. Thanks also to Steve Lucas, another glorious example of how fatherhood does not make a man more mellow (not between three o'clock and quarter to five on a Saturday, anyway . . .). Thanks to Paul Garner too, a mine of information, a fading beacon of sportsmanship surrounded by fanaticism (or three fanatics at least, while he's having his lunch . . .).

Many thanks to my Mum and Dad, the world's finest parents now become the world's greatest grandparents.

Extra special thanks to my wife, Belinda, who continues to love and support me and who presented me with such a precious gift in November '95. Thank you.

As ever this book is for you, my readers. I thank you for your continued support, those who have been with me from the beginning and those just joining the ride.

Let's go.

Shaun Hutson

For my daughter

PART ONE

Hell is for children.
And you shouldn't have to pay for your love
With your bones and your flesh

Pat Benatar

Do you hear the children weeping, O my brothers,
Ere the sorrow comes with years?

Elizabeth Barrett Browning

One

If he hurried, he might just make it, thought Peter Hyde as he scuttled across the crowded concourse of Euston Station. He glanced at his watch, apologising as he bumped into a woman dragging a large suitcase on a set of wheels. It looked as if she was taking the luggage for a walk, Hyde mused, weaving his way through the maze of bodies which thronged the busy area.

He was torn between the options of using his brief-case as a weapon to clear a path through the milling throng or holding it close to him in case he accidentally struck anyone with it. Ahead of him he saw a young man with an enormous back-pack turn and slam into an older man in a grey suit who was sweating profusely, perspiration beading on his bald head. The suited man slapped angrily at the back-pack and marched towards the platforms.

Hyde glanced beyond him and saw what he sought.

He had minutes if he was lucky.

Would there be time?

He pushed past two porters who were standing pointing at the huge departures and arrivals board which towered over the concourse and he heard them speaking loudly to a foreigner who was having diffi-culty understanding their accents. Hyde thought that it would have been hard enough for someone English to

3

decipher the words of the porters, jabbering away as they were in a curious combination of South Asian tinged Cockney.

Not far now.

Another few yards and he should make it.

He saw his objective come into view.

Up above him, the huge clock on the board clicked round to 18.00 hours.

Now or never.

The doors were actually closing before him.

Hyde slipped through the narrow gap and smiled broadly at the assistant in the Knickerbox shop.

'I know you're closing,' he said, smiling even more broadly. 'I won't keep you two minutes.'

The assistant, a girl in her teens wearing an enormous pair of Doc Martens, nodded and returned to her till where she was cashing up.

Hyde glanced around the rails at the array of silk and cotton underwear.

He began to browse.

He knew that Maggie loved silk. He wasn't averse to the feel of it himself. Especially when it was wrapped around his wife's slender form. He smiled to himself as he gently rubbed the material between his thumb and forefinger, running approving eyes over the range of lingerie.

Basques, body suits, camisoles and knickers.

Heaven, he thought, almost laughing aloud.

He selected a camisole in burgundy.

Very nice.

Now, which size?

Oh, shit. Ten or twelve? Or maybe even fourteen?

No, if he took a fourteen home she'd go crazy. She

4

wasn't that big, he was sure of it. A twelve should do it.

He selected a pair of knickers to go with the top, and crossed to the cash desk, laying the garments beside the till, reaching for his wallet.

The assistant dropped them into a bag and took his money, watching as he slipped the underwear into his briefcase.

She smiled at him and then he was gone, once more part of the crowd heading towards the escalators like some immense amoebic mass.

As Hyde stepped onto the escalator he glanced at his watch. He had arrived back in London earlier than he'd expected. For once the train from Birmingham had been on time and the meeting he'd attended there had finished two hours earlier than scheduled. Maggie would be surprised to see him. He glanced down at his briefcase, amused by the thought of its secret silk contents, and wondered what her reaction would be to his little present.

As he stood on the crowded moving stairway, he smiled to himself, picturing her in the flimsy attire. All around him, stern faces met his gaze, and Hyde felt he was the only one who looked happy. Two or three men were attempting to read newspapers as the escalator carried them deeper into the bowels of the earth. He glanced across to his right and saw several people pushing their way hurriedly towards the top of the up escalator. Late for a train, Hyde reasoned, or perhaps simply rushing out of habit.

The ticket area was even more crowded.

He moved as swiftly as he could through such a dense mass, and headed for the next set of escalators, glancing back to see a man trying to push his suitcase

5

through the automatic gates, ignoring a porter's attempts to help him.

Hyde didn't stand on the next set of steps: he followed the line of hardier souls who had decided to walk down.

At the bottom he turned to the left, and was hit by the warm air of the subterranean cavern. The familiar stale smell, tinged with what he recognised as the smell of scorched rubber, clawed at his nostrils.

He made his way down onto the platform, groaning inwardly as he saw how crowded it was. It was going to be sardines all the way to East Finchley, he thought. He'd left his car at the station there; it was a short drive from the tube once he got there. Hyde wondered if the Northern Line would be plagued by its usual delays. He moved down the platform a little way, pushing past a tall man wearing a Walkman and tapping his fingers on his shoulder bag in time to the inaudible rhythm. Close by, another man was reading his strategically folded broadsheet. Somewhere further along the platform, Hyde could hear a baby crying, its shrill calls echoing around the cavernous underworld. He decided to head back the other way: he didn't fancy making his journey crushed up against some howling infant.

A couple in their early twenties were kissing passionately, oblivious to the dozens of eyes turned in their direction, which quickly turned away again when the couple paused for breath. Hyde ducked past them, glancing back momentarily.

The girl was pretty. Tall, dark hair.

A little like his Maggie, only not as good looking.

He'd thought, when he first met her, that she was the most beautiful woman he'd ever seen, and even now, after eight years of marriage, he still thought the same way. She was perfect.

And she'd look even more perfect in this silk stuff, he thought to himself, glancing down at his briefcase as if the underwear inside were some kind of illicit secret which only *he* knew about.

He heard a rumble, felt a blast of warm air from the tunnel mouth, smelled its familiar odour of dust and metal.

The train was coming.

About bloody time.

The mass of people on the platform prepared itself for the impending squeeze onto the tube, ready to fill every available gap.

Hyde saw lights in the tunnel, heard the rumbling grow louder.

Soon be home now.

The train burst from the tunnel like some oversized, jet-propelled worm, the blast filling the station.

Hyde thought about Maggie and smiled.

He was still smiling when he threw himself in front of the train.

Two

Manchester

In less than two hours it would be dark.

She feared the coming of the night but she also knew that she would be away from this place by then.

Away from *them*.

Shanine Connor pushed a pair of leggings into the hold-all, cramming trainers, knickers and T-shirts in with them. There was no order to her packing, she merely shoved in whichever item came to hand next.

She hurried through to the bathroom and picked up her toothbrush and toothpaste, which she pushed into a plastic bag, before dropping that into the bag along with her clothes.

As she crossed in front of the window she paused to look out, ensuring that she was hidden from any prying eyes by the sheet of unwashed nylon that passed for a net curtain. She could see no movement on the ground floor, three storeys beneath her own flat. A couple of kids were kicking a ball about in the small playground over the road. Another child, no more than seven, was trundling around happily on a tricycle, careful to avoid the football which was bouncing back and forth.

She spotted a car parked a little way down the road and screwed up her eyes in an effort to see inside it.

It seemed to be empty.

She swallowed hard.

Could she be sure?

For interminable seconds she stood squinting at the stationary vehicle – then the moment passed and she remembered the urgency of her situation.

She hurried back into the kitchen and pulled open a drawer, scanning its contents.

She pulled out a long-bladed carving knife, hefting it before her, satisfied with its weight.

As she turned to go back into the sitting room she caught sight of her reflection in the mirror on the wall above the Formica-topped table.

She looked older than her twenty-three years. More

sleepless nights than she cared to remember had left her looking pale and puffy-eyed. Dark circles nested beneath her eyes and her skin was the colour of uncooked pastry. Her shoulder-length brown hair needed combing, and she ineffectually ran a thin hand through it before returning to her task.

Shanine slid the knife into the side pocket of the bag. It would be easy to reach should she need it.

She glanced at her watch.

Come on, hurry up. You've taken too long already.

She heard a shout from downstairs and crossed back to the window.

The two kids with the football were kicking it against the low fence surrounding the play area, banging it as hard as they could, shouting encouragement to each other.

The car was still parked.

Waiting?

Shanine finally zipped up the hold-all and pulled it onto her shoulder.

She was about to open the door of the flat when she heard footsteps climbing the stairs outside, echoing on the concrete surface.

She sucked in an anxious breath, one hand sliding towards the knife.

The footsteps drew nearer.

They were almost on her landing now. She looked at the door expectantly, her hand now touching the hilt of the weapon.

Silence.

The footsteps stopped.

Shanine took a step nearer to the door, her heart thudding against her ribs.

9

She closed her eyes for a second, trying to still the mad beating, afraid that whoever was on the other side would be able to hear it.

The moment passed and she heard the footsteps heading up the narrow corridor, away from her door towards one of the other flats.

She waited a moment longer, then opened the door and peered out.

Two or three doors down there was an old woman carrying two bags of shopping, her face flushed with the effort. She looked disinterestedly at Shanine then pushed her key into the lock and stepped into her own flat.

Shanine stepped out onto the landing, locked her door and hurried down the concrete steps, avoiding a mound of dog excrement a few steps down. Graffiti had been sprayed on the walls in bright blue letters. She glanced at the words UNITED ARE CUNTS as she scurried down to the next landing.

As she reached ground level she slowed her pace.

Don't make it look as if you're running.

The car was still parked further down the street.

Still motionless.

Still waiting?

Her attention was torn from it by a loud shout from one of the kids across the street. She looked at him blankly for a moment, aware that he was staring back at her, his gaze never wavering.

Shanine finally began walking, aware of the watchful eye of the boy, her back to the parked car.

If it was *them* they would know by now. They would have seen the hold-all and they would know.

She quickened her pace.

10

There was a bus stop at the end of the road. She could catch a bus into the city centre from there. One should be due any minute.

She prayed it wouldn't be late.

The last thing she wanted was to be standing around, in plain sight, for all to see.

For *them* to see.

She glanced behind again and saw that the car was still there. Ahead of her she heard the rumble of an engine and saw the bus pulling in.

She ran towards it, waiting as passengers clambered off, then she hauled herself up inside, fumbling in her jacket pocket for some change. She didn't have much. About a pound in coins, less than ten pounds in the pocket of her worn jeans.

She got her ticket and retreated to the back of the bus, glancing anxiously around her as it pulled away, past the kids kicking the football, past the parked car.

The journey to the city centre should take about fifteen minutes.

She looked at her watch nervously.

As she sat on the back seat she hugged the hold-all comfortingly, allowing one hand to rest on the part of the bag where the knife was.

As the bus rounded a corner, Shanine took one last look out of the back window.

The car was gone.

She felt her heart begin to thud more heavily in her chest.

Had it been them?

She looked at her watch again, as if repeatedly doing so was going to hasten the journey.

She shifted uncomfortably in her seat.

11

Time, it appeared, was running out faster than she had realised.

Clouds gathered more thickly in the sky.

Night was coming.

She wondered what was coming with it.

Three

A sickly sweet smell filled the air, which James Talbot recognised as burned flesh.

It was a smell not easily forgotten.

Six years earlier, when he'd been a Detective Sergeant, he'd attended a fire at a house in Bermondsey. Some old guy had fallen asleep and allowed his chip-pan to catch fire. The whole house had gone up in less than twenty minutes, and the old boy had been incinerated along with the contents.

Talbot remembered that smell.

Acrid, cloying. It caught in your nostrils and refused to leave.

The chip-pan fire had been an elaborate ruse to cover up a burglary. Two kids, no more than seventeen, had stolen what little there was of value in the house, then battered the old man unconscious and ignited the chip-pan to make it look like an accident.

Simple?

Except that they'd left fingerprints on the hammer they'd used to smash his skull.

Silly boys.

Both were doing a nine stretch in Wormwood Scrubs now.

It was that case which had secured Talbot's promotion to the rank he now held.

The Detective Inspector walked slowly up the platform at Euston, which was clear but for a number of uniformed men: London Transport employees, police and ambulancemen.

One of the Underground workers was standing on the track with two ambulancemen and two constables, staring down at a blackened shape which looked more like a spent match than a man.

The train was gone. The line was closed. The power off.

Talbot could imagine the annoyance of other travellers delayed because of the incident.

Inconsiderate bastard. Throwing himself on the track. Didn't he know people had homes to go to?

Talbot saw blood on the edge of the platform close to the tunnel exit. Large crimson splashes of it, congealing beneath the cold white lights of the station. There was more on the track itself. A large red slick had even spattered one of the advertising posters on the far side of the track.

The faces of a male and female model smiling out from a poster of Corsica looked as if they'd been smeared with red paint.

'Discover the beauty' screamed the shoutline.

A little further along, also lying on the track, was a briefcase, its contents scattered for several yards. Papers, typewritten sheets, pens. A Knickerbox bag.

Talbot stopped at the chocolate machine on the platform and fed some change into it. He punched the button for a WholeNut but nothing happened. He hit it again.

Still nothing.

'Shit,' murmured the DI.

'His name was Peter Hyde,' a voice beside him said.

Talbot nodded but seemed more intent on wresting the chocolate from the machine.

He struck the button a little harder.

'All that about the King's Cross fire being started by a match,' said Talbot. 'That's crap.' He eyed the machine irritably. 'It was someone trying to get a bar of chocolate out of one of these fucking things.'

He slammed his hand against the machine.

The WholeNut dropped into the slot at the bottom and Talbot smiled, retrieved it, and held it up like a trophy.

'See, that's all they understand. Violence.' He looked at Detective Sergeant William Rafferty and nodded triumphantly, breaking off a square of chocolate and pushing it into his mouth.

'What else?' the DI wanted to know, pacing slowly up the platform with his companion.

'He worked for a firm of accountants in the City,' Rafferty told him. 'Good salary. Married. No kids. Almost thirty-one.'

Talbot offered him a piece of chocolate but the DS declined.

'I'd rather have a fag,' he said, gruffly.

'Smoking's bad for you.'

'Yeah, and so is eating ten bars of chocolate a day. You've been worse since you gave up smoking.'

'Fatter but healthier,' said Talbot smugly, patting the beginnings of a belly which was pushing rather too insistently against his shirt. 'Anyway, a bit of exercise will get rid of that.'

'You'll be like a bloody house-side before you're forty,' Rafferty told him, smiling.

'Four years to go, Bill,' Talbot murmured, pushing another square of chocolate into his mouth. 'Thanks for reminding me, you bastard.'

They continued their leisurely stroll up the platform.

'Why did the Transport Police call us in?' Talbot wanted to know. 'They don't usually for a suicide.'

'They're not sure it *was* a suicide.'

'How come? Did someone see him pushed?'

Rafferty shook his head. 'They just think—'

Talbot cut him short. 'It's a suicide, Bill, take it from me,' the DI said, stopping and motioning behind him. 'The bloodstains on the platform and track are right near the tunnel mouth. He wanted to make sure that if the live rail didn't fry him then the impact of the train would kill him. Some of the dickheads who try and kill themselves down here jump from the middle of the platform. That gives the driver plenty of time to see them so he hits the brake and, nine times out of ten, the train doesn't even hit them. Runs over them maybe. They might lose an arm or leg, get some nasty burns from the live rail, but that's it. They jump from the middle because they're not sure.' He shrugged. 'Same as the ones who cut their wrists, you know that. If they cut across the veins of the wrist they bleed slower. They *want* someone to find them. The ones that do it from elbow to wrist, now *they're* not fucking about. They're sure. So was Hyde, that's why he went off near the tunnel mouth.'

'We couldn't get much out of the driver, poor sod's still in shock,' said the DS.

'I'm not surprised. What about the other witnesses?'

'We're taking statements upstairs now.'

Talbot nodded.

'Even money he topped himself,' the DI said, looking down at the group of uniformed men gathered around the body. They moved aside.

'Shit,' muttered Rafferty, staring at the corpse.

The stench of burned flesh was almost overpowering now.

'Where's his right leg?' Talbot wanted to know.

'The train took it off at the hip, we found it ten yards further down the track,' Rafferty replied.

'I want a full autopsy report as soon as possible,' the DI said. 'And one other thing, Bill,' Talbot pushed another piece of chocolate into his mouth, 'someone had better tell his wife.'

Four

Catherine Reed felt sweat beading on her top lip. She tasted the salty fluid as she licked her tongue across it, her breath coming in gasps now.

Her long dark hair was plastered across her face and neck, the flesh there also covered in a sheen of perspiration.

She tried to swallow but her throat was dry, she could only manage a deep moan of satisfaction as the sensations grew stronger. She lifted her feet, wrapping her slender legs around the form above her.

Phillip Cross had his eyes closed, his own body and face covered in sweat as he kept up a steady rhythm, supporting his weight on his fists as he drove swiftly, deeply, into Cath.

'Oh Jesus!' she murmured, her legs gripping him tighter, her fingers now clawing at his back and buttocks as if to pull him deeper. 'Go on. Go on.'

He opened his eyes and looked down at her pleasure-contorted face, an expression of joy etched on his own features as he continued with the hard thrusts.

The phone rang.

'Shit,' gasped Cross, slowing up slightly.

'Don't stop,' Cath moaned.

The phone continued to ring.

Cross withdrew slightly.

'Leave it,' grunted Cath.

The answering machine clicked on.

Cath hardly heard the voice on the other end of the phone, her own growing exhortations drowned it out.

She pulled Cross closer to her.

'I know you're there, so pick up the bloody phone,' said the voice, sharply.

Cross looked across at the phone and the machine on the bedside table.

He slowed his pace, his own breathing still laboured.

'Leave it,' Cath implored.

'Phil,' the voice continued. 'Pick the fucking thing up, this is important.'

They both recognised the voice.

Cross shrugged and ruefully eased himself free.

Cath allowed her legs to slide from his glistening back, her chest heaving, perspiration running in rivulets between her breasts.

17

Cross snatched up the phone.

'Cross here,' he said, clearing his throat.

Cath didn't wait to hear what he had to say. She swung herself off the bed and padded through to the bathroom, the blood pounding in her veins. She twisted the cold tap and splashed her face with water, studying her reflection in the mirror as she looked up. Her dark hair was ruffled, still matted with sweat at the nape of her neck. She eased it away with one hand. Naked, she stood before the mirror, glancing at the image which greeted her. Her smooth skin was tinged pink, particularly around her face, neck and breasts. She let out a deep breath, catching the odd word drifting through from the bedroom.

Why the hell couldn't he have let the bloody thing ring?

She heard Cross say something else, then the sound of the receiver being replaced.

Cath stood where she was, finally seeing Cross's reflection in the mirror behind her.

He too was naked and, she noticed, still sporting an erection.

'That was Nicholls.'

'I gathered that,' she said. 'Do you always jump when you hear his voice?'

There was an edge to her tone which Cross chose to ignore.

'I've got to go to Euston. Now,' he told her. 'Some geezer's just topped himself, Nicholls wants pictures. Do you want to come?'

She looked at him and raised an eyebrow.

'If you hadn't picked up that bloody phone I would have done,' she said, a slight smile touching her lips.

'Ha, bloody ha. So, what's your answer? I'm going to

18

be gone about an hour. Nicholls said he called me because he knew I was nearer.'

'How convenient for him,' Cath said, heading back towards the bedroom where she lit up a cigarette. 'It's a good job you live in Camden and not Chelsea, isn't it?'

Cross was already pulling on his jeans. 'Are you coming or not?' he said irritably, looking round, seeing one of his cameras on a cabinet close by.

'Why not?' she answered, already collecting her leggings, socks and trainers which earlier had been discarded beside the bed.

They dressed quickly in silence, then Cath spoke again.

'What's so interesting about a suicide, anyway?'

'Nicholls just asked me to take some pictures. I'm a humble photographer, I do what I'm told.' He smiled. 'You never know, there might even be a story in it for you. I thought reporters were always on the look-out for a story.'

'Yeah, very funny. A suicide at Euston. Real front-page stuff,' she chided.

'That's the point,' Cross said. 'It might not have been a suicide.'

Cath's expression changed.

'Who *was* the bloke?' she demanded.

Cross snatched up his camera bag and pointed to the name he'd scribbled on a notepad by the phone.

Cath looked at the name and nodded slowly, running a hand through her hair.

She was already heading for the door.

19

Five

James Talbot watched impassively as the four uniformed men lifted the body of Peter Hyde up onto the stretcher laid out on the platform edge.

Ambulancemen expertly fastened the plastic body bag around the corpse, but before the zip was closed Talbot looked at what was left of Hyde's face.

The skin around the right cheek and jaw was burned black, the remainder was a vivid red. One eyelid had been scorched off, leaving the orb glistening in the socket. It seemed to fix Talbot in a baleful stare as he looked on.

He watched as the severed leg was passed up from the track, and tucked neatly into the bag along with the body.

At the far end of the platform, two cleaners stood waiting, mops in hand. Ready to wash away the blood.

The DI swallowed the last square of chocolate and nodded permission to the ambulancemen to seal the bag once and for all. The zip was fastened.

As Talbot turned he saw a white light which momentarily blinded him.

'Fucking press,' Rafferty snapped.

'How did they get down here?' Talbot asked wearily.

20

'We only closed off this platform,' Rafferty informed him, striding towards the figure at the far end of the platform.

Phillip Cross continued snapping away. At the blood-stains. At the rails. The policemen.

The black body bag.

Catherine Reed followed him, glancing around her as if trying to commit what she saw to memory, anxious not to miss a detail.

She saw a bloodied tooth lying close to the platform edge.

Smashed loose by the impact of train and body, she assumed.

'Who's in charge?' she wanted to know.

'Get off the platform, please,' Rafferty said. 'You haven't been given official clearance to be down here.'

'Was it suicide or was he murdered?' she persisted.

'There'll be a statement issued in due course.'

'You must think it's murder,' Cath said, nodding towards the approaching figure of Talbot. 'Why else would a DI be here?'

As Talbot drew nearer he slowed his pace, seeing the dark-haired woman dressed in a loose-fitting sweatshirt and leggings. He recognised her. He knew those features.

He knew . . .

'What the fuck are *you* doing here?' he hissed, his gaze fixed on Cath.

'The same as you, DI Talbot, my job.'

Both Rafferty and Cross watched the journalist and policeman as they faced one another.

'You haven't got permission to be down here, so piss off,' Talbot snarled.

'Are you treating this as a murder investigation?' Cath said.

'No comment,' Talbot grunted.

Cath considered Talbot for a moment and then asked matter of factly, 'When did you get promoted?'

'What the hell does it matter to you?'

'Just curious.'

'Yeah, curiosity's part of your job, isn't it?' Talbot rasped.

'A Detective Inspector,' she said. 'You've done well.'

'Fuck off, Reed. I told you, you're not supposed to be down here. Now move it, before I have you arrested for obstruction.'

'As charming as ever, nice to see some things never change.'

'I'm only going to tell you once more. Piss off.'

'When can we expect an official statement?' Cath wanted to know.

'You just had it,' Talbot responded as he turned his back on her and walked back up the platform.

Cath watched him for a second then she and Cross ducked back through the archway which led to the escalators.

'What the hell was that about?' Cross asked as they rode the moving staircase.

Cath exhaled deeply.

'Did you get plenty of pictures?' she said, sharply.

'I asked—'

'Forget it, Phil,' she said, looking back down towards the platform area.

Talbot was standing in the middle of the raised area, arms folded across his chest, an expression of anger on his face.

22

'Do you *know* her?' Rafferty asked him. Talbot nodded slowly, watching as the body was lifted.

'You could say that,' he murmured.

Six

The air inside the pub was thick with smoke and James Talbot inhaled deeply as he headed towards the table in the corner.

What he wouldn't give for a cigarette!

He tried to push the thought from his mind as he weaved carefully around other drinkers, anxious not to spill any of the liquor he carried.

The pub was in Eversholt Street, just across the road from Euston, and it was busy. The sound of a dozen different conversations mingled with the noise of a jukebox which seemed to Talbot to have been turned up so high that it necessitated everyone in the pub to raise their voice to be heard.

Two young women cast him cursory glances as he passed, but Talbot seemed more concerned with reaching his designated table with full glasses than he did with their fleeting attention.

One of them, a tall woman with short blonde hair and cheek bones that looked as if they'd been shaped with a sander, smiled at him, and the DI managed a barely perceptible smile in return, glancing back to run appraising eyes over the woman's shapely legs as he reached the table.

He set down the two glasses, sipping his own Jameson's, feeling the amber fluid soothingly burn its way to his stomach.

Rafferty nodded gratefully and took a mouthful of his shandy.

'I can't stay too long, Jim,' he said, almost apologetically.

'One drink isn't going to hurt, is it?' Talbot muttered. 'What's your rush?'

'I want to see Kelly before my wife puts her to bed.'

'How *is* your kid?'

'Beautiful,' the DS said, proudly.

'She must get her looks from her mother, then,' Talbot mused, glancing at his companion.

'It was her first day at school today,' Rafferty began. 'I wanted to—'

'Who was on duty up top this afternoon?' Talbot interrupted, apparently tiring of Rafferty's conversation.

'What do you mean?' the DS asked.

'I want to know how those fucking press arseholes managed to get down onto the platform.'

Rafferty contemplated his superior for a moment then cleared his throat. 'Look, Jim, you can tell me to mind my own business, but who the hell *was* that reporter? You don't usually react to press like that.'

Talbot took a long swallow of his whiskey. 'Fuck them, they're all vultures anyway,' he snarled.

'You said you knew her.'

The DI exhaled deeply and sat back in his seat.

'She did a story on me about two years ago,' he said, looking down into his glass. 'It was all over the paper she works for, I forget which one. Not that I really give a

24

shit.' He looked at the other man. 'You know what I'm talking about, don't you?'

Rafferty nodded slowly. 'Paul Keane.'

'Yeah, Paul fucking Keane.' Talbot downed what was left in his glass.

'Was it true? About you beating him up during questioning?'

'Her fucking allegations got me suspended for two weeks, didn't they? Her and her "sources". Maybe I did rough him up a bit, but I'll tell you something, I wasn't the only copper who did.'

'He did some kids, didn't he?'

'Three of them. The fucking nonce. He raped two five-year-old girls and sodomised a three-year-old boy. Whatever he got, the bastard had it coming.' Talbot pushed away his empty glass. 'Three years old, can you imagine that? Jesus.' He sucked in an angry breath. 'But that bitch cried "police brutality" and splashed it all over the front of her fucking rag and there was an investigation.'

'No charges were ever made against you though,' Rafferty offered.

'That's not the point,' Talbot hissed. 'She crucified me. She could have ruined my career, and do you know who her source was? Keane's solicitor. He was more bent than his client. Keane nearly got off because of what she wrote. He could have been walking the streets *now* because of her. Newspapers. Wrapping up fish and chips or wiping your arse, that's all they're any good for. All of them.'

He looked down at Rafferty's empty glass. 'Another?' he asked.

'I've got to get off, Jim,' the DS said, getting to his feet.

'When are you expecting the autopsy results on Hyde?'

'Tomorrow.'

'And you still reckon it was suicide?'

Talbot nodded.

'I don't know how anyone can do that,' Rafferty said. 'Kill themselves. I mean, they reckon it's a coward's way out, but I reckon you need a lot of guts to top yourself. How could things ever get so bad you'd want to end your own life?'

Talbot shrugged. 'It could happen to any of us,' he said, quietly.

'Not me,' Rafferty said, heading for the door. 'I've got too much to live for.' He chuckled. 'See you tomorrow.'

And he was gone.

Talbot waited a moment then returned to the bar and ordered another Jameson's.

The woman with the finely chiselled cheekbones was still there, only now she was talking animatedly with a man slightly younger than Talbot. She didn't even see him this time as he passed her. As he sat back down he could hear her laughter, even over the jukebox.

Talbot glanced at his watch.

It was too early to go home.

Besides, there was nothing there for him anyway.

He sipped at his drink.

'Too much to live for,' he murmured, remembering Rafferty's words. The DI raised one eyebrow. 'You're lucky.'

He swallowed some more whiskey, the smell mingling with the stale odour of cigarette smoke.

He'd have another after this.

Maybe two.

It would take that before he could face the trip home.

Seven

Catherine Reed rolled onto her back, her chest heaving, her breath coming in deep, racking gasps.

'Jesus,' she murmured, trying to slow her breathing.

Beside her, Phillip Cross was also trying to get his breath back. He reached across to the bedside table and retrieved the can of Carlsberg there, taking a swig, wincing when he tasted warm beer.

'Can I have some of that?' Cath asked, taking the can from him.

'It's warm,' he told her. 'I'll go and get us a couple more.'

She too sipped at the lukewarm fluid, watching as Cross swung himself out of bed and walked naked across the room.

Cute arse.

She smiled to herself, stretching her long legs, then bending them, clasping her hands around her knees as if she were preparing for some kind of exercise routine.

Cross looked back at her and grinned.

'I thought you were going to get the beers,' she said, looking at him, framed in the doorway.

He nodded and disappeared through into the sitting room. She heard rattling around by the fridge in the kitchen and, moments later, he returned and sat down on the bed beside her, holding out a cold can for her. As she went to take it he pressed it to her left breast, rubbing her already stiff nipple with the cold metal.

She yelped and slapped his shoulder, chuckling.

At thirty, Cross was two years her junior, but his face was heavily lined for one so young. Cath was aware of lines on her own face, but around the eyes she preferred to call them laughter lines. It was as good a euphemism as she could think of.

'Do you think anyone at the office knows about us?' Cross said, taking a sip of his drink.

She lay back, stretching her legs again, admiring their shape herself.

Cross ran a hand along her right calf and thigh, stroking the smooth flesh there.

'I doubt it, we've been pretty discreet. Besides, nobody gives a shit. They're too concerned with their own lives or how to fill the paper. Nobody cares about what *we're* doing.'

'What about you?' he said, looking into her green eyes. 'Do *you* care?'

'Phil, don't start this again,' she said, smiling.

'It's not funny,' he snapped.

'I'm not *laughing*, am I?'

'You smiled.'

'What do you want me to do? Break down in tears?' she swigged her beer. 'Look, what we do together is fun, right? I enjoy being with you, but it's not a big romance.'

'Is that because you don't want it to be?'

'Can we save the big inquests for some other time, please?'

'We just finished making love, I think that's a fair enough time to ask about feelings, isn't it?'

28

'Phil, we just finished *fucking*,' she smiled and touched his cheek. 'There *is* a difference.'

Cross looked at her with accusing eyes. 'You can be a right bitch sometimes,' he said, acidly.

'Sorry,' she said, shrugging, taking a sip from the can. 'I just don't want you getting carried away with what's going on between us.'

'According to you, there's not much to get carried away with anyway.'

Cath took one last sip of beer then clambered off the bed, pulling on her leggings.

'What are you doing?' Cross demanded.

'Getting dressed. I'm going home.'

'I thought you were staying the night.'

'I didn't say that, did I?' she retorted, pulling on a denim shirt and fastening it.

'I just thought . . .'

She kissed him on the forehead.

'You think too much,' she said, pushing her feet into her trainers.

He pulled on his jeans and followed her through into the sitting room, watching as she gathered up her handbag and jacket, checking in the pocket for her car keys.

'I'll call you tomorrow,' she said, kissing him lightly on the lips.

Cross pulled her more tightly to him, easing his tongue past the soft flesh, happy when she responded.

'You're a pain in the arse,' he said, attempting a smile. 'No wonder that copper at Euston got so uptight when he saw you.'

She nodded.

'I suppose he had his reasons,' she said dismissively,

29

then turned and headed towards the hall. 'I can find my own way out, Phil, and besides . . .' she nodded towards his crotch, 'you don't want to frighten the neighbours, do you?' She giggled.

Cross looked down to see that his flies were undone.

As he hurried to zip them up, Cath stepped out.

He heard the door close behind her.

The photographer stood alone for a moment then sat down on the edge of the sofa, running both hands through his hair.

He could smell her perfume on his fingers.

He'd be able to smell it in the bedroom too.

He always could.

As he got to his feet, the phone rang.

Eight

'What's your name?'

Shanine Connor jumped slightly in her seat as the silence inside the car was suddenly broken.

She glanced across at the driver who took his eyes off the road momentarily and smiled at her.

Her own expression remained blank. Instead, she ran cautious eyes over the driver's features. He was in his early forties, his face a little on the chubby side, his hair thick and lustrous, although in the gloomy interior of the Astra it was difficult to tell what colour.

The only other light was supplied by the lamps on the M60. There wasn't much traffic travelling in either direction, and even when vehicles did pass by on the opposite carriageway, Shanine hardly noticed their headlamps. She was too concerned with checking the wing mirror beside her. Glancing in it every few moments.

Checking.

She was sure she'd seen a dark blue Nissan tuck in behind the Astra about twelve miles back.

She couldn't be sure it wasn't still there.

Following?

The Nissan had had plenty of opportunities to overtake, but she was sure it had sat in the inside lane, keeping a respectable distance, sometimes dropping back out of sight, sometimes coming closer.

Wasn't it?

She held the hold-all close to her, one hand resting on the side of the bag where she had secreted the kitchen knife.

The driver had offered to put the hold-all in the back seat for her but she'd shaken her head vehemently, preferring to keep it near.

He'd told her his name but she'd forgotten it. He'd been trying to make conversation for the last fifteen miles, ever since they left Manchester. All she could remember was that he'd said he was heading back home to Liverpool but otherwise her attention was elsewhere.

Like on the Nissan that was following?

Following?

She gazed into the wing mirror again and could see no sign of the vehicle.

Her heart began to thud a little faster against her ribs.

'I said what's your name?' the driver repeated, again looking at her.

'Shanine,' she told him without looking round.

'That's a nice name,' he said, tapping on his steering wheel gently, muttering to himself.

The car began to slow down.

'What's wrong?' Shanine asked, a note of anxiety in her voice.

'Bloody roadworks,' the driver groaned. 'It's going down to one lane. We'll be at a crawl for the next few miles.'

Shanine shot a glance at the wing mirror.

No sign of the Nissan.

'They're always doing something to this road,' the driver continued. 'Soft bastards.' He looked at her and smiled. 'Excuse my French.'

Shanine managed a nervous smile.

'So why are you leaving Manchester?' the driver asked. 'I mean, I can understand why, but I was just curious, like. I mean, I only go there because I have to work there.'

She didn't answer, preoccupied with what was visible in the wing mirror.

The Astra had slowed right down to around twenty miles an hour now, as the driver guided it between two rows of plastic bollards.

'You seemed in a hurry to get away,' he said, grinning. 'Someone chasing you?'

She turned to face him, the colour draining from her face.

'What makes you say that?' she demanded.

He glanced across at her, saw the concern etched across her features.

'Just joking,' he said, almost apologetically.

Shanine spotted the Nissan.

The road had opened out into two lanes again, and the Nissan was moving up fast behind the Astra.

They were approaching a slip road, leading to a service area.

'Can you drop me off there?' Shanine asked.

'I can take you all the way to Liverpool if you want.'

'No,' she said, watching as the Nissan swept past, its rear lights disappearing.

She felt her heart slow its frantic pounding and slumped back in her seat.

'Where are you going, anyway?' the driver asked.

'Drop me on the slip road, you don't have to drive right up to the service station,' she told him, ignoring the question.

'Don't be soft,' he muttered, indicating, guiding the Astra up the incline.

She was reaching for the door handle as soon as he began to slow down.

'Thanks,' she said, clambering out.

'I can take you further . . .' he began, but she was already out of the car, walking hurriedly towards the Little Chef which lay beyond the petrol station area of the services.

The Astra driver watched her for a moment, then stuck the car in gear and drove on. As he passed he saw her entering the restaurant. She paused at the door and looked anxiously around her before stepping inside.

The driver glanced into his rear-view mirror, wondering about Shanine.

What *was* she running from?

Boyfriend? Parents?

As he guided the car back onto the slip road that took him back to the motorway, he pondered.

Had he known the truth he might well have been relieved she was no longer in his car.

Nine

Catherine Reed could hear the sound as she turned the key in the door.

A high-pitched beeping noise which came every three seconds. The audio alert on her answering machine. There were messages.

She pushed the door of the flat closed and locked it, pulling the chain across; then she put down her car keys and door key on the small wooden table just inside the hallway.

The drive from Camden Town to her flat in Hammersmith had taken longer than usual. There'd been some sort of security alert in Central London and traffic had been diverted. Cath felt as if she'd been stuck behind the wheel of her Fiat for hours.

She pressed the Play button on the answering machine and the metallic voice announced that she had five messages.

She turned up the volume on the machine and wandered into the sitting room where she kicked off her trainers, sitting on the edge of the sofa as she massaged her feet.

The first message was from a friend, asking if she wanted to meet up for a few drinks in a couple of days' time.

Cath padded across to the TV set and flicked it on, pressing the mute button on the remote so that just the picture glowed before her.

The second message was a guy called John Linley. She'd met him at the opening of an art exhibition about a week ago and, for reasons which she couldn't remember now, she'd given him her number. The message invited her to call back.

Cath shook her head.

She sat looking at the silent TV screen as the messages continued.

A wrong number.

The caller had even waited for the tone to apologise.

On the screen, two politicians were gesturing at each other, their posturing somehow more interesting without the benefit of their empty words.

She changed channels.

Boxing.

Cath pressed another button.

A seventies sit-com – at least she guessed it was, from the way the characters were dressed.

She pressed again.

A Western. She peered at it for a moment, recognised William Holden and Ernest Borgnine and smiled to herself.

'*The Wild Bunch*,' she said, chuckling as the ad break caption confirmed her guess.

The fourth message on the machine was from her brother.

Cath got to her feet and walked back to the machine, jabbed the Replay button and listened more carefully to the words.

'Cath, it's Frank. Give me a call tomorrow night will you?

I need to talk to you. Any time after nine o'clock. Hope you're well. See you.'

She scribbled a note on the small pad beside the phone and listened to the last message.

It was from her publisher.

They loved the book, there were just a couple of points they'd like to discuss if she had the time tomorrow. Could she ring the senior editor?

Thank you. End of messages.

Perhaps they were going to tell her the publication date, she mused. Inform her when they were going to pay her the remainder of the advance. She'd already spent the first part. The flat had needed decorating and it had come in handy for that. The publisher seemed to have a great deal of faith in the book though: 'true crime', they had told her, was a big seller. With her background in journalism she had the contacts. The book had been relatively easy to write and she'd finished the first draft in under three months.

Mind to Murder was Cath's examination of some of the twentieth century's most notorious murderers and, more to the point, the public fascination with them. What was it about people like Brady and Hindley, Peter Sutcliffe, Charles Manson, Dennis Nilson, Fred West and dozens of others like them that the public found so intriguing?

Cath had already been commissioned to write a second book along similar lines about violence in the movies, but that was a long way off. She hoped the two non-fiction books could be a stepping stone to what she really craved: to have a novel published.

She pressed Rewind and listened to her brother's message again.

He sounded fine. Chirpy, in fact.

Surprising, considering the circumstances he was caught up in at the moment.

She glanced at her watch and wondered whether she should ring him now, then decided against it.

She went into the kitchen and switched on the ghetto-blaster, which was propped on top of the microwave: the sound of Clannad filled the room. Cath filled the kettle and switched it on, dropping a tea bag and some milk into a mug which she first rinsed beneath the tap.

While she waited for the kettle to boil she walked back into the sitting room, glancing at the silent TV screen, watching as the bridge the Wild Bunch had rigged with dynamite exploded, sending Robert Ryan and his bounty hunters into the river below.

Cath stopped for a moment, struck by how incongruous the brutal image was with the lilting sounds drifting from the kitchen.

From the top of the television two photos stared back at her.

One was of her parents.

They had emigrated to Canada six years ago.

Cath hadn't seen them since. She spoke to them every two or three months. They seemed to be enjoying themselves there, both retired. And they were proud of her achievements. Proud of both their children.

She wondered what they would have thought of Frank's situation.

It was he who looked out at her from the other photo.

Five years older than Cath, he was powerfully built with a bushy moustache, flecked with grey like his hair.

In the picture he was sitting on a park bench with her, smiling happily, his arm around her shoulder.

The photo had been taken about eight years ago, the day after she began working for the *Express*, and shortly after he'd secured the deputy headmaster's job at the school where he taught.

Happy days.

And now?

She crossed to the photo and picked it up, studying his features more carefully.

It was obvious the photo was old.

Frank was smiling.

He had something to smile *about*.

Cath heard the kettle boiling and set the photo back in position atop the television.

She'd spoken to him three days ago. His message seemed to imply there was something new to report.

As she headed back towards the kitchen she wondered what it could be.

It had got to the stage where she feared his calls.

Ten

The silence enveloped James Talbot like a shroud.

He pushed the front door shut behind him, muttering to himself as he stepped on the letters lying on the mat. He picked them up and carried them through into the sitting room, dropping the mail onto the coffee table without even glancing at it.

Christ, he needed a cigarette!

Instead he crossed to the drinks cabinet and poured

himself a large whiskey, swallowing most of the soothing liquid in one gulp.

The cabinet, like most of the furniture in the house, was old. Some was in need of repair, some of replacement. It was like stepping back into the fifties, walking inside the place. A huge mahogany chest of drawers stood against one wall, the dark wood matching the coffee table and also the small table upon which the television was perched. The electronic contraption looked out of place amidst such relics of the past.

The walls needed a lick of paint too.

Talbot could remember that sickly shade of magnolia from when he was a small child.

His father had painted the whole bloody house in that colour.

His father.

Was it really twenty-six years since he'd died?

It seemed like an eternity. Sometimes it felt as if he'd never even lived. Like a fading photograph, the image of his father had slowly grown more and more faint in Talbot's mind, until he could barely recall the man's features.

He heard shouting outside and crossed to the window, peering out to see a group of young lads passing by, chatting loudly and animatedly.

The street was littered with pieces of crumpled paper and rubbish, blown about like bizarre tumbleweeds as the cold breeze swept through the streets.

The streets always looked like this after a match.

From the front window of the house in Gillespie Road, Talbot could see the outline of Arsenal's stadium.

His father had taken him along to matches when he'd been a child, at first too young to realise what was going on, aware only of the crush and throng of so many bodies packed into terraces. Then, as he'd got older, he'd travelled the short distance to the stadium for every home game. Then he'd started going to away games too.

It gave him an excuse to get out of the house for a few hours.

To get away.

To be alone.

Strange, he'd always thought, to seek solitude amongst thirty thousand people, but it seemed to have the desired effect.

And then he would return.

To the smell of the drink. The shouts and screams.

The blood.

Talbot swallowed what was left in his glass and poured himself another. He crossed to the sofa where he flopped down on the large flower-patterned seats, rolling the whiskey glass between his large palms, gazed at the letters on the table, as if the very effort of reaching for them required some superhuman feat of will.

He took another sip of whiskey and tore open the first.

Phone bill.

He put it to one side.

A couple of circulars.

He tossed them into the bin beneath the table and picked up the last envelope.

Crisp. Pristine white. It seemed to gleam in his hands as he tore it open, noticing that his fingers were trembling slightly.

He pulled out the single typed sheet and unfolded it.

The heading on the paper stood out starkly: Litton Vale Nursing Home.

He sighed, wearily, and began to read.

Eleven

It was far too beautiful a day to be surrounded by death, Andrew Foster thought as he trudged up the narrow gravel path which led off from the main walkway.

It had been on a day like this, a day of clear blue skies and gentle breezes, that death had first touched their lives, and the memory seemed to grow stronger with each successive visit.

Croydon Cemetery was bathed in the soft warming rays of a sun which had risen proudly to take its place in a sky the colour of washed denim.

The scent of flowers, some freshly laid, wafted on the breeze. The scene was idyllic, even down to the birds perched in the leafy trees whistling happily, oblivious to the misery below them, unaware that for every joyful note they uttered in those branches, a tear had fallen below them: tears of pain, helplessness, regret and anger.

Andrew had felt every one of those emotions the day he'd been told his son had died.

Ahead of him, his wife Paula walked with her usual purposefulness, moving surefootedly over the path and grassy ridges, stepping around the many other graves as they made their way to their usual destination.

They were both in their early twenties. They should be playing with their baby boy now, not bringing flowers to lay on his grave. A grave so small that Andrew could reach from one end to the other without stretching his arms.

Suffocation, the doctors had said. The child had been strangled by its own umbilical cord while still inside the womb.

He'd stood at his wife's side as she sobbed and screamed in her efforts to birth a child who was already dead.

Andrew had cried when he'd seen that tiny body removed, wrapped in a sheet. Cried with sorrow and rage. Why did it have to be *their* child?

Paula had taken it remarkably well, but the doctors had warned him there could be a delayed reaction to her grief. They'd rattled off some psychological bullshit names for the condition, most of which he'd forgotten.

He'd heard her crying at night.

He'd woken in the darkness, disturbed by his own nightmares, and he'd heard her weeping in the next room; sometimes he went to her to share her pain, and other times he allowed her to grieve in private.

Two weeks had passed since their son's death, and Andrew was struck by the appalling irony – they had been expecting the beginning of a new life with his birth, but instead had witnessed only death. Birth and death had become inseparable. They'd become one.

His wife had given birth to a dead child.

And the weather outside on that day had been so beautiful. A day full of the promise of life had brought only pain.

A day like today.

They passed graves bearing fresh flowers, and some which needed tending; some where the headstones sparkled in the early morning sunlight: others where the stones were dull and neglected.

It seemed they were the only two people in the cemetery. They'd seen an old man almost every morning, visiting, Andrew assumed, the grave of his wife. He always nodded a greeting to them. But not this morning.

This beautiful morning seemed to have been created solely for them.

Andrew sucked in a deep breath but it tasted sour. He noticed Paula slow her pace as she reached the path leading to their son's grave.

It lay beneath a small oak tree, the branches dipping low over the tiny grave. A sparrow was perched on one of the lower branches, chirping gaily.

The sound grated on Andrew's nerves and he was relieved to see the bird fly off.

He watched it rise and disappear from view as it flew towards the sun. He shielded his eyes to protect them from the glowing orb.

Then he heard Paula gasp.

She had stopped dead and was pointing ahead of her with one shaking hand.

The flowers she had been carrying had fallen to the ground. Andrew almost trampled on them as he brushed past her, his own eyes now bulging wide as he took in the horrific scene.

He paused, his breath coming in gasps, his mouth open as if he was about to say something. But no words would come. What could he say? What feeble exhortations could express the feelings that swept through him now? What words could begin to describe what he saw?

43

The grave of Stephen Foster had been dug up, flowers and wreaths scattered across the dark, overturned soil.

The coffin, so tiny in its small resting place, was visible through the earth.

A split snaked across the top.

The brass nameplate had been smashed off.

And, all around, dirt had been scattered. It looked as if the coffin had erupted from beneath the ground, spraying earth in all directions.

From behind him he heard Paula sobbing hysterically, and now he found the voice for one astonished cry of his own.

It felt as if it was wrenched from his soul.

He dropped to his knees in the disturbed earth.

Twelve

Phillip Barclay's office at New Scotland yard was small and incredibly well kept. It seemed to mirror the man himself. Immaculately dressed, not a hair out of place, he was the picture of efficiency as he set down two files on his desk, arranging them with almost manic neatness. He then sat down, brushing a speck of dust from his sleeve.

Across from him, DI James Talbot was snapping a Kitkat into four separate pieces. He balled up the silver paper and left it on Barclay's desk, watching as the coroner frowned and pushed an ashtray towards him, indicating the foil with an accusatory glance.

Talbot made an exaggerated gesture of picking up the silver paper between his thumb and forefinger and dropping it into the ashtray.

'You'll make someone a lovely wife one of these days, Phil,' the DI said, smiling.

Barclay pulled the ashtray away then glared at Rafferty, who was in the process of lighting a cigarette.

'Not in here, please,' snapped Barclay.

Rafferty looked at him in bewilderment.

'No smoking,' Barclay reminded him, watching as Rafferty replaced the cigarette in its box.

'So, come on, Phil, what's the story on Peter Hyde?' Talbot got down to business. 'Did he top himself or what?'

Barclay flipped open one of the files and glanced at its contents.

'The autopsy showed no sign of alcohol, drugs or anything stronger than caffeine in his bloodstream at the time of the accident,' said the coroner.

'Could he have fallen?' Talbot asked.

'He could, but it's doubtful. I've seen victims of tube accidents before. There are usually severe burns to the palms of the hands and the upper arms, where they've tried to break their fall. There were no such marks on Hyde's hands. That would seem to indicate that he wasn't pushed either.'

'Suicide, then?' Talbot murmured.

'Plain, simple suicide,' echoed the coroner. 'No suspicious circumstances. If I were you I'd close this one, Jim.'

Rafferty looked at his superior. 'What if it was made to *look* like an accident?' he prompted.

Talbot chuckled. 'Piss off, Bill. Hyde killed himself, just like I said. That's it. End of story.'

45

'I'm sorry to cheat you out of a murder enquiry,' Barclay added.

Rafferty shrugged.

'Terrible waste of life,' Barclay said. 'A man so young. It makes you wonder what his reasons were for killing himself.'

'As far as we could tell, he didn't have any,' Rafferty said, shaking his head in bewilderment. 'He had a good job, a beautiful wife, lovely home, everything.'

'You don't know what was going on inside his head,' Talbot offered. 'Just because the guy *seemed* happy doesn't mean he *was*. Never judge a book by its cover and all that shit. You should know that, Bill, you've been on the force long enough.' The DI chewed a piece of chocolate. 'So, he didn't look like a bloke who'd top himself: since when have you been able to tell someone's state of mind from their appearance? If we could do that there wouldn't be a criminal on the streets, we'd grab all the bastards if they even *looked* dodgy. I mean, Nilsen didn't look like a mass murderer, did he?'

Rafferty shrugged. 'Oh, I don't know,' he said, smiling.

Talbot got to his feet. 'Thanks for your help, Phil,' he said, heading for the door.

Rafferty got up to follow.

'I don't know if that makes it worse for his wife, knowing he killed himself,' the DS said. 'At least if he'd been murdered she'd know there was a reason why. She might *never* know why he killed himself. She might blame herself.'

Talbot sighed.

'You're in the wrong game, Bill,' he said. 'You should have been a bloody social worker. Give me some change.'

46

Rafferty fumbled in his pocket. 'What's it for?'

'The coffee machine. Come on, I'll buy you a cup of hot, brown water,' Talbot chuckled.

'You're all heart,' Rafferty told him.

'That's my middle name. Come on.'

They closed the door behind them and Barclay heard their footsteps echoing away up the corridor.

He waited a moment then took the file on Peter Hyde and slid it into one of the bottom drawers of his desk.

Thirteen

The barrel of the .357 Magnum glinted beneath the banks of fluorescents, the cylinder clicking as it was turned.

Neil Parriam pulled back the hammer and wiped the firing pin with the same oily cloth he'd used to clean the frame of the gun. The smell of gun oil was strong in the air, mingling with the less acrid aroma of coffee. Parriam put down the weapon, laying it on a cloth he'd spread out on the table. He wiped his hands on the edge of the cloth then took a sip of his coffee.

'How long have you known?' asked the man seated to his right.

Parriam beamed at him.

'About a week,' he said, happily. 'We weren't going to tell anyone until Lynn had her first scan, but then we thought what the hell.'

'I don't blame you,' said Jacqui Weaver. 'It's not every day you find out you're going to become a father, is it?'

47

She squeezed his arm. 'I reckon you're a clever boy.'

The other three men seated at the table broke into a chorus of chuckles.

Parriam felt his cheeks redden and he nodded humbly.

Jacqui retreated back behind the counter, glancing up as the buzzer on the main door sounded. She checked the closed circuit TV screen behind the desk, recognised the man waiting outside and buzzed him in. She recognised most of the members of the gun club. A good percentage of them were regulars, turning up at the same time on the same night, week in week out.

Parriam was a regular. Every Tuesday he booked a lane, seven o'clock until eight. He'd been a member of the club in Druid Street for the last five years. It was the only hobby he'd ever had in his life which had made him truly relax. He felt no competitive drive here. No need to be the best shot at the club, no burning desire to be top dog.

Lynn had encouraged him to join. Her brother had introduced him to the delights of pistol shooting and he'd found the pastime instantly addictive but, over the years, the social side of the activity had taken on added significance for him. The gun club was somewhere to meet friends on a weekly basis, somewhere to unwind, to forget about the pressures of work, although, if he was honest with himself, his job brought very little pressure. He loved what he did and he got well paid for it.

Rumour had it that he was likely to be made a partner in the firm of architects he worked for. And he had yet to reach his thirtieth birthday.

And now to learn that he was to become a father.

As far as Neil Parriam was concerned, life couldn't get much better.

A child seemed to be the one thing missing, the only remaining piece to be fitted into the jigsaw.

He'd wanted to keep it secret until they were sure the baby was going to be perfect. He and Lynn had both agreed to wait until the third month before releasing the news to friends and family, but neither had been able to contain their excitement.

They'd already been out and bought a cot.

So much for patience.

Parriam smiled to himself and sipped his coffee.

He intended decorating one of the spare rooms next weekend in preparation for transforming it into a nursery.

Nursery.

Even the word made him glow inside.

'Have you thought about names yet?' Graham Rogers asked.

Parriam shrugged and continued cleaning the .357.

'Kelly if it's a girl, or Nicole,' he said. 'Sounds a bit exotic, doesn't it?'

'What if it's a boy?' Rogers wanted to know.

'I haven't thought about boy's names, I think we both want a girl so much.'

Parriam pushed the wire brush through each of the cylinder chambers, holding the gun up towards the light to check if there was any excess oil left in the chambers.

He reached for the box of ammunition close by and flipped it open, pushing the heavy grain shells into the chambers one by one.

The door to the range opened and the range-master stuck his head out. 'Your lane's free when you're ready, Neil,' he said.

'Cheers, Bert,' Parriam called as the other man disappeared back inside.

'Are you going to be there at the birth?' Jacqui asked, pouring herself a cup of coffee and crossing to the table where she sat down opposite Parriam.

'Bloody right I am,' said Parriam, chuckling. 'I might even video it.' He pushed another slug into the cylinder.

'I'm sure Lynn will appreciate that,' Rogers laughed. 'You can show it to your friends over dinner. They'll love it.'

'My old man was there for the birth of our first,' Jacqui said. 'He passed out.'

The men around the table laughed.

'One minute he was telling me to push and that he could see the baby's head, the next he went down like a sack of spuds,' she said, grinning. 'Men!' She shrugged. 'I hope *you* don't pass out, Neil.'

'No chance, Parriam assured her. 'Anyway, I'm staying up the end without the blood.'

'Chicken,' Rogers chided, nudging him.

'Were *you* there when your wife gave birth, Graham?' Parriam asked, thumbing the final shell into the cylinder.

'I was there in spirit,' Rogers said.

Parriam looked puzzled.

'I was in the pub getting pissed. When I got there I said to the doctor, "Can you put a couple of extra stitches in down below, she's never been very tight."'

Rogers let out a cackling laugh, Parriam joined him.

Jacqui slapped Rogers on the arm and scowled in mock outrage.

'Bloody chauvinist,' she said, grinning.

Parriam was shaking with laughter. 'I must remember that, Graham,' he chuckled.

Then, in one fluid movement, he spun the .357 around, pushed the barrel into his mouth and pulled the trigger.

Fourteen

James Talbot paced back and forth across his office, occasionally stopping to look out of the window, gazing down on the streets which led into New Scotland Yard.

Every now and then he would walk back to the desk and take a square of chocolate from the bar of Fruit and Nut he'd broken up. He chewed thoughtfully, seemingly oblivious to the gaze of Rafferty who watched his superior as he paced.

'Was the gun his?' Talbot asked, turning back to his desk, peering at a collection of ten by eights which lay there.

'Everything was in order,' the DS said. 'The certificate of purchase was in the carrying case, so was his FAC.'

Talbot picked up the first picture.

It had been taken by a police photographer less than ten minutes after Neil Parriam had shot himself.

The body was still upright in its seat, the gun still clutched in one fist.

It looked as if the wall behind Parriam had been coated with red paint.

'There were at least four witnesses who saw him do it,' Rafferty said. 'No question of foul play, the autopsy report backs that up anyway.' Rafferty jabbed the manilla file beside the photos.

Talbot looked at the second photo.

It showed a rear view of the dead man's head.

The exit wound was large enough to accommodate two fists; a gaping hole which showed the full extent of the damage wrought by the heavy grain bullet.

'There were powder burns on his lips and tongue,' Rafferty added. 'The bullet took out three of his back teeth on its way through.'

Talbot chewed another square of chocolate.

'One of the ambulancemen pulled part of it out of the wall behind where he was sitting,' the DS added.

'Any family?' Talbot asked.

'A wife. She'd just found out she's pregnant. Apparently Parriam was over the moon about it.'

'So happy he blew his brains out,' Talbot mused, looking at a third photo. 'Has official identification been made?'

'They took the body to Guy's. His wife identified it. They've taken her back home now, she's sedated.'

'I'm not surprised.'

'She left his personal effects at the hospital.'

Talbot looked puzzled.

'He was carrying a wallet, credit cards, that sort of shit,' Rafferty elaborated.

'I'm not with you, Bill,' the DI muttered.

'He had a pocket diary with him too: one of the uniformed men at the hospital went through it – don't ask me what he was looking for.'

'And?'

Rafferty ran a hand through his hair.

'There weren't many entries in it, but one of them

caught his eye and he called me. He's a good man. Observant. He was on Euston the same day we pulled Peter Hyde off the tracks, that's why the entry in the diary made him sit up.'

'Bill, what the fuck are you talking about? Are you trying to excuse the actions of one of our men who went through the private belongings of a dead man because he had nothing better to do?' Talbot snapped.

'There was an entry in the diary for two weeks ago. It said "Call Peter at Morgan and Simons". Morgan and Simons is the firm of accountants that Peter Hyde worked for. Parriam *knew* him.'

Talbot stopped pacing and looked quizzically at his companion 'So what?' he said, finally.

'Jim, two men commit suicide within days of each other, both for seemingly no reason and now we find out that they *knew* each other. Doesn't that strike you as strange?'

'One entry in a diary doesn't make them bosom buddies, and even if it does it still doesn't prove a link between the two suicides.'

'It's a hell of a bloody coincidence though.'

'Yes it is. But that's *all* it is, Bill. A coincidence.'

The two men locked stares, then Rafferty took a defiant drag on his cigarette. He inhaled then blew out a long stream of bluish-grey smoke, watching it dissipate in the air.

'So that's it,' he said. 'End of story?'

'What the hell else do you *want* me to do?'

Rafferty didn't answer. 'I suppose you're right,' he conceded finally.

'You *know* I'm right. If I thought it was worth investigating we'd be on the case now, but what are we going to look for, Bill? Why they killed themselves? No one but Hyde and Parriam is ever going to know that. Fuck knows what made them do it, but then again I'm a copper not a psychiatrist. I can't read minds. Especially dead ones.'

Rafferty nodded slowly.

'Fancy a drink?' Talbot asked.

'Are you buying?'

Talbot nodded.

Rafferty got to his feet. 'Let's go then.'

As they left the office, Talbot glanced back at his desk, at the photos of Neil Parriam.

One was a close up of the dead man's face, eyes still staring wide. The corners of the mouth were turned up slightly. Talbot could have sworn Parriam was smiling.

Fifteen

'I tried you twice earlier on but I couldn't get an answer,' said Phillip Cross.

Catherine Reed continued gazing at the screen of the word processor, scanning what she'd already written. It flickered there in green letters, almost accusingly. She waited a moment longer then pressed Delete. The screen went blank.

'Sorry, Phil, what did you say?' she asked, the phone balanced between her shoulder and ear.

'Jesus, are you listening?' Cross chuckled.

'I was working on something; I was miles away. Sorry.'

'Was it the guy who blew out his brains in that gun club in Druid Street?'

'No, I didn't cover that. I've been at the Dorchester most of the day.'

'Nice work if you can get it. What happened?'

'Some visiting Arab ambassador went ape-shit and strangled one of his wives, or tried to, according to some of the staff I spoke to. She's in hospital. I've been tearing around like a blue-arsed fly trying to speak to doctors, nurses and Christ knows who. The embassy guys and security were pretty jumpy.'

'What did you hear about the suicide?'

'Put a gun in his mouth, didn't he? Did you take the pictures?'

'No, Porter covered it. I've been in Croydon Cemetery today.'

'What for?'

'One of the graves had been dug up, the headstone had been smashed.'

'Shit,' she murmured, sitting forward in her seat. 'What else?'

'The coffin had been tampered with, apparently it's not the first time it's happened in that cemetery.'

'Who did the grave belong to?'

'A kid. A baby. I made a note of the name, don't ask me why. I reckon I've been around *you* too long.'

At the other end of the phone she heard the rustling of papers.

Cath pulled a pad towards her and wrote on it: *Desecration?*

'Stephen Foster, that was the kid's name,' Cross said at last.

Cath scribbled it on the pad and drew a ring around it.

'Did you say it wasn't the first time it had happened there?' she asked.

'The vicar was there when I arrived, I overheard him talking to the police about it. I didn't catch it all.'

She sat staring at the word *Desecration*, chewing on the end of her pen.

'Probably just some sick bastard pissing about,' Cross added.

'Mmm,' Cath responded distractedly.

'So,' the photographer said. 'What are you doing tonight? Are you coming over here or—'

She cut him short. 'I'm expecting company, Phil.'

'Anyone I know?' Cross asked frostily.

'My brother.'

'Oh, right,' he murmured, sounding relieved. 'What about tomorrow?'

'I'll call you.'

'I just think there's things we should talk about,' Cross protested.

'Not now, Phil,' she told him, wearily. 'I'll see you for lunch tomorrow, all right?'

There was a protracted silence at the other end of the line.

Cath exhaled deeply.

'Yeah, OK,' Cross said, reluctantly. 'See you.'

He hung up.

Cath replaced the receiver, got to her feet, and headed for the kitchen. It was hot; three pots were bubbling on the cooker. She lifted the lid of each and checked its contents, smiling to herself. Then she passed back into the sitting room and picked up her wine glass, taking a sip. She had laid the table close to the window, even draped it with a clean, freshly ironed table cloth. Cath wasn't the most domesticated of women but even her mother would have been proud of the table, she mused, glancing across at her parents' photo on top of the TV. There was music playing softly in the background, the volume turned low. Cath hummed as she wandered back to the kitchen, glancing at her watch.

Almost time.

It wasn't like him to be late.

The doorbell sounded at exactly eight o'clock and Cath headed towards its source, a smile already on her face.

She checked the spy-hole and saw him out there.

She opened the door.

'Hello, mate,' said Frank Reed, grinning, holding a bunch of flowers before him.

He stepped inside, into her welcoming arms.

Sixteen

The lights inside the tube train hurt her eyes.

Shanine Connor blinked hard and lowered her head momentarily.

When she looked up again she noticed that the man seated opposite was staring at her.

Wasn't he?

He was in his mid-forties, dressed in an open-necked shirt and dark trousers that were far too short. As he crossed and uncrossed his legs, the material rode up to reveal the pure white of his flesh.

57

Shanine looked at his hairless legs. Anything rather than hold his gaze, which she felt boring into her.

Standing at one end of the carriage was a couple in their twenties, both dressed in jeans and leather jackets. They were kissing passionately, oblivious to the other passengers in the carriage.

A young woman with a dark complexion was studying a map of the Underground intermittently, glancing up at the map opposite for reassurance.

The man next to her was reading a well-thumbed paperback, chuckling to himself, unable to hear his own giggles over the sound of his Walkman.

Shanine glanced across at the man with the white legs and was relieved to see that he was gazing down the carriage at the leather-clad couple.

She pulled the hold-all closer to her, hugging it tightly as if it were a sleeping dog.

She couldn't remember how long she'd been on the train. Only that her journey had begun in natural light, overground, only to become swallowed by the tunnels as the tube had drawn closer to Central London.

Her eyelids felt as if someone had attached lead weights to them.

Christ, she was tired!

It felt as if she'd been travelling for days on end. From the service station she'd found a lift easily enough, but the journey down the motorway had seemed interminable.

And now this.

She needed sleep more than she needed food, but her stomach rumbled noisily to remind her of *that* particular requirement too.

Where should she get off?

She didn't even know where the hell she was going.

The train pulled into Leicester Square station: Shanine glanced out of the grubby windows and saw the signs.

The man with the white legs opposite looked across at her.

He was staring at her.

Wasn't he? It was obvious.

She shifted in her seat as the doors slid open.

Stop staring.

The leather-clad couple got out; so did the young woman with the dark complexion. Shanine saw her looking around helplessly on the platform seeking the way out.

Other people stepped on to replace them.

A young woman no older than herself sat a couple of seats away, brushing her long blonde hair away from her face, catching Shanine's eye.

Shanine smiled.

The young woman ignored her and began thumbing through a copy of *Cosmopolitan*.

The train moved off.

How many more stops?

Piccadilly Circus.

Shanine looked around anxiously.

Should she get off here?

She hesitated a moment longer, then jumped to her feet just as the doors were sliding shut. The man with the white legs watched her as she jammed a hand between the doors to force them open again. She stepped out onto the platform as the doors closed behind her.

Shanine stood motionless, gazing around, searching for the Exit sign while dozens of other people walked, scurried or pushed past her. She followed the largest group and saw the way out.

She rode the escalator behind a man who carried the pungent odour of sweat on him, the smell mingling with a stench like burning rubber. The moving stairway creaked protestingly as it rose, and Shanine looked to her right and left, at the posters which lined the escalator and at the profusion of faces on the down escalator to her left.

The ticket hall with its low ceiling seemed to amplify every little sound, and the noise crowded in on her. She could hear music coming from close by – many voices, some raised.

She passed through the automatic barriers, looking down at an old man who was seated cross-legged by one of the exits, a dark stain across his crotch, his grey beard resembling a hedgehog that somebody had stapled to his chin. He had a battered brown fedora on the floor in front of him with some coins in it.

Shanine passed him by, the smell of urine and alcohol strong in her nostrils.

She took the first flight of steps she came too, emerging into the cool evening air, the sound of cars and buses almost deafening. It hit her like a wall.

For a long time she stood motionless looking out across Piccadilly Circus, at the buildings towering above her and the constantly flashing neon of so many signs and hoardings. It hurt her eyes almost as much as the glaring white of the tube lights.

There was a Dunkin' Donuts to her left and she fumbled in her pocket and found a couple of pound coins.

At least she could attend to the problem of her hunger.

And what about sleep?

She crossed the road, saw people emerging from the main entrance of the Regent Palace Hotel. Four of them, two couples, laughing and talking loudly. Americans. She heard the accents.

One of the men looked at her.

Didn't he?

She got her doughnut and coffee and sat down, one foot resting on the hold-all.

Shanine took a couple of bites of the doughnut and looked at her watch.

She'd been gone almost eighteen hours.

They would know by now.

They would be looking.

For all she knew, they already were.

Her hand was shaking slightly as she took a sip of her coffee.

Seventeen

'That was beautiful,' said Frank Reed, pushing the empty bowl away from him. 'Which branch of Marks and Spencer did it come from?'

'You cheeky sod,' Cath said, nudging him as she retrieved the bowl and carried it to the sink. 'That was all my own work. You should feel privileged. That's the first meal I've cooked for a man in over six months.'

'And was *he* as appreciative?'

'We split up a week later, but I don't think that was

61

anything to do with the meal,' Cath chuckled, spooning coffee into a couple of cups.

She stood by the draining board, waiting for the kettle to boil.

'Next time, why don't *you* cook *me* a meal?' she asked.

'I'll take you out instead.'

'Typical teacher. You spend most of the year on holiday but you can't even take the time to cook your own sister a meal.'

He smiled.

'I don't cook much. *You* know what it's like when you're on your own, Cath.'

'*I'm* alone out of choice.'

'Are you sure?'

'What's that supposed to mean?' she asked, smiling. 'What are you going to do now? Psychoanalyse me?'

'You're a very attractive woman, Cath. I'm just surprised you never settled down. It wasn't as if there was any shortage of men.'

'Now you're making me sound like a tart,' she said, pouring hot water onto the coffee.

'You know what I mean,' he said, quickly.

She returned with the coffee, nodding towards the sitting room.

Reed got up and walked through to the other room, seating himself at one end of the sofa.

Cath sat at the other end, slender legs drawn up beneath her. She sipped her coffee and looked at her brother. He looked dark beneath the eyes and his skin was pale. There was a small shaving cut on his chin which looked even more starkly red against the pallor of his flesh.

'You make it sound wrong for me to be alone,

Frank,' she told him at last. 'Mum and Dad were always nagging me to get married. I don't think they ever understood what I was doing. How much my work meant to me.'

'I wasn't preaching at you,' he teased.

She stretched out one leg and prodded him with her bare foot.

'I know that,' she murmured, in mock irritation.

Frank caught her foot and ran his fingers slowly over the instep, pausing to massage her toes gently.

She kept her foot there, pressed against his thigh as he began to knead her sole with his fingertips.

'So,' he continued, glancing at her, holding her gaze 'how come you never settled down?'

'You've heard of Mr Right?' she said. 'I found too many Mr Wrongs.'

Reed chuckled, his finger tracing patterns between her toes, across the nails and joints, stroking, squeezing.

She watched as the smile on his face gradually faded.

'Perhaps you were right not to get married,' he offered, finally.

'Have you heard from Ellen lately?' she asked, sliding down slightly, pushing her foot further into his gentle, skilful hand.

'We spoke on the phone about a week ago. 'A sternness had crept into his tone.

'Was it that bad?'

'It's getting worse, Cath. *She's* getting worse. This bastard she ran off with, Ward or whatever the hell his name is, she's obsessed with him.'

'Is she in love with him?' Cath asked quietly.

Reed didn't answer.

Cath studied his profile, saw his eyes narrow slightly.

63

'It isn't love,' he said, finally. 'She doesn't make a move without his bloody say-so. He controls her, like some fucking pet.' Reed was breathing harshly now, unable to control the anger in his voice. 'Every time I mention meeting her she says she's got to ask Jonathan.' He emphasised the name with disgust. 'All I want to do is talk to her. Be alone with her for a few hours. I want *her* to tell me it's over between us.'

'And if she does?'

'Then I have to accept it, don't I?' Reed snapped, reaching for his coffee.

Cath left her foot pressed against his thigh, pressing lightly against the material of his jeans.

'When was the last time you saw Becky?' she wanted to know.

'A month ago. Ellen says she doesn't want me to see her, she says it would be too upsetting for Becky.'

'You're her father, Frank, you've got a right to see her. You've got rights under the law. Ellen can't keep Becky away from you.'

'And what am I supposed to do? Kidnap her back?'

'Go through the courts.'

'Can you imagine what that would do to Becky? Christ knows, she's been through enough already. She's seven years old, Cath, and she's seen her mother walk out on me, take her and move in with some guy she's only been seeing for six months. Well, six months that *I* know about anyway.'

'Are they still living at Ward's place?'

He nodded.

'I've been round there,' Reed told her. 'But either they won't answer the door or they're never there.' He clenched his fists angrily. 'Perhaps it's a good thing. If

I got hold of that bastard I'd probably kill him. *And* Ellen.'

'That wouldn't do anybody any good, least of all Becky. Think about her.'

'I *do* think about her,' Reed snarled. 'Why the hell do you think I feel this way? My wife cleared off five months ago and took my daughter with her. Twelve years of marriage pissed away. Flushed down the fucking toilet, Cath. And for what? So she could be with some . . .' He shook his head. 'Jesus, I don't even know what he does for a living. I don't know where they're getting their money. He could be a fucking pimp or a drug dealer for all I know.'

'I'm sorry, Frank,' Cath said, softly.

'I want my daughter back,' he said, angrily. 'And it's getting to the stage where I don't care *how* I get her.'

They sat in silence for what seemed like an eternity, then Reed got to his feet.

'I'd better be going.'

Cath rose with him.

'Frank, if there's anything I can do to help—' she began.

He cut her short. 'What, like drive the getaway car when I snatch Becky?'

'Don't say that.'

She walked with him to the door of the flat, watching as he slipped on his jacket. He turned to face her.

'I won't lose Becky,' he said.

Cath embraced him, holding him close to her, feeling his warm breath against her cheek.

She kissed him lightly on the lips.

'Sorry to spoil the evening,' he said, apologetically.

'You didn't. I understand how you must feel.'

65

'No you don't, Cath. I hope you *never* have to understand what it feels like.'

He kissed her again, his lips pressing a little harder against hers.

'Call me tomorrow,' she said as he stepped out into the hallway. She watched him walk to the lift then closed the door, leaning against it.

'Shit,' she sighed, wearily.

Eighteen

The boy knew that the man was coming for him.

He came for him most nights.

Sometimes he stank of drink.

Then he would come with anger and there would be pain.

At other times he came with kindness and there would be little suffering. He would speak to him softly, reassure him, praise him. Sometimes even smile at him.

Tonight there were no smiles.

The boy heard the banging of the door as it was hurled open, rocking back on its hinges, and he saw the man silhouetted in the bedroom doorway.

The figure paused, swaying uncertainly, then lurched towards the boy, who drew the sheets more tightly around his neck, perhaps hoping they would form an impenetrable cocoon to protect him.

Above him the figure bent down, then gripped the sheets and tore them away, exposing the boy's frail body.

And then the boy caught that smell.

The stink of alcohol, the acrid stench of sweat and another stronger odour. A musky, choking stench which seemed to grow stronger.

The boy wanted to scream.

He opened his mouth but no sound would escape; then when he felt the blow across his cheeks, first one then the other, he knew he must remain silent.

And he knew he must keep his mouth open.

God help me.

But then why should he help tonight? He turned his back every other time.

Somebody help me.

He wanted to scream.

He had to scream.

And finally, he did.

James Talbot sat bolt upright, eyes staring, dragged from the nightmare by invisible hands.

There was a bellow of pain and rage echoing in his ears.

His own bellow.

'Jesus,' he gasped. 'Jesus. Jesus.'

He smelled his own sweat.

'Fuck,' he panted.

Talbot tried to swallow but it felt as if his throat had been filled with chalk.

'I'm as mad as hell and I'm not going to take it any more...'

The voice shouted at him.

Talbot stared frantically around him.

'Who...' he began.

'Let me hear you, I'm as mad as hell and I'm not going to take this any more...'

He looked at the television screen, saw the source of the voice.

Talbot jabbed the Off button on the remote.

Silence.

'Fuck,' he whispered. 'Fuck.'

He sat forward in his seat, leaning his elbows on his knees, and rubbing his forehead with his fingertips. Talbot kept his eyes closed tightly but the fragments of his dream floated into view, fractured images which only disappeared when he opened his eyes. He took several deep breaths, trying to slow the thunderous pounding of his heart, afraid it would burst.

He glanced across at the clock on the mantelpiece.

11.42 p.m.

He didn't know how long he'd been asleep. Couldn't remember.

Didn't fucking care.

He got to his feet and wandered through into the kitchen where he spun the cold tap over the sink, scooping water into his sweating palms. He splashed his face with the cold water, then drank some from the gushing stream, forcing away the dryness in his throat. He gripped the edges of the sink for a moment, eyes closed again, water running down his face.

Then he turned and headed for the hall, where he picked up his car keys and, slamming the front door behind him, stepped out into the night.

Talbot had no idea how long he'd been driving.

The streets were quiet at such a late hour. He'd passed the usual traffic on main roads but the less populated thoroughfares of Finsbury Park, Tottenham Hale and Harringay were virtually deserted.

The DI sat behind the wheel of the Volvo, arms resting on it, gazing across the darkened street.

From where he was parked he could see only the low stone wall which fronted the building opposite.

It was in total darkness apart from a light burning outside the main entrance. There were a couple of cars parked outside, but certainly no sign of movement either inside or outside the building.

Talbot sat motionless for what seemed like an eternity, only his fingertips moving gently, rhythmically, on the steering wheel.

As he switched on his headlights the name plate on the low wall opposite was illuminated: LITTON VALE NURSING HOME. He stuck the car in gear and swung it around in the street, intent on heading home.

He didn't know how long it would take him.

He didn't care.

Nineteen

'They knew they were going to die,' said Frank Reed, pressing his fingertips together. 'Most of them wanted to.'

'Why, sir?' a voice from the back of the class called.

'Because they were stupid,' another answered.

There was a ripple of laughter.

'Because they were French,' another added.

'Same thing,' the second voice echoed.

The whole classroom erupted into a chorus of loud and raucous laughter.

Even Reed smiled as he got to his feet and crossed to the map pinned to one side of the blackboard, leaving the rest free for him to write on.

He stood beside it, scanning the faces of his pupils. Girls and boys: girls and boys aged eleven to twelve. He glanced at the row of faces: thirty-eight in his class.

It was too many. *He* knew it, his colleagues who were dealing with similar size classes knew it. Everyone knew it except the Government, it appeared to Reed.

He walked across to the window of the classroom and looked out. From his position he could see the Employment Exchange and, beyond that, the Adult Education centre. St Michael's Secondary School had been built close by them, and Reed wondered if he was the only one who saw the irony. Most of the kids he taught faced a life without work and, for many, a little further down the way in Old Street was Hackney Police Station and Magistrates Court. For most of his temporary charges, Reed felt that at some time in their lives they would encounter either one or the other.

Life didn't hold too much promise for the young *or* old in this part of Hackney.

He waited until the laughter had died down, then returned to the map.

It showed the battlefield of Waterloo.

'Napoleon's Old Guard were elite troops,' Reed continued. 'They were the Emperor's personal body-guard and they felt it their duty and an honour to die for him. They were also the final rearguard for the defeated French army. They stood and fought long enough for the rest of the army to run away and for Napoleon to escape.'

Eyes followed him expectantly as he paced back and forth.

70

'Does anyone know what the Old Guard's officer shouted back when asked to surrender?' The teacher looked around expectantly. 'Come on, you should have read it last night.'

A hand went up close by.

A young boy with a very short haircut and frayed sleeves on his blazer.

Reed nodded.

'He shouted back "The Guard never dies", sir,' said the boy.

'That's very good. He actually said "The Guard dies but never surrenders". Historians have interpreted his answer this way. He actually shouted "*Merde*."'

There was a chuckle from the front of the class.

Reed suppressed a smile. 'And what do you want to share with us, David?' he asked.

David Morris coloured slightly.

'Well, my sister does French, and when I asked her what that word meant she said it meant—'

Reed interrupted him. 'I'm sure she told you what it meant, but that wouldn't look too good in the history books, would it?' he said, smiling.

'What does it mean, sir?' an excited voice called.

'It means shit,' Morris whispered. 'Sorry, sir,' he added, rapidly, looking warily at Reed.

The teacher was no longer able to suppress his grin, and the rest of the class erupted into a chorus of laughter.

'Right,' Reed said over the din. 'So you all know that the commander of the Old Guard used to swear.'

'I d swear if I was about to get shot,' a voice added.

'My mum and dad swear all the time and no one's ever tried to shoot them,' another offered.

More laughter.

Reed looked around at the faces. Happy faces.

Except one.

A boy sat alone at the back of the classroom, his head slumped on his arms, his eyes gazing blankly at the top of his desk as if he were tracing the pattern of the wood. He ran one chewed fingernail gently over the back of his hand, seemingly oblivious to the sounds of merriment around him.

Reed knew the boy as Paul O'Brian. Twelve years old. A tall lad with thin lips and fine black hair.

He was about to call to the boy when the strident ringing of the bell cut through the air.

It was the signal for frenzied activity. Books were snatched up and shoved into bags, pencils were pushed back into pockets, exercise books gratefully stowed.

'Read chapter twelve tonight,' Reed called out. 'You can find out if Napoleon used to swear, too.' He smiled to himself, returning to his desk as the children filed out quickly.

Paul O'Brian followed, alone. Shuffling as fast as he could, head down.

As he passed in front of Reed's desk, the teacher saw that the boy was shivering. 'Paul, can I have a word with you?' Reed said. 'It won't take a minute.'

O'Brian stopped, his gaze still lowered.

'If I've done anything wrong . . .' he murmured almost inaudibly.

'You haven't done anything wrong,' Reed assured him, noticing how the boy never met his gaze. He merely stood motionless before him, arms at his sides.

'I just wondered if you were feeling OK,' Reed said. 'You were very quiet today. Usually I can't shut you up.' He smiled reassuringly.

O'Brian clasped his hands in front of him.

Reed frowned.

Around both the boy's wrists there were vivid red marks.

As if aware of Reed's gaze, O'Brian pulled down the sleeves of his jacket to hide the abrasions.

'Are you sure you're all right?' Reed persisted.

O'Brian nodded.

Reed saw another mark on his neck, close to the open top button of his shirt.

It was bluish-black. Like a bruise, the extremities yellowing and mottled.

'Can I go now please, sir?' O'Brian asked, head still lowered.

Reed sighed. 'Yes, go on. You'll be late for lunch.'

O'Brian was gone as hastily as his spindly legs would carry him.

Reed sat down at his desk, his brow furrowed.

He could understand the boy's silence. His baby sister, Carla, had died just a week earlier. The atmosphere at his home must be distressing. That could account for the boy's withdrawn state.

And the marks on his wrists and neck?

Reed administered a mental rebuke. Perhaps he was overreacting.

But those abrasions on the wrists had looked bad. Raw in places.

The teacher shook his head.

There would be a perfectly logical answer.

There had to be.

He picked up his bag and left the classroom.

Twenty

James Talbot brought the Volvo to a halt in the car park of Litton Vale Nursing Home and switched off the engine. He remained behind the wheel, gazing at the building, then he swung himself out of the car, scooping up the Cellophane-wrapped bunch of flowers in the process.

The gravel of the short pathway leading up to the main entrance crunched beneath his feet as he walked, and a light breeze rustled the flowers.

Litton Vale was built of grey stone, but the ivy climbing its walls and the beds of immaculately kept flowers which formed a frontage to the stonework helped to soften the forbidding appearance of the place. It was Victorian in origin but a new wing had been added only ten years earlier. It looked somewhat incongruous with its red bricks, nestling against the great grey bulk of the main building.

The scent of blossom was strong in the morning air but Talbot hardly noticed it. He continually switched the bunch of flowers from one hand to the other, aware that his palms were sweaty.

Nervous?

He climbed the short flight of stone steps to the main entrance and walked through into the reception area. To his right was the day room, to his left a staircase which led to the first storey. There was a chair lift attached to it and, in addition, at the bottom of the corridor behind him, there were lifts.

The thick carpet seemed to muffle sounds within the building, even Talbot's own footsteps as he moved down the corridor.

To one side of him there were rooms, and to his left was an enormous picture window looking out over a pond, which was surrounded by a Japanese garden.

Several wooden benches were set up there and he saw people sitting on them.

Men and women.

He recognised one or two.

At the end of the corridor he pushed his way through a set of double doors, walking through what looked like an enormous sitting room. There were sofas and chairs dotted all around, but mainly pointing towards a large television set close to an open fireplace.

The television was on, the sound turned up high.

Seated in one of the chairs close to the set was a woman in her eighties.

She smiled broadly at Talbot as he passed through, and he returned the gesture, again switching the bunch of flowers from hand to hand.

His heart was beating that little bit quicker now.

What is there to be afraid of?

The walls were covered by a warm lemon-tinted wallpaper and adorned with many gaily coloured paintings. Everything in the home was designed to be welcoming, soothing to the eye.

As he passed through the next set of double doors he almost bumped into one of the staff members.

She was in her mid-forties, dressed in the familiar dark

blue uniform which Talbot had come to know so well.

'Hello, Mr Talbot,' she said, cheerfully. 'Nice flowers.' She bent forward and sniffed them. 'Lilies, aren't they?'

'I'm a copper, not a florist, Mary,' he said, smiling.

'If all coppers were as good looking as you, I wouldn't mind getting arrested,' the woman said, chuckling.

'I've got my handcuffs with me.'

She slapped him playfully on the arm.

'Cheeky,' she giggled, then disappeared into a room to the right.

Talbot paused for a moment.

They all think you're so fucking wonderful, don't they?

The smell of the flowers was beginning to make him feel nauseous.

Talbot paused at the next set of doors.

Through the glass panels in each of them he could see out into the gardens beyond. Immaculately kept lawns, flanked by flower beds and conifers. There were more wooden benches too. Two sparrows were perched on the edge of a birdbath close to the door.

They flew off when he stepped out into the garden.

Talbot watched them fly away, disappearing over the line of conifers, then he spotted what he sought.

The single figure was seated in a white-painted wooden seat on a patio nearby. There was a walking stick propped against the chair.

Come on. Get it over with.

He swallowed hard and set off towards the figure.

The smell of freshly cut grass mingled with the aroma of so many flowers. Somewhere off to his left he could hear the sound of a lawnmower. There was even laughter coming from behind him but he couldn't see its source.

Laughter.

As he drew closer, the figure turned to face him and Talbot held out the bunch of flowers as if he were warding off some predatory beast. He managed a broad smile which never touched his eyes.

You bastard. At least try and be convincing.

'Hello, Mum,' he said, softly.

Twenty-one

Dorothy Talbot rose shakily to her feet, smiling, her arms extended.

She was dressed in an immaculately pressed green two-piece suit and her white hair was held in place by hair laquer. As Talbot embraced her he felt her head brushing against his shoulder. She gripped him tightly to her, then stood back and kissed him on the cheek. Her own face was ruddy and she looked remarkably healthy, more closely resembling a woman who has spent her life in the countryside than one who had hardly ever set foot outside London for her whole life.

She gripped Talbot's hand and he felt the swollen veins beneath the flesh as he squeezed it, helping her to sit down again. He pulled another chair across and sat down opposite her, watching as she looked gratefully at the flowers he'd brought.

'They're beautiful,' she said. Then she squeezed his hand again. 'It's so good to see you, Jim. I wasn't expecting you today.'

'I can't stop long, Mum,' he said quickly.

'I know, dear.'

Jesus, did she have to be so fucking understanding?

Talbot shifted uncomfortably in his seat.

'Are you busy?' she asked.

'I'm *always* busy, Mum. But never mind me, how's your leg?'

She rubbed gently at her thigh and shrugged.

'They keep telling me I might have to have one of those frames if it gets any worse but I don't fancy that,' she said, dismissively.

'Can you manage with your stick?'

'I've been managing for the last twenty years. I've been taking tablets for the last week or so, I've had a little pain from it.'

Talbot squeezed her hand more tightly.

'I'm lucky,' she said, smiling. 'He could have broken more than just my leg.'

'I thought he did, the bastard,' snarled Talbot, his tone darkening. A long silence followed as they both sat, lost in their own thoughts.

'Did you ever *try* to leave him?' he asked at length. 'Just run away, I mean.'

'I thought about it, Jim. All I wanted to do was get away from him, especially when I found out what he'd been doing to you.' Her voice trailed away into a whisper and she glanced at her son.

Talbot saw tears in her eyes.

'I was terrified of him,' she said, quietly. 'You know that. If I'd tried to run he'd have killed me, probably killed both of us. Like I said, I was lucky he only broke my leg.'

'Did you ever tell anyone what he did to you? Or to me?'

She shook her head.

'I think everyone round about knew what he was like anyway, especially after he'd had a few drinks in him. They never knew what he did to you, though. I never let anyone know that.'

Talbot swallowed hard.

'I wasn't the only wife to get a beating, you know,' Dorothy continued. 'There were plenty round our way in the same boat.'

'Not all of them ended up in a hospital with a compound fracture of the right leg and a dislocated shoulder,' Talbot reminded her.

'I was trying to protect you. I would have done anything to stop him hurting you. I tried the best I could. I'm sorry for what happened, Jim.'

'It wasn't your fault. It was that bastard.'

Talbot got to his feet and paced back and forth in front of her.

'It's just a pity he didn't die sooner,' he snapped.

'I know, but we managed, didn't we?' she said, softly.

Talbot stopped pacing, turned his gaze towards her.

There was an almost unearthly serenity about her.

'When can I come home, Jim?'

He'd been dreading the words.

'Mum, we've talked about this before,' Talbot told her, sitting down again. 'If there was any way you could, don't you think I'd have sorted it before now?'

'I've been in here for six years now. I don't want to die in here.'

'You're not going to die in here or anywhere else for that matter; stop talking like that. You're not going anywhere, Mum.'

'I don't belong here, Jim. The other people are older than me.'

'You're seventy-one, Mum,' he said, a small smile on his face.

'But there're people in here with Alzheimer's or whatever it's called, there are some who are dying. It's turning into a hospice, not an old people's home. I want to be in *my* house, not here with strangers.'

'I thought you liked it here.'

'The staff are nice but it isn't where I belong. I don't need people to look after me.'

'Yes you do, Mum. That's why you're here. Don't you think that if there was any other way I'd have found it? This is the best I can do for you, Mum. Christ knows, I feel bad enough about it.'

'You shouldn't, Jim.'

But I fucking do.

He could barely bring himself to look at her.

'Just speak to the doctors, ask if I can come home,' she persisted.

'Mum . . .' he began but then merely nodded.

He got to his feet and kissed her on the cheek.

'I've got to go,' he told her. 'I'll be back at the weekend, I'll try and stay a bit longer.'

She held his hand, as if reluctant to let him go. 'I'm very proud of you, you know. What you do, what you made of yourself.'

He kissed her on the other cheek.

'Please speak to them,' she whispered, tears in her eyes.

He nodded.

'I love you, Jim,' she called after him.

He turned and waved as he reached the doors leading him out of the garden.

Hidden from her view he stood in the corridor, sucking in huge breaths. He felt as if he was suffocating, as if the walls were crushing in on him.

'Fuck it,' he snarled under his breath, then walked up the corridor to the reception area.

To his left was another corridor and he walked briskly down it, scanning the nameplates on each door until he found the one he sought. He knocked and waited, finally invited to enter by a voice on the other side.

As Talbot entered the room, Dr Maurice Hodges rose.

He was a tall, slim man, five or six years older than Talbot, his hair greying at the temples, his forehead deeply lined.

'I got your letter,' Talbot said.

'Have you seen your mother today?' the doctor enquired.

The DI nodded. 'She looks fine. Does she know?'

'Not yet,' Hodges told him. 'We thought it best to inform you first; besides, if we tell her it could cause an acceleration. The shock sometimes does.'

Talbot ran a hand through his hair and exhaled deeply. 'So, Doctor,' he said, looking at the physician unblinkingly. 'When are you going to tell my mother she's got cancer?'

Twenty-two

Shanine Connor woke suddenly, her heart slamming hard against her ribs, the breath catching in her throat.

81

Something was touching her face.

She sat up, barely suppressing a scream, her movement causing the fly which had been crawling across her cheek to take off.

It buzzed somnolently in the stale air, the sound it made amplified by the emptiness of the room.

Shanine shielded her eyes from the rays of sunlight pouring in through the windows.

For a long time she sat in the corner, legs drawn up before her, arms hugging them to her chest. She watched the motes of dust twisting and spinning back and forth in the sun's rays, her heart gradually slowing from its frenzied beating.

Outside the building she could hear the sound of traffic and voices.

She didn't know what the building was. She hadn't known the previous night when she'd stumbled upon it, barely able to walk another step due to the bone-crushing weariness that overwhelmed her.

She had wandered up Regent Street from Piccadilly, glancing in shop windows on the way, looking up at the glittering lights and beyond into the night sky. She'd kept to the main streets, pushing her way through the throngs of people, happier to be surrounded by others than to be walking dark streets alone.

She hated the night.

Feared it.

The presence of others went some small way to allaying that terror.

She'd stood across the street from Selfridge's and gazed at the huge department store, watching as people passed through its main doors. Like a child mesmerised by the lights on a Christmas tree, she'd remained transfixed by the huge building for what had seemed like hours.

Behind her she had watched people coming and going from a Burger King and a couple of small restaurants. The smells were tantalising; she hadn't eaten much since she left home and her stomach had rumbled unceasingly as she'd sat on a bench outside, the hold-all beside her.

When she'd seen two young men leave the fast-food place and toss a hamburger carton into a nearby wastebin she couldn't help herself.

She'd grabbed the container from amongst the other refuse almost before they'd turned away. There had been a half-eaten cheeseburger inside.

She'd eaten without thinking. The food was still warm, that was all that mattered. It stopped the pains in her stomach for an hour or so.

She'd walked up Duke Street and noticed several To Let signs outside some of the terraced properties leading into Manchester Square.

Maybe one would be empty.

Easy to gain access to?

She'd tried five doors before finally discovering one which was unlocked.

Shanine didn't care who was to blame for this security fault. All she knew was she had somewhere to sleep. A roof over her head for at least one night.

She'd lain down on the dusty floor and fallen asleep almost immediately. There had been dust sheets in the room, half-empty paint pots. She had no idea when the decorators would return, but that hadn't mattered. She'd pulled one of the grubby dust sheets over herself and slept.

If there had been nightmares, then she could no longer remember them as she sat motionless, gazing at the warming rays of the sun.

She glanced at her watch.

10.06 a.m.

Her stomach rumbled protestingly. A sound she was becoming used to.

She had to get something to eat. Something substantial.

Shanine crawled across to the hold-all and pulled out a clean T-shirt. Balling up the one she removed, she used it to wipe her face and arms before stuffing it into the bag. As she was donning her fresh T-shirt, she looked down at her thin body. The slight smell of body odour she knew would get worse. But, at the moment, food was her most pressing concern.

The sunlight glinted on the blade of the kitchen knife.

She had to get some food or some money. Both, preferably.

Shanine touched the cold steel.

She *must* eat. No matter what.

Shanine ran a hand through her hair and, hauling the hold-all over her shoulder, got to her feet.

Twenty-three

The doorman of the Grosvenor House Hotel nodded almost imperceptibly at Talbot as the DI walked in, not even glancing at the uniformed attendant.

His eyes, and his mind, were elsewhere. He passed through into reception. One of the receptionists glanced across at him briefly, then returned her attention to the computer before her. Talbot could hear the printer chattering away as he passed.

A couple was checking in, the woman leaning against the counter looking around. Talbot noticed that she slipped her right foot in and out of her shoe as she waited.

Two men in their early fifties walked past him, heading for the lifts, both of them speaking in hushed, almost reverential tones, as if they were reluctant to disturb the stillness of the lobby.

Cigarette smoke accosted him as he entered the Gallery Bar. Although there were only half a dozen people in there, the stale air made it seem as if each of them was already half-way through their second packet of the night. The smoke seemed to refuse to disperse, gathering instead like some invisible cloud which enveloped him as he entered.

Christ, he wanted a cigarette!

A couple of heads turned as he walked in, slowing his pace, gazing around.

Searching.

He saw her sitting at the bar, just a glass for company.

As Talbot approached her, he noticed that she was fumbling in her leather clutch bag for something. He ran appraising eyes over her.

The long blonde hair, brushed gently over the shoulders of her charcoal grey jacket, which was fastened by two gold buttons. Beneath it she was wearing a white blouse and, as she crossed her legs, the black skirt she wore slid up an inch or two to reveal her shapely thighs. She looked down and brushed a piece of fluff from one of her black suede high heels.

Talbot sat on the stool beside her, aware that she still hadn't seen him.

The barman, on the other hand, *had* and he ambled towards the policeman.

'I'll have a Jameson's please,' said the DI. He looked at her. 'And whatever the lady's having.'

Gina Bishop looked first at Talbot then pushed her glass towards the barman who moved off to refill it.

'Talbot,' she said, managing a small smile. 'What are *you* doing here?'

'Looking for you,' he told her.

She pulled a packet of Silk Cut from her handbag. He watched as she lit up, the flame of the lighter reflecting in her large brown eyes.

'You still trying to give up?' she said, pushing the packet towards him.

He nodded, reaching for a handful of peanuts from a bowl on the bar.

The barman returned and set down the drinks.

'That's a nice outfit,' Talbot told her, allowing his gaze to travel up and down her shapely form.

'It's Louis Féraud,' she told him, smugly.

'A present?'

'I bought it myself. From Harrods.' She took a sip of her drink.

'You must have had a good week last week.'

'*Every* week's a good week.'

He smiled and took a swig of whiskey, feeling it burn its way to his stomach.

'How did you know I'd be here?' she wanted to know.

86

'I've already tried the Dorchester and the Hilton. This was the only one left.'

'You're not a detective for nothing, are you?' she said, a hint of sarcasm in her voice.

'I knew it had to be one of the three. You've been working this same beat since you were twenty. That's when I first arrested you, remember?'

'How could I forget?' She sucked on her cigarette, then blew the smoke in the policeman's direction. 'Look, I've changed a lot in five years.'

'Yeah, you're more expensive now.'

'But I'm worth it.'

'Then how come business is slow tonight?'

'I was going to ask you the same thing. What's wrong, no one else to arrest?'

Talbot sat back on the bar stool, drink in hand, and looked at her.

'What are you looking at?' she demanded.

'I bet that outfit cost more than I earned last month,' he commented finally.

'Probably,' she said, amused. 'We're both the same, Talbot. We both get fucked, it's just that I get paid more.'

He ran a finger over the sleeve of her jacket.

'Louis who?' he said, looking at the material.

'Féraud,' she said, indignantly. 'I didn't expect you to have heard of him.'

He nodded.

'And whose designs were you wearing the first time I picked you up? Dorothy fucking Perkins, wasn't it? You've come a long way, Gina.'

'Look, Talbot, did you come in here to reminisce or is there a reason for all this?'

87

'What do *you* think?'

She nodded, finishing her drink.

'My place?' she asked.

'It's closer, isn't it?' Talbot said, downing what was left in his glass. He left a five-pound note on the bar top, waited for his change and pocketed it.

'Aren't you going to leave him a tip?' Gina said, picking up her bag. She pushed the portable phone inside.

'For bringing two drinks?' he said, incredulously.

'You haven't changed a bit, Talbot. You're still a cheap bastard.'

He grinned crookedly at her and offered her his arm, which she took.

They left the bar together.

Twenty-four

He wasn't afraid of death.

Why should he be?

At thirty-eight years of age, the Reverend Colin Patterson had already stood over enough burials and interments to know that those who went beyond went somewhere better. It was always the relatives his heart went out to. He hated to see suffering, and many times in the past ten years he had struggled to find the words to ease the suffering of those who had lost someone close. It was never easy. It wasn't always possible. But he did his best. That was all God had ever asked, that he did his best.

He would do his best in the army too.

Patterson had thought long and hard about his decision to join the army as a chaplain but he felt that he could do more good there than here in this part of southeast London. He needed a challenge and, despite his family's protests, he felt that challenge would come amongst fighting men, not amongst the parishioners he'd known and ministered to for the last decade.

His mother had mentioned Bosnia, Belfast and the Falklands, although he'd respectfully pointed out that particular conflict had been over since before his ordination. She had been unimpressed. It could happen again. If not there then some other godforsaken corner of the world.

Patterson had listened attentively to all her arguments, but his mind had been made up before he'd even mentioned it.

He paused beside one of the graves near by and straightened a metal vase which had been blown over by the wind. As he straightened up he glanced at the headstone: IN LOVING MEMORY OF A DEAR FATHER AND HUSBAND. Patterson smiled affectionately and continued his walk.

The cemetery gates were opened at nine and he'd already seen a number of people moving around the large necropolis which was Croydon Cemetery.

A number of them he knew by name, the others he was on nodding terms with.

The priest glanced at his watch.

He was due to conduct a burial at eleven.

Plenty of time.

There was a bench to his left, beneath a large oak tree which had already shed several dozen of its large leaves:

they lay like a yellow carpet over the graves beneath the tree.

A bird was singing higher up, its shrill calls wafting pleasingly on the gentle breeze.

Patterson made for the newer area of the cemetery where the more recent interments were sited. The path on which he walked sloped down gently, past a tap which was dripping water. He stopped and turned it off as he passed.

Lives were like drops of water, one of his teachers had told him shortly before his ordination: fragile, precious and so quickly gone.

Patterson wondered how many he would see go in his position as a chaplain, lives taken not by old age or disease but by violence. By explosions, by bullets. By war.

He would see men die, he knew that. But he had no fear for his own life. Why should he?

As he rounded a corner he saw the first splash of colour.

Red. Vivid and almost dazzling.

The colour of blood.

It took him a second to realise that the paint was spattered across a headstone.

Patterson took several hesitant steps towards the stone, his eyes narrowed against the sun which was burning so brightly above him.

He saw that the paint was also on another stone.

He made out letters this time. Words.

GOD IS FUCKED

smeared on a white marble stone.

CHRIST CUNT

scrawled over a plinth.

'Oh no,' Patterson whispered.

Another headstone had been smashed, shattered by a heavy instrument. Pieces of stone were scattered over the dark earth.

He saw something else on the ground near by, on a grave.

It was excrement.

More of it was smeared on a white marble headstone close to him.

Patterson shook his head.

Not again.

One of the graves had been dug up.

He hurried across to it and saw that the stone had not been touched but, instead, daubed with something. A symbol. A shape?

Earth was scattered everywhere. The coffin was lying at the graveside, the top smashed in. There was more paint on the polished wood, more writing.

CUNT

Further on, to his left, he saw more earth had been disturbed. Another box had been disinterred, dragged from its resting place so that it stood almost vertically in the dirt.

There was black paint on the lid of that box and, again, no words, just a symbol. The same symbol as had been painted on the gravestone.

It took Patterson a moment to realise what it was. His mind was reeling.

In red on the stone. In black on the casket.

The sign he saw was a pentagram.

Twenty-five

There was a sharp crackle as another wasp flew into the 'Insectocutor' mounted on the wall of the café.

Catherine Reed looked up and noticed that there were already half a dozen charred shapes displayed on the glowing blue bars, like tiny hunters' trophies.

Apart from herself and Phillip Cross, there were only five people in the café. A couple was chatting and laughing at a table close to the door. Over to her right a man was poring over a newspaper, one finger constantly pushing his tea cup from side to side on the Formica-topped table.

One of the white-aproned waiters was chatting to a young woman who had a map of London laid out on the table before her. Cath watched as the waiter pointed to the map every now and then.

An older man, rugged and unkempt, sat alone in one of the booths at the far end of the café, an overcoat wrapped around him, despite the warmth inside the building. Steam rose in a steady cloud from the top of the tea urn perched behind the counter, where two more members of staff were talking while one buttered bread.

A television set, the sound turned down, sat high in one corner close to the door, the performers speaking and moving silently for those who cared to glance at them.

The air smelled of fried food and coffee.

Phillip Cross took a sip of his tea and looked at Cath. 'How did your meal go last night?' he asked, trying to inject some kind of interest into his voice. 'Your brother, wasn't it?'

Cath regarded him silently for a moment.

'He's got a few problems at the moment,' she said, quietly.

'What time did he leave?'

'About eleven. Why?'

Cross shrugged.

'Just curious,' he said, pushing a forkful of chips into his mouth.

'It was my *brother*, Phil,' Cath said, irritably.

'Well, I've only got your word for that, haven't I?'

'Are you calling me a liar?' She leaned forward, lowering her voice slightly. 'Look, even if it wasn't my brother, it's none of your fucking business *who* I have at my flat.'

'What about us?'

'What *about* us? We're not married, for Christ's sake. When are you going to accept that this isn't some big bloody romance, Phil? We both agreed we didn't want any ties.'

'*You* didn't want any ties,' he corrected her.

'So now what? You want a commitment from me?' she snapped.

There was another sharp hiss of electricity as one more wasp struck the glowing blue bars.

'Look, I don't mean to pressure you, Cath,' Cross replied. 'Maybe you're right. Perhaps I'm coming on a bit too strong. But I think a lot of you.'

She smiled. 'Thanks.'

'Why do I get the feeling that it's not reciprocated?' Cross added bitterly.

'I've been on my own a long time, Phil,' she told him. 'I like my own company. I've been in relationships before and they always end up getting too heavy.'

'It was with the wrong guys,' he offered.

She looked at him over the rim of her cup.

'And what if you're the wrong guy too? Where does that leave me?'

'Me. I. Myself. This conversation is a bit one-sided, isn't it? Haven't you ever stopped to think about *my* bloody feelings?'

'This isn't the time or the place, Phil—' she began.

'It never is,' he hissed.

They sat in silence for what seemed like an eternity.

Cath reached into her handbag and pulled out a packet of cigarettes.

'Do you mind?' she asked, noticing that he was still eating.

Cross shook his head.

She lit up.

'So, what sort of morning have *you* had?' she asked, a smile hovering on her lips.

Cross shook his head, trying to keep a straight face but failing.

'I should fucking hate you,' he said, grinning.

'I wouldn't blame you if you did.'

'All I'm asking is that you see things from my point of view. I don't think you realise how much I think of you.'

She took a drag on her cigarette and nodded slowly.

'I think I do,' she said quietly.

The face of a newsreader glared out at her from the silent television screen.

Something flashed onto the screen. Uniformed policemen.

A graveyard.

The caption at the bottom of the picture read: Croydon Cemetery.

Cath got to her feet and hurried across to the TV set, curious glances following her sudden movement. She turned up the sound and stood close to the set, staring at it as if hypnotised.

She heard the voice of the priest. The caption told her his name was Colin Patterson.

'. . . *third time this kind of thing has happened here in less than two months. I find it disgusting and I think the people who did this need help. It's appalling . . .*'

'Wasn't that where you said there'd been desecrations a few days ago?' Cath called to Cross, who had now turned in his seat to look at the screen.

Other faces, too, were glancing at the set.

'I've still got the pictures at home,' the photographer said.

'We never ran anything on it, did we?'

'They stuck a couple of columns inside. I think they used one small photo.'

'Croydon Cemetery,' Cath murmured to herself.

The picture changed, the story shifted. The newsreader was talking about a new school in Hampstead.

Cath turned the sound back down.

As she sat down at the table she ground out what was left of her cigarette.

'Didn't you say there'd been other desecrations there, before you took those photos a couple of days ago?' she asked, her gaze fixed on Cross.

'I only overheard the vicar talking to a couple of

people while I was there,' Cross explained. 'He reckoned there'd been stuff going on for months.'

'What kind of stuff?'

'I didn't hear properly.'

Cath was already on her feet.

'Where the hell are you going?' Cross demanded.

'Croydon Cemetery. I want to speak to that priest. Fancy a drive?'

'Cath, I can't, I'm due at Heathrow this afternoon, Madonna's flying in, they want pictures . . .'

'Then I'll see you later.'

'Cath, wait,' Cross called, fumbling in his camera bag. 'Here, take this.' He handed her a small pocket camera. 'You might need it.'

She smiled at him.

Then she was gone.

Cross looked up, watching as another insect perished amidst a loud crackle.

The scorched fly dropped to the floor.

He drained what was left in his tea cup.

Twenty-six

Cath had never seen so many cars at a cemetery.

The car park and most of the street outside were crammed with vehicles.

Inside it was swarming with people, many of whom, she assumed, had also seen the report on lunchtime TV and come fearing that the resting places of their own relatives might have been disturbed.

She could only guess at how many people had converged on Croydon Cemetery during the two hours it had taken her to drive there.

Once within the sprawling churchyard she'd had little difficulty finding the Reverend Colin Patterson. He had been walking agitatedly back and forth, speaking to anyone who came to him or who he felt was in need of some comforting words.

In his black robe and standing over six feet tall, he was an imposing, almost threatening, figure and, Cath noted somewhat guiltily, rather good looking. Not the kind of priest she would normally expect to find.

After a brief introduction, she got straight down to business. 'Have you any idea who might have done this?' she asked, pulling the pocket camera from her handbag and looking through the viewfinder.

She focused on a gravestone which bore the words GOD IS FUCKED in large red letters. She snapped away.

'No idea,' Patterson told her, sighing.

'Could it be a personal thing, against you?' she enquired, moving closer to another of the headstones.

This one was smeared with excrement. The smell was strong in the air. Flies buzzed round excitedly.

'Priests don't make many enemies, Miss Reed,' said Patterson.

'Besides, if it was personal, whoever did this would have come after *me*.'

'Not necessarily,' she told him, snapping off more shots.

Patterson walked a couple of paces behind her as she moved amongst the disturbed earth and the smashed stones.

'Did you call the police?'

'They've been and gone. They took samples of that,' he pointed disgustedly to the pile of excrement that had been left on top of one grave. 'They dusted the headstones for fingerprints.'

'Did *they* have any ideas who might be responsible?'

'No.'

'Were any bodies actually removed from their coffins?'

'No, thank God. A couple were broken but no remains were touched.'

Cath took several pictures of one such battered coffin, leaning forward to look at the nameplate. LOUISE BANKS. She glanced at the black marble headstone which bore the same name. It was spattered with red paint.

Cath read the inscription: LOUISE BANKS. AGED 16 MONTHS. SLEEP IN PEACE.

She took a step back, glanced at another headstone, this one smeared with excrement.

She read it.

And the one next to it.

She took photos of them both.

'Father, have you noticed something about the graves which have been desecrated?' Cath asked.

Patterson looked at her. 'They're all children,' he said, softly.

Cath nodded.

'Not one of them over the age of four,' she murmured.

She moved along to another headstone.

'Why children?' she mused.

Patterson had no answer for her. 'I'm afraid I can't help you, Miss Reed. I can't begin to understand the type of mind that could do this.' He made a sweeping gesture with one large hand, designed to encompass all the devastation.

'When it happened before, were the graves which were disturbed children's graves too?'

'Yes.'

'Do you have a list of names of those graves that I could see?'

'What good will it do?'

'There could be a link between them. If we find that link, we might find the reason it was done.'

'What reason could *anyone* have for disturbing the body of a child once it's been laid to rest?' Patterson rasped.

Cath snapped another of the shattered headstones. On the plinth was a roughly drawn pentagram.

She looked at the priest.

'The list?' she asked.

'I keep it in the church,' he told her. 'And while you're there, there's something else I think you should see.'

Twenty-seven

She knew they were watching her.

Shanine Connor walked slowly through the perfume department of Selfridge's and she knew that the women behind the counters were looking at her. Plastered with make-up and smelling of expensive scent, they followed her every movement with their mascara-shrouded eyes.

Some of the other customers glanced at her too as she made her way through the maze of glass counters, occasionally picking up one of the many testers and spraying her wrist. She didn't even bother to sniff the fragrance, but the collective aromas helped to smother the more acrid smell of her own dried perspiration.

Shanine caught sight of her own reflection in one of the many mirrors and saw how pale and drawn she looked. Her hair needed washing and she ran a hand through it, wiping that hand on her grubby jeans.

She moved onwards, through the torrent of shoppers, all of who seemed to be moving in the opposite direction. In the jewellery department she paused and inspected some gold-plated chains hanging from a felt board.

The assistant behind the counter moved across and smiled efficiently at her.

'Can I help you' she asked, no softness in her voice.

Shanine shook her head and walked on, past the bracelets and watches, through stationery and pens.

Her stomach rumbled as she smelled food.

To her left, up a short flight of steps was the food hall.

The exquisite aroma of freshly ground coffee wafted invitingly on the air and Shanine inhaled deeply.

She looked around, at the confectionery which seemed to surround her. She put out a hand and scooped a couple of wine gums into her palm, pushing them quickly into her mouth before anyone noticed.

As she moved slowly up the steps towards the main food hall, she spotted a security camera overhead.

Fuck it. She hadn't expected things to be easy.

She passed a fresh fish counter, the smell of seafood almost overpowering. Two Americans, distinguishable by their size and appalling taste in clothes as well as accents, were busy prodding a large salmon which the assistant had laid out for their inspection.

Shanine wandered by, picking up a basket as she entered the small maze of shelves lined with all manner of tinned, packet and fresh foods.

Come on. Do it quickly.

She walked awkwardly with the hold-all over one shoulder, aware that it made her more conspicuous and, as she rounded a corner, she bumped into a woman who was leading a child around, practically dragging the youngster by his arm.

Shanine put a loaf of bread into her basket.

A packet of bread rolls she slipped into the hold-all.

Tins of corned beef.

No good. How the hell would she get them open?

She found the packet meat. Slipped two packs of luncheon meat into her basket, two more into the bag.

Come on. Come on.

The woman with the child was just ahead of her, inspecting some fresh fruit.

Shanine bagged up some apples and bananas and dropped them into her basket, accidentally knocking several of the Golden Delicious onto the floor as she turned. Cursing, she dropped to her knees and started to retrieve them.

She pushed three inside the bag.

The woman with the child kneeled down and helped her pick up the other two.

'Thanks,' said Shanine.

The woman smiled, glanced at Shanine's basket then at the hold-all.

Did she know?

Shanine moved around into the next aisle.

A member of staff was stacking shelves there, pricing each can before placing it carefully in position.

She too gave Shanine a cursory glance.

Above her, she saw another security camera.

She moved into the next aisle.

Bars of chocolate. Sweets.

She scooped several Mars Bars into the hold-all.

Enough's enough.

She headed for the check-out, saw that only one till was open. There was a small queue.

The exit door was just beyond.

No doorman.

She stood in the queue, her heart pounding.

No one watching the door.

She never saw the woman with the child beckon a member of staff to her.

Never saw her pointing at Shanine.

Two to go, then she was at the check-out.

Shanine turned, trying to look unconcerned, despite the fact that she felt her heart was about to burst through her ribs.

She saw the uniformed member of staff walking down the aisle, gaze fixed on her.

That's it.

Shanine dropped the basket, leaped to one side and hurdled the chain next to the other till, dashing for the door.

She heard shouts behind her.

Shanine crashed into the door, hurled it open and dashed out into the street, glancing behind her.

She saw two members of staff emerge seconds behind her. One of them shouted something which she didn't hear.

Shanine turned the first corner and ran as fast as she could.

When she finally looked back there was no one following.

She kept running.

Twenty-eight

The steps leading down to the crypt were narrow, the stonework shiny with hundreds of years of wear.

Cath wondered how many feet had traversed these steps over the centuries.

The staircase wound down in a tight circular shape, the fusty odour which she'd detected when Patterson first opened the door now becoming more overpowering the deeper they went. Exactly how far beneath the ground they were she had no idea but she was aware of a growing chill too. Even the walls were icy to the touch, the very stone itself cold beneath her fingertips.

'How did they ever get the coffins down here?' she asked, her voice echoing slightly in the subterranean stairwell.

Patterson didn't answer, he merely walked a few feet ahead of her, the powerful beam of his torch cutting a swathe through the blackness.

Cath slipped on one of the stairs.

'Shit,' she hissed.

Patterson looked round at her.

'Sorry,' she said, quickly.

The priest smiled.

103

'Watch your step,' he said, grinning. 'You could break your ankle down here.'

They continued to descend.

'Who uses this place now?' Cath wanted to know.

'No one. The last body laid to rest here was in the 1920s,' he told her. 'I think most people tend to see crypts and tombs as archaic, something belonging in horror films. Besides, even in the old days they were the preserve of the wealthy.'

'What was wrong with burial?' Cath asked, her breath clouding before her.

'Families used to remain together even in death. A family vault or crypt was quite a status symbol.'

'The family that plays together decays together,' Cath murmured.

'You could say that,' Patterson chuckled.

'Who did this crypt belong to?'

'The Parslow family. It was built in the late eighteenth century. The family owned the land on which the church was built. Before it was a cemetery it was private land, they were a rich family. The crypt used to be above ground.'

'Why move it?'

'They wanted it beneath the church. Perhaps they thought it would bring them closer to God.'

Cath sucked in a deep breath, the smell of damp strong in her nostrils. She could see motes of dust turning lazily in the bright beam of Patterson's torch. The steps were getting smaller, levelling out.

'Look, Reverend, this is fascinating stuff but what's it got to do with the desecrations?' Cath asked, almost stumbling the last couple of steps.

Patterson shone the light at the far wall.

'Jesus Christ,' Cath whispered, transfixed.

'I don't think Christ had anything to do with *this*, Miss Reed,' Patterson commented, playing the torch beam around the crypt.

It was large, fully twenty feet from end to end and side to side, the sarcophagi piled on top of each other, reaching to a height of almost fifteen feet, close to the damp ceiling of the crypt.

On the far wall an enormous pentagram had been drawn.

It looked as if it had been hacked into the stone itself with a chisel.

There were figures too.

Cath moved closer, gazing at the crudely painted outlines.

On either side of the pentagram they stood like sentinels: one of a man sporting a huge, erect penis, the woman adorned with bulbous, thick-nippled breasts.

Cath took a couple of pictures, the flash from the camera bathing the crypt in cold white light each time she pressed the button.

'When did you find this?'

'About two weeks ago,' Patterson informed her. 'I arrived at the church one morning and found that someone had broken in. I checked to see if anything had been stolen inside and noticed that the crypt door had been forced. I came down and found this.'

Again the flash of cold light. 'Did you show the police?'

'They said it was vandals.'

'Is that what *you* think?'

'I don't know *what* to think, Miss Reed.'

Cath took a step closer to the wall, closer to the

obscene figures and the massive pentagram, her eyes fixed on something else scrawled on the cold stone.

Words. Symbols.

NEMA REVE dNA REVEROF

She could feel the skin prickling on the back of her neck.

YROLG eHT dNA REWOPeHT

It suddenly seemed much colder inside the crypt.

MODGNIK eHT SI ENIHTROF

'What the hell is it?' she murmured.

LIVE MORF SUREVILED

Patterson kept the torch beam steady on the meaning-less scribble.

'It took me a while to work it out,' he said, softly.

Cath looked at him, seeking an answer.

'It's the Lord's Prayer written backwards.'

Twenty-nine

'So who the fuck is he?' demanded Talbot, his eyes never leaving the front entrance of the shop.

'No one knows,' Rafferty replied, his own gaze also directed at the building.

'What about the girl, do we know *her* name?' the DI persisted.

'Emma Jackson. She works in there.'

'Who saw it?'

'One of the customers,' Rafferty told his superior. 'She'd just opened up, about an hour ago now. This geezer walks in, pulls a knife out of his pocket, tells the customer to fuck off, then went for the girl. As far as we can tell she's not hurt.'

'Not yet,' murmured Talbot.

The Ann Summers shop in Wardour Street looked deserted, apart from the lifeless shapes of the models standing in the window. They seemed to stare back at Talbot.

What had those blank eyes seen? he wondered.

'Is the back sealed off?' he enquired.

Rafferty nodded. 'There's no way he's coming out of there,' the DS said, a hint of satisfaction in his voice. Traffic to the north and south had been diverted, the road closed. Red and white barriers had been erected across the thoroughfare. Uniformed policemen stood by them. At both, Talbot noticed, crowds had built up, maybe a hundred people on either side, anxious to see what was going on.

Morbid fuckers.

He even caught sight of a camera held in one set of eager hands.

'Has anyone spoken to him yet?' Talbot asked.

'One of the uniformed men,' Rafferty replied.

'And?'

'He said he just wants to talk to the girl.'

Talbot looked incredulously at his companion.

'He doesn't want money, he doesn't want a getaway car. He just wants to talk to her,' the DS said.

'For fuck's sake,' sighed Talbot clambering out of the Escort. Rafferty followed him, watching as his superior brushed some dust from the sleeve of his jacket.

'What do you want to do, Jim?' the younger man asked.

'Get inside there,' Talbot answered, already taking a couple of paces towards the shop.

Rafferty joined him. 'What about the girl?' he asked anxiously.

'If he's already killed her then we may as well go in now. If he's *thinking* of killing her it could take him all fucking day to make up his mind, but, if I'm right, then he doesn't want to hurt her.'

'What makes you so sure?'

'Ever heard of a gut feeling, Bill?'

'And what if you're wrong, what if he *does* want to kill her?'

'Have an ambulance crew standing by,' Talbot said, indifferently.

He strode across the street, watched by the hordes of uniformed men and the curious crowd.

The man with the camera snapped off a couple of shots as the DI approached the door.

Rafferty scurried across to join him.

From either side, crouching low to the pavement, uniformed men edged nearer.

Talbot waved them back.

He banged hard on the door, leaning close to it, trying to see through the dirty glass.

The lights were off inside, it was difficult to make

out shapes. All he could see clearly was a rack of basques hanging close to the entrance.

There was a counter to his right, glass topped and fronted. He could see a selection of vibrators inside.

Something moved towards the back of the shop.

He saw a figure move a couple of paces towards the door.

A young man, no more than twenty-five.

He was carrying a short-bladed knife in his right hand.

'Fuck off!' he screamed at Talbot.

'Open the door or I'll break it down,' the DI said, impassively.

He watched as the man retreated a few feet then grabbed at something hidden by the counter. Talbot saw him drag a young woman into view.

About twenty-four, petite, pretty.

The man hauled her in front of him and pushed the knife to her face.

'You try coming in and I'll hurt her,' shouted the man who was dressed in jeans and a black shirt.

Rafferty looked at his superior. 'What do you reckon?' he said.

Talbot shook his head. 'Open the door now!' he bellowed.

The young man looked at the girl, then at Talbot. 'I'll cut her,' he called back, his voice cracking slightly. 'I mean it.'

'He's scared shitless,' Talbot said.

'Be careful, Jim,' Rafferty said, softly.

'Keep them back,' the DI told his companion, motioning towards the uniformed men near by. 'I'll sort it.'

Rafferty took a couple of paces back and barked

109

something into the two-way radio he pulled from his jacket pocket.

Talbot kicked at the door, the glass rattling in its frame. He drove another powerful boot into it and it flew back on its hinges. The DI found himself standing inside the shop.

It smelled of cheap perfume and sweat.

Talbot looked at the girl's face.

Apart from some puffiness around her eyes she looked unharmed. Her make-up was smudged and there were mascara stains on her cheeks but, as far as he could see, no wounds of any description.

'Put down the knife,' Talbot said.

'You shouldn't have done that,' said Black Shirt, through clenched teeth.

'Just put it down before someone gets hurt,' Talbot continued. He took a step forward.

'Stay there,' black shirt shouted.

Talbot moved forward more cautiously.

The knife blade was hovering close to the girl's cheek.

'Just let her walk away,' Talbot said, still taking slow deliberate steps towards Black Shirt and his hostage.

'If you come one step closer I'll stab her,' Black Shirt babbled, none too convincingly.

'Go on, then.'

It was the girl's turn to look surprised.

'Go on then, you little prick,' snapped Talbot. 'Kill her.'

Black Shirt was breathing rapidly now, perspiration had already beaded on his forehead.

'You're already looking at aggravated assault, possible ABH, maybe even kidnapping. You want to add murder to that list? Be my fucking guest.' He moved closer, pushing aside a rail hung with silk knickers. 'Go

110

on, hard man, fucking cut her. Slice her up. Impress me.'

'You're fucking nuts,' Black Shirt blabbered.

'Let her go.'

'He didn't hurt me,' the girl said, seeing the DI drawing nearer.

'Good. Then *you* ask him to let you go. Do you *know* him?'

She nodded.

Bingo.

'Boyfriend?' the DI continued, his progress even.

'Look, things got out of hand,' said Black Shirt, uncertainly.

'Let her go.'

The knife was lowered a fraction.

Talbot was about three feet from the couple now, his eyes fixed on the watery gaze of Black Shirt.

He could hear him breathing, smell his sweat.

'Let her go.'

Two feet.

Black Shirt allowed the knife to waver a little lower but he kept his grip on the girl's shoulder.

'Come on, I'm not playing fucking games,' hissed Talbot. 'Let her go.'

Black Shirt looked at Talbot, then at his captive, and pulled his hand away.

She stepped away from him, leaning against the counter.

'Drop the knife,' Talbot ordered.

Black Shirt stood motionless, the knife held before him now.

Talbot extended one hand, palm up. 'Give me the knife.'

Black Shirt was shaking now, barely able to control

his own breathing. He looked across at the girl who nodded almost imperceptibly.

'The knife,' Talbot repeated.

Black Shirt reached out to hand over the blade.

Talbot gripped the proffered wrist, twisted and simultaneously wrenched the younger man towards him. In one swift movement, he drove his head forward, slamming his forehead into Black Shirt's face.

The impact broke the younger man's nose, blood bursting from it, spilling onto the floor, some of it spattering Talbot.

The girl shouted something and ran towards him.

Talbot felt a blow against his back.

'You bastard,' shouted the girl but Talbot merely pushed her away.

Rafferty came scurrying into the shop, four uniformed men behind him, one of them an ambulanceman.

He saw the girl standing against the counter, saw Black Shirt crouching on the floor, blood gushing through his fingers as he clapped both hands to his face.

'Get them out of here,' Talbot instructed, turning towards the door. 'And move that fucking crowd from the street, the show's over.'

Behind him he could hear the girl crying.

Thirty

Frank Reed looked at the phone perched on the corner of his desk.

What are you waiting for?

He leaned back in his chair, stretching his arms in front of him, hearing the joints of his elbows crack.

Outside his office he could hear voices and, swivelling around in his chair, he saw a group of children walking unhurriedly across the playground towards one of the more modern blocks of classrooms. He couldn't see the face of the teacher who led them, but he recognised the broad back and the worn tweed jacket: Don Hicks, Biology.

Reed smiled to himself.

Hicks was a couple of years older than Reed and the two men got on well. Indeed, as Deputy Head, Reed had a good rapport with all of his colleagues. Even the older ones didn't seem to resent the fact that a man young enough to be their son, in some cases, held such a lofty position. Even if the salary didn't match the responsibility, Reed mused.

He turned back to face his desk.

And the phone.

The door of his office was open slightly and from the outer office he could hear the sounds of a typewriter being pounded by the secretary both he and the head-master shared. No new-fangled technology for her. No computers or word processors. She was loyal to her old electric typewriter.

He got to his feet and crossed to the door, closing it, then returned to his desk and looked at the phone once more.

He picked it up and dialled.

Had he got the right number?

Unsure, he pressed down on the cradle and checked the number he wanted in his diary. He dialled again and waited.

113

It was ringing.

Come on.

And ringing.

Perhaps they were out.

Or busy?

He tapped agitatedly on his desk top with his finger-tips.

What are they doing?

Reed tried to push the thoughts from his mind.

Perhaps you're disturbing them. Perhaps they're in bed together. Perhaps he's fucking her.

'Pick it up,' Reed hissed.

They might not be able to hear it. Didn't she tell you he made her feel so good?

Reed ran a hand through his hair.

So good.

At the other end the receiver was picked up.

'Hello,' said a man's voice.

Reed was so lost in his own thoughts that it took him a second to react.

'Hello,' repeated the voice at the other end.

'Could I speak to Ellen Reed, please?'

There was a moment's silence followed by a little chuckle.

'Frank, how nice to hear from you,' said Jonathan Ward.

Don't you dare laugh at me, you bastard.

'Can I speak to Ellen, please?' the teacher said, trying to contain his irritation.

'And how are *you*, Frank? Keeping well?' Ward said, that trace of derision in his voice. 'We haven't heard from you for so long we were starting to get worried.'

'Yeah, I bet you were. Just put Ellen on, will you?'

114

'I don't know if she wants to speak to you, Frank,' Ward told him dismissively.

'Just get her,' Reed snapped, his free hand now balled into a fist.

'What did you want to speak to her about?'

'That's between her and me. It's none of your business.'

'Ellen and I have no secrets from each other, Frank. She'll tell me if I ask her, anyway.'

'Yeah, she'd do anything for you, wouldn't she?' Reed spat.

Ward sniggered. 'You're probably right, Frank,' he said. Then all Reed heard was the sound of the receiver being laid on a hard surface.

'Bastard,' the teacher murmured under his breath.

He waited.

At the other end he heard the receiver being lifted.

'Hello,' said the woman's voice.

'Ellen, it's Frank.'

Silence.

'Ellen, I said—'

'I heard you. What do you want?' she asked curtly.

'I need to talk to you.'

'We've got nothing to say.'

'We've hardly said a dozen words to each other since . . .' He allowed the sentence to trail off.

'Since I left you?'

'How's Becky?'

'She's fine.'

'And how are you?'

'Oh, Christ, you're not going to make small-talk are you?'

'We need to talk, Ellen,' Reed said, angrily. 'About Becky, about *us*.'

'There is no *us* any more,' she told him, flatly.

Reed swallowed hard. 'How's Becky?'

'She's fine.'

'I want to see her, Ellen.'

'We were thinking of going away for a few days – it isn't convenient now.'

'You're talking about *my* daughter,' he rasped. 'I want to see her.'

'Look, I'll call you, right?'

'Ellen. You can't do this to me. She's my daughter. If I have to get the police I will. You won't keep her from me. I'll do—'

'Do what you fucking want,' she snarled and slammed down the phone.

He sat at his desk, the receiver still pressed to his ear, the buzz of a dead line the only thing he heard.

Very slowly, he slipped the phone back onto its cradle.

Fucking bitch.

Reed waited a moment then snatched up the phone and dialled another number.

And waited.

Thirty-one

Sean Harvey thought how aptly named the restaurant in Hays Mews was.

The Greenhouse was more like a large, immaculately decorated, conservatory than an eatery. He sat glancing

116

around at the faces of the other diners, relatively few for a lunchtime, his gaze turning towards the restaurant's main door every so often.

He glanced at his watch.

She was late.

Despite the fact that the windows near him were open, it was very warm inside the restaurant, as the sun hovering high in the sky overhead blazed down. The plants potted carefully all around the tables, obviously responded to the temperature and blossomed.

Harvey felt a bead of perspiration forming on his forehead.

He wasn't sure how much of it was apprehension.

He looked at his watch again.

What if she didn't turn up at all?

He looked at his menu, sipped his Perrier and attempted to look nonchalant.

The gesture failed miserably.

Harvey glanced towards the main entrance again and this time he saw her.

Thank Christ.

He stood up as she made her way towards his table, smiling at him, brushing her blonde hair away from her face.

Hailey Owen was dressed in a short, rust-coloured skirt and matching jacket. She walked gracefully in a pair of high heels, the tips clicking on the tiled floor of the restaurant. Harvey couldn't resist an appreciative glance, allowing his gaze to linger on her slender legs.

'Sorry I'm late,' she said, sitting down opposite him.

'You're not, I was early,' he told her. 'Do you want a drink?'

She nodded as he called the waiter to him and

ordered another Perrier for himself and a Bacardi and Coke for her.

'I would have been here earlier,' Hailey told him. 'But I couldn't get away. Debbie wanted me to go for lunch with *her* – I had to make up an excuse about shopping. I said I was going to a wedding and had to get a dress. Then she wanted to come with me to help me pick it. I thought I was never going to get away.'

The waiter returned with the drinks.

He watched as Hailey took a sip of hers.

'No one knew where you were going?' he asked.

She shook her head. 'What about you?'

'I told my secretary I was meeting a client, I said I might be late back,' he announced.

'You don't think anyone knows, do you, Sean?'

He shook his head.

'We've been careful so far.'

'We've been *lucky* so far,' she reminded him.

'We don't even work on the same floor, Hailey, why should anybody suspect we're . . .'

'Having an affair?'

'Three lunches and two dinners hardly constitute an affair, do they?'

'Your wife might disagree if she found out. Where did you tell her you were the other night?'

'She knows I work late, that I meet clients. She doesn't suspect anything, trust me.'

'*You* might be used to this, Sean, but I've never had an affair before. I just don't want anything to spoil it.'

'Stop worrying.'

He pushed a menu towards her.

'Let's order,' he said, smiling.

Harvey watched her as she ran her gaze up and down

the list of offerings, one hand pulling lazily at her long hair.

She noticed his attention and smiled. 'What are you looking at?'

'I'm just looking. You don't blame me, do you?' he said, quietly.

She shook her head and giggled.

'You're a real smoothie, aren't you?'

Beneath the table he felt her foot brush against his calf.

Briefly. Tantalisingly.

She sipped her drink, wondering what the dark shadow was that had suddenly fallen across the table.

It was as if a cloud had passed before the sun.

But this was too small, too dark to be a cloud.

They both looked up.

Harvey opened his mouth.

Hailey didn't even manage to give voice to the scream.

The man's body plunged down towards them, slamming into the glass roof of the restaurant.

Glass exploded inwards, the strident eruption of splintering crystal mingling with a deafening crash as the body came hurtling through.

It struck the table where they sat, crushing glasses beneath it, overturning the table as more shards of glass rained down, exploding on the tiled floor.

And there was something hot and red splashing Hailey now.

Blood, jetting madly from a dozen wounds on the body, lacerated by the glass and the impact, spurted in all directions, some of it across her face and hair.

Finally, Hailey managed to scream.

119

The body flopped over onto its back, face shredded by the glass fragments, one long sliver embedded in the eye like a crystal spear.

Harvey fell away from the blood-spattered table, trying to control his churning stomach, aware that there was already a dark stain spreading across the front of his trousers.

Blood began to spill rapidly around the corpse which lay motionless amidst the shattered glass, broken crockery and scattered cutlery.

Other diners looked on in horror, one or two glancing up at the gaping hole in the glass roof left by the plummeting body. Pieces of broken glass were still dropping from the edges of the break.

Hailey felt a searing pain in her left hand and realised that the back of it had been sliced open by a piece of glass the size of a dinner plate.

But her own pain was all but forgotten as she stared down at the body, aware that the widening pool of blood around it was now lapping at the toes of her shoes.

Harvey saw that one piece of glass had torn away most of the flesh at the side of the dead man's face. The skin had been sliced raggedly from the corner of his mouth to his cheekbone, exposing his teeth and gums.

It looked as if he was smiling.

Harvey lost his battle and vomited.

Hailey continued to scream.

Thirty-two

The air was heavy with cigarette smoke, and Detective Inspector James Talbot inhaled deeply as he walked back and forth, chewing on a handful of chocolate peanuts which he was taking from a wrinkled paper bag.

The other men in the room either watched him or sat glancing down at their notes.

Phillip Barclay opened a window close to him and tried to waft some of the smoke out.

Rafferty grinned and lit another cigarette.

Of the two other men present, one was also smoking, twisting his cigarette in his fingers, watching the ash drop into the plastic cup which had contained coffee. His companion, a younger man dressed in a black suit and white shirt which looked a size too small for him, was drawing circles on a piece of paper with his Biro.

Talbot finally stopped pacing and turned to the noticeboard behind him.

'Craig Jeffrey,' he began, tapping a black and white ten-by-eight of a smiling man. 'Thirty-two years old, surveyor, engaged. Due to be married in three months' time.'

'Maybe that's why he topped himself,' mumbled the man in the black suit.

The other men laughed.

Talbot smiled wanly.

'They reckon it's difficult to get a table at that bloody restaurant,' the man next to Barclay offered. 'Perhaps he was desperate.'

More laughter.

Detective Constable Colin Penhallow ground out his cigarette in the plastic cup.

'Enough of the fucking cabaret,' Talbot said, chewing on another peanut. 'Any ideas?'

'Are we sure it was suicide?' Rafferty asked.

Talbot looked at Barclay. 'Phil,' he said and all eyes turned to the coroner.

Barclay cleared his throat. 'The autopsy showed no trace of any substances, legal or illegal, in his blood. Further examination showed no reason to suspect that he was murdered. I think we can rule out foul play.'

Talbot shrugged.

'What was he doing in that house in Hays Mews, anyway?' Rafferty wanted to know.

'He was doing a survey for a building society,' Talbot replied.

'So, while he was inside, he decided to climb up onto the roof and chuck himself off,' Penhallow mused.

'That's what it looks like,' Talbot added, chewing more peanuts.

'No drink, no drugs. No reasons why he should have done it,' Rafferty interjected. 'Just like the other two.'

Talbot nodded.

'Three suicides inside eight days,' he continued. 'All professional men. A surveyor, an accountant and an architect. All with stable home lives, as far as we know, all well paid, settled. None of them had any reason that we know of for committing suicide. But they did.'

'People kill themselves every day, Jim,' Penhallow

122

offered. 'What makes these three geezers so special?'

'That's what we need to find out,' Talbot told him.

'Have the wives or girlfriends been any help?' DC Stephen Longley asked, brushing at the sleeve of his black jacket.

Talbot shook his head.

'They all gave statements: none of them reported noticing any changes in behaviour in any of the three men. They also weren't aware that any of the men were under undue pressure. As far as they're concerned, there's no logical reason for the suicides.'

'So what do we do now?' Rafferty asked.

'Guv, if you don't mind me asking,' said Penhallow, raising a hand. 'Why are we investigating three suicides when we *know* that's what they were? I mean, there isn't a hint of foul play in any of them, is there?' He looked at Barclay.

The coroner shook his head.

'There's something not quite right here,' Talbot said. 'I want to know if there were links, I want to know if they knew each other.'

'Parriam knew Hyde,' Rafferty offered. 'I told you about that entry in his diary.'

'And I told *you* that one entry didn't make them close friends,' the DI reminded him. 'But I agree with you, Bill, it's a coincidence. It's also a coincidence that all three were professional men. Men who may have moved in the same circles. Find out if they did.'

'What'll it prove, Jim?' Penhallow enquired.

'It might just tie up a few loose ends,' Talbot said.

'What loose ends?' Longley asked. 'They topped themselves, no one knows why. Sorry and all that, but tough. Where's the investigation?'

123

'Just check it out in your spare time, I'm not asking for a full-scale investigation. Indulge me, Steve,' Talbot said. 'I'm curious.'

He turned and looked at the photos of the three dead men.

'What were you thinking?' he murmured, his gaze travelling slowly over the three faces. The DI finally turned to face his men again. 'OK, fellas, that's it for now. I want reports in three days.'

The other men rose and headed for the door.

'Phil, hang on a minute, will you?' Talbot called to the coroner.

Barclay hesitated and closed the door as the last of the officers walked out.

'You said the autopsies showed no trace of drugs, right?' Talbot said.

Barclay nodded.

'Could you have missed anything?' the DI pondered.

'If you're questioning my abilities . . .'

The DI held up a hand.

'I'm not questioning anything, Phil. I just wondered if there could be some kind of drug that might have been absorbed into the blood stream so fast that it didn't show up on the autopsies.'

'Taken voluntarily?'

Talbot didn't answer.

'You think someone might have *made* them commit suicide?' Barclay offered.

'Yeah, it's crazy, I know. I think it's called clutching at straws.'

The coroner leaned on the back of a chair and looked at Talbot.

'If it wasn't a drug, how about something else?

Hypnotism, something like that?' Talbot persisted.

'I doubt it, Jim, and, even if it was, even if someone *did* force them to kill themselves, you still have to find out why. What reason could there be for wanting those three men dead?'

The DI nodded slowly.

'You're right,' he said, glancing at the black and white pictures again. 'And if we find the *why*, we have to find the *who*. But just suppose it was possible. Just suppose that someone wanted those three men dead.' He pointed at the pictures. 'It's perfect. No suspect, no murder weapon. No clues.'

'I thought you were supposed to be the cynical one.' Talbot grinned.

'Like I said, Phil, just clutching at straws.' His grin faded slightly.

He continued gazing at the photos.

Thirty-three

Terence Nicholls ran a hand through his short, greying hair and turned over the next photo.

He considered each one carefully, studying every aspect of the image, like an art connoisseur.

Occasionally he would sit back in his chair, particularly intrigued by an image. When he did sit back he made a conscious effort to pull in his sagging stomach muscles. The buttons of his shirt were straining just a little uncomfortably against his belly. But it was the only part of his body that carried any excess fat. The rest of his frame was lean. His face most notably was thin, almost gaunt, his grey-flecked hair giving him the appearance of being older than his thirty-nine years. His fingernails, despite being immaculately manicured, were dirty. Grimy with newsprint and ink. Like the pads of his fingers which he wiped every now and then on the corner of a handkerchief protruding from his trouser pocket.

His desk was unnaturally tidy for a newspaper editor. No stray pieces of paper left lying wantonly on the wooden top. No scattered paper clips or pens. Everything was in its place. The only thing incongruous amidst this neatness was his coffee mug, which was so darkly stained inside, even the strongest detergent couldn't restore the original colour of the china. In fact, he'd given up washing it weeks ago. The stains were as much a part of the design as the logo: SHIT HAPPENS AND YOU'RE LIVING PROOF. Behind him, bookshelves were laden so heavily with hundreds of different-sized volumes, it seemed they would collapse at any moment. Blu-tacked to one shelf was a crayon drawing with DADDY scrawled beneath a multi-coloured figure. A gift from his three-year old son.

'Jesus,' said Nicholls finally, pushing the pile of photos back across his desk towards Catherine Reed. 'Did you take *all* of those?'

Cath nodded.

'This has been going on for the last three months, Terry,' she said. 'Graves dug up, headstones smashed, graffiti on tombs.'

'And the police know about it?' he enquired.

"They say it's vandalism.'

'Maybe it is, but it's a bit different to smashing car windows or writing "bollocks" on somebody's front door, isn't it? What does the priest there make of it?'

'He seems to think it's vandals as well, but it's upset him.'

'Have you spoken to any of the relatives of those whose graves were dug up?'

'Not yet.'

'And they've always been kids, you say?'

Cath nodded.

'There's a story here, Terry. Something big, I reckon.'

'What's your angle?'

'How far vandals will go these days. What sort of people would do this.' She prodded one of the photos. 'How much worse can it get? Is there a purpose to it? That kind of thing.'

He nodded and pulled half a dozen of the pictures back towards him. 'I remember this sort of shit happening at Highgate Cemetery a few years ago. Graves were dug up. Some coffins even had the bodies removed. There was some bloke who claimed there was a vampire loose in there.' Nicholls chuckled. 'I was assistant editor at the *Highgate Herald* then. We had front pages of the stuff for about a week. A few people reckoned they'd seen this vampire.'

He turned over the pictures again.

'Have you thought about the witchcraft angle?' he said, quietly, his gaze riveted to a shot of the giant pentagram on the wall of the crypt.

'Witchcraft?' said Cath, sounding surprised.

'Desecrated graves, pentagrams, the Lord's Prayer written backwards. It's worth investigating,' he continued.

127

'The punters usually go for that kind of thing. Find out if there've been any animals sacrificed there, too. Check with the local police to see if anyone's reported their cat or dog missing – somebody might have used it in some sort of ritual.'

'Are you serious?' she said, grinning.

'Of course I'm serious,' Nicholls told her. 'Talk to the local RSPCA, too.'

'You don't honestly believe that this is about witchcraft, do you, Terry?'

'A bunch of fucking druggies out of their heads on something, dancing around in cloaks and having an orgy. As far as I'm concerned that's close enough to witchcraft to make it interesting for your average reader.'

'Do *you* believe in it?'

'Do I fuck! But some of the dickheads who do might just be stupid enough to dig up a few graves, smash a few headstones and paint signs on a church crypt wall. It's not the devil they want, it's a quick shag. They're playing at it, Cath, but it makes good copy. It sells papers.'

'Perhaps I should do some research about black magic too,' she chuckled.

'Whatever you want. Find as many angles as you can. Milk it. I agree with you, it could be big.'

'I'm talking about doing a serious investigation into the causes and nature of vandalism, and you're talking about witchcraft.'

'I'm talking about selling papers,' Nicholls told her, scanning some more of the pictures. 'Has it only happened at Croydon Cemetery so far?'

'As far as I know.'

'Check out some others.' He grinned. 'Just be careful no one puts a spell on you.'

'I'll get my broomstick and black cat and get going, then,' Cath joked, getting to her feet. She paused as she reached his office door.

'Terry, what if it turns out to be real?'

He looked puzzled.

'If it really *is* linked to black magic,' she prompted.

'Then we'll run it on the front page next to the interviews with Father Christmas and the fucking tooth fairy.'

He heard her laughter as she closed the door.

Nicholls reached for the phone as it rang.

Thirty-four

Frank Reed sat at his desk glancing out of the classroom window into the corridor beyond.

He could see the heads of dozens of children as they hurried by, some using as much restraint as they could muster to stop themselves from running. But the final bell had sounded. They could go home and that was exactly what they were doing, with undue haste and delight.

Reed cleaned the blackboard behind him and dropped the chalky eraser onto the ledge beneath it, wiping his hands to remove the dust. He massaged the back of his neck with one hand, feeling a dull ache growing more intense there.

He gathered up his text books and shoved them into the battered leather briefcase he always carried them in.

Ellen had bought it for him for their first wedding anniversary.

Ellen.

He looked at the case and gritted his teeth.

Bitch.

As he left the classroom he locked the door, twisting the handle to ensure it was correctly secured.

Two young boys sprinted past him up the corridor.

'Don't run,' Reed shouted, smiling to himself as he saw them stop dead and continue at a more leisurely pace.

He watched them reach the door at the end of the corridor and was about to turn when he saw a familiar figure heading towards him.

As ever, she was dressed in a grey tracksuit, her long blonde hair pulled back and fastened in a pony tail. She seemed to bounce along on her immaculately clean trainers, and Reed smiled as he saw her.

Judith Nelson was six years younger than Reed, the head of the Physical Education department at St Michael's for the last five years now. A divorcee who now lived alone, she'd joined the school about a fortnight after Reed.

'Do you always have to look so bloody healthy?' he said, smiling. 'It's very depressing for the rest of us.'

'Fresh air and exercise,' Judith said, smiling. 'You look like you could do with some, Frank.'

They headed off towards the staffroom.

'I could do with *something*,' he said, wearily.

'Problems at home?' she enquired.

'I wouldn't bore you with it, Judith.'

'Why not? I bored you with *my* problems when I split up with my husband.'

Reed didn't answer.

'Come on, Frank,' she persisted.

'You didn't have kids, did you?'

'No, but splitting up still wasn't easy.'

'It's always more complicated with kids, Judith.'

'Is that the problem, then?'

'Ellen won't let me see my daughter.'

'She can't stop you, can she?'

'Not legally, no. I can take it to court, fight her for custody, all that shit. But I don't want to do that unless I have to. For Becky's sake. I don't want her to see me and her mother fighting over her. The problem is, I think that's what it might come to. I'm not letting her go without a fight.'

'Has she said why she won't let you see her?'

'Look, Judith, no offence but forget it, will you? I appreciate your concern but. . . .' He allowed the sentence to trail off.

'Just trying to help.'

They entered another corridor and Judith glanced into one of the empty classrooms.

'Not again,' she murmured, her attention caught by something inside.

Reed followed her gaze and saw a figure seated at the rear of the classroom.

He followed Judith inside.

The young girl who sat at the back of the room, satchel clasped on the desk before her, was about eleven; she was pale, thin-faced and a little scruffy. The cuffs of her dark blue cardigan needed mending and he also noticed a button was missing. The white socks she wore were badly in need of a wash, as was her grey skirt.

When she saw the two teachers she seemed to sink back against the wall, as if trying to blend in with its yellow-painted brickwork.

'Didn't you hear the bell, Annette?' Judith asked. 'Home time.'

The girl lowered her gaze, reluctant to meet the stare of the teachers.

'All your friends have gone,' Judith prompted.

'I'm sorry,' the girl said, almost inaudibly.

'Go on, run along now,' Judith said, softly, one hand touching the girl's shoulder.

She pulled away sharply, her head still lowered.

Reed looked on curiously.

'Are you feeling all right?' Judith asked.

The girl nodded and got to her feet.

As she eased herself out from behind the desk, Reed saw a large bluish-yellow bruise on her calf.

Aware of his prying gaze she hurriedly pulled up her off-white sock and made for the door.

'Anyone would think you didn't want to go home,' Judith called after her.

The two teachers watched as the young girl disappeared out of the door and went slowly up the corridor.

'That's three times in the past week I've found her here after last bell,' said Judith.

'What's her name?' Reed asked.

'Annette Hilston.'

'I know the name. Big family, aren't they? Five or six kids.'

'I think Annette's the youngest. I can't understand it. She used to be such a happy kid – chatty, friendly – but over the last few weeks she's become very withdrawn.'

Reed frowned. 'Did you see that bruise on her leg?' he asked.

'I've seen other marks on her, too. In the changing rooms, when the girls have been getting ready for sport.'

'More bruises?'

Judith nodded.

'And marks on the wrists?' Reed persisted.

'How did you know?'

'One of my lads, Paul O'Brian, he's the same. Withdrawn, unsociable, and he had what looked like burns on his wrists. He says there's nothing wrong, but if I didn't know better I'd say he was acting as if he was scared of something.'

'Like what?'

Reed shook his head. 'His parents, maybe?'

'Do you think that's the problem with Annette, too?'

'It's possible. Just do me a favour will you, Judith? Keep an eye on her. If you see any more injuries on her, let me know.'

'You think the parents did it?'

'I didn't say that, and this conversation doesn't go any further, right?'

Judith nodded.

'There's probably a perfectly logical explanation for it,' he said, none too convincingly.

'For the bruises and marks, you mean?' Judith said, her words hanging in the air.

'For the sake of those kids,' said Reed, 'I hope to Christ there is.'

Thirty-five

'She should be in fucking hospital,' shouted Talbot, angrily.

From behind his desk, Dr Maurice Hodges watched the policeman pacing angrily back and forth.

'Your mother *fell*, Mr Talbot, she didn't *collapse*,' the physician said, finally.

'She should be in hospital anyway,' the DI persisted.

'They can't do any more for your mother in hospital than we can do for her here. She's been examined, she's fine.'

'She's got cancer, in case you'd forgotten, Doctor. That's a bloody strange definition of "fine",' Talbot rasped.

He ran a hand through his hair and finally sat down. 'Jesus,' he muttered.

'I can understand how you feel,' Hodges told him.

'Can you?'

A long silence followed, finally broken by the doctor.

'She knows about the cancer, Mr Talbot,' Hodges said, quietly. 'When she fell, earlier today, we took her to St Ann's for a precautionary x-ray. We wondered if she might have cracked a rib when she fell.'

'Yeah, so?' Talbot said, challengingly. 'What's a broken rib got to do with fucking lung cancer?'

'She asked to see the x-rays and the radiologist showed her. She saw the shadow on the lung and asked me about it when she got back.'

'So you told her?'

'I thought it was right.'

'The radiologist showed her the x-rays,' Talbot said, incredulously. 'What the fuck was he doing that for?'

'Look, that was nothing to do with us, Mr Talbot, if I'd known . . .'

The DI got to his feet again.

'Well, Mrs Talbot, the good news is your ribs are fine, the bad news is you're dying of cancer. Was *that* it?' He rounded angrily on Hodges.

'Did you want to tell her yourself?' Hodges responded.

Talbot exhaled deeply and shook his head.

Hodge watched as the policeman sat down once more.

'She's been asking me to take her home for a while now,' Talbot said, finally. 'I keep telling her it's impossible.'

'Is there no way?' Hodges asked.

'Why do you think I put her in here in the first place? There isn't a day goes by without me feeling guilty about locking her away here like some family secret.'

'I'd hardly call it locking her away, Mr Talbot.'

'That's what it feels like to me.'

'There are people who can look after her at her home if that's what you want. The Macmillan nurses are a fine organisation – they tend to cancer patients in their own homes, visit on a daily basis.'

Talbot shook his head.

'Then you might have to think about finding her a place at a hospice when the time comes,' Hodges said, softly.

'No way,' Talbot snapped. 'I'm not sticking her in one

135

of those places. It was bad enough putting her *here*.'

'You haven't any family who—'

'No.' Talbot snapped. 'No family.'

No fucking family.

He got to his feet once again, this time walking towards the door of Hodges' office.

The doctor rose and followed him.

'I'm sorry about this, Mr Talbot,' he said, quietly.

The DI smiled humourlessly and, when he spoke, there was a crushing weariness in his tone.

'So am I, Doc,' he murmured.

He held the physician's gaze for a moment, then turned and walked away.

Cath saw him enter the office and smiled briefly before returning her attention to the screen before her.

Unlike her editor's desk, Cath's was organised chaos. Notebooks, pieces of paper, books, even a piece of half-eaten cheesecake, all looked as if they'd been piled on the desk in some bizarre kind of competition to see how much rubbish could be placed on one single piece of furniture. There was scarcely room for her wordprocessor. She sipped from a plastic cup as she worked, oblivious to the noise around her; the constant symphony of ringing phones and chattering voices, of shouts and occasional laughter.

'Did you find what you wanted this afternoon?'

The voice startled her and she spun round in her seat to see Phillip Cross standing beside her.

The photographer was looking at the screen glowing before Cath.

'At Croydon Cemetery,' he continued. 'Was it worth the trip?'

'It was incredible,' she said, excitedly. 'Phil, look at these.'

She pushed some of the photos she'd taken towards him, watching as he inspected each one carefully.

'You could have done with a bit more backlight on some of these,' Cross said, grinning.

Cath eyed him irritably.

'Not bad for a beginner,' he said, still grinning.

'I didn't want your professional opinion,' she snapped, snatching the pictures back from him.

'Excuse *me*,' said Cross holding up his hands.

She returned her attention to the screen once again.

'You saw what was done to those graves,' she said, fingers skipping over the keyboard. 'It's the same as what was done a few days ago. The pictures *you* took there.'

'Same idiots,' he said, shrugging. 'What's the big deal?'

'Can I have those pictures, Phil?'

'Why, don't you think your own are good enough?' Cross chuckled. He looked at his watch. 'What time are you getting out of here tonight?'

'Why?'

'I wondered if you wanted to get a takeaway, we can go back to my place and—'

'Not tonight, Phil,' Cath cut in.

'Why not?'

'I'm working on this story, and besides, tonight's no good anyway, I'm seeing my brother about something.'

'Again? Are you sure it's your brother?'

'Don't start that again. Tomorrow night, OK?'

He looked down at her. 'Maybe, I'll have to check my diary,' he snapped and walked away.

Cath turned to say something then decided against it.
She looked at the screen, then at her watch.
Another hour.
She went back to work.

Thirty-six

Shanine Connor still had most of the food left. As she sat
on the pavement in Leicester Square looking around her
at the dizzying array of neon, she slipped a hand inside
the hold-all and pulled out a Mars Bar.

As she did, her hand brushed against the knife.

Two girls, no older than she, passed by and shot her
curious glances.

As they moved away from her, Shanine saw one turn
and look back briefly.

She watched as they headed across the road towards
a club which seemed to be lit entirely by red and blue
fizzing lights. She saw others approaching the doors. A
sign which read 'BUZZ' glowed brightly in the night,
above the entrance. The bouncers, dressed in black
suits, stood impassively, expressions hidden behind the
dark glasses they wore.

Shanine watched the two girls approach the entrance.
Girls like her.

One was dressed in a short black dress which clung to
her slim form like a second skin, a black silk jacket slung
casually around her bare shoulders. Her blue-black hair
seemed to gleam in the reflected glow of the neon.

Her companion was wearing a trouser suit, immaculately tailored.

Shanine pulled at a rip in her grubby leggings, running one filthy hand through hair which needed washing.

The girls had disappeared inside the club.

Girls like her.

She got to her feet and hooked the bag over her shoulder.

Leicester Square was busy, this night and every night. Constant streams of people criss-crossed *en route* to or from restaurants, cafés or cinemas, forming one enormous amoebic mass until each face became indistinguishable from the next. Shanine moved among them, glad of the anonymity the crowd offered.

She chewed at the Mars Bar as she walked, the craving in her belly satisfied long ago. The food should last her another day or so she guessed.

And then what?

It was money she was desperately short of.

The smell of body odour that tugged at her nostrils was, she knew, her own. Jesus, what she wouldn't give for a nice long soak in a bath, followed by a soft bed.

Perhaps if she could find a hostel. She knew there were plenty in London. If she could find one . . .

What if *they* found her there?

For all she knew they were already searching for her.

How would they know she was in London?

They seemed to know *everything*.

They knew her thoughts before *she* did.

Ahead of her the lights grew even brighter and she heard music blasting out into the night. Loud and powerful.

She paused at the door of The Crystal Room, looking in at the massive array of electronic games, the noises they made competing with the music for supremacy. She could see people inside. Mostly young men.

There were some young women, mostly in groups of three or four. Some standing talking, others playing the machines.

Girls like her.

She stepped in, looking around. The music seemed to engulf her.

'With the lights out, it's less dangerous . . .'

One or two of the occupants of the place glanced at her.

'Here we are now, entertain us. . . .'

She had no idea what she was looking for in this place.

Was it help she sought?

'I feel stupid and contagious . . .'

Standing beside one of the motor racing games, a tall man with a barrel chest and neck as thick as chopped oak watched her from behind his sunglasses.

'Here we are now, entertain us. . . .'

Shanine heard rattling behind her as money spilled from one of the machines and the happy winner scooped up his bounty.

Money.

She looked at it as a starving man would look at food.

The tall man watched her.

Shanine wandered slowly around The Crystal Room, the music still thundering in her ears.

'A mulatto, an albino, a mosquito, my libido . . .'

Some of the faces in here were pale and gaunt like her own.

140

Lost. Afraid.

She walked towards the exit.

No help in there.

The tall man watched.

The music blasted on. A deafening litany.

'A denial. A denial. A denial . . .'

It swept her back out into the night.

Thirty-seven

He couldn't remember the last time he'd cried.

Fifteen years.

Twenty.

Longer?

James Talbot sat in his armchair, the glass of whiskey clutched in one hand, his head lowered, his cheeks streaked.

He took a sip of the whiskey, feeling it burn its way to his stomach.

How many was that?

He'd lost count.

He'd drink the entire contents of the bottle if he had to. All he wanted was oblivion. At the moment he was even being denied *that.*

Fuck it.

He looked across at the TV set, the screen blank. His own reflection was the only thing that showed there; slumped in the chair gripping the glass.

Just like his father used to be.

His father.

That fucking, stinking, drink-raddled piece of shit.

'Cunt,' hissed Talbot, sniffing back more tears.

From the top of the TV set, the photograph of his mother gazed back at him.

He couldn't hold that blank gaze, and downed what was left in his glass rather than face her stare.

Accusing. Denouncing.

It'll be your fault if she dies.

He shook his head.

You left her to rot in that place. You said you did it for her sake but you lied, didn't you? It was for you. You couldn't cope with her. You didn't want to cope with her. You couldn't be bothered. Your career came first. You discarded her like a dirty tissue.

'No,' grunted Talbot. He reached down the side of his chair and pulled up the bottle of Jameson's, pouring a large measure into his glass, swigging it.

She'll die there now. Because of you.

He shook his head, felt more tears pouring warmly down his face.

The tears used to come afterwards, didn't they?

How long since he'd cried? Twenty years?

Try thirty-two.

That was when it had first started, wasn't it?

He'd been four years old when he'd first smelled that whiskey stink in his face, felt those hands on his body, felt them touching him, forcing him to touch too.

Four when he'd felt that agony for the first time.

Penetration.

Talbot took another hefty swig.

It made him cough. *Choke.*

142

Remember that sensation too. Choking. Gagging as it was forced into your mouth. That salty, bitter taste, then the oily, tingling sensation in your throat and the smell of the whiskey. The rough hands.

Talbot sat forward in his chair, hands pressed to his temples as if he feared his head would explode, so full of memories was it.

Vivid and painful like cuts across his consciousness.

Jesus it was all fucking pain.

It was *then* and it was *now*.

But she'd been there to help sometimes. She'd tried to help. *To help you.* She'd fought with him. She'd fought with your father until he'd beaten her bloody, then he'd returned to you, her blood on his hands. Your blood on his hands, too.

Christ, the fucking pain!

Penetration.

But you'd stopped crying after the first half a dozen times.

You'd learned to endure it, in silence.

No tears. No tears for thirty-two years.

Until now.

Talbot gripped his glass in one fist, squeezing more tightly. His body was racked by sobs.

He looked across at the photo on top of the television set.

'Mum, I'm sorry,' he whispered.

Too late for apologies.

She was dying.

Leaving you.

Alone with your pain.

He squeezed the glass more tightly, tears scalding his cheeks.

143

The glass shattered in his hand, lumps of crystal slicing into his palm, splitting the skin effortlessly. Blood spurted from the cuts, gushing from a particularly deep wound at the base of his thumb, dripping to the carpet, mingling with the whiskey.

Talbot turned his palm and stared at it, the burning sensation of the liquor in the wounds agonising.

He stared at the ravaged hand, pieces of glass sticking out of the torn flesh.

Blood was running down his arm.

Fuck it. Fuck it.

Who fucking cared?

He hurled what was left of the glass at the wall, watching as it exploded into hundreds of tiny beads of crystal, spraying all around the room like transparent shrapnel.

Frozen tears.

'You fucker!' he roared at the top of his voice, his head tilted backwards, then he slumped in the chair once again, his bleeding hand dangling uselessly at his side.

Pain. Rage. Guilt. Anger. Memories.

He didn't know what had brought these tears, but as Talbot sat sobbing in the chair he wondered when they would stop.

Or even if they *could*.

Thirty-eight

When Cath walked back into the room she noticed her brother was holding something, gazing down at it.

As she sat down opposite him she saw that it was a small, pink teddy bear.

'I found it the other day when I was tidying up,' Reed told her, still looking at the stuffed toy, seeing his own distorted reflection in its blank eyes. 'It must have been the only thing of Becky's that Ellen didn't take when she left.'

Cath watched him silently for a moment as he ran a thumb over the bear, ruffling its smooth fur.

'You still haven't heard from her, then?'

He shook his head.

'If she's hurt Becky, her or that fucking arsehole she lives with,' he rasped, still staring at the teddy. 'If either of them has hurt Becky, I'll fucking kill them, I swear to Christ, I . . .'

Cath frowned, leaning forward in her seat.

'Frank, what are you going on about?' she said in bewilderment. 'Why would Ellen want to hurt Becky? She loves her as much as you do.'

'Then why the hell did she take her away from me?' Reed snarled.

'Just because she took her away doesn't mean she's going to hurt her, Frank. What makes you think that?'

He dropped the teddy onto the sofa beside him and rubbed both hands over his face. 'Shit, I'm sorry, Cath,' he murmured. 'There's two kids at the school – I'm worried about them. The boy in particular. I think he might have been . . .' Reed was struggling for the words. 'Roughed up, knocked about or something. It made me think of Becky.'

'You think it's the parents?'

'It looks like someone's given him a bloody good hiding.'

'Could it be one of the other kids?'

'I doubt it. I'd say it was the parents.'

'If it is, Frank, it's nothing to do with you, is it?'

'It is if I think that child is being beaten.'

'Come on, Frank, that's a bit strong, isn't it?'

'You didn't see him. He had bruises on him the size of your fist, and marks on his wrists too. Like weals.'

'Maybe his mum or dad just got a bit carried away. Dad used to wallop *us* when we were little.'

'A slap on the backside is a bit different to leaving bruises, Cath. Besides, this kid isn't the only one. There's a girl too, I saw her today. Same bruises, same marks.'

'So, two sets of parents decide to get a bit heavy with their kids. That doesn't mean Ellen's going to start knocking Becky about, does it?'

Reed regarded her impassively.

'Ellen wouldn't, but what about Ward? I don't know anything about that bastard,' Reed spat.

'Frank, why should he?'

Reed got to his feet and crossed the room to a small mahogany cabinet. He took out a bottle of Courvoisier and two glasses, pouring himself the larger measure.

146

He returned and handed the other glass to Cath.

'You know, you'd better be careful, Frank,' she advised. 'You can't go yelling abuse all over the place. It's a dangerous word. The parents of those kids could sue you unless you can prove it. How would *you* feel if someone accused you of hurting Becky? What are their names, anyway?'

'Annette Hilston and Paul O'Brian, they're both about ten.'

'O'Brian?' Cath said, frowning.

Why did that ring a bell?

'Paul's sister died a few months ago. She was only a baby and—'

Cath was already on her feet, heading across the room towards her briefcase.

Reed watched as she flipped it open and rummaged around inside.

'Where was she buried?' she asked.

Reed looked puzzled. 'How on earth should I know?' he said, watching in bewilderment as Cath sat down beside him, a set of photographs in her hand.

'Do you think it might have been Croydon Cemetery?' she asked.

'It's possible, the family moved from there after her death. What makes you think—'

She handed him a photo.

It showed a broken headstone.

The name on it was Carla O'Brian.

'Jesus,' murmured Reed. 'And this was taken in Croydon Cemetery?'

She nodded and handed him the other pictures.

Reed flicked slowly through them, his forehead creased, a look of dismay on his face.

'If it's a coincidence, it's millions to one,' she said. 'Same name, same age, same cemetery.'

'That's why I thought the boy was quiet in the beginning, I knew his sister had died . . .' He let the sentence trail off. 'Who the hell did this?'

'No one knows yet. That's what *I'm* trying to find out. Who and why.'

He paused at a picture showing a shattered headstone with a pentagram scrawled on it, peering at the name and age on the remains of the stone.

'Another child,' he whispered.

'All the graves belong to kids, all the ones desecrated,' Cath elaborated.

'Oh Jesus,' Reed hissed, looking at a picture of a coffin that had been hauled from its resting place. The lid had been split, the woodwork riven and scarred.

He came to the ones taken in the church crypt.

Cath watched him as he studied them.

'How much do you know about witchcraft, Frank?'

Reed looked at her blankly.

'Are you serious?'

'My editor told me to play up the black magic angle. I just wondered what you knew.'

'Are you asking me in my capacity as a history teacher or as an ordinary member of the public?'

'Both.'

'As a history teacher I can tell you about the Inquisition, the Salem Witch trials, Matthew Hopkins the Witchfinder-General, even Hitler's interest in the occult. Is that good enough for starters?'

'And as an ordinary member of the public?'

'I think it's bollocks.'

'You don't believe in it?'

'Whoever did *that*,' he gestured dismissively at the pictures, 'they were sick bastards, but I doubt if they were witches.'

'So you think the O'Brian family would talk about what happened to their daughter's grave?'

'Are you asking as my sister or as a muck-raking, sensation-seeking journalist?' he asked, smiling.

'I prefer investigative news reporter,' she retorted, feigning indignation. 'Would they talk, Frank? You could put me in touch with them. Give me an address.'

Reed looked down at the photos again.

'I might even be able to find out whether or not you're right about the parents whacking their kid if I speak to them,' she persisted.

He looked at her.

'*Excuse me, Mr and Mrs O'Brian, how do you feel about your baby's grave being dug up, and by the way have you beaten up your son lately?*' he said, sardonically.

She held his gaze.

'The address, Frank,' she murmured. 'That's all.'

He glanced down at the top picture.

A headstone, cracked, smeared with excrement.

Sick.

When he looked up, she was still gazing at him.

Waiting.

Thirty-nine

James Talbot dropped two Alka-Seltzer into the glass of water and watched as they started to dissolve, turning the liquid opaque, fizzing loudly. He watched bubbles rising to the top of the fluid, following their journey from the bottom of the glass to the surface with disproportionate fascination.

Across the table from him, William Rafferty watched his superior, noticing how pale he looked.

The other two men in the room didn't seem to notice.

DC Stephen Longley was more concerned about the temperature in the room, fidgeting uncomfortably in his seat and occasionally tugging at his shirt collar as he felt the heat building.

His companion, DC Colin Penhallow, was turning a cigarette lighter abstractedly between his thumb and forefinger, tapping it on a file which lay before him.

Talbot used the end of his pen to stir the Alka-Seltzer, licked the Biro dry and took a large swallow of the white fluid.

'Rough night?' Rafferty asked.

'You could say that,' Talbot murmured, clambering to his feet and crossing to a nearby window, which he pushed open. The noise of traffic from below was loud, the stink of engine fumes strong, even three floors up. He closed the window again.

'OK, fellas, what have you got?' he said, turning to face his colleagues.

'A *little* bit more than we knew a few days ago,' said Penhallow. 'But not much.' He lit up a cigarette, watched almost longingly by Talbot who swigged from his glass again.

'Thrill me,' Talbot said, flatly.

'It's mostly background stuff, guv,' Penhallow said. 'Upbringing, work, family life. That sort of shit.'

'Anything to connect them?' the DI wanted to know.

150

'Now that *is* the interesting thing,' Penhallow contin-ued.

Talbot drained what was left in the glass, grimaced and sat down, his gaze fixed on his colleague. 'Don't tell me, they all went to the same boarding school,' he said, a thin smile on his lips.

'They're all masons,' Longley chuckled.

'I wouldn't say that too loud around here,' Talbot reminded him, and all four men laughed.

'They were all working on the same building project,' Penhallow announced, taking a drag on his cigarette. 'There are some old warehouses near the West India Dock Pier, along Limehouse Reach. They've been empty for five or six years now. Somebody bought the ware-houses and the land they stand on. It's going to be a new development. Flats, that sort of stuff.'

'More yuppie hideaways,' Rafferty added.

'Do we know who bought the land?' Talbot asked.

'Believe it or not, it was a firm of accountants,' Penhallow informed him.

'Morgan and Simons,' Rafferty elaborated. 'The firm Peter Hyde worked for.'

'Part of Hyde's job was to cost out the project,' Penhallow offered.

'What about the houses nearby?' Talbot enquired. 'Had there been any complaints about this building project from local residents?'

'None that we could find,' Rafferty replied.

'So, how are Parriam and Jeffrey linked to this?' Talbot enquired.

'Jeffrey was a surveyor, right? Guess what he was working on when he topped himself?' Rafferty said.

'And Parriam had already designed two office blocks

and fifteen different types of apartment that were to be built on that land once the warehouses were levelled,' Penhallow added.

'There's your link, guv,' Longley finished.

'That still doesn't explain why they all topped themselves,' Talbot said. 'If they'd been murdered then I'd say let's find out who didn't want those warehouses being knocked down, find out who had a reason for wanting them dead, but it still doesn't make any sense, does it?'

The policemen sat around in silence for a moment, the stillness finally broken by Talbot.

'None of them was connected to anything to do with villains, were they? None of them taking backhanders from anybody who might run that manor or want a bit of the cream once those new flats were built?'

'Backhanders?' Longley chuckled. 'They were in the building trade. How many honest builders do *you* know?'

The other men laughed.

'You know what I mean,' the DI added, smiling.

'Not a sniff of villainy with any one of them,' Rafferty told his superior. 'If they'd smelled any sweeter you'd have seen them on a fucking perfume counter.'

Talbot rubbed his chin thoughtfully. 'Who stood to benefit by the three of them dying?' he asked.

'No one that we know of,' Longley responded.

'And that's the only link between the three of them, this building project?' the DI continued. 'Looks like we're fucked.'

'There was something else,' Rafferty told him. 'And this *is* weird.'

Talbot turned to face his colleague.

'In the two weeks leading up to their deaths, all three men reported having been burgled,' Rafferty said. 'Either their houses, their offices or their cars were turned over, but – this is the weird thing – nothing of any value was taken. None of the places was wrecked or even damaged. Whoever broke in knew exactly what they were looking for. They never touched TVs, videos, money, tapes, CDs. Nothing.'

Talbot frowned.

'Someone went to the bother of breaking into Hyde's, Parriam's and Jeffrey's,' Rafferty continued. 'They could have cleaned them out. But, in each case, the only thing stolen was a photograph of the dead man.'

Forty

The ringing of the phone startled him.

Frank Reed heard the high-pitched tone and shook his head, as if to rouse himself from his stupor.

Lying on his sofa, feet up, he'd drifted in and out of sleep, his attention barely gripped by the programme on the television, which still glowed before him.

He swung himself upright and walked across to the small desk where the phone stood, alongside a pile of exercise books, which he knew he had to finish marking.

Later.

He picked up the phone, running a hand across his face as if that simple gesture would restore his alertness.

'Hello,' he croaked, clearing his throat.

'Frank.'

He didn't recognise her voice at first.

'Frank. It's Ellen.'

He pressed the phone more tightly to his ear, gripping the receiver hard.

'Ellen,' he said, finally. 'What a pleasure.'

'I'm not disturbing you, am I?'

He sat down at the desk.

'Well, if my own wife can't disturb me, who can?' Reed said, sardonically. 'I suppose I should be grateful you found the time to fit me in.'

'If you're going to be a smart-arse, I'll hang up now.'

'And deprive me of your attention. No, please don't do that.'

'How are you keeping?'

'As well as can be expected, and don't make small-talk please, Ellen, it's embarrassing. What do you want?'

'I've been thinking about what you said. You're right, we do need to talk.'

He swallowed hard.

'About us?' he asked.

'About Becky. You're right, she's your daughter, you do have a right to see her. I spoke to Jonathan about it and—'

'Well, as long as Jonathan agrees that's all right, isn't it? She's *my* daughter, Ellen, not his. I don't want him making any decisions to do with her.'

'Don't dictate to me. *He's* her father now.'

'He's *not* her father and he never will be,' Reed snarled, angrily. 'Just because you walked out on me for that bastard doesn't mean he can ever take on my role in Becky's life.'

'Becky thinks a lot of him.'

Reed felt something like physical pain.

'I suppose you've told her how wonderful he is, how good he makes you feel. Have you got around to telling her how wonderful in bed he is yet?'

'Look, Frank, I rang you because I wanted to do the right thing—'

He cut her short, trying not to shout, but struggling.

'Then leave Ward and come home,' he said, angrily, gripping the receiver so tightly it seemed in danger of snapping.

'My home is with Jonathan now, and so is Becky's,' she told him, defiantly.

Fucking bitch.

There was a long silence, finally broken by Reed.

'So, what *do* you want?'

'You want to see Becky, spend some time with her. That's fine. How about this weekend?'

He swallowed hard, not daring to believe what he'd heard.

'Jonathan and I are going away for a couple of days and I thought—'

He interrupted. 'You needed a babysitter, is that it?' he snapped. 'You want me to babysit my own daughter while you and lover boy fuck off somewhere, right?'

'You either want to see her or you don't, Frank.'

'You *know* I want to see her.'

'So you'll take her this weekend?'

'And that's it? One weekend, because it's convenient for you? What about after that, Ellen? What about every weekend? What's wrong with that? Or does Jonathan have plans for Becky?'

'If you take her this weekend we'll see about you having her on a more regular basis.'

'Not just when it suits *you*,' he spat.

'Will you do it this weekend?'

'Of course I will.'

'I'll drop her off on Saturday morning.'

'You can remember how to get here, can you?' he asked, acidly.

'Just leave it, Frank.'

'And don't bring lover boy with you when you drop Becky.'

'Jonathan's busy in the morning anyway.'

'I'll bet he is.'

'I'll be round about ten.'

'I'll be waiting.'

'I thought you might have had the decency to thank me,' Ellen told him.

It was all Reed could do to prevent himself slamming down the phone.

'Ten o'clock Saturday morning,' he said through gritted teeth, then slipped the phone back onto its cradle, staring down at it .

He didn't know whether to jump for joy or punch a hole in the wall.

Forty-one

The pain was deep in her belly.

Shanine Connor knew that it wasn't hunger. She had come to recognise, only too well, that gnawing discomfort.

This was stronger, more intense.

156

It felt as if someone had wrapped a red hot band around her stomach and was slowly tightening it.

She groaned loudly and clutched at her belly, running her hands over it as if to soothe the pain, but it didn't help.

It had woken her, dragged her from her fitful sleep, and now, huddled in the doorway of an empty shop on the Strand, she curled up into a foetal position, hugging her knees, eyes tightly closed.

Perhaps if she stood up . . .

She struggled slowly to her feet, the pain intensifying and, for a moment, she thought she was going to faint.

A car passed by, the driver glancing at her as the vehicle was forced to stop at a set of traffic lights.

It was just after two in the morning; there were few vehicles on the road now. The continual stream of traffic had slowed just after one and now was virtually a trickle. Late-night revellers and tourists were probably safely tucked up in bed by now.

Jesus, what she wouldn't give for a bed. For a proper night's rest.

Shanine walked a couple of yards, one hand pressed to her belly, still watched by the lone driver waiting at the lights. She was a convenient diversion for him while he waited for the green light to come, which it finally did. He drove off without a second glance, leaving her to her pain.

She walked another few steps, passing a huddled shape in another doorway, unable to see if it was human or not. It looked as if someone had hurled a pile of dirty clothes into one corner of the shop doorway.

It moved slightly as she passed, and Shanine heard what sounded like low, guttural snoring.

She paused before the shape.

Should she ask for help? Should she shake this untidy bundle and see what lay beneath?

She decided against it, taking another few paces instead, the pain still intense.

Shanine was trying to control her breathing, panic beginning to set in as the spasms showed no signs of abating. She kept her hands clapped firmly to her belly then turned and walked back down the street towards her own sheltering doorway.

Again she swayed uncertainly, fearing she would faint, but she kept a grip on consciousness and shot out a hand to support herself, mouthing words silently to herself as she stood there.

The pain receded slightly and Shanine swallowed, hardly daring to believe that it might leave her, but as she walked tentatively back and forth in front of the shop doorway she realised that the spasms were indeed lessening in ferocity.

She sucked in a deep breath, taking the stale, grimy air deep into her lungs. She rubbed her stomach and sat down again, pulling the hold-all nearer to her, as if it were a long-lost friend. The only friend she had.

The pain had all but gone now and she lay back, eyes closed.

Shanine slid a hand down the front of her leggings, inside her knickers, withdrawing it hastily, her heart pounding faster again when she felt moisture there. She lifted her palm, terrified of seeing a dark stain but she saw only glistening perspiration.

No blood.

The pain hadn't been what she had feared.

She massaged her belly gently.

No blood.

She smiled.

As far as she knew, the baby she carried was still safe.

Forty-two

He didn't sleep because with sleep came dreams.

Those dreams.

Talbot stood in the kitchen, waiting for the kettle to boil, coffee already spooned into his mug.

He stood silently, watching as the gas flame flickered beneath the kettle, blue tongues lapping at the metal above.

So, what are you going to do? Stay awake all night?

Every night?

He knew he couldn't run.

How can you run from something inside your own head?

Talbot knew he couldn't run, but he could at least hide occasionally. By drinking. By stopping the intrusion of dreams.

The DI turned and walked into the sitting room, glancing down at the files that were scattered haphazardly over his sofa and coffee table.

There were photos on the front covers of each.

Peter Hyde.

Neil Parriam.

Craig Jeffrey.

All dead.

Lucky bastards.

And yet, what had they had to run from? Talbot mused. Why had they found it so easy to take their own lives, when he continued to survive, continued to live with the pain.

They were braver than you.

He wandered back into the kitchen, saw that the kettle was boiling. Talbot lifted it clear of the gas flame, but didn't turn off the burner, his gaze drawn to it like a moth to bright light.

They escaped. Why can't you?

He stared at the gas flame until it hurt his eyes. Then, slowly, he passed his hand through it.

The hairs on the back of his hand shrivelled immediately and he felt a stab of pain but Talbot kept his hand there a moment longer, teeth gritted.

Have you got the guts?

He could smell the flesh on the palm of his hand beginning to burn, the skin seared by the flame.

He pulled his hand away, his breath coming in gasps.

Talbot held the reddened palm before him, inspecting the damage, seeing the blisters which were already beginning to form.

For interminable seconds he gazed at the hand then, with a shout, he slammed it down on the worktop. 'Fuck!' he roared at the top of his voice.

He sagged against the sink.

'Fuck it,' he whispered. 'Fuck it.'

The gas flame still flickered.

'I would never ordinarily have dreamed of calling you at this time in the morning,' said the Reverend Colin Patterson. 'But I thought you had to see this.'

Cath Reed pulled her jacket more tightly around her

and walked alongside the clergyman, her trainers crunching on the gravel of the pathway which led to the church.

'You didn't disturb me, I was working,' she told him, but the clergyman seemed not to hear her.

The church loomed above them, large and imposing, the night closed around it like a black glove.

Glancing around, Cath could see the odd light in houses near the cemetery but, apart from the torch Patterson carried, they were immersed in blackness.

'I don't know what woke me,' Patterson told her as they drew nearer to the church. 'Some kind of noise perhaps. I looked out and saw that the chains on the cemetery gates had been pulled off. I ran straight across here.'

'Where from?'

'I have a small house across the road,' he explained. 'It goes with the job.'

'Did you call the police?'

'No, I called you first.'

Patterson stopped in his tracks and shone the torch at the main doors of the church.

'Oh God,' Cath murmured, her stomach contracting.

The cat had been decapitated, the head lay close to the door in a spreading pool of blood.

The body of the creature had been nailed to the heavy oak doors of the church, a large metal spike driven through each of its four paws.

Cath noticed that the body was upside down, the stump of the neck facing the ground, still dripping blood onto the gravel.

Patterson held the torch beam steady, allowing her to inspect every inch of the dead feline.

There was a slit which ran from its breast bone to its genitals, the stomach walls pulled open, the intestines hanging freely like the bloated tentacles of some bloodied octopus.

'Shit,' she murmured, reaching into her jacket and pulling out the pocket camera.

As Patterson held the torch, Cath began taking pictures.

Forty-three

Talbot pressed hard on the buzzer of Flat 5b, Number 23 Queens Gardens, keeping the digit so firmly against the button that the tip of his finger began to turn white.

The building, like the rest of the road, was in darkness apart from a light which burned brightly in the covered porchway.

Talbot looked up at it and winced.

Fucking thing.

It hurt his eyes.

He heard a crackle and then a voice from the speaker on the wall next to the panel of buttons.

'Who is it?' said the voice, a little uncertainly.

'Open the fucking door,' Talbot rasped back into the other speaker, pressing his face close to it.

There was a moment's silence.

'Come on, Gina, for Christ's sake, open the door,' Talbot said again.

'Talbot?' said the voice on the other end. 'What the hell—?'

'Open it,' he persisted.

There was a loud buzzing sound followed by a metallic click and the policeman pushed against the front door, which swung open to admit him.

He stood motionless in the spacious hallway for a moment, looking around at the closed doors of the other flats, then he headed for the stairs, thudding up them with almost purposely loud steps.

Gina Bishop appeared in the doorway of Flat 5b, her blonde hair unkempt, her body covered by a short white towelling robe.

Talbot smiled at her but found the gesture wasn't reciprocated.

As he stepped past her into the flat he ran one hand over the soft material of the robe.

'Calvin Klein?' he said, haughtily.

She shot him an angry glance.

'What the hell is all this about?' she cried. 'It's two-thirty in the morning.'

Talbot sat down on the sofa and lay back, eyes closed.

'You've been drinking,' Gina said.

'Brilliant deduction.'

'How did you get here?'

'I drove. Did you think I fucking walked all the way from north London? Good job I didn't get stopped by the police, wasn't it?' He cracked out laughing.

'You're drunk.'

'Not yet, but if you're offering I'll have a whiskey.'

Gina hesitated a moment then crossed the sitting room to a drinks cabinet. She took out a bottle of Scotch and a glass and walked back to Talbot, handing them both to him.

163

'Here,' she muttered. 'You might as well finish the job.'

She watched as he poured himself a large measure and swallowed most of it in one gulp.

'Not joining me?' he asked, watching as she sat down on the seat opposite, pulling the robe around her as best she could.

She crossed her arms, covering her chest even more.

'A sudden attack of modesty?' chided Talbot. 'Surely not.'

'Look, Talbot, just finish your drink, do whatever you came here to do and fuck off, will you?'

'You know, you're not the best hostess sometimes, Gina.'

He poured himself another drink. 'Did I interrupt something?'

She shook her head.

'You weren't entertaining, then?' he asked.

'I got back about an hour ago.'

'Busy night?'

'What do *you* care?'

'Perhaps I'm interested. Perhaps I want to know what you did. Who you did it *with*?'

'What are you going to do? Arrest me?'

'If I wanted to do *that* I'd have done it five years ago.'

'Sometimes I wish you had. At least it might have got you off my bloody back.'

'An unfortunate turn of phrase,' he grinned. 'Just remember, it's only because of me that you haven't been pulled in before now. The only reason you're out there doing business every night is down to me.'

'Am I supposed to be grateful for that? I keep up *my*

164

end of the bargain, don't I? You always get what you want.'

He poured himself another drink and glanced around the room, his gaze drawn to a photograph on top of the stack system. The DI got to his feet and crossed to it.

'Who's that?' he asked, indicating the picture.

'My mum and dad.'

'Are they still married?'

Gina looked puzzled. 'Yes. Why?'

Talbot ignored the question.

'You look like your mum,' he said softly, touching the photo with the tip of his finger. Then his tone changed. Hardened. 'Do they know what you do for a living?'

She snorted incredulously. 'Oh, yeah, of course they do, Talbot. The first thing I did was tell them I'd left the escort business and become a call girl. What do *you* think?'

'So, what do they think you are? They must have seen this place. They'd know you couldn't live in a flat in Bayswater on a shop assistant's wages. What do they think you do? Air hostess? Brain surgeon?'

'They think I work in a PR company.'

He laughed.

'PR. *Prick* relief,' he snorted. 'Very appropriate.'

Gina got to her feet, her expression darkening.

'Look, I know what you came here for,' she snapped. 'So just get it over with. This is what you want, isn't it.'

As Talbot watched she pulled at the cord around her waist and opened her robe, shrugging it from her shoulders, allowing it to drop to the floor. She stepped away from it and stood naked before him, watching as his eyes

165

flickered back and forth, his gaze passing from her small, rounded breasts, down her smooth belly to the small triangle of light hair between her slim legs.

'Well,' she said, sitting down again, lying back in the chair, one hand brushing the hair away from her face. 'Come on.'

Talbot took a step towards her.

'Do you need some help?' she asked, allowing her right hand to glide over her breasts, her thumb scraping across one nipple. She used the nail delicately, rubbing until it rose into a stiffened bud.

Talbot watched impassively, the whiskey tumbler still in his hand.

'Still nothing?' she said, scathingly. 'Does this help?'

He watched as she slid both hands down to her softly curled pubic hair, the index finger of her left hand tracing featherlight patterns across the mound.

She moved one leg so that it was dangling over the arm of the chair, and simultaneously she pushed her right middle finger into her mouth, drawing it glistening from that warm refuge. Using the slippery digit, she drew the gleaming saliva over her cleft, rotating it gently.

Talbot took another step towards her, looking down at her, at that finger.

'Do you just want to watch me tonight?' she purred.

Talbot stooped, picked up the robe and dropped it on her. 'Put it on,' he said, turning his back on her.

She pulled on the robe, fastening it haphazardly.

'If you don't want that, what the hell *do* you want?'

He sat down opposite her, head bowed. 'I just wanted to talk,' he said, wearily.

'Talk about what?' Gina snapped. 'Talk dirty? Is that

166

what you want tonight?' She dropped to the floor, crawled across to him and placed one hand on his thigh, looking up into his face. 'I'll talk dirty for you, baby. I'll get you hard, I'll make you feel so good. I'll make you come. It'll feel great. My mouth on your cock, so soft. Sucking. Licking. Until you come in my . . .'

He grabbed her hand, pulled her upright so that her face was inches from his.

'I just want to talk to somebody,' he snarled, pushing her away.

His voice dropped to a whisper. 'Just talk,' he murmured, and when he looked at her she saw there were tears in his eyes.

He put down his glass and got to his feet.

She saw that he was heading for the door.

'Talbot, wait,' she called.

He was already turning the door handle.

'Thanks for the drink,' he said quietly, then stepped out, shutting the door behind him.

She heard his footfalls on the stairs. Receding.

'Fucking idiot,' she hissed.

She heard the front door slam.

He was gone.

Forty-four

The relative silence of the classroom was broken by a muffled yelp of pain.

It was followed by several muted giggles.

167

Frank Reed looked up from the book he was reading and surveyed the faces before him, or rather the tops of heads. Most of the classroom occupants were hunched over sheets of paper, hurriedly scribbling down the passage in one of their text books which he'd instructed them to copy.

He looked in the direction of the yelp and the giggles but saw nothing to alert him. Hiding a smile, he paused a moment to run an appraising gaze over his wards before continuing with his own reading.

Paul O'Brian was seated at the back of the room again, head bent so low over his desk it looked as if his forehead was resting on the wooden top.

Reed watched him for a few minutes before returning his attention to his book.

There was a loud snapping sound.

Another yelp.

More giggling.

Reed caught the slightest hint of movement out of his eye corner.

He saw one of the boys towards the back of the class turn around, saw another flick a rubber band at him.

'Right, that's enough,' the teacher said, jabbing a finger towards the culprits. 'If you want to indulge in target practice, don't do it in *my* time,' he told the lad with the rubber band.

'Sorry, Mr Reed,' the lad said, humbly, returning to his book.

Other eyes turned in his direction. More giggles.

'All right,' Reed told the class. 'The cabaret is over, get back to work.'

He noticed that Paul O'Brian hadn't taken much

interest in the disturbance. In fact, the boy hadn't even raised his head.

And yet, he didn't seem to be writing.

His head was still bent low over his desk, the pen still gripped in his hand.

His forehead was on the desktop.

It took Reed a second or two to realise that O'Brian wasn't moving at all.

The teacher hurried from behind his desk and towards the back of the classroom, other eyes turning to watch.

Reed's only concern was O'Brian.

As he drew closer he could see how pale the boy's skin was.

His eyes were closed.

'Paul,' Reed said, gripping the boy's shoulder.

He didn't stir.

Reed squeezed harder, sucking in a deep breath as O'Brian slid to one side.

Reed managed to catch him before he slid off the chair, scooping him up into his arms, holding him as if he were some kind of lifeless doll.

The rest of the class had turned their attention fully to the scene at the back of the room now. They looked on as Reed held the boy, looking down at his milk-white face.

There were scratches on his neck. They stood out vividly against the whiteness of his skin.

'Gary, Mark,' Reed snapped, nodding towards two boys near the front of the class. 'Run along to Mrs Trencher now, tell her that Paul's ill and that I'm bringing him along immediately. Go on.'

The two boys didn't need to be told twice, both

scooting to their feet and hurtling out of the door. Reed heard their footsteps pounding away up the corridor as he advanced through the rows of desks, carrying his limp cargo.

'Is he dead?' a voice called.

Reed looked down at Paul O'Brian's gaunt face.

And the scratches.

'No, he's not dead,' Reed replied, reaching the door. 'You all just get on with your work until I get back.'

He headed out into the corridor, carrying the frail form of the boy with little difficulty. So little that he found he could run.

The school nurse's office was about a hundred yards away but Reed sprinted along with his unconscious cargo.

O'Brian hadn't stirred.

Reed ran a little faster.

Speed suddenly seemed important.

Forty-five

'What happened to him?' asked Amy Trencher, removing the cuff of the sphygmomanometer from Paul O'Brian's arm with a sound resembling ripping fabric.

'I haven't got a clue,' Reed told her, looking down at the boy who was semi-conscious now, his eyes flickering open every few seconds. 'He passed out. Blacked out. I don't know.'

'His blood pressure is low,' the nurse told Reed. 'I'd better listen to his heart.'

Reed watched as she began to undo the buttons of the boy's shirt, gradually easing back the material on both sides.

'Jesus,' whispered Reed, his eyes fixed on the boy's torso.

It was criss-crossed in several places by long, red marks.

Weals.

Scars, he noted, across the belly and close to the shoulders.

Amy hesitated a moment then pressed the stethoscope to O'Brian's chest.

Reed also moved closer, running his gaze over the emaciated body. O'Brian's ribs pressed so insistently against his pale flesh it seemed they must tear through the thin covering.

The boy stirred slightly, as if embarrassed by his own condition, and he pulled at one side of his shirt with a thin hand.

The nurse helped the boy to sit up, slipping the shirt from him.

There were more marks on his back, some of them vivid red against the pallidity of the skin.

Amy pressed the stethoscope to his back in several places, her brow furrowed.

Again Reed stepped closer to get a better look at the marks, reaching out to touch a dark line running from shoulder blade to lumbar region.

He felt the hard, coarse surface of a scar.

Amy was shining a pen-light at the boy's eyes, watching as his pupils dilated and contracted with each flash of light.

171

'Paul,' she said, softly. 'We're going to have to take you to hospital, do you understand?'

It was as if the boy had suddenly been hit by a 25,000-volt cable.

He leaped to his feet, pulling his shirt back on, anxious to cover his body, his eyes wide and staring.

'No,' he said, pleadingly. 'Please. I'm all right.'

'I want a doctor to take a look at you,' Amy said, trying to slip an arm around him.

He pulled away violently, crashing into a trolley, overturning it.

It struck the floor, the instruments which had been laid upon it scattering over the tiles.

O'Brian backed into a corner.

'Leave me alone,' he said, his eyes filling with tears.

Reed took a step towards him.

'We just want to help you, Paul,' the teacher assured him, extending a hand.

The boy drew back even further.

'Who did this to you?' Reed asked.

O'Brian was panting madly, his eyes bulging wildly in their sockets as he looked anxiously from the teacher to the nurse.

'Don't call a doctor, please,' he implored.

'Why not?' Reed asked. 'They'll help you.'

'No. I mustn't tell.'

'Tell what?' Reed asked. 'Tell who did this to you?'

The boy was buttoning his shirt with one hand, keeping the other before him to ward off the teacher.

Reed saw bruises on the boy's wrist. More red weals.

'Have you been told not to tell who did this?' the teacher persisted, taking a step back.

'Don't get a doctor, please,' the boy repeated.

Reed sat down on the nearest chair, trying to keep the tone of his voice as low as he could.

'Who told you not to tell, Paul?' he asked, softly. 'What do you think will happen if you do?'

O'Brian was quivering uncontrollably now, his eyes still bulging as he looked from the teacher to the nurse and back again.

Reed saw tears begin to trickle down his cheeks. 'They told me not to tell,' he stammered.

'Who?' Reed demanded.

'Please,' O'Brian sobbed.

'Were you told something would happen to you if you told, Paul?' Reed persisted.

The boy wiped his eyes with the back of one shaking hand.

'Did someone threaten you?'

No answer.

'Did the people who did this to you threaten to hurt you if you told?' the teacher coaxed.

Amy looked at Reed, mesmerised by the tableau unfolding before her.

'Did your mum or dad do this?' Reed asked, his voice even.

'They said they'd kill them,' O'Brian blurted, his body shaking uncontrollably.

'Who? Your parents? Someone threatened to kill your parents if you told what happened? Is that it?' Reed asked, swallowing hard.

Take it easy. Be patient.

He held out a hand to the boy, beckoning gently.

'Just take your time, Paul,' Reed said, softly, his hand still extended. 'We just want to help you.'

Reed got to his feet and took a step forward.

O'Brian pushed himself more tightly to the wall, tears now streaming freely down his cheeks. 'Please don't tell anyone,' he pleaded, his voice cracking.

'I'm not going to,' Reed assured him. 'I just want you to tell me who did this to you. Did someone hit you?'

O'Brian looked at the extended hand. 'They said they'd kill my mum and dad,' he repeated.

'So it wasn't your parents who did this to you?' Reed asked.

No answer.

He could almost touch the boy now.

Another step.

'I can't remember,' the boy said, weakly.

Reed reached out and clasped his hand gently. It felt so frail. So cold.

O'Brian suddenly ran to him, wrapped his arms around Reed's waist, and the teacher felt the boy sobbing hysterically into his midriff. He closed his arms around the thin form and held on.

'It's OK,' he whispered. 'No one's going to hurt you now.'

'They'll kill my mum and dad *and* my sisters,' O'Brian blurted. He suddenly looked up into Reed's face, his eyes wide and bulging.

'Please help us,' he wailed, then buried his head in Reed's comforting arms once again, his body shaking madly.

Reed looked at Amy.

'Fetch Hardy,' he said, softly. 'I want him to see this.'

Forty-six

'Fucking garbage,' snorted Talbot, dropping his copy of the *Express* onto the table.

Rafferty looked up from his own paper and glanced first at his superior, then at the newspaper which was folded open at the centre pages.

Talbot took a sip of his coffee and ran both hands over his face.

He felt the perspiration on his skin, and when he looked at Rafferty it was through eyes rimmed vividly red, the whites criss-crossed by dozens of blood vessels.

Sleep had eluded him for most of the previous night. Two or three hours of oblivion at most had come to him. He'd been up since five, standing beneath the shower trying to reactivate his mind as well as his body. Now, five hours later, he felt as if someone had spent the night systematically beating him about the head with a plank of wood.

Too much whiskey usually had that effect.

The café in Charing Cross Road was empty but for himself and Rafferty, both men sitting at a corner table, Talbot periodically gazing out into the street at the passers-by.

So many faces.

'Read that shit,' the DI said disdainfully, pushing the folded up paper towards his colleague.

Rafferty scanned the words, glancing too at the photos which accompanied the piece.

Talbot took another swig of coffee as he sat watching Rafferty who finally looked across at him.

'What's the problem, Jim?' he asked.

'See who wrote it?' Talbot said, irritably. He jabbed a finger at the name. 'That stupid cow I spoke to at Euston the day Hyde topped himself. Remember?'

Rafferty nodded.

'She says it's been going on for a while,' the DS offered. 'Those pictures seem to back her up.'

'Do *you* believe it, Bill?' Talbot wanted to know.

Rafferty shrugged.

'She's just shit-stirring again,' Talbot said before his colleague had time to answer. 'Catherine fucking Reed.' He pushed the paper away from him.

The headline blared from the centre spread, photos of the desecrated graves and crypt at Croydon Cemetery adding silent weight to the large black letters which screamed across the two pages: VANDALISM OR SATANISM?

'Do you think they'll talk?' asked Terry Nicholls, scratching his head with the end of a pencil.

'I don't know,' Cath told him, shifting position in her seat. 'My brother didn't say what they were like.'

'Your brother knows them?'

'Their son attends the school where he teaches.'

'You're going to have to be careful, Cath,' the editor told her. 'Now this story's broken, every paper in the country is going to be crawling over it. I don't want anyone else getting info we don't have. This is your story, you make sure you follow it up. We should be able to run features on this for the next week or so. Find out what the other families think, too. Speak to the O'Brians, by all means, find out how they feel about their daughter's grave being desecrated, but speak to the other families it happened to as well. If they won't talk to you, then speak to their neighbours, their relatives, anyone who might be able to tell you more.'

Cath nodded slowly.

Nicholls tapped the paper on his desk.

'This is good stuff,' he said, smiling. 'Get some more.'

Cath grinned and got to her feet.

When the pigeons took off it sounded like the applause of a thousand invisible hands.

Shanine Connor sat on the bench in Trafalgar Square and watched the birds rise into the clear blue sky.

However, for every one that had left there seemed to be two more in its place. The entire pavement seemed to be alive with them. She sat watching them as they strutted back and forth in front of her, heads bobbing back and forth, bright eyes occasionally looking up at her as if to ask for food.

Christ, she barely had enough to feed herself.

The man seated on the bench next to her was flicking through his copy of the *Express*, impressed neither by Shanine's close proximity nor by the mass of pigeons all around.

He was dressed in trousers and a shirt and tie, and Shanine thought how hot he looked.

She watched as a bead of perspiration popped onto his forehead, then ran down his nose.

She suppressed a chuckle and glanced at his paper.

The word struck her like a hammer.

He had the paper open at the centre pages.

Shanine edged closer to him, trying to read over his shoulder.

She could see the photos from where she sat. She could make out the headline, but the rest of the piece was a blur to her.

The man scanned the story quickly and turned the page.

Shanine felt like grabbing the paper from him, telling him she wanted to read the story that covered the middle pages. Instead, she just sat looking at him, turning away quickly when he glanced in her direction.

She gripped the hold-all closer to her, eyes fixed on two pigeons close by pecking at discarded fruit where someone had missed the nearby waste-bin. Wasps buzzed frenziedly around the bin, the sound of their wings a constant accompaniment to the noise of the pigeons and the more powerful sound of traffic passing by.

The man glanced at his watch and got to his feet.

Shanine watched as he rolled the paper into a funnel, then stuck it into the waste-bin, heading off across the square, scattering birds in his wake.

She pulled the paper from the bin and tore it open at the centre pages.

Despite the warmth of the day, as she read, she felt the hairs on the back of her neck begin to rise.

Forty-seven

'You saw that boy,' snapped Frank Reed. 'You saw what had been done to him. You *must* call the police.'

Noel Hardy sat forward in his chair, hands clasped together as if in prayer. He was a short man and the large desk which bore his nameplate seemed to dwarf him even further. Reed had sometimes wondered if the furniture in the school had been designed to suit the importance of the person who sat behind it. Predictably, as Headmaster, Hardy sat behind a desk of almost ludicrously oversized proportions. For a man of fifty-five he looked remarkably sprightly, the only flecks of grey visible on him being in his eyebrows which hovered like bloated furry caterpillars above his dark brown eyes: eyes which now seemed to be gazing into space as if seeking some kind of answer.

As he looked across his office, his stare focusing on the vase of fresh flowers on a table near the door, he was aware of Reed leaning on the front of the desk.

Hardy could hear the younger man breathing.

'Come on,' Reed said, irritably. 'Why wait any longer?'

'It's not that easy, Frank,' Hardy said, finally, blinking hard. The spell, it seemed, was broken. 'We have no proof.'

'You saw the marks on his body. He didn't do that to

himself. That kid is terrified. God alone knows what he's been through. The only way to help him is to call the police. They have to find out what's been done to him.'

'There are other considerations.'

'Such as?'

Hardy lowered his gaze again.

'The publicity,' he said, sheepishly. 'This kind of thing could reflect badly on the school.'

'Jesus Christ!' Reed snapped, exasperatedly. 'There's a kid here that's been beaten, possibly by his parents. Not just slapped around but badly abused physically and mentally. You don't have to be a bloody social worker to see that. And all you're worried about is the reputation of the school. What matters more to you, Noel? The state of St Michael's or the wellbeing of its pupils? So what if it does attract some publicity? Good. It might stop some more kids from being mistreated.'

'What makes you think there are others?' Hardy wanted to know.

'Ask Judith Nelson. She's seen one of her girls in more or less the same state.'

'Which girl?'

'Annette Hilston. She lives about two streets away from the O'Brian boy.'

'So what do you want me to do? Have every home in that area investigated, just *in case* the children there might be in danger?' Hardy glared at his assistant. 'Frank, you're a parent yourself, how would you feel if someone started yelling abuser at you? If they accused *you* of harming your child?'

'If my daughter looked and behaved the way Paul O'Brian does then they'd have every right to accuse me, because the chances are they'd be right. That boy needs our help, Noel, and the only way he's going to get it is by you calling the police. Now.'

Hardy got to his feet and crossed to his window. It looked out over part of the school playground. He could see children out there now, some standing around in groups talking, others running about. Some boys were kicking a football against the wall opposite.

There were a number of houseplants on the window sill and, as he stood there, Hardy gently stroked the smooth leaves of a spider plant.

'You say you've seen injuries on another pupil too?' the Headmaster said, quietly.

'*I* haven't but, like I said, Judith Nelson said *she* had. Call her in if you want to.'

Hardy shook his head slowly, his back still to Reed.

'There are serious ramifications for everyone concerned if your allegations are right *or* wrong, Frank,' he said, still gently stroking the plant leaves.

'I realise that. But I'm prepared to take that chance.'

Hardy turned to face him. 'Yes, *you're* prepared,' he snapped. 'I'm not sure *I* am. As I said, perhaps, if we had more proof.'

'Come on, for Christ's sake! What are you going to do? Wait until a child is killed? Will *that* be proof enough for you?' Reed pushed the phone angrily towards his colleague. 'Call the police, Noel.'

Hardy held up a hand as if to silence Reed.

'Assuming you're right,' he said, returning to his desk. 'What will the police do? Visit the boy's family? Ask a few questions? If they find nothing to support your allegations then you could make it worse not just for the school but for the boy himself. Perhaps you haven't considered *him*, Frank.'

'He's my *only* bloody consideration,' Reed snapped.

'We're not responsible for those children once they're outside our care,' Hardy said, defensively.

'So what do we do? Turn our backs on them when they need help?' Reed demanded. 'That boy needs help. You *know* that. We're the only ones who can give it to him.'

The two men stared at each other in silence for what seemed like an eternity.

It was Reed who finally spoke again.

'Call the police, Noel,' he said, pushing the phone nearer to the Headmaster.

The older man glanced at the phone.

Reed kept his gaze fixed upon him.

Hardy looked at him, his face pale.

'And if you're wrong?' he said, the words hanging in the air.

Reed pushed the phone a little closer.

'Call the police, Noel,' he said, quietly.

Forty-eight

All Phillip Cross saw when he answered the door of his flat was the bottle of Möet et Chandon dangling before him, gripped by two slender fingers.

The photographer smiled even more broadly as Catherine Reed stepped into view, clasping the bottle to her as if it were a child.

'Peace offering,' she said, indicating the champagne.

Cross ran appraising eyes over her, over the long dark hair, which he could smell: freshly washed. There was a vibrance to her features which he'd not seen for a while. If he'd harboured any thoughts of giving her a hard time they vanished quickly. She remained before him in the doorway and crossed one shapely leg in front of the other, the split in her skirt opening to reveal the smooth skin beneath. She raised her eyebrows quizzically.

'Come in,' Cross said, chuckling, stepping aside as he ushered her into the flat.

Cath put down the bottle and wrapped her arms around him, feeling his lips press urgently against hers, his tongue probing beyond the hard edges of her teeth. She responded fiercely, pulling him more tightly to her.

When they finally separated, it was Cross who spoke first.

'What have I done to deserve this?' he asked, grinning. 'Not that I'm complaining.'

She shrugged and sat down on the sofa, kicking off her shoes, drawing her legs up beneath her, watching as he retreated to the kitchen to fetch a couple of glasses. He returned a moment later with two large tumblers, blowing in one to remove the dust.

Cath watched him as he uncorked the champagne and poured some into each of the tumblers. She smiled.

'That's really classy, Phil,' she chuckled as he passed her the glass.

He raised his own glass and tapped it gently against hers. They both drank.

'You still haven't told me why,' Cross said, sitting beside her, snaking one arm around her shoulder.

Cath shrugged. 'I've been working hard lately. I think I've been a bit of a bitch to you.'

'I'd like to argue with you but I can't,' he said, smiling as she punched him playfully on the arm.

'I haven't meant to be,' she persisted. 'But this story I'm working on is big.' She sipped her champagne. 'It's important to me, Phil.'

'You didn't come round here to tell me how much your career means to you, did you? I already know that. I've never wanted you to change the way you think about your work; I know how much it means to you. I just don't see why I have to be separate from it. We are in the same business, after all.'

'Feeling left out, were you?' she chided, pulling at his cheek.

His smile faded and he caught her face in his hand, holding her there, gazing into her eyes.

'I miss you when I can't see you,' Cross said, quietly. 'I like being around you, Cath.'

He ran his hand through her hair, then gently stroked the back of her neck, kneading the flesh there between his thumb and forefinger.

'I don't want to talk about work tonight,' she said, softly, sliding closer to him.

'Good, that makes a change. What *do* you want to talk about?'

She lifted her head and looked into his eyes.

'I don't *want* to talk,' she murmured, leaning forward, kissing him hard on the lips, one hand fumbling with the buttons of his shirt.

He felt her slim fingers gliding across his chest, his

184

own hand slipping down to her thigh, stroking gently, pushing up beneath the material of her skirt, moving higher.

His fingers brushed something smooth, soft.

Cross realised with delight that it was her gently curled pubic hair.

He pulled back slightly, smiling.

Cath grinned at his reaction.

'So,' he said, his breathing now more rapid. 'What time are you leaving me tonight?'

She leaned back, fumbling inside her handbag, pulling something free that she held up before him.

They both began to laugh.

Cath was brandishing a toothbrush between her fingers.

Talbot slumped wearily in the chair, head back, eyes closed.

The silence inside the house was, as usual, oppressive, and he thought about switching on the television just to shatter the solitude but, finally, he decided against it.

The DI poured himself a whiskey, then sat back down, rolling the tumbler between his palms, gazing down into the soothing fluid as if seeking some answers in the bottom of the glass.

Fucking bitch.

He'd tried the Grosvenor House, The Dorchester and the Hilton. He'd even wandered around to the Park Lane Hotel, taking a drink in each of their bars before driving to number 23 Queens Gardens.

There had been no answer there either from Flat 5b.

Gina Bishop was nowhere to be found.

Bitch.

He snatched up the phone and tried her number.

It rang twice, then the metallic whine of her answering machine began: *'Hi. I'm not here now, but if . . .'*

Talbot pressed down on the cradle, waited a moment then dialled another number.

Her mobile.

Ringing.

'Come on,' he whispered.

Then a voice.

'The Vodaphone number you have dialled is not in use . . .'

'Fuck!' he snarled and slammed the receiver down.

Mind you, if she was with a client she wouldn't have the bloody thing turned on, would she?

Fucking bitch.

He took a hefty swallow from the glass, then dialled again, her home number this time, waiting for the message to end, for the long beep to signal he should start talking.

He heard it and tried to speak but found he couldn't say the words.

The tape was recording silence at the other end.

He pressed the receiver hard to his ear, his eyes closed.

Say something.

Tell her to call you. Tell her you'll meet her somewhere.

He gripped the handset more tightly.

'Gina,' he said, finally then he heard another long beep.

Time up.

'Fucking bastard!' he roared at the phone, at the answering machine.

At himself?

He dropped the phone back onto its cradle and got to his feet, refilling his glass.

And if she'd answered, what would you have said to her?

He glared at the phone.

He needed to talk to her.

To anyone.

Talbot walked back to the phone and dialled again.

PART TWO

. . . Let me show you how I love you.
It's our secret, you and me.
Let me show you how I love you,
But keep it in the family . . .

Megadeth

. . . The sleeping and the dead
Are but as pictures; 'tis the eye of childhood
That fears a painted Devil.

Macbeth, Scene II, Act II

Forty-nine

He thought he'd wet himself.

Doug O'Brian rolled over in bed and slid a hand down towards his groin, his eyes half open, his head still clouded.

He felt no moisture, just the wrinkled skin of his scrotum. O'Brian also touched his penis.

Checking.

He must have been dreaming.

Only then did he become aware of the pressure inside his bladder.

No wonder he'd dreamed he'd pissed himself.

He swung himself quickly out of bed, pulled the cord of his pyjama bottoms tighter and headed for the bedroom door.

Half-way across he tripped on one of his own discarded shoes and almost overbalanced.

He muttered something under his breath and kicked the offending article out of the way, tugging open the bedroom door, his haste to reach the toilet now increased.

The floorboards on the landing creaked protestingly as he crossed, past two other closed doors and another to his right which was slightly ajar.

He peered in and saw two of his children sleeping, one of them hanging precariously close to the edge of the top bunk.

O'Brian thought about tiptoeing in and pushing the child back, but his desire to empty his bursting bladder proved too strong.

The window on the landing was letting in the first, dirty rays of dawn and O'Brian squinted, as if the dull, greyish-blue light was too much for him.

Another day.

A day just like all the rest. They had become indistinguishable from one another, or so it seemed to O'Brian. Get up, work, go to bed.

Sandwiched between were worries about his job (he'd heard that fifty were to be laid off from the Bankside Power station in Southwark where he'd worked for the last fifteen years), his family and his car, which looked like packing up on him again. Bloody thing. It hadn't run right for more than a week since he'd bought it from his brother-in-law three years ago.

But, at the moment, the only thing which concerned Doug O'Brian was relieving himself.

He pushed open the bathroom door, flipped up the seat and began urinating.

The relief.

He smiled to himself, catching a glimpse of his reflection in the bathroom mirror. His black hair was sticking up at one side like a wayward punk rocker, his eyes looked puffy and he needed a shave.

Otherwise he didn't look too bad for such an early hour.

He finished urinating but chose not to flush the toilet, not wanting to wake anyone, least of all any of the children. Especially the youngest. She'd be in their bedroom like a shot if he disturbed her. O'Brian wondered if he might just get another hour's sleep before the alarm woke him. If the youngest heard him moving about he had no chance.

He tiptoed back onto the landing, glancing out of the window, pausing a moment.

There were two police vans parked in the road outside.

He could see uniformed men moving about, pointing to various houses. They were talking to a couple of smartly dressed civilians, one of them a woman.

O'Brian rubbed his eyes.

What the hell were the law doing out there at this time in the morning?

He glanced at his watch.

5.16 a.m.

More uniformed men climbed from the back of a third van, which pulled up and parked on the other side of Luke Street.

The men paired up and O'Brian watched as they headed off in different directions, some towards the front doors of houses.

He blinked hard, as if the uniformed men might disappear.

Perhaps they were part of his dream, too.

Then he saw two of them approaching his house.

The loud knocking on the front door that he heard seconds later convinced him this was no dream.

Two streets away in Blackall Street, there were no vans, just police cars.

Each officer had a plain clothes companion as he approached his designated house.

They all seemed to pause outside the doors of those

houses chosen, then, as if a signal had been given, they knocked.

Annette Hilston had watched the police vans draw up in Weymouth Terrace, crouched on her bed, the eyes of a dozen pop stars glaring blankly at her from the posters festooning her walls.

She had seen them approach the house.

She had heard them bang on the door.

Now she listened to shouting. Her father and her mother were yelling at someone, but she heard no words in reply.

Annette remained kneeling on her bed, hands clasped together, clutching a key-ring with a picture of the lead singer of her favourite pop group on it. She carried it everywhere, for luck.

Now she gripped it like some kind of rosary.

Downstairs she could still hear the shouting and swearing.

She continued gazing out of the window.

Even when she heard footsteps coming up the stairs.

Some rose meekly, shocked.

Some wanted to fight back.

Some tried.

Tempers frayed like old rope, stretched and finally snapped.

There were tears, screams, curses but no arrests.

And there was anger.

Fear.

By 6.00 a.m. that morning, it looked as if the entire might of the Metropolitan Police Force had invaded Hackney.

By 7.00 a.m. it was all over.

Fifty

Catherine Reed heard the voice and thought it was part of her dream. Only when she felt the hand on her shoulder did she stir, sitting up quickly, almost knocking the mug of tea from Phillip Cross's hand as he stood over her.

'Morning,' said Cross, grinning.

Cath looked at him and blinked myopically, then she too smiled and reached for the mug, burning her fingers. She hissed and set the tea down on the bedside table.

'What time is it?' she asked, flopping back against the headboard.

'Half seven,' he told her.

She ran two hands through her long, dark hair and groaned.

'What day is it?' she murmured, smiling. 'Where am I? *Who* am I?'

Cross chuckled.

'I'm going to have a shower,' he said, glancing at her naked breasts.

She watched as he walked from the bedroom, her gaze fixed on his naked backside.

'Thanks for the tea,' she called, smiling as he turned. 'And for everything else.' She looked at his groin and raised her eyebrows. 'I must have been good, to get tea in bed.'

'Not bad,' he said, grinning.

She threw a pillow in his direction, listening as he made his way towards the bathroom. A moment later she heard the hiss of the shower.

Cath picked up the remote control from the bedside table and pressed the standby switch. The small portable TV fixed to a bracket on the bedroom wall sputtered into life.

She flicked channels.

A cartoon on one channel.

Some self-important so-called celebrity enjoying his fifteen minutes of fame on another.

More cartoons.

An overdressed woman plugging her new book, whining on in a grating Anglo-American accent.

Nice to know some things never changed, thought Cath, and the mediocrity of breakfast TV was certainly one of life's constants.

She jabbed the buttons again, checked Ceefax and Teletext for the headlines, then ran through the channels once again.

This time she found some news.

Picking up her mug of tea she lay there listening to a report on the latest famine in Africa.

Some things never changed.

She glanced around the room and saw her clothes were scattered around the floor, left in untidy heaps along with Cross's. She chuckled to herself when she saw his underpants hanging on the back of a chair opposite.

From the bathroom she could still hear the sound of the shower and she was about to call to the photographer to hurry up, when her attention was caught by something on the television.

The camera was showing a street in London. The caption beneath the reporter said Hackney.

Cath turned up the sound, annoyed with herself that she hadn't heard the beginning of the report.

'. . . haven't released an official statement yet, but it's thought that up to fifty or sixty officers and members of Hackney Social Services carried out the dawn raids.'

Cath sat forward.

'More than twenty houses were raided and, as far as we know, something like fifteen or sixteen children were taken by the Social Services. Again, we have no official word as yet, but it appears that police are investigating a possible child pornography ring.'

'Jesus Christ,' murmured Cath.

She slid across the bed, picking up the phone from the other bedside table.

With one eye still on the screen she jabbed out a number and waited.

Fifty-one

The room was twenty feet square and, to Talbot, it appeared that every single inch of floor space was covered by large, brown cardboard boxes. Each one about three feet deep and two feet wide.

There were yellow labels attached to each one with a name and address written in marker pen.

197

At one end of the room, a couple of uniformed officers were searching through the boxes; another, seated at a desk, was scribbling down the nature of the contents as his companions inspected every object they removed, looking at it closely before returning it.

All three men wore transparent rubber gloves.

Detective Inspector Gordon Macpherson lit up a cigarette and offered the packet to Talbot who shook his head.

'I've given up,' he said, quietly, his eyes fixed on the array of boxes.

Macpherson nodded and pushed the pack inside his jacket before running a hand through his thin blond hair.

He was three years older than Talbot; a slightly over-weight, red-cheeked man whose features were almost boyish. His eyes darted constantly back and forth as if he were watching some invisible tennis match: a habit all the more disconcerting when Talbot looked him directly in the face.

However, at the moment, the younger man was concerned only with the boxes filling the room of the police station in Theobald's Road.

'How many kids?' he said, finally.

'Seventeen,' Macpherson told him. 'All aged from three to sixteen.'

'How come you've got the stuff here, Mac? Because you're closest?'

Macpherson nodded.

'Someone from the Yard's coming to fetch it. We're just doing the spade work. Inventory and boxing it up. They want to know what came from each house.' He looked at Talbot and smiled.

'I thought that's what *you* were here for, Jim,' the older man said. 'To collect it.'

Talbot shook his head.

'Where are the kids now?' he wanted to know.

'Hackney Social Services have got them, interviewing them.'

'Who tipped you off about what was going on?'

'We don't actually know anything *is* going on yet, Jim. It's a precautionary measure. Social Services requested it.'

'Social Services requested a fucking dawn raid?' Talbot snorted. 'I'd call that a bit more than a precautionary measure, Mac.'

'One of the local schools, St Michael's, called us in. They reckoned two, maybe more, kids there were being knocked about by their parents.' He shrugged. 'We checked it out, sent a report to Hackney Social Services and they thought there could be something going on.'

'Who reported it?'

'A teacher.'

'When was this?'

'Two days ago.'

'How the hell did Social Services get wardship orders so quick?'

'You tell *me*.'

Talbot wandered across to the nearest box and peered in.

It was full of books, videos, magazines, and he even noticed some clothes in the bottom.

'It's the same in all of them,' Macpherson told him, reaching inside another of the boxes. 'What do you reckon?' He held up a magazine which showed a young woman kneeling in front of a man, gripping his penis with one hand, her lips closed over the end.

'Don't fancy yours much,' said Talbot, dismissively, glancing at the title: *Wild Cum Party*.

'We found loads of them,' Macpherson said, indicating more of the magazines. He flicked through another.

'No law against *those*, Mac,' Talbot reminded him.

'Some of the stuff's going to the Vice Squad, some of the heavier stuff.'

'Like what?'

'In two of the houses we found paedophile magazines and photos. And that's just what's been checked *so* far.'

'How bad?'

'Kids as young as two.'

'Shit,' muttered Talbot.

'We raided twenty-three houses, took stuff from every one, and we've done inventories on twelve so far. Out of those twelve we've found enough porno magazines and videos to decorate a block of flats, and we're not finished yet.'

'Anything else?'

'Like what?'

'Equipment. Bondage gear. Anything that might have been used on the kids.'

'Not unless you count three vibrators, a blow-up doll and some of those fucking love eggs.' He smiled. 'You know, those things women stick up their—'

'Yeah, I know what they do with them, Mac,' Talbot interrupted.

He wandered over to another of the boxes and looked inside.

More magazines. More videos.

He pulled one out.

'*Cannibal Ferox*,' he read aloud.

'And video nasties,' Macpherson added. 'We've found plenty of those. *Driller Killer. I Spit on your Grave. S.S. Experiment Camp*. The lot. *The Exorcist*—'

Talbot interrupted him.

'I've got a copy of that,' he said.

'So have I,' Macpherson echoed. 'I'm just telling you what we found.'

'Not all from one house?'

'No. I wish it *had* been: we might have been able to nail someone quicker. If there was one geezer supplying the rest of the neighbourhood it'd make things much easier, but it seems to be spread around.'

'So how much have you got to go on? What's the likelihood it *is* a child abuse ring?'

'We're not going to know that until Social Services finishes questioning the kids. *That* could be days. Then there's the medical reports if they *do* find any physical damage.'

'Damage isn't always physical,' murmured Talbot.

'What did you say, Jim?'

'Nothing,' he lied.

You know all about that, don't you?

Talbot reached into one of the boxes and pulled out some Polaroids.

Damage isn't always physical.

They showed a naked woman spreadeagled on a worn and battered sofa. She was sucking one index finger. She was skinny. The outline of her ribs showed clearly.

There were only red dots where her pupils should have been.

Talbot shook his head, flicking through the remainder of the pictures.

The same woman holding a cucumber to her mouth, licking the tip.

The absurdity of the pose was striking.

There was one of a naked man, gripping his penis in one large fist.

Another of the skinny woman with her middle finger pushed into her vagina. She looked back with that familiar red-eyed expression.

Talbot noticed that there was a budgie cage in the background behind the sofa on which she was spread-eagled.

'Whoever took them was no fucking David Bailey, was he?' said Macpherson chuckling. 'And she's no Cindy Crawford.'

'How many times have *you* seen Cindy Crawford pose with a cucumber?' Talbot asked, smiling.

'We can all dream, can't we?' Macpherson smiled, taking another drag on his cigarette.

Talbot stepped away from him as he blew out a stream of smoke.

He could do with one now.

He dropped the photos back into the box.

'You don't mind if I have a look around, do you, Mac?' he asked.

'Help yourself,' Macpherson told him, watching as the younger man moved slowly from box to box, his gaze drawn to the contents of each one.

'You looking for anything in particular, Jim?' Macpherson asked.

Talbot chose not to answer him.

Jesus, the fucking press would have a field day with this lot.

'If you don't mind me asking, Jim,' Macpherson said, cautiously, 'what's *your* interest in this?'

'What makes you think I've got an interest?' Talbot snapped without looking at his colleague.

'You're here, aren't you?'

The two men regarded each other silently for a moment then Talbot spoke again.

'You remember, a couple of years ago I was suspended for slapping some fucking nonce around.'

Macpherson nodded.

'Let's just say that case aroused my interest in this sort of thing,' he lied, nodding towards the boxes. 'If there *is* a child abuse ring in operation here then I want to know about it.'

Fifty-two

'It looks pretty quiet,' said Phillip Cross, his voice hushed almost reverentially.

Catherine Reed peered out of the side window of the Fiat, her eyes drawn to one particular house, then she glanced at the computer print-out spread across her lap.

There was nothing moving in Luke Street, Hackney, apart from a motley-looking Labrador, which was padding back and forth across the street.

Cath watched as it stopped to cock its leg against a hedge before disappearing up the pathway of a house.

Cross pulled a camera from his bag and focused.

'That house,' Cath told him, pointing at the building almost opposite them.

She sat gazing at it, listening to him clicking off shots.

'Are you sure it's the same O'Brian family?' the photographer asked.

'I double-checked the address with my brother,' she said. 'The kids go to the school where he teaches.'

'And they're the same ones whose kid was dug up in Croydon Cemetery?' Cross continued.

Cath nodded, her eyes still on the house.

'I hope that list's right,' Cross said, nodding towards the computer print-out.

'These are the houses that were raided this morning,' she said, flicking the paper with her middle finger. 'Nicholls got it from a contact of his at the Met.'

'Off the record, presumably?' Cross said, changing lenses.

Cath looked at him and raised one eyebrow. 'What do *you* think?'

She folded the print-out and pushed it into the glove compartment then opened the driver's side door and swung herself out.

'Let's have a closer look,' she said, pausing beside the car, her gaze fixed on the house opposite. She set off without waiting for Cross who scuttled up alongside her.

The gate at the end of the short path creaked as she pushed it open. As she approached the front door she noticed that the milk was still on the doorstep.

Cath knocked three times and waited.

Cross looked up, trying to spot signs of movement inside the house.

There was no answer.

She tried again.

'Perhaps they're out,' Cross offered.

Cath knocked once again then crossed to the front window, cupped one hand over her eyes and tried to see inside.

She could see very little through the curtains, only that she was staring into the sitting room.

Cross imitated her action, squinting through the window on the other side.

'Cath,' he called. 'I think there's someone inside.'

She hurried across to join him.

'I thought I saw someone moving in there,' he assured her.

She could see nothing.

'I think they saw me looking in,' Cross continued.

Cath returned to the front door and knocked again. Harder this time.

'Why don't you leave them alone?'

The voice came from behind her.

'You're reporters, aren't you?' the voice said, and now Cath turned to find its source.

The woman standing in the garden of the house next door was in her early thirties, long reddish-brown hair reaching past her shoulders. She had both hands tucked in the pockets of her jeans.

'I just wanted to speak to Mr and Mrs O'Brian and—' Cath began.

'And what?' the woman snapped. 'Stick your fucking nose in where it's not wanted. Why don't you just piss off?'

'Take it easy,' Cross interjected.

'You want some pictures?' the woman said, raising two fingers. 'Take one of that.'

'How well do you know the O'Brians?' Cath asked.

'Don't expect *me* to talk to you. I'm not answering any of your fucking questions.'

'Did you have children taken this morning?' Cath persisted.

The woman took a step towards the low hedge which separated the two gardens, her expression dark.

'I told you,' she hissed, 'I'm not going to talk to you, I'm not going to help you write your fucking lies.'

'I'm just trying to find out the truth,' Cath told her.

'Jesus. Since when have newspapers been interested in the truth? You couldn't care less what you write about people, how you hurt them, could you? As long as you get a story. You're all the same. You're scum.'

The front door suddenly opened and Cath turned to find herself looking into the haggard features of Doug O'Brian.

'Fucking reporters, Doug,' said the red-haired woman, scathingly.

'What do you want?' O'Brian said, looking at Cath with red-rimmed eyes.

Cross snapped off a couple of shots of him.

'Bastard,' snapped the redhead.

'My wife's indoors crying, would you rather get a picture of *that*?' O'Brian said, turning his attention to the photographer.

'I just wanted to speak to you, Mr O'Brian, just a quick word,' Cath said. 'I wondered if you knew why your children had been taken away. What reasons could the police and Social Services have for taking them?'

'Just go, will you?' said O'Brian, half closing the door.

'Yeah, piss off,' shouted the redhead.

'You've got a right to give *your* side of the story,' Cath told him.

'And that's what you're here for, is it? To let me have my say?'

'People will make up their own minds from what they read. You deserve a chance to put *your* point of view forward.'

'I don't know what I hate about you people the most, your lies or your hypocrisy,' said O'Brian and slammed the door.

'Just fuck off,' the redhead continued.

Cath shot her a withering glance, then turned and headed back towards the car, Cross close behind her.

As she slid behind the wheel of the Fiat she noticed that the red-haired woman had retreated to her front step. From there she was still shouting, gesturing angrily towards the car, but Cath could barely hear her furious exhortations.

Just before she pulled away, Cath saw a figure peering from behind a curtain in an upstairs room of the O'Brian house.

Watching.

Then, like an apparition, the shape was gone.

Fifty-three

Nikki Parsons was shaking.

As she tried to light the cigarette the twenty-nine-year-old found that she could scarcely keep the tip steady in the flame of the match. She took a heavy drag and blew out a stream of smoke.

Beside her, Janice Hedden, a year younger, merely kept both hands clasped around her mug of coffee and gazed vacantly ahead of her, occasionally glancing at her companions.

Besides herself and Nikki, there were three other women in the room, all seated around a large table. The walls of the room were dotted with a variety of leaflets distributed at various times by Hackney Council and Social Services. Leaflets on giving blood, on how to cope with multiple sclerosis, AIDS, suicide, drugs.

It was their daily routine.

Janice and her companions were used to dealing with suffering.

With pain.

She had wondered if she would ever become immune to it. Able to distance herself from some of the frightful tales of deprivation and suffering which she heard on a daily basis. Like her companions, she walked a fine line between compassion and efficiency, solace and practicality. She, like her colleagues, walked that line every day, rarely touched by what they heard, able to walk away from it at the end of the working day. It was, after all, a job.

Until today.

Maria Goldman was the senior official amongst them: senior in experience if not in years. At thirty, she'd worked in Brixton and Islington before moving to Hackney.

She'd found no resentment from her older colleagues.

One of them was in the room now.

Valerie Weston swept her short brown hair away from her forehead in a gesture that implied habit rather than necessity.

A nervous habit perhaps.

At the moment she had plenty to be nervous *about*.

Juliana Procon chewed the end of her pen, her eyes fixed on a sheaf of papers spread before her. There were drawings on some of them. She swallowed hard and pushed one of the drawings out of sight beneath more paper, her attention drawn towards the head of the table where Maria Goldman coughed, kept her hand over her mouth for a moment, then finally raised her gaze to look at her companions. She could feel the beginnings of a headache gnawing at the base of her skull.

It was almost 1.46 p.m.

It had already been a long day and she feared there was much more to come.

She took a sip of coffee, wincing when she found it was cold; then she cleared her throat again and glanced around the table at the other women.

She found it hard to disguise the weary look on her face.

'I thought it best to call a break,' Maria said, looking at her colleagues. 'I think we all need it.'

Nikki Parsons nodded, her hand still shaking slightly.

'I wondered if anyone had any comments to make before we examine the first set of statements,' Maria continued.

The women seemed reluctant to speak, but it was Janice Hedden who finally broke the uneasy silence.

'How many more children are there to interview?'

'Eight,' Maria told her.

'Same age range?'

Maria nodded.

'The ones I spoke to seemed very afraid,' Janice continued. 'Mainly that they weren't going to see their parents again. The younger ones in particular.'

'That's only natural,' Maria said.

'It seems to be about the only thing concerned with this case that *is*,' Val Weston offered.

'I've never seen or heard anything like it,' Nikki Parsons echoed, her voice low.

'Do you think any of them are lying?' Maria asked.

'It's possible, but most of the stories seem too complex to have been invented,' Nikki continued. 'Especially by children so young.'

'Janice, you said the children you spoke to seemed afraid,' Juliana interjected. 'I noticed that too, but not so much afraid of their parents as of . . .' she shrugged, struggling to find the words. 'Of what might happen to their parents. They didn't seem afraid for themselves, just puzzled by what had happened to them.'

'Some of them spoke out without too much prompting,' Val Weston said. 'The others were difficult, some still haven't spoken.'

'Any physical evidence of abuse?' Maria wanted to know.

'On two of them,' said Nikki.

'One,' Janice added.

'Three of them I interviewed,' Juliana said.

'Val? What about yours?' Maria asked.

'Just the odd scratch or bruise,' Val Weston said.

'I saw one boy who was scarred quite badly,' Maria confessed. 'He told me *how* it happened but he wouldn't show me the injuries *below* his waist.' She swallowed hard. 'He said that a stick had been pushed into his bottom, that it was painful when he went to the toilet.'

'When's the doctor arriving?' Nikki asked.

'He's here now,' Maria replied. 'He's examining all of the children.'

'A three-year-old boy and a six-year-old girl I spoke to reported having objects pushed into them,' Val added. 'The girl drew that when I asked her to describe the object.'

Val pushed a piece of paper towards Maria.

On it was a cylindrical object scrawled in red crayon, round tipped and about six inches long.

Maria nodded slowly.

'There were no physical signs, though,' Val continued.

'And you're all sure that none of the children had a chance to speak to each other before you interviewed them?' said Maria, looking at the other women. 'There's no way they could have worked out stories between them?'

The others shook their heads.

'All right,' Maria said, wearily. 'We'll look at the statements now. I'll start.' She lifted the top sheet from the pile of papers at her left elbow and scanned it, her eyes narrowing slightly. 'This is from a four-year-old, Alex Cutler.' She traced the words with the tip of her finger as she read: '"They make you stand in a circle and they laugh at you and sometimes I cried but then some more uncles and aunts come and they put the baby on the floor and then everyone walks around with their arms up and they shout. And you can see their willies. And then one of my uncles jumped on the baby."'

211

'Aunts and uncles,' murmured Nikki. 'The children I spoke to called them that.'

'It's common. The abusers make the children feel as if they're some kind of extended family members. Aunts and uncles covers a multitude of sins,' said Maria, cryptically. 'In more ways than one.'

She flipped through the sheaf of papers before her.

'This is from a six-year-old,' she said, sucking in a tired breath. '"I loved my puppy but they killed it. They cut off its head and put the blood in a cup."'

'"Sometimes they used animals and they stuck a knife in them and then they put the blood in a jug,"' Nikki read, holding a piece of paper before her.

'"They stick swords in the cats and kill them and they made me drink the blood,"' Janice added.

Maria ran a hand through her hair and sat back in her seat.

'Nearly every statement mentions the killing of animals,' she murmured.

'Not the usual paedophile pursuit, is it?' Juliana offered.

Maria shook her head.

'Why animals?' Janice asked.

Maria had no answer. She had her eyes fixed on the sheet of paper in front of her, the drawing on it.

'The children I spoke to mentioned cameras,' Val Weston said. 'That one of the uncles always had a camera, that he was taking pictures of them when they had no clothes on.'

'"*I saw one of those video cameras taking pictures of the baby,*"' Juliana read.

'"*They made me touch Uncle Paul's willy. I had to put my hands on it and he put it in my mouth and it tasted funny*'

212

and they took photos,"' said Nikki, quietly. 'That statement is from a six-year-old boy.' Her jaws were clenched
tightly together, the knot of muscles there pulsing
angrily.

'We'll finish interviewing the other children today,'
Maria told her colleagues. 'Once we've been through all
the statements and I've got the medical reports from the
doctor, we'll run through what we've got again.'

'I would have thought it was obvious what we've got,
Maria,' Nikki said, scathingly. 'A paedophile ring. How
much proof do you need?'

Maria Goldman kept her gaze fixed on the sheet of
paper before her, eyes tracing the outlines of the shape
which had been drawn there.

'I have no doubt that you're right, Nikki,' she said,
touching the scrawled image with her finger. 'I just hope
that's *all* we've got.'

As she looked at what had been drawn on the paper,
she felt the hairs on the back of her neck rise.

Fifty-four

'What the hell are *you* doing here?' said Frank Reed, a
broad smile spreading across his face.

Cath raised her eyebrows as she slipped inside his
office and smiled back.

'I thought you'd have been out gathering information
for some Pulitzer Prize-winning article,' Reed chuckled,
offering her a seat.

'Not quite, Frank,' she answered, accepting it. 'But this *isn't* a social call. I need your help on something.'

'So, what else is new?'

'You've seen the papers this morning? The news?'

'The police raids, you mean?'

She nodded.

'I didn't expect things to go quite this far,' he said, softly.

'Jesus, Frank, what did you think was going to happen? You scream child abuse and it warrants more than a few polite enquiries by the neighbourhood bobby on the beat.'

'I heard somewhere they'd raided twenty-three houses.'

'That's right.'

'Cath, what I did, I did for the good of those children. It *had* to be reported. What the hell was I supposed to do, sit around and let it just happen?' he said, challengingly. 'Anyway, what's *your* problem? It's given you something to write about, hasn't it?'

'Look, take it easy, I'm on *your* side, right?'

He sat back in his seat, glancing out of his office window. There was a group of children crossing the playground, chattering loudly until the teacher leading them called for silence.

'So, what can I do to help?' Reed said, finally.

Cath reached into her handbag and pulled out the computer print-out which had spent most of that morning stuffed into her glove compartment. She stood up and walked around the desk so that she was standing next to her brother; then she laid the print-out down before him, smoothing out the creases as best she could.

'It's a list of the families whose houses were raided this morning,' she told him. 'I want to know how many of the kids go to school *here*.'

Reed looked up at Cath, then at the print-out.

'Why?' he asked.

'I'm looking for links, Frank, anything that ties these cases together.'

He spotted one name immediately.

Paul O'Brian.

Reed jabbed a finger at it.

'I know. I've already been there this morning. The parents, well, the father at any rate, wasn't very co-operative,' she informed him.

Reed studied the list.

He pointed to another name.

'What about the address?' said Cath.

The door to Reed's office opened unexpectedly and both he and Cath watched as Noel Hardy entered.

The Headmaster glared at Cath, then at her brother, paused in the doorway a moment, then slammed the door behind him and strode across to the desk.

'Haven't we had enough of the press already today?' the older man said, acidly.

'I hate to tell you, Mr . . .'

'Hardy,' the older man snapped. 'In case your brother hadn't told you, I'm the Headmaster here. This is *my* school. I'd appreciate it if you'd leave.'

'You said that other members of the press had been here today. I think I'm entitled to the same courtesy you may have extended to them,' Cath said, officiously.

'There was no courtesy extended to any of them,' Hardy assured her. 'But I'll give you the same statement I gave the rest of them. No comment.'

'A number of the children taken into care attended your school,' Cath informed him. 'Doesn't that bother you?'

'Are you trying to infer that the school is somehow to blame for what has happened to these children?'

'I'm not trying to infer anything, Mr Hardy, but if you're worried that inference might be attached to yourself *or* your school . . .' She allowed the sentence to trail off.

'I knew nothing of this . . .'

'Abuse,' Cath said, with an air of finality.

'Nothing's been proved yet,' the Headmaster reminded her.

'Come on, Noel,' snapped Reed. 'You know what's going on here. We all do.'

'I warned you,' Hardy snapped, angrily. 'I said that if this was reported it could damage the reputation of the school, whether you were right or wrong.'

'So what matters more to you?' Reed wanted to know. 'The welfare of the children or the reputation of the school?'

'I have to take into consideration the damage this publicity could do to St Michael's,' said Hardy.

'What about the damage that's already been done to those kids?' snapped Reed.

'That's nothing to do with this school.'

'Then why worry about it?' Cath interjected. 'It's not you or your school that's on trial, Mr Hardy. I'm just looking for the facts.'

'Journalists' cliché number one,' Hardy snorted, as he moved towards the door.

'Look, I didn't come here to see you, I came to see my brother,' Cath said, irritably.

216

Hardy opened the office door and let it swing wide.

'Then do it somewhere else,' he said, angrily. 'If you're not off these premises in thirty seconds I'll call the police.'

Cath shrugged, gathered up the computer print-out and pushed it back into her handbag.

'Nice to see you again, Mr Hardy,' she said flatly, as she reached the door. Then, turning to her brother 'I'll speak to you later, Frank.'

Hardy slammed the door behind her.

'You can't run away from this, Noel,' Reed told him.

'I'm trying to protect this school.'

'And I was trying to protect those kids.'

Hardy turned to leave, pausing in the doorway briefly. 'Perhaps you should start thinking about your own job,' he said menacingly.

'Are you threatening me?'

'I'm just protecting the school,' Hardy snapped then he was gone, the door slamming behind him.

Reed sat back in his chair, exhaled deeply then looked down at the phone.

He waited a moment, then dialled.

Fifty-five

Dorothy Talbot sipped at her tea, then carefully replaced the cup and saucer on the table close to her, the china rattling.

James Talbot shot out a hand to steady the cup,

217

fearing it would overbalance, but he withdrew it just as suddenly when he saw his mother push the cup further onto the table.

'It's all right, Jim, I can manage,' she said, smiling. 'I'm not a cripple, you know.'

No. You're just dying of cancer.

They were the only two people in the day room at Litton Vale. The other residents, or a party of twenty of them, had been driven in to the West End to see a film. Dorothy couldn't remember the title but she hadn't fancied it. Some Victorian-based thing, she'd said.

'You should have gone, Mum,' Talbot said. 'You might have enjoyed it.'

She shook her head.

'It didn't sound very exciting,' she told him. 'Anyway, you know me, I like a good Western. Like the ones I used to take you to see when you were little.'

Talbot tried to hold her gaze but found that he couldn't.

Guilt, perhaps?

'You took me to see all sorts,' he said, chuckling as brightly as he could. 'We saw *Planet of the Apes* four times when I was ten. You hated it, I remember you saying. But you still went back with me.'

She reached out and touched his hand.

'What's wrong, Jim?'

Could she read his fucking mind too? See inside him?

He forced himself to look at her, noticing that she looked pale, a little drawn around the eyes.

He thought about asking her if she was in pain.

'There's nothing wrong,' he lied.

'Is it work?' she persisted. 'You should try and get a rest, and I bet you're not getting enough sleep.'

'Mum, *I'm* fine, *you're* the one who's ill . . .' The sentence trailed off.

She squeezed his hand more tightly, gripped it with surprising strength.

He met her gaze and held it.

'Jim, I don't want to die in here,' she whispered.

'Mum, you're not going to die.'

'Doctor Hodges told me how far advanced the cancer is.'

'You're not going to die,' he said, angrily, as if his fury would somehow reprieve her.

But you know she is.

'These bloody doctors they don't know shit,' he snapped.

'Just don't let me die in here, that's all I ask.'

He could face her no longer.

Talbot got to his feet and walked across the day room, looking out into the immaculately kept gardens beyond. The sun was shining. He could hear birds singing.

It was a beautiful day.

Yeah, fucking brilliant.

He cleared his throat but didn't turn to face her.

'Have they given you anything?'

'I take some tablets, I can't remember what they're called,' she informed him. 'I'm not even sure what they do. Doctor Hodges *did* tell me but I can't remember.' She laughed humourlessly. 'I think I'm going senile as well.'

'Are you in pain?'

There, now you've said it.

'No.'

'You wouldn't tell me if you were, would you?'

He turned to face her, saw she was sipping at her tea again. As he looked at her, Talbot felt more helpless than

219

he had ever done in his life. Helpless to ease her pain, helpless to comfort her.

How often did *she* help *you*?

He walked back and sat down beside her.

'I've been reading in the newspapers about those children,' she told him. 'Isn't it terrible? It made me think about what your father did. How he hurt you.'

'Forget it, Mum. That's in the past.'

'But it never goes away, does it, Jim? The memories never go. I hated him for what he did to you. I hated myself for not stopping him.'

'You tried. Every time you tried.'

'I should have killed him. After the first time he did it to you I should have killed him.'

He saw her eyes misting over.

'I didn't even have the guts to leave him,' she said, softly. 'To take you away from him.' She gripped his hand. 'Jim, I'm sorry.'

A single tear rolled down her cheek.

'Jesus Christ, Mum, *you're* not the one who should be sorry,' he told her, watching as she wiped the tear away with a hankie.

It should be me. For putting you in this fucking place.

As she shifted position in her chair he saw a flicker of pain on her face.

'Are you OK?' Talbot asked.

She smiled and nodded almost imperceptibly.

'All I'm asking is that you let me come home, Jim,' she pleaded quietly.

He sucked in a breath and got to his feet.

'I'll speak to the doctor,' he said.

Fucking liar.

Talbot embraced her.

220

She kissed him on the cheek and smiled up at him.

'I love you,' she said.

'I know,' he told her and she watched as he walked towards the exit, turning to wave as he left.

Dorothy Talbot winced, held her breath against the pain, waiting for the spasm to pass.

It didn't.

She reached into her handbag for the morphine.

Talbot strode down the corridor towards the main entrance, slowing his pace slightly as he reached the door which bore the nameplate DR M. HODGES.

He paused.

Go on, you bastard. Go in.

He raised his hand to knock.

Do it.

He wheeled away from the door, almost running from the building to his car, leaning against the Volvo, eyes closed.

It was a long time before he moved.

Fifty-six

Maria Goldman heard the knock on the office door but continued reading, her attention fixed on the piece of paper before her.

When the second knock came, more insistent this time, she finally managed to mutter something which passed for an invitation to enter.

The door opened slightly and Nikki Parsons stepped inside.

'Maria,' she said, quietly, looking at her colleague who was still staring at the report she held.

When she finally lifted her head, Nikki saw how pale she looked.

'I'm sorry, Nikki,' she said, softly. 'I was miles away. Sit down.'

The younger woman did as she was asked, peering towards the stack of papers on Maria's desk.

'The doctor's reports?' she said, although it sounded more like a statement than a question.

Maria nodded.

'Did he examine *all* the children?' Nikki wanted to know.

Again Maria nodded.

'And?'

Maria sat back in her chair and blinked hard. It had been a long day and it seemed to be getting longer.

'Where do you want me to start?'

'"Considerable bruising around the entrance of the vagina and on the inner thighs,"' she read from one report. '"Evidence of anal penetration."' She turned to another sheet of paper. '"Pelvic injuries, caused by crushing. Possible damage to the bladder." "Cervical rupture." "Penetration by a sharp instrument, possibly a stick, causing internal lacerations of the anus."' She put down the reports. 'How much more do you want to hear?'

Maria handed the reports to her colleague, watching as Nikki read them for herself, shaking her head slowly as she scanned the words.

'Rape,' she said, softly. 'The doctor's report specifies evidence of rape in the case of three of the girls.'

'All under eleven,' Maria added.

'And anal rape of six of the children, either that or penetration of some kind.'

'Coupled with numerous cuts, bruises, contusions and burns in nearly every case.' Maria closed her eyes. 'I think it's worse than any of us first thought.'

'It says that most of the cuts and bruising were on the ankles or wrists. As if they'd been tied up at some stage.'

'Some of the children specified that in their statements, didn't they?'

'They also mentioned sex, sometimes with one particular person.'

'*Person?*' said Maria, challengingly. 'Some didn't mention people, some mentioned animals. Some of these children were forced to have sex with animals, Nikki, if we believe these reports, if we believe *them.*'

'Why shouldn't we?'

'We know that the children we interviewed were kept apart from the time they were brought here. There's no way they could have invented stories like this together. No way they could ensure that each one gave evidence to support his or her friends' statements. That may be true with older children but not with four- and five-year-olds. You need a good memory to be a liar.'

'Are you saying that some of the children are lying about what they saw, about what happened to them? How can you? You've got the medical evidence there to back up their statements.'

'I'm not accusing any of them of lying. Far from it, but just because *we* might believe them doesn't mean the police will. These statements wouldn't be enough to secure a conviction.'

'Even with the medical evidence to back them up?'

223

'It's still not enough. No one is named. Who are they going to arrest?'

'But the parents—'

Maria cut her short. 'We don't know that.'

'So you're telling me that the parents of these children had no idea of what was happening to them?'

'Are any of them named in any of the statements? No. The only references are to aunts and uncles. Not one of them says "Daddy did this or Mummy did that". Even *we* don't know how involved the parents are.'

'I think it's safe to assume that some *are*.'

'The police will need more than an assumption, Nikki. I know, I've seen it before. Abused children given back to the people who abused them because there's not enough evidence against them.' She exhaled wearily. 'I don't want that to happen this time. *Especially* not this time.'

'You said something earlier today about us having a possible child abuse ring on our hands, hoping that was *all* we had. What did you mean?'

'I didn't push it this afternoon; I was worried the rest of you might think I was overreacting. But these statements, some of the things the children say – there's a uniformity to them that frightened me. I can't think of any other word to describe it.' She found the piece of paper she sought and tapped it with a pencil, running the tip down a list. 'The sacrifice of animals and being made to drink the blood. Having their bodies painted. Being filmed or photographed while they were being abused. Penetration by sticks. Being given pills and drinks that made them feel funny. Enclosure in cupboards or boxes. A figure who hurt them, people dressing as clowns or monsters. Latin chants.' She looked at Nikki. 'This isn't ordinary abuse.'

224

'What do you mean?' said the younger woman, frowning.

'I think there could be a ritual element to it. When we asked the children to draw a picture of the person who hurt them, this is what one of them drew.'

Maria handed a sheet of paper to her colleague, watching her expression as she scanned it.

The drawing showed a large figure wearing what appeared to be a cloak. Red crayon had been used to colour in where the eyes should have been. There was also red crayon on the figure's hands. But it was the head which held Nikki's attention. It was crudely sketched but it resembled the head of a sheep or goat.

There were two horns protruding from above the eyes.

'As far as that child was concerned,' said Maria, 'it was hurt by the Devil. How many six-year-olds do you know who'd draw something like that?'

'But, Maria, it's just one child.'

Leaning forward, Maria laid four more sheets of paper before her colleague.

Each one showed the same horned figure.

Fifty-seven

Frank Reed inspected his reflection in the bedroom's full-length mirror, running a hand through his hair yet again.

He looked across at the clock on the bedside table, and then at his own watch.

She was late.

He felt his heart quicken.

What if she didn't come?

What if there'd been an accident?

Perhaps she was ill, or . . .

The front doorbell rang and Reed hurried down the stairs, slipping the chain off, pulling the door wide.

Rebecca Reed stood before him, smiling up at him.

'Becky,' he beamed, sweeping her into his arms, kissing her.

It felt like an eternity since he'd seen her last.

'You look so big,' he told her, cradling her in his arms. 'I think you're getting too heavy for me to hold.' He pretended to drop her.

Becky chuckled as he set her down.

'There's something for you in the living room,' he said.

She looked round, as if seeking reassurance from the woman who stood impassively on the doorstep.

Ellen Reed nodded and Becky ran off, disappearing from view through a door on the right.

'Thanks for bringing her,' said Reed, his smile fading. 'Do you want to come in for a minute?' He stepped back and extended an arm.

An invitation.

'Jonathan's waiting in the car,' Ellen told him. 'I can't be long.'

'I thought I asked you not to bring him with you,' Reed said.

'He's in the car, Frank,' Ellen said, irritably, stepping inside.

She followed him through into the kitchen where he boiled the kettle, glancing at her as she stood by the kitchen table.

'You can sit down, you know,' he told her. 'This *is* your house too.'

'It used to be, Frank,' she reminded him, pulling out a chair. 'You've kept it neat.'

'Did you expect me to start living like a pig just because you walked out on me?' he snapped.

He handed her a mug of tea and sat down opposite, pushing the sugar bowl towards her.

She took a sip.

'What happened to your sweet tooth?' he asked. 'It used to be three spoonfuls in a mug didn't it?'

'Jonathan said I was putting on a little weight, so I've cut out sweet stuff.'

'Oh, well, if *Jonathan* says you're getting fat . . .' he said, his voice heavy with sarcasm. 'Has he specified an optimum weight and size he'd like, or will he just tell you when you've completed the task?'

'I didn't come here to argue, Frank,' she told him, sipping her tea.

'I can't see too much wrong with you,' Reed told her.

He ran appraising eyes over her and thought how good she looked. Her hair was cut in a short bob, the blonde tresses gleaming. She wore little make-up except for a touch of eye-liner, but her skin seemed to glow. She was dressed in a dark green two-piece suit and a white blouse, immaculately pressed.

'Did he pick those out for you, too?' Reed asked, nodding towards her. 'Is he a fashion expert as well as a weight-watcher?'

As she closed her hands around the mug, Reed pointed to her left hand. 'Where's your wedding ring?'

'When I left, I took it off. We're not together any more.'

227

'But we're still married. Or was *that* Jonathan's idea too?'

'Just leave it, Frank. It's down to him that Becky's here today. He suggested I let her see more of you.'

'How fucking magnanimous of him! What am I supposed to do, run out and tell him how grateful I am that he's agreed to let me see my own daughter?'

'You can't blame him for everything that happened, Frank.'

'He took you away from me: I can blame him for that.'

'He didn't take me. I chose to go.'

'Yeah, and take *our* daughter with you.'

They both heard footsteps hurrying back towards the kitchen and, a moment later, Becky rushed in clutching a GameBoy, brandishing it like a trophy.

'Look, Mum,' she said, staring at the screen. 'It's got Mario on it.'

She handed the GameBoy to Ellen then rushed across to Reed and threw her arms around him.

'Thanks, Dad,' she beamed, kissing him on the cheek.

He squeezed her tightly for a second, then let her slip from his lap, watching as she reclaimed the game and scurried off into the living room again, blonde hair flying behind her like wind-blown silk.

'Don't you think that's a little advanced for a seven-year-old?' Ellen asked. 'And a little extravagant? You can't buy her back, Frank.'

They eyed each other coldly then Ellen spoke again.

'I thought you didn't approve of those things for kids. I'd have expected you to buy her a set of encyclopaedias or something more educational,' she said.

'Perhaps Jonathan can teach her how to use it,' Reed snapped. 'He seems to be an expert on everything else.'

Ellen got to her feet. 'I think I'd better go.'

Reed followed her out into the hallway.

'I'm going now, Becky,' she called and the little girl ran out from the living room once more, still clutching the GameBoy.

Reed watched as the two of them embraced, then Becky retreated from sight again.

'I'll pick her up at eight on Monday morning,' Ellen said.

'You'd better hurry,' Reed said. 'You'll keep Jonathan waiting.' He closed the door behind her and stood there for a moment, listening to the sound of her footsteps receding down the path. Then he headed for the living room.

Fifty-eight

'What the hell are you playing at, Talbot?'

Gina Bishop stood before him in the bar of the Holiday Inn, Mayfair, lowering her voice, aware that several heads had turned upon her entrance.

Talbot was convinced it was because of the black, double-breasted jacket and short skirt she wore that the attention of some of the other drinkers was momentarily diverted. She towered above him on her heels, blonde hair falling forward as she leaned towards him, whispering her words through clenched teeth.

'Sit down,' he said, running his eyes over her slender legs. 'You make the place lock untidy.'

She paused for a moment, then slid into one of the chairs opposite him, catching the attention of a white-coated waiter who hurried across towards her. His speed increased when she crossed her slender legs and her short skirt rode a little further up her thighs.

'What can I get you, madam?' he said, smiling.

'I'll have a spritzer,' she said, brushing strands of hair from her face.

'Another Jameson's, please,' Talbot added, and the waiter retreated almost reluctantly.

'Been raiding the piggy bank again?' Talbot said, nodding towards her suit. 'Or has work been particularly good lately?'

'I've told you before. Work's always good.'

'It's not bad,' he said, almost approvingly.

'Not bad? It's Gianni Versace, for God's sake. The shoes are Manolo Blahnik,' she said, indignantly.

Talbot plucked at the sleeve of his own jacket.

'Man at C&A,' he said, smiling.

The waiter returned with the drinks, set them down, then scuttled away to another table.

'So, what do you want, Talbot?' she asked, taking a sip of her drink. 'You interrupt my afternoon, *tell* me to be here tonight, you stop me working on one of my busiest nights. Do you know how much I could have made tonight? I had to cancel two appointments because of you. I could have made three grand tonight.'

'A special, was it?' he said, sardonically.

'Two Japanese businessmen.'

'Japs. You don't advertise in the Tokyo Yellow Pages too, do you?'

'I was recommended,' she told him defiantly.

'Two of them, eh? Both at the same time?'

'If that's what they'd wanted. The Japs tip well, too.'

'Fuck your appointments. You wouldn't have any at all if it wasn't for me letting you work that beat.'

'I'm *so* grateful,' she said, scornfully.

They regarded each other in silence for a moment, then Gina spoke again.

'So, what *do* you want?'

'I want to talk.'

'Like you wanted to talk the other night?'

'I wondered if you wanted to get something to eat. We could walk down the road, there's a pizza place.'

'Do me a favour, Talbot, you don't have to wine and dine me. You know that. If you want to fuck me, let's go back to my place now and get it over with.'

'I offered to buy you a meal.'

'In a bloody pizza parlour. Do you think I'm walking into Pizzaland dressed in an outfit that cost more than their staff earn in a year?'

'It's only a fucking suit, for Christ's sake.'

'Clothes say a lot about a person, Talbot. I mean, look at the state of yours.'

'You think those designer labels you insist on wearing mean anything?'

'They mean something to me.'

'Maybe, but shit's still shit, even if it's wrapped in silver paper.'

'I don't have to put up with this,' she snapped.

'Wrong,' he said, downing what was left in his glass.

'You're a cunt,' she hissed.

'Careful, Gina, the mask's slipping.'

'You *are*.'

'Who's arguing? Now, are we going to eat or not?'

'Not in a fucking Pizzaland,' she told him and he

231

watched as she opened her bag and pulled out her mobile phone, stabbing digits. She smiled when she heard a voice at the other end.

Talbot watched her.

'Hello, it's Gina Bishop, I was in the other night. I was wondering if you had my usual table, I know you must be busy but . . . Oh, you can, that's wonderful. I'll be there in five minutes. Thank you.' She switched off the phone and slipped it back into her bag.

'One of your customers own a restaurant?' Talbot asked.

'I eat there a lot. They know me.' She got to her feet. 'Come on, Talbot, let's go. We'll get a cab. Don't worry, I'll pay for it.'

He joined her, leaving a ten-pound note on the table to cover the cost of the drinks.

They walked through the reception together, Gina a step or two ahead of him.

The blue-clad doorman nodded at them as they walked out.

'Can you get us a taxi, please?' Gina asked, and the man hurried into the road to hail one.

As they climbed in, Gina sat behind the driver, aware that he was looking at her in his rear-view mirror.

'If I'm going to listen to your shit all night,' she said to Talbot, 'I might as well do it in comfortable surroundings.' Then to the driver: 'Overtons please.'

Talbot looked across at her.

She was staring out of the window, away from him.

The taxi pulled out into traffic.

232

Fifty-nine

'Did any of those names you showed your brother check out?' asked Phillip Cross, spooning rice from the foil container closest to him.

Catherine Reed, kneeling beside the coffee table on the carpet next to Cross, nodded, her eyes flicking back and forth over the array of takeaway food. She picked up several forkfuls of meat and dropped them into the bowl with her rice.

'Nine of the kids on that list attended the school where Frank teaches,' she told Cross.

'Did any of the parents talk?'

'Two closed doors, two fuck-offs and five that either wouldn't or couldn't answer,' Cath told him.

'What do *you* think is going on, Cath?'

She sat back against the sofa, one eye on the TV screen, but her mind concentrated on the question Cross had just asked her.

'There's abuse of some description going on, I'd bet money on it,' she said, taking a mouthful of rice. 'But no one will talk about it and I don't really blame them. Although, if they've got nothing to hide . . .'

'You think it's the parents who are doing the abusing?'

'Some of them must be involved either directly or indirectly. I'm not saying they've actually done damage to their own kids, but they must have known what was

233

going on.' She ran a hand through her hair. 'I need to speak to someone from Hackney Social Services, see what kind of statements the kids made.' She continued staring blankly at the TV screen, the sound turned down. 'Something's been bothering me too. I mean, there's probably no connection but one of the families, the O'Brians, their boy was taken away by the Social Services, right? A couple of weeks before that, the grave of their dead baby daughter was desecrated. You remember all that shit that was happening at Croydon Cemetery?'

He nodded. 'The smashed headstones, the graffiti and all that?'

'Some of it was pretty heavy.'

'You're not trying to say that the O'Brians were involved in what went on there, are you? I mean, they're hardly likely to dig up their own kid's grave, are they?' Cross snorted.

'Maybe *they're* not. It could be someone with a grudge against the family.'

'So what about the other graves that were desecrated? And that cat that was nailed to the church door. Was that a grudge thing, too?'

'Phil, I haven't got a *clue* what it was. For all I know, Nicholls could be right, it could have been some kind of witchcraft thing.'

'So you think this is satanic abuse?'

'It wouldn't be the first time it'd happened, would it? What about those cases in Cleveland, Nottingham and the Orkneys? They were supposed to be satanic abuse cases.'

'And none of them was ever proved,' Cross said, flatly.

Cath pushed a forkful of food into her mouth.

'Don't try looking for a story that isn't there, Cath,' Cross told her.

'Don't tell me how to do my job, Phil,' she said, irritably. 'I don't tell you how to take pictures.'

'I didn't mean it like that,' he responded. 'I just don't want you making a fool of yourself.'

She was about to say something else when the phone rang.

Cath got to her feet and crossed to it, lifting the receiver.

'Hello,' she said.

Silence.

'Hello.'

Still nothing.

The line went dead. Cath replaced the receiver and returned to her dinner. 'If I can get someone from one of the families who had kids taken away to talk, or even someone who knows them,' she said, excitedly, 'then I might have a chance of finding out what's going on.'

'And you think they're going to talk to you?' Cross said, shaking his head.

'Someone will talk, they always do.'

The phone rang again. Cath muttered something under her breath and prepared to haul herself up off the floor again but Cross put his hand on her shoulder, swinging himself off the sofa.

He picked up the phone. 'Hello.'

Again, only silence.

'Listen, I think you've got a wrong number.'

There was a click as the line went dead once again.

He was about to sit down when it rang again.

'Jesus,' Cross muttered.

235

'Leave it,' Cath told him. 'I'll let the answering machine take care of it.'

She heard her own voice on the tape, then the beep, then nothing.

Barely ten seconds had passed when the phone rang again.

Cath jumped to her feet and snatched up the receiver. 'Hello, again,' she said, smiling.

'Catherine Reed?' said the voice.

'Yes.'

'Keep your fucking nose out, you slag. Keep it out of other people's business, right? Are you fucking listening to me?' The voice was low, guttural.

'Who the hell *are* you?' Cath demanded.

'Back off, bitch, or you're fucking dead.'

At the other end the phone was slammed down.

Cath held the receiver for a moment then gently replaced it.

'Are you OK?' asked Cross, seeing how pale she looked.

She nodded, still looking down at the phone.

Waiting.

It was another thirty minutes before it rang again.

Sixty

Talbot was too busy eating to notice Gina Bishop glance at her Cartier watch.

She sighed.

Ten-thirty.

Jesus Christ, how much longer was he going to be?

She puffed agitatedly at her cigarette, gazing at the policeman through a thin film of smoke.

Around her, the low buzz of conversation from the other diners seemed to rise and fall in volume, the chink of cutlery on crockery the only other sound disturbing the relative peacefulness of the restaurant.

Talbot finally took a last mouthful of food and pushed his plate away.

'Very nice,' he said, raising his eyebrows. He glanced around at the other customers.

'How many of this lot do you know?' he asked.

She looked puzzled.

'Any of them help to pay for that outfit?'

'What's wrong, Talbot?' she snapped. 'Fed up with talking about your mother now?'

He shot her an angry glance.

'You've done nothing but talk about her since we got here, why change the subject?' Gina said, acidly.

'I said I wanted to talk, I didn't ask for your fucking opinions, I just needed someone to listen.'

'And why was I singled out for that honour?'

'Because there isn't anyone else,' he said, quietly.

'What, no friends? Mind you, I'm not surprised.'

'Do you think I'd choose to speak to *you* if I had other options?'

They regarded each other in silence.

She took another drag on the cigarette and blew smoke into his face.

'What about your colleagues?' she asked. 'Surely they'd listen to you.'

'I wouldn't bother them with my problems.'

'How considerate, but you'd bother me.'

237

'Their time's important. Yours isn't.'

He took a swallow of his drink, watching as she drew on the cigarette.

'So what *are* you going to do about your mother?' she asked, eventually.

'I don't know,' he muttered.

'Why not let her come home?'

'Who the hell is going to look after her?'

'Pay someone.'

'That's what I do now. They don't let her stay at Litton Vale out of the kindness of their fucking hearts. It costs money.'

A man sitting at the next table glanced across at Talbot who met his glance with a withering stare.

'If she comes home you'll save money that you're paying at the hospice—'

'It's *not* a hospice.'

She shrugged.

'Whatever. You'll save the money that you spend keeping her there. Spend it on a nurse to look after her at home. That seems pretty logical to me. It won't cost you much, anyway. From what you've said, she's not going to be around very long.'

Talbot glared at her furiously.

'Or is it that you don't want her home, Talbot?' Gina said, flatly.

He had no answer.

Well, is that the reason?

He downed what was left in his glass and banged it down hard on the table, drawing more glances from the other diners.

'You said earlier on that you owed her,' Gina told him. 'What did you mean?'

He shook his head slowly.

'Forget it,' he said, quietly.

'Tell me.'

'Fuck you.'

'You wanted to talk, Talbot. I'm talking. You wanted me to listen. I've listened.'

'All part of the job, isn't it?' he snapped. 'You listen to dirty old men, sad fucking bastards who can't get it up with their wives. Who have to pay you. Or you talk to them and you tell them how good they are, while you're watching the clock and adding up the pounds. You talk, you listen. You do anything for money. *For* anybody and *with* anybody. As long as the price is right.'

'I'm not like the others and you know that.'

'You're a tart. Pure and simple. The only difference between you and the slags that work around King's Cross is that you wear designer clothes to cover the dirt.'

'And you need me, Talbot. That's why you hate me, isn't it? You've got nobody else. No friends. No family. Nothing. I'm all you've got.'

He ran his finger slowly around the rim of his empty glass, watching her as she ground out her cigarette.

'I told you before, we're both the same. The only difference is I wouldn't let *my* mother die in an old people's home. If you do *that*, Talbot, then don't ever have the nerve to call *me* scum again.'

He eyed her malevolently, watching as she caught the attention of a waiter who scurried off to fetch the bill.

When he returned, Gina laid a Gold American Express card on the plate with the bill. The waiter scooped them both up and disappeared again.

239

'Money talks,' she said, a thin smile on her lips. 'Bullshit walks.'

The waiter reappeared and she signed the blue slip. Then she got to her feet and Talbot followed her out into the cool night air.

A taxi was approaching and Gina stuck out an arm to flag it down.

'My place?' she said, unenthusiastically.

Talbot had already begun walking up St James's Street towards Piccadilly.

The taxi pulled into the kerb.

'Talbot,' she called after him.

He kept walking.

Gina waited a moment, then climbed into the cab.

It sped off.

She didn't look round as she passed him.

Sixty-one

'Cath, you've got to call the police,' said Phillip Cross. 'You don't know what kind of fucking maniac might be making these calls.'

Cath sat on the sofa, legs drawn up beneath her, eyes fixed on the telephone.

There had been two more calls since the last one.

Both violently abusive.

But, she thought, different voices.

'They can trace where these calls came from,' Cross insisted.

'Whoever's making them isn't on long enough for the police to set up a trace,' Cath said, quietly, her gaze never leaving the phone.

At any second she expected it to ring again.

'At least ring them,' the photographer said, angrily.

'It's probably the parents of one of the kids who've been taken into care,' she observed. 'They told me to back off.'

'They also threatened to kill you. What's next after the phone calls. Someone banging on your door? Petrol poured through your letterbox? Ring the police, Cath.'

She shook her head.

'There's no way I'm leaving you alone tonight.'

She smiled at him, touching his hand as he squeezed her shoulder. 'I didn't want you to leave anyway,' she whispered, moving closer to him.

Cross enveloped her in his arms and she clung to him fiercely.

'How the hell did they get your number anyway?' he wondered. 'I thought you were ex-directory.'

'I am,' she said, softly.

'Jesus Christ, Cath,' he exclaimed. 'If they can find that out what else can they do?'

She moved away from him, got to her feet and crossed to the window of the flat and peered out into the night.

'They're probably using a public phone,' she mused. 'It'd be harder to trace.'

"Whoever's doing it probably hasn't even thought about that,' said Cross, dismissively.

'There's been nothing for two hours now,' she said, still gazing out into the blackness. 'I think they've finished for the night. Probably fed up. They think they've

241

made their point.' She turned to face Cross. 'Let's go to bed.'

He nodded slowly, watching as she flicked off the lamp on top of the TV set, glancing down at the photo of herself and her brother that took pride of place there.

She reached out and touched the photo, touched the image of his face briefly.

Cross had already wandered across the hallway to the bedroom.

Cath took one last glance across at the telephone, then flicked off the main light, closing the sitting-room door behind her.

Outside, hidden by the enveloping shroud of night, prying eyes saw the light go off.

The flat was in darkness.

Now it was just a matter of time.

He watched her as she slept, crouching inches from the side of the bed.

Frank Reed watched the steady rise and fall of his daughter's chest, listened to the faint hiss of her breathing.

She looked so beautiful. So peaceful.

He reached out and, very gently, brushed a strand of hair away from her mouth.

She rolled over in her sleep and Reed took a step back, fearing that he'd woken her, but she remained still.

He leaned forward and kissed her softly on the forehead.

'I love you,' he whispered, then rose to his feet and walked slowly from the bedroom, pausing in the doorway, his gaze still upon her.

He wouldn't lose her.

No matter what it took.

He'd already lost his wife: he didn't intend losing his daughter.

He pushed the bedroom door shut.

Maria Goldman woke with a start, her eyes staring wide, the last vestiges of the nightmare still imprinted on her mind.

She looked anxiously around the room, searching for that huge cloaked figure which had pursued her through her dreams.

The horned figure.

Was it hiding in the shadows of the room? Skulking in the blackness?

She let out a frightened gasp as she felt the hand touch her back.

Her husband, woken by her sudden movement, ran one hand over her soft skin and asked her if she was OK.

Maria nodded and moved closer to him, feeling his arm around her, sliding towards sleep, drifting quickly into oblivion once more.

She wondered if the horned figure would be waiting in the dark recesses of her dreams.

He couldn't remember how long he'd been walking or even where.

Talbot might as well have been walking in circles.

Each street looked the same, every building indistinguishable from the next.

The darkness had grown colder as night had become early morning.

And still he walked, collar turned up to protect him

from the biting wind that whipped down some of the side streets, tossing waste paper and empty cans before him.

Hands dug deep into his pockets, he walked on.

Sixty-two

Detective Sergeant Bill Rafferty knocked on the door of the office, waited a moment, then stepped inside.

The room was empty.

Talbot's desk was unoccupied.

Rafferty muttered something under his breath and glanced to his left and right along the corridor. He spotted a uniformed man heading for the exit doors at the far end.

'Have you seen DI Talbot this morning?'

'No, sir,' the uniformed man called back.

Rafferty went back into the office, perched on the desk, and turned the phone to face him. He jabbed one of the buttons on it and waited.

He recognised the voice on the other end.

'Colin, it's Rafferty here,' said the DS. 'Have you seen Talbot this morning?'

'I haven't seen him for a couple of days,' DC Colin Penhallow told him. 'What's the problem, Bill?'

'He's not here, *that's* the problem. I've had two messages from Macpherson over at Theobald's road saying he wants to talk to him, but so far, no sign.' The DS looked at his watch.

'Sorry, I can't help you, Bill,' Penhallow said apologetically. 'What does Macpherson want with him anyway? He's in charge of that child abuse case; isn't he? That's nothing to do with us.'

'Try telling that to the DI. It seems to have been the only thing on his mind in the last few days.'

'Why the hell is he so interested?'

'That's what I'd like to know.' He glanced down and saw a red light blinking on the console. 'Look, I've got to go, there's another call on three. Cheers, mate.'

Rafferty jabbed the third button.

'DI Talbot's phone.'

'Bill, is that you?' said the voice at the other end.

It was low, rasping.

'Who's this?' Rafferty asked.

'It's me.' A cough. 'Talbot.'

'Jesus Christ, I've been trying to get hold of you for the last hour, are you all right?'

'Yeah. Listen, can you pick me up from home in about an hour?'

'No problem. Jim, Macpherson's been on the line this morning, something to do with this child abuse case in Hackney.'

'What did he want?'

'He said he's seen the medical reports on the kids that were taken into care. A number of them were physically abused. He also left the name of the woman at Hackney Social Services who he said you wanted to talk to.'

'Right, pick me up as soon as you can. I want to talk to her.'

'Jim, if you don't mind me asking, what the fuck is going on?'

'What do you mean?'

'This case at Hackney. Why the interest? We've got enough shit of our own to deal with. This is Macpherson's problem.'

'Right, you get on with what *you've* got to do – just give me this woman's fucking name,' rasped Talbot.

'Jim, I just asked. It seems like you've become obsessed with this bloody case and—'

'The name,' Talbot snapped.

'Maria Goldman.'

'Right. Look, if you've got other stuff to do, then get on with it. I'm going to speak to this Goldman woman.'

'I'll pick you up,' Rafferty said, wearily. 'We've been digging around on those three suicides, too. Remember, the case we were working on *before* this shit at Hackney came up?' the DS said, sarcastically.

'And?' Talbot said.

'Apparently, two of the three dead men had reported strange phone calls about a week before they topped themselves.'

'What do you mean, strange?'

'Parriam and Hyde *both* got calls warning them off.'

'How come this has just turned up?'

'We spoke to their secretaries.'

'You mean it's taken this fucking long?'

'Hyde's had been away on honeymoon; Parriam's has just come back from sick leave.'

'Were threats actually made?'

'They were told to back off. That's all.'

'What about Jeffrey?'

'Nothing strange there.'

'Look, Bill, just pick me up as quick as you can, right? We'll go over this shit later.'

'I think it's important—'

246

Talbot cut him off. 'So is this abuse case, now get a fucking move on.'

He slammed down the phone.

Rafferty looked at the handset for a moment then slipped it gently back onto the cradle.

Frank Reed held his daughter tight, feeling her warm breath against his cheek.

'Did you have a good time?' he asked her, glancing up at his wife who looked down at them impassively.

'Come on, Becky, we'll be late,' said Ellen glancing at her watch.

Becky kissed her father on the cheek. 'I love you, Dad,' she said then turned towards the door.

'Go on, run out to the car,' Ellen told her.

'I could have taken her to school,' Reed said, irritably.

'It's on my way to work,' Ellen said, picking up her daughter's small hold-all. She turned to leave.

'Thanks, Ellen,' he said, almost grudgingly.

'For what?'

'For letting me have Becky for the weekend. I know I've got every right to access but . . .'

'I'll be in touch, Frank,' she told him and turned away.

He watched as she walked down the path towards the waiting car. Becky was already in the back, waving to him.

He waved back.

Christ, it hurt to see her leave.

Ellen slid behind the steering wheel and started the engine.

'That's it, Becky,' she said, a smile touching her lips, 'You wave goodbye to your Dad.' She glanced across and looked blankly at Reed for a moment, silhouetted in the doorway. 'It might be a while before you see him again.'

The car pulled away.

Sixty-three

'As I explained to you when you rang, I can't let you see any of the children,' said Maria Goldman, holding open the door of her office.

Catherine Reed entered, glancing around the small, immaculately tidy room. She accepted the chair offered to her and sat down opposite Maria.

The journalist afforded herself a brief glance around the office. She spotted a small television set and a video, set up in one corner, the clock on the video flashing constantly. The walls were a mass of filing cabinets and shelves and what spare space there was seemed to be covered with a collection of posters and leaflets.

'Have you finished with them all yet?' Cath enquired.

Maria nodded.

Cath reached into her pocket and pulled out a small notepad.

'You don't mind if I use this, do you? I've got a lousy memory.' She smiled.

'Would you like a coffee?'

'Thank you. No sugar.'

Maria got to her feet and headed for the office door.

'The machine's just down the corridor,' she explained. 'I won't be a minute.'

248

As she disappeared, closing the door behind her, Cath sat motionless for a moment, then crossed to the door and peered through the tiny crack between frame and partition. She could see Maria standing in front of the vending machine, feeding coins into it.

Cath hurried back to the desk, stepping around Maria's side, glancing over the stacks of papers arranged there.

She saw a large book that looked like a ledger of some description.

Cath flipped it open, scanning it for anything which resembled a list of names.

Nothing.

She pulled open the top drawer of Maria's desk.

Manila files but no names.

In the next drawer there was a framed photo of a man in his early thirties.

Smart, good looking.

She was about to open the next drawer when she heard footsteps heading back up the corridor.

Cath scuttled around to the chair and sat down, sucking in a deep breath, picking up her pen and drawing rambling circles on the top of the page.

Maria entered carrying two styrofoam cups of coffee. She pushed the door shut with her backside and handed one of the cups to Cath.

'Now, what can I do for you, Miss Reed?'

'Call me Cath, please,' she said, sipping her coffee. 'I wondered if you'd finished interviewing all the children that were brought in.'

'Yes, we have.'

'And from what you've heard, are you satisfied that there is child abuse involved?'

249

'Unfortunately yes.'

'In every case? There were seventeen children seized, weren't there?'

'*Seized* sounds a bit melodramatic,' Maria said, smiling.

'Well, dawn raids *are* pretty melodramatic, aren't they? You obviously felt the need to go through with them.'

'We felt that there were children at risk.'

'Why were those *particular* homes targeted?'

'They were random, apart from two. We had received reports . . .'

'Was one of those houses the O'Brian house?'

Maria looked stunned.

'My brother was the teacher at St Michael's who made the initial report,' Cath explained. 'I know that the O'Brian boy was one of the children taken into care.'

'How much more do you know?' Maria asked, cupping both hands around the styrofoam container.

'Not enough. There are too many loose ends already, things going on which may or may not be linked to this child abuse ring.'

'I didn't say it was an abuse ring,' Maria interjected.

'You said abuse was involved, though.'

'Not all of the seventeen children we brought in had been abused, at least not physically.'

'How many had?'

'Nine.'

'Including the O'Brian boy?'

Maria nodded slowly.

'Do you think it was the parents?'

'That's not for me to say, Miss Reed. You'll have to ask the police.'

'Have they been informed of the physical abuse?'

'They've seen the medical reports. Whatever further action is taken, and who it's taken against, is up to them.'

Cath sipped her coffee, glancing around the office again.

'What's the video for?' she asked.

'In certain cases, like this one, evidence is recorded on audio *and* videotape, as well as written statements being taken.'

'But video evidence isn't permissible in court, is it?'

'It's mainly to help our people here, to make sure we get all the facts, everything the children tell us.'

'Did any of them mention graveyards?'

The question was unexpected and Maria couldn't disguise her surprise. For a long time she merely gazed at Cath.

'Why do you ask?' she said, quietly.

Cath sighed.

'It's probably nothing,' she said. 'But the O'Brians lost a baby a little while ago, it was buried in Croydon Cemetery. I don't know if you're aware, but there've been . . . desecrations, for want of a better word, going on there for the past few weeks. Graves dug up, headstones wrecked, stuff written on them. Even the church itself there has been vandalised. The grave of the O'Brian baby was one of those dug up. I just wondered if any of the other children might have mentioned graveyards in their statements.'

'What kind of vandalism?' Maria wanted to know.

'As I said, mainly the smashing of headstones, and graves being disturbed, but there was an incident with a cat. Some sicko nailed a cat to the church door.'

'And cut its head off,' Maria added.

It was Cath's turn to be shocked. She nodded slowly.

Maria reached into the bottom drawer of her desk and pulled out some pieces of paper which she laid before Cath on the desk top.

Cath noticed that some of the drawings were done in crayon. Some in pencil. A number were rough, almost impossible to distinguish, but others, in their crude way, were easily recognisable.

One was of an animal spreadeagled. From the long tail she guessed it was meant to be a cat. There was a great scrawl of red crayon beneath it then a round object with two slits for eyes and a couple of ears. The long whiskers made it obvious the artist intended it to be recognised as a cat. The head was also surrounded by red.

'That was drawn by a six-year-old,' said Maria.

Cath looked carefully at the other drawings.

She recognised a pentagram, drawn with remarkable dexterity.

There were more pictures of animals, usually headless.

Another pentagram.

Then some writing.

At first it looked like meaningless scrawl, then Cath looked more closely. She swallowed hard. 'I've seen this before,' she whispered, looking at the roughly drawn letters.

'We couldn't make it out,' Maria said.

Cath reached into her handbag and pulled out a small make-up mirror then she held up the piece of paper, turning it towards Maria.

'How old was the child who wrote this?' the journalist asked.

'Eleven,' Maria told her, trying to pick out the letters in the mirror.

She studied each one carefully, the words running into each other.

'I still can't see what it says,' she said, quietly.

'I saw this in the crypt of the church at Croydon,' Cath explained, pointing out the reversed words. '"The power and the glory, for ever and ever, Amen."'

'The Lord's prayer.'

'Written backwards.'

She lowered the mirror and the piece of paper.

'Is that reversed too,' Cath asked, pointing at more words written on a piece of paper below a large grey block that had been carefully shaded in.

Maria shook her head.

'No,' she said. 'It's Latin. Written by a seven-year-old. The grammar's probably wrong but we managed to work out the meaning. "*Deus mihi mortuus.*" It means "God is dead to me." Now where the hell would a seven-year-old learn that?'

The social worker got to her feet and crossed to the closest filing cabinet.

Cath continued staring at the Latin words.

From a seven-year-old?

'Look at these,' said Maria, laying out five more pieces of paper before the journalist.

Each one bore the sketches, some rough, some more detailed, that had invaded Maria's dreams.

The horned figure.

'That's the person the children say hurt them,' she told Cath.

Cath traced the outline of the horns with her finger.

'The children have been kept apart ever since they

253

were brought in,' Maria told the journalist. 'They couldn't have copied this figure from each other. They would have to have seen it.'

'But each drawing is almost identical.'

'In other abuse cases children have reported being touched or hurt by people dressed as clowns, even Father Christmas, but this is the first time I've seen any draw . . .' She was unable to finish.

Cath gazed blankly at the drawings.

'The Devil,' she whispered.

Sixty-four

For a long time the two women stared at the pictures of the horned figure, then Cath pointed to something else on the sheet nearest to her.

It was in the top left-hand corner.

About half-way down the page on another sheet.

At the bottom on another.

'What are these meant to be?' she asked, indicating the shapes.

They were all rectangular, box-like constructions, all of them shaded in black or grey.

In one or two, windows had been drawn.

'The children say that's where they were taken,' Maria explained. 'We don't think they're houses. Children usually draw very simplistic houses – a square with a slanted roof, four windows and a front door.'

'Coffins?' Cath offered.

Maria shook her head. 'Whatever they are, they're on nearly every drawing. There's a uniformity about what they're telling us that makes it difficult to think they're lying.'

'Why should they lie?'

'It has been known. Kids with a grudge against their parents have screamed abuse. The parents have been pilloried by the press.' She looked at Cath and raised her eyebrows.

'But you don't think *these* children are lying?'

'The stories have too many common threads, too many similarities, and they're too detailed. In some statements, children talked about smells and tastes. Sensations they could only know by having experienced them. They didn't see them on TV or read about them. They went through them.'

'And the Latin? The backward writing? The figure?'

'They would have had to have seen them.'

'Here?' Cath said, pointing at the grey rectangular shapes on the paper before her.

'Possibly,' Maria muttered, taking a sip of her coffee. 'If only we could find out what that is.'

There was a knock on the office door and Nikki Parsons stuck her head inside.

She smiled at Cath, then at Maria. 'There are two policemen here to see you.'

'I *am* popular this morning, aren't I?' Maria said, wearily.

Before she could say anything else the office door was pushed open. Talbot strode in, Rafferty close behind him.

He shot a withering glance at Cath.

'What are *you* doing here?' he snapped.

255

'My job, the same as you,' she told him.

They locked stares for a moment.

'You two know each other?' Maria asked.

Talbot ignored her question, pulling his ID from the inside pocket of his jacket. Rafferty did likewise.

'It's getting a little crowded in here,' Maria commented, an amused smile on her lips.

'Yeah, it is. Why don't you piss off, Reed? This is none of your business anyway,' Talbot hissed.

'Hackney's not your usual *beat* is it, Talbot?' she said, scornfully. 'What's wrong, don't you trust the local coppers to do the job as well as you? Frightened there might be some suspect you'll miss? One you could slap around a bit?'

'Why don't you fuck off, you're in the way.'

'I had an appointment with Mrs Goldman, I haven't finished yet.'

'You have *now*. On your bike.' He hooked a thumb in the direction of the door.

'I'm sorry to interrupt,' said Maria. 'But this is my office, and if you two are going to have a running battle, I'd rather you didn't do it here.' She smiled efficiently at Talbot. 'Miss Reed and I *had* almost finished, if you could wait just a couple of minutes.'

'Fine,' said Talbot, nodding. 'We'll wait here.'

He picked up his chair and moved it to one side of the desk.

Rafferty stood beside him.

There was a moment of awkward silence, broken by the DI. 'Well, go on, don't let *us* stop you,' he said. 'We wouldn't want to get in the way of a great journalist doing her job.'

'Why don't you make yourself useful?' Cath hissed at

him. 'What do you make of that?' She handed him one of the drawings of the horned figure.

'If this is evidence you shouldn't even be looking at it,' he barked, snatching it from her.

'What does it look like, Talbot?' the journalist persisted.

'A kid's drawing,' he said, dismissively.

'What of?'

'The Devil,' said Rafferty, looking over his colleague's shoulder.

'How the hell do *you* know?' Talbot demanded.

'That's what a kid would draw. I should know, my Kelly's five,' the DS told him.

'And the child who drew that was a year older,' Cath informed him.

'So, that's our suspect, is it? The Devil,' Talbot sneered. 'Well, we should be able to pull him in pretty quick, we'll just put out identikits of a bloke with a goat's head, a cloak, a pitchfork and cloven hooves. Should have him banged up by the end of the week. Well done, Reed, you've cracked the case.'

She glared at him.

'What's your explanation, then?' she demanded. 'How come five different children have, independently, all drawn almost identical pictures of the person they say hurt them? They've seen this, Talbot. Whatever it is. They haven't imagined it.'

'I'm sure they *have* seen it,' the DI snapped. 'As you probably know, amongst the stuff seized from some of the houses were horror videos including *The Devil Rides Out, To the Devil a Daughter, The Exorcist, Devil Within Her*. Shall I go on?'

'That's bullshit,' Cath said.

'You want to find out where those kids saw this *Devil*, then watch those films.'

'But what about the things they couldn't have seen on film, Detective Inspector?' Maria interjected. 'I've already told Miss Reed that some of the things they described they could only have experienced first hand.'

'Such as?' the DI demanded.

'The smell of blood, the taste of it,' Maria said.

'They read it in a book,' Talbot told her.

'Some of the sexual acts described,' the social worker persisted.

'There was pornographic literature *and* videos seized,' Talbot said. 'The kids could have seen it.' He laughed. 'They might even have walked in on their parents some time.'

'Jesus Christ, Talbot,' Cath said, exasperatedly.

'I know you, Reed. You journalists are all the fucking same. I read that shit you wrote in the paper about satanism going on at Croydon Cemetery.'

'I didn't say it *was* satanism.'

'You *wanted* it to be. It made a better story. Just like this.' He jabbed the piece of paper in front of him. 'The Devil. Pentagrams. Cats and dogs cut up. You couldn't have found a better story if you'd invented it yourself.'

'These children aren't lying about having been abused, Detective Inspector,' Maria interjected. 'I'm sure of that. There *has* been abuse.'

'I don't deny that,' Talbot conceded. 'But not by the Devil.' He shook his head. 'Those kids were abused by someone *dressed* like fucking Satan or they thought he was because they were drugged or they'd been watching videos with the Devil in. It's simple logic.'

'So, it's simple logic the kids who described the taste

of blood had read it, right?' Cath said, scornfully. 'Four-and five-year-olds? Bullshit, Talbot.'

The policeman turned towards Maria. 'You're the expert, what do *you* think?'

'I would say that, from my experience and from what I've read and heard, there is evidence of ritual abuse in this case,' Maria said.

'Just because five of the kids drew a picture of the Devil?' Talbot said, dismissively.

'No, not just because of that, because of the other things they've said in their statements. Too many incidents point to ritual abuse,' Maria insisted. 'And these children are terrified. Not just for themselves but for their families. They're afraid of *something* hurting their parents and grandparents. Something that has already hurt *them*.'

'It's an abuse ring, pure and simple,' Talbot said.

'What makes *you* such an expert?' Cath snapped.

If only you knew.

Talbot felt the hairs at the back of his neck rise. 'I know,' he said, quietly, avoiding eye contact with Cath.

She studied him thoughtfully for a moment, wondering where the brashness and abrasiveness had gone momentarily. For bewildering seconds Talbot seemed to change visibly before her, his features softening.

Come on, get a fucking grip.

Aware of three sets of eyes upon him he managed to shrug off the painful recollection.

'What are these?' he demanded, pointing at the grey rectangular shapes on each piece of paper.

'That's what we've been trying to find out,' Maria said. 'It's where the children say they were taken, where they were hurt. It seems to be a building of some kind.'

Talbot looked at several more of the sketches.

'And this?' he said, showing the sketches to Rafferty.

On several of the drawings, the rectangular blocks had squiggly blue lines drawn in front of them.

'It's meant to be water, isn't it?' the DS mused.

'Big grey buildings close to water,' Talbot echoed.

Rafferty swallowed hard. 'Jesus Christ,' he whispered. 'I think I know what they are.'

All eyes turned towards him.

'The warehouses at Limehouse Reach,' the DS continued. 'The big buildings with only a few windows, the water nearby. That's what they're meant to be, I'd bet money on it. *That's* where these kids were taken.'

Sixty-five

'You explain it then, Jim,' said DS Rafferty, glancing across at his companion who was gazing out of the side window of the car peering at two young women on the zebra crossing. He seemed more concerned with the duo than with the words of his colleague.

One of the young women turned and saw Talbot staring at her. She said something to her friend, both of them laughed then waved at him. He looked away.

'Jim,' Rafferty said, more loudly.

Talbot looked at the DS.

'If they're not the warehouses, what are they?' Rafferty persisted.

'I'm not arguing with you about the possibility they might be.'

'And you don't find it just a little bit curious that the unexplained suicides of three men we've investigated could be linked with those same buildings?'

'Come on, Bill, you're clutching at straws now.'

'Why? We don't know that Jeffrey, Hyde and Parriam weren't involved.'

'In child abuse?' Talbot shook his head.

'Maybe that was why they killed themselves. Perhaps they were scared of being found out.'

Talbot exhaled wearily.

'Come on, Jim, for Christ's sake, at least admit that there *might* be a link,' the DS said, exasperatedly.

'We don't even know if the things that those kids drew *were* those warehouse, do we? If we're wrong, then—'

'Then we're wrong,' Rafferty snapped. 'But it's worth checking out.'

'You said that two of the three men had received threatening phone calls shortly before they topped themselves, right?'

'It could have been parents of the abused kids. Perhaps they knew who was doing the abusing. Hyde and Parriam were told to back off.'

'If they'd been found out as child molesters, don't you think the callers might have done more than just warned them off?'

'So what the fuck do *you* think?' snapped Rafferty.

'I think that everyone's overreacting. The social workers, the media. I don't doubt for one minute that this is a genuine child abuse case, but linked with satanism? Do me a favour. And now *you're* trying to tell me that three unexplained suicides might come into the same picture. There's too many loose ends, Bill.'

261

'But if the warehouses where those kids were molested—'

Talbot held up a hand to silence his companion.

'No one knows that's what those drawings are meant to be,' he said, quickly. 'We're assuming. Because if we're right then maybe, and it's a *big* fucking maybe, we've got something a bit more substantial.' He ran a hand through his hair. 'Until then, we're no closer.' He looked at his watch.

The traffic was heavy.

It would take them another hour or more to get to Limehouse Reach.

Catherine Reed had tried his mobile number.

Nothing.

Now she tried to reach Phillip Cross by his pager, wondering where the hell he was and, more importantly, how long it would be before he called her back.

Where was he?

Almost as a last resort, she tried his home number. The phone rang.

Cath waited.

And waited.

Frank Reed wandered slowly back and forth in the main hall, peering alternately at his watch and the rows of children seated in the hall, heads down over their papers.

The only thing that interrupted the silence was the odd cough or sneeze and, on one occasion, the particularly loud rumbling of a child's stomach.

Reed smiled to himself and performed his slow, measured trek once more before returning to his desk, which was set on top of the stage overlooking the hall.

As he sat down he glanced out of one of the large picture windows which ran the length of the hall on either side. To his left he could see the street beyond.

He'd first noticed the police car parked there over an hour ago.

It hadn't moved.

From his vantage point he could see that there were two uniformed men seated inside. The driver kept removing his cap, adjusting the headgear as if it was too tight or uncomfortable.

Reed watched them for a moment longer, then picked up the book he'd been intermittently glancing at.

When he looked out again, thirty minutes later, the police car was still there.

The time had come at last.

She knew the one she sought. She knew where to find her.

She even knew what she looked like. There had been a photo next to an article she'd found a day or two earlier.

But she felt fear.

It was an emotion she knew well.

They would find her soon, she was convinced of that.

Shanine Connor rubbed her swollen belly.

She took one last look at the photo of Catherine Reed, then folded the piece of paper and pushed it back into her jeans.

Sixty-six

'Where the hell do we start?' murmured Rafferty quietly, looking at the high wire fence which faced them.

Beyond it stood the closest of the warehouses: large, monolithic buildings which appeared to have been hewn from one massive block of stone rather than constructed piece by piece.

Each one was as grey as a rain-sodden sky.

From where the two policemen stood neither of them could see any windows in the structures.

What must once have been a service road ran from the gate before them, splitting off into several narrower Tarmac sections, linking the buildings like grey arteries.

Just beyond the gate there was a large wooden sign which read: ACQUIRED FOR MORGAN AND SIMONS.

There were a number of dents in the sign where someone had, over the past few months or weeks, hurled stones or bottles at it. Talbot could see several broken beer bottles littered around near by. The service road itself was strewn with pieces of broken concrete. There was even the rusting frame of a bicycle lying just beyond the gate.

Talbot approached the gate and found there was a chain twisted through the entryway, woven around the wire mesh. He tugged on it, relieved to find there was no padlock.

The chain looked new, the steel gleaming.

Alongside the rusted, neglected air of everything else on the site, the chain seemed even more incongruous.

The DI pushed open the gates, hinges that hadn't tasted oil for years squealing protestingly.

He walked back to the car and climbed into the passenger seat, glancing around as Rafferty slowly guided the vehicle up the service road.

'They *look* like some of those drawings,' said the DS glancing up at the large grey warehouses.

'The kids who drew them could have been past here a hundred times,' Talbot said, dismissively.

'What, *all* of them?' Rafferty challenged.

He brought the car to a halt and looked at his superior, who was still gazing up at the buildings, as if mesmerised.

'What now, Jim?'

'We take a look around,' Talbot told him, fumbling in the glove compartment. He pulled out a half-eaten Mars Bar and took a bite. 'You take those two,' he indicated the two warehouses to the right, the ones closest to the water. 'I'll check these.'

'What if we find anything?' Rafferty asked.

'Just shout,' Talbot told him, swinging himself out of the car.

He stood surveying his surroundings: the warehouses towering over them, the dark choppy waters of the Thames just beyond. Across the water he could see the outlines of cranes thrusting up towards the heavens like accusatory fingers. Seagulls wheeled and dived in the air above the Thames, some coming to rest on the roof of the nearest warehouse. They seemed to look down warily on the two men beneath them.

A small boat went chugging past on the river, tossed and bumped by the seething brown waves which spread across the surface. Even from where he stood, Talbot could smell the salty odour of the river. But it was tinged with something more pungent: the stench of neglect and decay which seemed to hang around the warehouses like an invisible cloud. As Talbot took a step closer he felt as if that cloud was enveloping him, sucking him in.

'We'll meet back here in an hour,' he said, gesturing towards the car. 'Unless one of us finds something first.'

Rafferty looked at his watch and nodded.

Talbot watched as his companion walked away in the direction of the other two warehouses.

The DI hesitated a second longer, then headed towards the building nearest him.

Above him, a seagull circled, its mournful cries echoing through the air.

As he glanced up he noticed dark clouds were gathering.

Sixty-seven

The door was padlocked.

Rafferty kneeled down and inspected the lock, pulling at it uselessly for a second before taking a pace or two back and peering up at the warehouse.

The concrete edifice towered above him, the padlocked main entrance barring his way.

He muttered something under his breath and headed

off around the side of the building, picking his way along a path which was overgrown with yellowed grass and weeds, some of which stood as high as his knees. The DS looked to his left but he could see no sign of Talbot.

Perhaps, he thought, his superior had already gained entry to one of the other buildings.

Ahead of him he saw a door set in the side of the warehouse.

Rafferty pressed his face against it, cupping a hand over his eyes, trying to see inside.

There was so much dirt on the glass it was practically opaque. He could see nothing but darkness inside.

His hand disturbed a spider's web as he brushed against the glass, the gossamer strands sticking to his fingers. The DS wiped the sticky threads on his hand-kerchief, recoiling as he saw a particularly large, bloated spider drop to the ground beneath him.

For one brief second, he felt the overwhelming urge to step on it, especially when he noticed that the purulent creature was holding a crane-fly securely in its fangs, but instead he watched as it scuttled off into the long grass.

He returned his attention to the door for a second, twisting the handle but finding, not with any great surprise, that it was locked.

Rafferty walked on, around the building, glancing up at it every so often, aware now of the odd drop of rain in the air.

The overgrown pathway took him to the rear of the large building and he paused for a moment to look out over the Thames. He was close enough to hear the water slapping against the bank, a fine spray rising into the air as each wave slammed against it.

A flight of steps rose before him, hugging the side of the warehouse, rising until they reached another door.

Rafferty paused a moment then began to climb, the steps slippery. He gripped the handrail, some of the blistered paint flaking away like leprous skin. Beneath there was rust. In places it had almost eaten away the metal handrail.

The DS hoped it hadn't done the same to the metal steps he climbed.

The thought made him slow his pace and he climbed more cautiously now, glancing down at his feet, wondering if the steps were about to give way. He was half-way up and more than fifteen feet above the concrete below. If the stairs *did* collapse he'd be lucky to escape without a few broken bones.

Pushing the thought from his mind, he continued to climb until he finally reached the platform at the top.

The door which confronted him, like the other he'd found, had glass panels in it and, like the first, these panels were also thick with accumulated dirt and dust.

Even the door knob itself was rusted and it squeaked when he twisted it.

It was loose.

Rafferty rubbed his hands together, the coppery smell of rusted metal strong in his nostrils, then he took a step back and kicked hard against the door knob.

It came away with the first impact and the DS smiled to himself. He pushed the door with one fingertip and it swung back on rusted hinges.

The darkness inside was impenetrable.

Rafferty fumbled in his jacket pocket and pulled out his lighter.

He struck it, raising it above his head.

The light scarcely cut through the enveloping black-ness.

Still, he reasoned, it was better than nothing.

He stepped inside.

Talbot walked around the entire perimeter of the first warehouse and found, like Rafferty, that the doors were all securely fastened.

However, gaining entry wasn't such a priority for the DI.

He was looking for something else.

Ignoring the weed-infested paths, he walked on, beginning another circuit of the warehouse, stopping at the main entrance first.

Two huge double doors, wide enough to accommo-date an articulated lorry with ease, seemed to form most of the front of the building.

They were secured by a padlock.

As he'd expected.

A rusted metal chain had been wound round the door handles, too.

Rusted.

Like the door knobs on the smaller doors at the side and rear of the building.

Rusted.

It hadn't struck him until he'd passed the padlock for the second time.

The lock itself was brand new.

No rust. No discoloration.

And there was something else.

Talbot saw marks in the dirt and grime that covered the doors.

Particularly at the bottom.

The doors were scratched.

He ran the pad of one thumb over the marks and felt rough edges.

A new padlock.

Scratch marks on the door.

The DI kneeled beside the locked entrance, now certain his hunch was correct.

These doors had been prised open recently and a new lock placed on them to keep them closed.

Someone had been inside here.

He turned and looked around, noticing that the concrete pathway surrounding the warehouse was cracked and broken in several places. He kneeled again, pulling at a chunk of concrete about the size of his fist.

It came free easily, woodlice scuttling for cover as the stone was lifted.

Gripping the stone like a club, Talbot turned towards the new padlock and struck it hard several times.

The padlock held, despite his efforts.

He struck again.

Still it held.

And again.

It was the chain that eventually broke.

The rusted links seemed to stretch, then snap, pieces of rotten metal spinning into the air like shrapnel.

The chain swung free, the padlock dropped to the ground.

Talbot smiled to himself and dropped the rock, digging into his pocket for a handkerchief which he wrapped around his fist. Then he took hold of the door handle and pushed.

The twin doors squealed protestingly then opened a fraction.

An almost overpowering stench of damp and decay belched forth, the dust so thick Talbot was forced to shield his nose and mouth from the noxious blast.

He paused a moment, squinting into the gloom inside, then cautiously he took a step inside, pushing the doors closed behind him.

The rancid half-light swallowed him up.

For a second he wondered where the yellowish light was coming from, then he realised.

There were four large skylight windows in the roof of the cavernous building, covered, like every inch of glass in the place, by thick dirt and grime.

The daylight could barely force its way through, but the filth allowed enough illumination for Talbot to see where he was going. He narrowed his eyes, trying to accustom his vision to the artificial twilight.

As he stood there he realised how large the warehouse actually was.

For interminable seconds he stood there, the thick dust and the stench of decay filling his nostrils, his eyes struggling to adjust.

He sneezed, the dust choking him.

He raised the handkerchief to his face, breathing through the cotton.

It was as he glanced down at the concrete floor that he thought he saw movement.

A rat?

He shook his head and took a couple of steps forward, the dust so thick it clung to his shoes.

High above him there was a soft pattering sound.

Like what?

Like tiny feet?

More rats?

271

It was only to be expected, surely? The place had been derelict for years and with it being so close to the riverside it was bound to attract vermin.

Again he heard the soft pattering above him.

He realised it was rain against the skylight windows.

Soft, gentle drops.

Talbot took another few steps forward then sucked in a polluted breath.

What he saw ahead of him stopped him in his tracks.

Sixty-eight

Frank Reed smiled broadly as he watched Judith Nelson light her cigarette.

The gym mistress noticed his obvious amusement and smiled back, not even sure why he was smiling. She swept her hair back and took a long drag on the Embassy.

'What are *you* laughing at?' she said with mock indignation, prodding Reed's leg with the toe of one of her trainers.

'You're a great example to your pupils, Judith,' he said, chuckling. 'A physical education teacher smoking.'

'You're not going to lecture me, are you, Frank?'

'What, me? God forbid,' he said, grinning. 'But, you know the risks.'

'Yes, and, as the man said, non-smokers die everyday. You don't smoke. *You're* dead too.'

They both laughed.

'How did your weekend go?' she asked him, finally.

'It was fantastic,' Reed answered, 'to have Becky around again, even if it was only for two days. We went to McDonald's, I took her swimming, we went to the pictures. That was the first time I'd been for months.' He smiled wistfully. 'It was like being a proper father again.'

'You never stopped being a proper father, Frank. It wasn't your fault your wife took Becky away from you.'

'Sometimes I wonder about that. I wonder if there was more I could have done to stop her.'

'Like what? Kidnap Becky back again?'

'It was great having her with me for the weekend, but now she's gone again it hurts even more.' He lowered his gaze momentarily.

'Is it going to be a regular thing?'

'Ellen and I haven't discussed it yet but, God, I hope so.' He began picking distractedly at the arm of the chair, pulling away loose pieces of thread.

'Perhaps she's come to her senses at last,' Judith offered. 'She probably realises she can't keep Becky away from you forever.'

'I don't know what she's thinking anymore, I . . .'

Judith leaned forward and touched his arm gently. 'It'll be OK, Frank,' she reassured him. 'You haven't lost Becky.'

He smiled at her.

Reed got to his feet and picked up his briefcase.

'I'm going home,' he said, smiling, glancing around the staff room.

Judith took another drag on her cigarette and nodded, watching him as he made for the exit.

The playground was empty as Reed crossed it, heading for his car which was parked behind one of the newer blocks. There were a number of vehicles still parked there including a large Triumph 750 which he knew belonged to one of the sixth-formers. The lad made a point of parking it close to Noel Hardy's car because he knew it irritated the Headmaster. The fact that the owner of the bike was also going out with a fifth-year girl seemed to annoy Hardy even more.

Reed crossed to his own car, fumbling in his jacket for the keys, whistling happily to himself as he slid the key into the door lock.

Perhaps Becky's visits would become a regular thing.

Even the thought of her cheered him.

Two days a week was better than nothing.

He never even heard the footsteps from behind him.

Just the voice.

'Mr Reed?'

He turned and saw the two uniformed policemen no more than three feet from him.

'Frank Reed?' the one on the left said.

The teacher nodded.

He looked past the two men, saw the marked car sitting there, engine idling. There was a third man behind the wheel.

His first thought was of Becky.

An accident?

'What's happened?' he asked anxiously.

'We need to ask you some questions, Mr Reed,' said one of the policemen, a tall man with reddish hair. 'About your daughter.'

'Oh God, what's happened?' he demanded, the colour draining from his cheeks.

'That's what we need to find out,' said the red-haired PC.

'What are you talking about?'

'We'd like you to follow us to Theobald's Road Police Station. My colleague will sit with you.'

'Not until you tell me what the hell is going on,' Reed said, his anxiety rapidly turning to annoyance. 'Is my daughter hurt?'

'No, sir,' said the red-haired man.

'Then what are you going on about?'

'As I said, we need to ask you some questions. If you'd just get in your car it would save a lot of time and aggravation.'

Reed held up both hands.

'I still don't know what you're talking about,' he said, wearily.

'A complaint has been filed against you, Mr Reed. There may be charges.'

'For what?' he said, angrily.

'Assaulting your daughter.'

Sixty-nine

In the dull half-light of the warehouse, Talbot had no doubt what the marks in the thick dust were.

He moved forward a foot or so, the carpet of grime so thick it deadened his footfalls.

Finally he kneeled, motes of dust spinning all around him in the dimly lit silence.

Footprints.

Some five-toed, indicating bare feet. Others from shoes of various sizes.

The carpet of dust was old. These footprints were not.

In places, the dust had been disturbed so badly that the dirty floor beneath the filth was visible.

Elsewhere, the footprints seemed to lead deeper into the cavernous building, towards the rear of it.

Talbot moved on, glancing around him.

There were high metal shelves on either side of him, some rising up to ten or fifteen feet into the air. What had once been stacked on them he could only guess. To his right lay several dust-sheathed wooden pallets, broken and splintered.

He saw what appeared to be a toolbox on one of the shelves. Like everything else inside the building it was covered by the same noxious blanket of grime.

Talbot flipped open the lid.

There was an old screwdriver inside.

He moved on, glancing down at the footprints.

The DI could only guess at how many feet had made these marks and over what period of time but, as he stopped again and kneeled over a particularly well-defined print, he saw that the covering of dust on what would have been the sole was very thin. This print looked no more than a week old.

He straightened up, scanning the area ahead of him.

The shelves continued practically to the back of the warehouse: beyond them he saw a door.

The only sound inside the warehouse was the rushing of the blood in his ears. The silence seemed to crush him, closing around him like an invisible fist which tightened by the second.

He reached the office door and twisted the handle.

Locked.

Talbot took a step back and thought about kicking it open, but then realised that he might destroy any fingerprints or other physical signs which might be on the partition. He spun round and headed back to where he'd seen the discarded toolbox.

He scooped out the screwdriver and returned to the door, cupping a hand over his eyes, trying to see through the small window in the centre of the door.

Whatever lay inside was in pitch blackness.

No windows to give him even the kind of paltry light currently battling through the thick grime of the skylight openings.

The DI steadied himself and slid the top of the screwdriver into the grooved head of a screw which secured the handle to the door.

He twisted, surprised at how stiff the screw was.

Again he tried, cursing when the implement slipped and gouged a lump from the door.

'Shit,' the DI hissed, even his low exhalation echoing in the thunderous stillness around him.

The sound seemed to bounce back off the walls, echoing like some brief sibilant rattle before dying, smothered by the carpet of dust.

He jammed all his weight behind the screwdriver this time, pushing hard against it with the heel of one hand, turning with the other.

The screw started to give.

Talbot grinned triumphantly and removed it, dropping it into his pocket.

He set to work on the second one immediately.

*

DS William Rafferty stood close to the guard rail which ran around the inside of the warehouse and looked over.

He held the lighter above him but the yellow flame could barely penetrate the gloom. Even with the sickly light coming through the filthy skylight windows he could barely see the floor of the warehouse from his high vantage point.

The DS flicked off his lighter, realising that it was doing little good, but also because it was growing uncomfortably hot in his hand. He dropped it into his pocket and walked along the raised parapet, glancing to his right and left.

The walkway along which he moved seemed to stop at each corner of the warehouse, terminating in a door. It was towards the nearest of these doors that Rafferty now headed.

The walkway creaked beneath him and, as with the metal stairs he'd climbed, the policeman wondered briefly if the entire structure might give way beneath him, but he pushed the thought aside and kept walking.

The first door he met was wooden and he pressed against it with his fingertips, surprised when it opened, swinging back on rusted hinges.

The room beyond was large: he guessed twenty feet square.

It was completely empty but for a metal filing cabinet in one corner, now dust-shrouded like the rest of the building.

Rafferty crossed to the cabinet and slid open the top drawer.

Nothing.

The second one was a little more recalcitrant and it let out a loud grating sound as he pulled it open.

Empty.

The third one slid out easily.

The spider inside it looked as large as a child's fist.

'Jesus,' the DS hissed, stepping back, his heart thudding.

It took him a second to realise that the creature was dead.

Probably choked on the dust, he thought, shaking his head, annoyed by his own reaction.

He peered into the drawer again.

It was indeed empty but for the dead spider.

Rafferty turned towards the door at his rear.

It would, he reasoned, lead out onto the gangway which hugged the rear wall of the warehouse.

The DS crossed to it and tried the handle.

To his surprise it opened.

He set off along the next walkway.

The third screw came free and Talbot dropped it into his pocket along with the others.

One more to go and he'd be able to remove the entire door handle. That would give him access to the room beyond.

He eased the head of the screwdriver into the groove of the screw and began to turn it, pieces of rust flaking off as he exerted more force.

'Come on, you bastard,' he muttered, using all his strength, pausing a moment when the screw remained stuck fast.

He sucked in a deep breath, coughing as the dust filled his lungs.

A bead of sweat formed on his forehead, welled up then ran down the side of his face as he resumed his exertions, determined to free the last screw.

It was rusty like the others, but this one seemed to have been welded to the rotten metal by the decay.

The screwdriver slipped again.

'Fuck,' snapped Talbot.

He was about to start again when he heard a sound from behind him.

A grating, tortured sound like rusted hinges.

Rusted hinges.

Someone had entered the warehouse through the main door which he himself had penetrated.

Talbot waited a moment, thought about calling out to Rafferty, shouting to him to come and help, but then he turned, squinted through the dull light of the dust-blanketed building.

He heard footsteps.

Slow, tentative.

Muffled by the dust but still hesitant.

Talbot saw a shape move in the gloom.

A shape which was moving slowly towards him.

And, in that split second, he knew it wasn't Rafferty.

Seventy

'This is bloody disgraceful,' said Frank Reed, angrily.

He got to his feet, gripping the back of the wooden seat he'd been sitting on. Apart from the small table, it was the only piece of furniture in the interview room at Theobald's Road Police Station.

The room was no more than twelve feet square and the presence of both Reed and the single uniformed man in there with him made the place look over-crowded.

'I've been here over an hour now,' Reed snapped. 'I haven't been charged, I haven't even been allowed to call my solicitor. What the hell is going on?'

'If you'd just sit down, sir,' said the constable quietly, motioning towards the chair with his eyes.

Reed still gripped the back of it as if threatening to use it as a weapon against the policeman but, after a moment or two, he sat down heavily.

He could smell the acrid odour of perspiration and realised that it was his own.

What are you afraid of?

He'd drunk two cups of coffee since being escorted into the room, his breath smelled of the brown liquid which was now going cold in the cup before him.

What the hell was going on?

His mind was reeling, words tumbling through it like collapsing building bricks. And each of those bricks carried a different word on it:

ASSAULT

CHARGES

COMPLAINT

INVESTIGATION

Jesus Christ!

He wanted to scream it.

WHAT THE FUCK IS GOING ON?

It was like some kind of bizarre nightmare from which he felt he must wake at any second. What did they call them? Lucid dreams? The ability to be aware of what you're dreaming while it happens.

Then wake yourself up. Get out of here.

But there was no waking.

No respite.

No end to it.

Whatever *it* was.

They said he'd assaulted his own daughter.

Sexually assaulted.

One of them had actually used that word when he'd arrived at the police station.

Sexual assault.

Dear God, even the words made him feel sick.

There had been a complaint. *By whom?*

He sat forward, head resting against his hands, palms pressed to his temples as if he feared his head would explode with so many fearful and conflicting thoughts spinning through it.

So many emotions were coursing through him, his body wired like some cocaine fiend, his mind hyperactive as it searched for answers when it didn't even have questions.

Sexual assault.

An image of Becky flashed into his mind.

How could anyone even think he would touch her?

Who would think it, let alone *say* it?

Who would . . .?

He swallowed hard.

Go on, you're supposed to be a teacher. Think. Use your brain. *Who would say it? Who?*

He clenched his teeth together so hard his jaw ached.

The uniformed officer cast him a cursory glance, then snapped his eyes forwards again as the door of the interview room opened.

Reed got to his feet and glared at the two men who had entered.

'Can one of you tell me what the hell is going on?' the teacher barked.

'Mr Reed, my name is Detective Inspector Macpherson, this is Detective Sergeant Collier,' said the larger of the newcomers.

Macpherson leaned against the table, the DS stood close to the door as if fearing Reed was going to make a run for it.

'Look, I've been sitting here for over an hour,' Reed snapped.

'That's a slight exaggeration, Mr Reed,' Macpherson told him. 'It hasn't been anywhere *near* that long.' The detective perched on the edge of the table and motioned for Reed to sit down, which he did.

'I want to know why I'm being held here,' Reed said, trying to control his temper.

'We received a report about you and your daughter,' the DI told him.

'From who?'

'Ellen Reed. I believe that's your wife.'

'Jesus Christ!' Reed rasped, leaning back in his chair. 'I should have fucking known. What did the bitch say?'

'You and your wife are separated, aren't you?' Macpherson said.

'I want to know what she told you.'

'We'll come to that, Mr Reed. If you could just answer these questions it would make things a lot easier.'

A heavy silence descended on the room, all eyes fixed on the teacher.

'Yes,' he said, finally. 'We're separated.'

283

'And she lives with a Mr Jonathan Ward and *your* daughter Rebecca. Correct?'

Reed nodded.

'Are you divorced?' Macpherson continued.

'No. She just walked out on me and took my daughter, but you'd better ask *her* about that.'

'Your daughter stayed with you over the weekend?' the DI asked.

'Yes. For the first time since my wife took her away.'

'What did you do?'

'What are you talking about?' Reed snorted.

'Where did you go? What did you do together?' the detective continued.

'Went out, saw a film, had some fun. We did what most normal fathers and daughters do,' Reed said, shaking his head.

'Did your daughter sleep in the same bed as you at any time?'

'Jesus Christ, don't be so ridiculous. Is that what Ellen said? Is that what all this is about?'

'Did she sleep in your bed at any time during the weekend?' Macpherson persisted.

'No.'

'She didn't get into bed with you at *any* time?'

'Well, she came and woke me up on the Sunday morning,' Reed said. '*She* woke up early, she came and woke *me* up.'

'And got into bed with you?'

'Yes. It's perfectly natural, you know. Seven-year-olds do that.'

'Was there any physical contact between the two of you while she was in bed with you?'

'For God's sake,' Reed hissed, angrily. 'If you mean

284

did I touch her the answer is no. No, sorry, I hugged her once or twice, is that against the law?'

'Were you fully clothed at the time?'

'I was in *bed*,' Reed blurted, incredulously.

'Naked?'

'I was wearing pyjama bottoms.'

'Did your daughter have a bath while she was with you?'

'Yes, on the Saturday night before she went to bed.'

'Did you bath her?'

Reed swallowed hard and glared at the DI.

'I ran the bath for her,' he snapped. 'I made sure she was OK, then I left her to it.'

'You left her alone.'

'I was in the next room, in case she needed me.'

'For what?'

'In case she slipped, in case she wanted to get out. In case she swallowed the fucking soap. What do *you* think?' Reed snarled.

'And when she'd finished?'

'She got out and dried herself.'

'Did you help her?'

Reed shook his head, letting out a weary breath. 'Yes, I helped her,' he said quietly. 'She asked me to help her. Then she got dressed.'

'On her own?'

'Yes.'

'But you dried her off?'

'I wrapped her in the towel, she was cold, she was damp. I helped her, then I left her to dress herself.'

'Which parts of her body did you dry?'

Reed gripped the edge of the table.

'Her feet, her toes, her back,' he said, quietly.

285

'Between her legs?'

The question hung in the air.

Macpherson's stare was unflinching.

'Did you touch your daughter between the legs?' he persisted.

'No, I did not,' Reed hissed.

'You didn't dry her there?'

'I may have . . . I . . .'

'Did you touch her vagina?'

'You sick bastard,' Reed breathed.

'Did you touch your daughter's vagina, Mr Reed?'

'No.'

'But you say you may have helped her to dry herself between her legs. Surely you must have touched it.'

'Perhaps I did, but not in the way *you* mean.'

'What do *you* think I mean?'

'Ellen says I molested Becky, doesn't she?'

Macpherson stood up, fumbled in his pocket and pulled out a packet of cigarettes. He lit one, blowing the smoke in Reed's direction.

'I just want *your* side of the story, Mr Reed,' the DI said.

Again a heavy silence descended, broken this time by Macpherson.

'You took your daughter swimming at the weekend, didn't you?' he said. 'Did you dry her off when she'd left the pool?'

'Of course not, she was in the changing rooms,' Reed said, irritably.

'So, you couldn't be sure if she was dry. If she'd dried herself properly?'

Reed gazed blankly at the DI.

'If you couldn't be sure, then why did you find it so

necessary to be sure after she got out of the bath?' Macpherson asked, quietly.

'This is ridiculous,' Reed said, his voice low. He swallowed hard.

'If it's so ridiculous, Mr Reed, then you've got nothing to worry about,' the DI told him.

'I'm not worried, I'm angry,' Reed snapped. 'Has Ellen actually pressed charges?'

Macpherson shook his head.

'Not yet,' he said, flatly.

'Then you have no reason to hold me here.'

'We thought you should have the right to give *your*—'

'Side of the story, yes I know, you already told me that,' Reed interrupted.

'Look, I can understand your feelings, Mr Reed.'

'Can you? Have *you* got kids?'

Macpherson shook his head.

'Then don't tell me you understand. If you had kids you'd *know* I was telling the truth,' Reed said.

The DI shrugged.

'I should warn you, Mr Reed, that charges will probably be made within the next day or two. You're not planning on going anywhere, are you?' the policeman wanted to know.

'Why should I? I've got nothing to hide.'

Reed got to his feet. 'Does this mean I can go?' he said, challengingly.

Macpherson nodded.

'I should be sueing you for wrongful arrest,' Reed barked.

'You weren't arrested, you came here voluntarily,' the DI reminded him. He held Reed in that unflinching gaze once more. 'Next time, it might be different.'

Seventy-one

Talbot pressed himself up against the metal shelves, using them, as best he could, for cover.

He held the screwdriver in one hand, ready to use it as a weapon if necessary.

The figure was less than fifteen feet from him now, moving slowly, staying in the shadows.

Talbot ducked down and scuttled towards it, using the shelves to cover his approach, knowing the thick dust would muffle his footsteps. Dust disturbed by his feet clogged in his throat and nostrils, and it was all he could do to prevent himself coughing but he held his breath, emerging through a gap in the high shelves.

The figure was ahead of him now, close to the office door.

The DI squinted in the direction of the intruder.

Whoever it was obviously hadn't heard *him*.

He began walking towards the figure, his hand now gripping the handle of the screwdriver so tight his knuckles were white.

He was ten feet away.

The figure was leaning close to the door, inspecting the damage.

Six feet.

Talbot tried to hold his breath, his heart thudding harder against his ribs.

Two feet.

The figure straightened up.

Talbot raised the screwdriver.

The figure turned.

Talbot shot out a hand, grabbed for the intruder's throat.

The scream which filled the warehouse was deafening, amplified by the cavernous structure.

Talbot took a step back. Catherine Reed swallowed hard and glared at him with bulging eyes.

'What the fuck are *you* doing here?' Talbot rasped. She looked at the screwdriver which he still held poised in his fist.

'Are you going to put that down?' she said, nodding towards the sharp implement.

He lowered his arm.

'I asked you what you were doing here,' the policeman continued.

'I followed you,' she told him.

'I could arrest you for interfering with police business.'

'Why not just stab me with the bloody screwdriver, as you were going to,' Cath said her heart hammering hard against her ribs.

'This is private land. You shouldn't be here.'

'This is news, Talbot, I'm doing my job.' She looked at the loosened handle on the office door. 'I see *you've* been busy too. Have you found anything yet?'

'What's it got to do with you?' he snapped, pushing past her.

Cath regarded him wearily as he stood by the door. 'You believe what Maria Goldman said don't you?'

'About those kids being ritually abused?' He shook his head.

'Then why are you here? It's because of what those kids drew, isn't it? You think this is where the abuse happened.'

'We're exploring every possibility,' Talbot said without looking at her.

'Why are you so resistant to the facts, Talbot?' Cath said angrily, watching as the DI set about loosening the last screw on the door handle.

'What facts?' he said, straining to release it, the veins at his temple standing out with the effort.

'The children's statements.'

'The mentions of the Devil? Give me a break.' The screw was coming free.

They both looked round as they heard the main door opening.

'Jim.'

Talbot recognised Rafferty's voice.

'Down here,' he called and the DS hurried to join his companion, slowing his pace when he saw Cath standing there.

'I heard a scream,' Rafferty said.

'It was her,' the DI told him. 'Sticking her nose in where it's not wanted again. She nearly got hurt.'

The screw was almost out.

'Did you find anything?' the DI enquired.

'Not a thing.'

'Well, somebody's been in here, and recently,' Talbot told his colleague.

The screw came away, the door creaked open an inch or two.

'What do *you* think about what you heard from Social Services?' Cath asked Rafferty. 'Do you believe there's ritual abuse going on?'

'Just ignore her, Bill,' said Talbot. 'She'll go away.'

'Well?' Cath persisted.

'I don't know,' Rafferty said, quietly, watching as his superior pushed the door further open.

It swung right back on its hinges.

Talbot took a step inside.

The room beyond was large, twenty-five feet square at least.

If it had been an office, it had been a big one.

Talbot looked down at the floor.

There was only a light covering of dust.

'Look,' said Cath pointing.

'I can see it,' Talbot murmured, glancing in the direction of her finger then further around the walls.

She stepped into the room with the two policemen.

'Jesus Christ,' murmured Rafferty.

There were a dozen large wooden boxes in the room, seven or eight of them in the centre, built up, stacked on top of each other in three block-like stacks.

Behind them, painted on the wall in black paint, was a massive pentagram.

'Don't touch anything,' Talbot snapped at Cath, then, turning to his companion, 'Bill, I want a forensics team down here now. I want this place gone over with a fine-tooth comb, got it?'

Rafferty turned and sprinted from the room.

There were several dark stains on the floor.

Talbot crossed to the closest and ran the tip of one index finger over it, sniffing the digit.

'Wax,' he murmured.

Cath was looking at the other symbols drawn on the walls.

A large upturned cross.

Another, smaller pentagram.

Some writing.

She recognised it as Latin.

Talbot saw another dark stain on the ground close to the piled boxes, more of the rusty coloured tint on the boxes themselves.

He moved towards another of the boxes and peered in, screwing up his face, struck by the stench coming from the box.

There was a sack in the bottom, covering whatever was giving off the rank odour.

The DI pulled a pen from his inside pocket and jabbed it under the sack, lifting the cover away.

'Shit,' he hissed.

Whatever lay inside, he guessed, must once have been a dog.

An Alsatian possibly.

The head was missing. The body had been slashed open from breast bone to genitals.

The intestines had also been removed, torn free like most of the internal cavity.

Talbot dropped the sack back into place and crossed to another of the boxes.

Cath pulled the pocket camera from her handbag and snapped off two or three shots, the cold white light of the flash illuminating the inside of the room.

She glanced around towards Talbot, waiting for him to admonish her, but he seemed more concerned with what was inside the box.

She took two more pictures.

Talbot slipped a handkerchief from his pocket as he reached for the object in the bottom of the box. He wrapped the linen around his hand, not wanting to disturb any fingerprints which might be present.

Again that stench of decay.

Of death.

'Reed,' he called.

She turned slowly, aware that Talbot had something in his right hand.

Something fairly large.

He threw it towards her.

Cath screamed as the object landed at her feet, her eyes fixed on it, staring down at it.

Talbot smiled humourlessly.

The journalist took a step back, her stomach somersaulting.

At her feet lay the head of a goat, a large portion of the hide still attached.

The eyes were gone, the entire object shrunken, bloodless.

Drained.

The hair of the hide looked dull and matted.

She put a hand to her mouth, eyes inspecting the long horns which jutted from the skull, bone visible in places where the skin had peeled away.

And there was that stench.

The rank odour of decay.

Talbot prodded the goat's head with his foot, then looked scathingly at the journalist.

'There's your Devil,' he snapped.

Seventy-two

The Jaguar Showroom in Kensington High Street looked deserted as Frank Reed scuttled across the street, bumping into people in his haste.

Most turned and shot him angry glances, one shouted something at him but Reed didn't hear the words.

He'd heard very little since leaving the police station in Theobald's Road over an hour ago, his anger and impatience directed towards the traffic and other drivers, all of who seemed to be conspiring to prevent him reaching his goal.

But now it was in sight.

He could feel perspiration soaking into the back of his shirt, beading on his forehead, and his skin felt hot.

He'd parked the car a couple of streets away and run, finding the effort more taxing than he'd imagined but, as he pushed open the door of the dealership, that effort seemed worthwhile.

He sucked in one or two deep breaths, trying to slow the pace of his breathing, to steady the thunder of his heart.

The fluorescents in the ceiling shone coldly, their white light reflecting in the immaculate and sparklingly clean paintwork of the vehicles arranged inside.

Reed barely saw them.

He headed towards the rear of the showroom,

towards a desk. Beyond it was an office, the door slightly ajar.

The phone on the desk was ringing.

Where the hell was everyone?

Where was *she*?

The phone was still ringing.

'Can I help you, sir?'

The voice came from behind him.

'Sorry, I didn't see you come in,' said the balding man who approached him. 'I was checking something on one of the cars.'

Reed saw the appraising look the man gave him.

'I want to see my wife,' said Reed.

'I can sell you a car, sir, not a wife,' said the balding man with the practised laugh of an experienced salesman.

Reed heard the irritating combination of servility and duplicity in the man's tone that he'd heard a hundred times before from salesmen of all kinds.

On the desk the phone was still ringing.

Ellen Reed emerged from the office, slowing her pace when she saw her husband facing her.

'You fucking bitch,' he hissed.

'Just a minute,' said the salesman, taking a step towards him, his forehead furrowed now.

'Keep out of this.' Reed glared at him.

The man took a step back.

The phone continued to ring.

'What are you playing at?' Reed snarled at Ellen.

'This isn't the time or the place, Frank,' she told him.

'I think it is.'

'I'm going to have to ask you to leave, sir,' the salesman said as bravely as he could.

'How could you do it to me, Ellen?' Reed said, ignoring the man. 'What did you make Becky say?'

'I didn't make her say anything,' Ellen told him, defiantly.

'You planned it, didn't you? Or was it *his* idea?' Reed hissed. 'Mr Jonathan fucking Ward. I knew you were a bitch, but this is a new low, even for *you*.'

'I've got nothing to say to you, Frank,' Ellen said, reaching for the phone. 'And if you don't mind I'd like to get on with my job.'

'Fuck the job,' he roared, sweeping the phone from the desk. 'This is my *life* I'm talking about.'

'I'm going to call the police,' the salesman told him, seeking refuge behind a car, 'if you're not out of here in thirty seconds.'

'You won't get away with this, Ellen,' Reed said fists clenched.

'Get out, Frank,' she said, her own heart beating that little bit faster now.

'I know what you're trying to do.'

Another man appeared from the office behind, a taller, older man dressed in a grey suit. 'What the hell is going on out here?' he asked.

'I told this man I'd phone the police,' the salesman said.

'I know what you're trying to do and it won't work,' Reed continued, oblivious to the other two men. His attention, and his rage, focused on Ellen.

The taller man hesitated, saw the fury on Reed's features.

'Call the police,' he said to the cowering salesman.

'Just go, Frank,' Ellen told him.

'You won't take my daughter,' he said raising an accusatory finger and pointing it in her direction.

'If you don't leave immediately we'll call the police,' the taller man insisted.

'YOU WON'T TAKE MY DAUGHTER!' Reed bellowed, then he turned and headed for the exit, his breath coming in gasps.

'It's over, Frank,' Ellen called after him.

'No it isn't,' he shouted back. 'It's only just started. I won't let you take her away from me, Ellen. I'll kill you before I let you do that.'

And he was gone.

Had he turned, he might have seen the slight, almost imperceptible smile which flickered briefly on Ellen's lips.

Seventy-three

Cath just caught the lift, calling to the single occupant to hold the doors as she hurried through the main entrance of the block.

She was carrying a bag of shopping in each hand and she didn't fancy walking up the steps to her flat with such a weight.

The man in the lift lived on the third floor.

She'd seen him occasionally since he moved in three months earlier.

They'd never spoken at any length. Indeed, she couldn't remember speaking to any of the other residents for more than three or four minutes at a time ever since she'd taken up residence in the block.

Everyone above, below and around her could be dead in their beds for all she knew. The residents didn't socialise much.

There were two couples about her own age on the floor below who she'd seen together sometimes but, apart from that, contact was limited to polite nods of recognition or perfunctory bouts of conversation in the lifts.

That was the way in London.

And that was the way Cath liked it.

She did manage a warm smile at her fellow lift traveller and received a similar gesture in return, aware of his gaze lingering on her legs, tightly clad in denim.

'I hate shopping,' the man said, nodding towards the two bulging carriers she'd put down on the floor.

'Me too,' Cath said, jabbing button one.

The lift doors slid shut.

'My girlfriend does all my shopping for me,' the man said, a little too smugly for Cath's liking.

She glanced at him again, saw him looking at her more intently.

When he noticed she was aware of his admiring glances at her legs and buttocks he did little to disguise the fact: merely smiled to himself.

'Are you married?' he asked.

She shook her head.

'I'm getting married soon,' the man told her.

'Isn't your girlfriend lucky?' Cath said, sarcastically.

As the lift bumped to a halt, she picked up her shopping and stepped out.

'See you around,' he said as the doors slid shut.

'Not if I see you first,' she whispered under her breath. *Jesus, what a creep.*

She reached the door to her flat and put down one of the shopping bags, fumbling in her pocket for her keys.

As she did she leaned against the front door.

It swung open.

Cath stepped back, shocked, her heart suddenly thumping heavily against her chest.

She put down the other shopping bag and stood at the doorway, ears straining to catch any sound from within.

Cath inspected the lock, noticed some small scratches on it. The metal was scored in several places.

She took a step inside.

Go and get help. Go now. Bang on the next-door flat.

She hesitated a moment, then moved another step into the hall.

'Oh God,' she murmured under her breath.

The pictures which had hung on the wall lay scattered across the carpet. The glass in the frames of two of them was shattered.

A small ornamental table and the plant which it held had also been overturned.

Glass crunched beneath her feet as she advanced towards the sitting room.

What if the intruder was still inside?

She stood motionless.

Get out now.

The flat was silent. She moved on, into the sitting room.

As she looked around, one word flickered in her mind.

Devastation.

Anything that *could* be broken, had been.

The three-piece suite had been overturned, ornaments had been knocked from their places, some shattered against walls. Pictures had been ripped from the walls and destroyed.

Her desk had also been overturned, the PC with it. Paper was scattered over the carpet. A vase of flowers which had stood on the coffee table lay in a dozen pieces close by, the flowers strewn over the floor.

Bookcases had been knocked over, their contents spilled wantonly.

Her mind reeling, she walked through into the kitchen.

Drawers had been pulled out, cutlery and broken crockery lay everywhere. Even the clock which hung on the wall had been pulled down and hurled across the room: it was lying in the sink.

Cupboards had been pulled open, the door of one ripped from its hinges by the ferocity of the intrusion.

She took a step backward, back into the living room, then beyond to her bedroom.

More damage.

The bedclothes had been pulled off, bedside cabinets overturned. The wardrobes stood open, and her clothes had been scattered over the bed and floor.

Coat-hangers had been pulled from the wardrobe and hurled across the room. One had struck the radio alarm clock, cracking the plastic window that covered the flashing red digits.

Cath could feel her head spinning, and for a second she thought she would faint, but the feeling passed and she sucked in several deep breaths, trying to regain her composure, moving back into the living room to find the phone.

She glanced around the room again, stepping over the printer of the PC which had been tossed to one side.

The printer.

Why hadn't they taken the printer?

Cath reached for the phone, and looked around her as she pressed three nines.

Why hadn't they taken the computer itself?

She frowned.

The stereo was still in position in one corner of the room.

Untouched.

Why hadn't they taken it?

The video was still there.

Untouched.

So was the television.

Cath swallowed hard.

By the time the voice on the other end of the phone asked her which service she required, her heart had slowed its mad thumping.

She announced that she needed the police, gave her name and address, then put down the phone.

Video untouched. TV untouched. Stack system untouched.

She went back into the kitchen.

The ghetto blaster was still there.

Untouched.

What kind of burglars were these?

The flat had been ransacked but, as far as she could tell, little, if anything, had been taken.

Cath returned to the sitting room and it was then, as she glanced around, she noticed that there *was* something missing.

301

Seventy-four

When she heard the knock on the door, Cath had looked anxiously at Phillip Cross.

The photographer had remained by her side for a moment, slowly getting up to answer it.

Cath glanced at her watch.

11.23 p.m.

Despite Cross's presence she felt suddenly afraid.

Burglars aren't going to knock, are they?

She ran a hand through her hair and sucked in a breath.

The last policeman had left the flat more than four hours ago. She'd called Cross and he'd come to the flat immediately. Together they'd cleared up the mess left by the intruders although there were still traces of the aluminium and carbon powders on various surfaces dusted by the police fingerprint man.

She shivered involuntarily as she saw the profusion of prints, but even as a layman she knew that most of the smudges were smooth.

Now she pulled her legs more tightly beneath her, listening to voices in the hallway.

A moment later Cross walked back in.

'Someone to see you,' he said.

DI James Talbot followed him in, looking briefly at Cath, then glancing around the room.

'Doesn't look like they did that much damage,' said the DI.

Cath regarded him silently for a moment. 'What do you want?' she said, finally.

'I heard about what happened here, I thought I'd come and have a look for myself.'

'If you've come to gloat you're a bit late,' she said, acidly. 'We've cleaned up the mess.'

'Who do you think it was?' the DI asked, sitting down uninvited.

Cath shrugged. 'Burglars.'

'And yet nothing valuable was stolen?'

'You're supposed to be the detective, Talbot. *You* tell *me* who did it.'

'Someone with a grudge. Someone who doesn't like you. Mind you, that narrows down the suspects to about half a million, doesn't it?'

'If that was all you came here to say, you can go now,' she told him, getting to her feet.

Talbot didn't move.

'What the hell did you come here for, anyway?' she persisted.

'The case interests me.'

Cath sat down again.

Cross looked at both of them, feeling somewhat helpless.

'Would you like a drink?' he asked the policeman.

Cath shot him a withering glance.

'Whiskey, please,' Talbot said, smiling. 'As it comes.'

'So, what's so interesting about *my* case, then, Talbot? What's fascinating enough to bring you here at this time of the night?'

The DI accepted the drink from Cross and took a swig.

'I'm interested in why they broke in here and then took nothing,' he said. 'Aren't you?'

'Intrigued.'

'Only they *did* take something, didn't they?'

Cath nodded.

'A photograph of you and your brother,' the DI said. 'That's all that was stolen.'

Cath watched as he took another sip of the whiskey.

'You remember that day at Euston, not so long ago,' the policeman asked, 'Some geezer had thrown himself under a train?'

She nodded.

'And you heard about the bloke at that gun club in Druid Street who blew off his own head? And the one who took a dive through the top of The Greenhouse restaurant?'

Cath sat forward.

'The same thing happened to them a week or two before they topped themselves,' Talbot told her.

'You mean they were burgled?'

He nodded.

'Either their houses or their cars,' the DI said. 'And in all three cases, the only thing that the intruders stole were photos of those three men. Just like you.' He drained what was left in his glass and put it down on the table before him.

'Do you think the same people broke into my flat?' she asked incredulously. 'Why would they do that?'

Talbot shrugged. 'It might be a coincidence,' he said. 'But it's stretching things a bit. Four similar break-ins in the space of ten days, no valuables stolen – just a photo of the victim. In three cases, less than a week after the break-in, the victim commits suicide. You might be number four.'

'If you're expecting me to kill myself, Talbot, don't hold your breath waiting,' she told him defiantly.

'A man can dream can't he?'

Despite her bravado, Cath felt the hair rise at the back of her neck. 'Who were these men?'

Talbot smiled. 'Now there's the funny thing,' he said, humourlessly. 'They were all professional men, all working on one project, all happy family men. All with plenty to live for.'

'What was the project?' Cath asked.

'Those warehouses at Limehouse Reach.'

'Jesus! Have you been investigating this?'

'What the fuck do you think I've been doing?' he snapped.

'And it wasn't murder?'

'I think I would have noticed the difference,' he answered, acidly.

'But why do you think I might be involved?'

'I didn't say you were, I just said it's a hell of a coincidence. Their places were robbed and only a photo was stolen. Now *your* place is turned over and nothing but a picture is nicked. The circumstances are the same, whether or not the perpetrators are remains to be seen.'

He prodded his empty glass, pushing it towards Cross who got to his feet and returned with the bottle, which he set down before the detective, watching as he poured himself a large measure.

'One thing, Reed,' he said. 'I don't want you bothering the families of those dead men. If I so much as sniff that you've been round to any of their places I'll arrest you.'

Cath smiled. 'You'd like that, wouldn't you?' she said, softly.

He eyed her malevolently.

'Why did you tell me all this, Talbot?'

'I thought you had a right to know.'

'And if it scared the shit out of me that was just a bonus, right?'

'Someone could be after you, I just thought I'd warn you,' he said.

She watched as he sipped his drink.

'By the way, have you had any weird phone calls or mail, any shit like that recently?' the DI asked.

Cath nodded.

'Some threatening phone calls,' she admitted.

'Did you report them?'

'No. I thought they might be something to do with this child abuse story I'm working on, you know, parents warning me off.'

'They actually made threats?'

She nodded.

'Two of the three dead men had threatening phone calls too. Looks like you might have more in common with them than you thought.'

The DI finished his drink and got to his feet.

Cross rose with him.

'I'll see myself out,' Talbot said, heading for the door.

'How do I know they won't come back, Talbot?' Cath called after him.

'You don't.'

'Then what about some sort of police guard?'

'Are you fucking serious? I've got better things for my men to do than stand around here keeping an eye on *you* twenty-four hours a day.'

'So what do I do?' she demanded, getting up and following him to the front door.

He hesitated in the doorway.

'Watch yourself,' he advised, a smile creeping across his face. 'Sleep tight.'

She slammed the door on him.

Seventy-five

Frank Reed hadn't slept well the night before, a fact confirmed by the haggard-looking reflection that stared back at him from the glass of the car window.

The teacher locked the door, transferred his briefcase to his other hand and set off across the playground.

He'd swallowed a couple of Panadol with his coffee that morning, but they seemed to have done little to relieve the gnawing pain thudding away at his temples and spreading over the top of his scalp. It felt as if the skin there was slowly contracting, squeezing his skull until he felt sure it would collapse under the pressure.

He raised a hand in greeting to one of his colleagues, whose car was heading for the teachers' car park. He winced at the sound of the engine as the vehicle passed him. Every sound seemed to be amplified.

He walked on.

At the staff-room window he could see some of the other teachers getting ready for the day ahead. Two of them were gazing out into the playground holding cups of tea, as if steeling themselves for what the day might bring.

They both saw him, but when Reed raised a hand towards them they both turned away from the window.

Perhaps he wasn't the only one who'd had a rough night.

Christ, that was an understatement.

He'd made a couple of phone calls, left a message on Cath's answering machine, wondering why she hadn't called back.

He'd even tried to phone Ellen.

Fucking bitch.

There had been no answer.

Perhaps they'd been at the police station giving statements. Even now, in the cold light of day, the absurdity, the inanity, of the whole episode seemed no clearer.

He had been accused of molesting his own daughter.

Even the thought made him feel nauseous.

What sort of mind could dream up such an obscenity? Ellen?

Or her fucking lover?

He had wondered if Jonathan Ward might be behind it. The thought had tormented him all the previous night. He knew how besotted Ellen was with the man. Just how far would she go to please him?

What had they said to Becky to make her agree to such outrageous claims?

Did she *really* believe he had touched her? Hurt her?

The questions tumbled over in his mind as they had done the previous evening. And, as before, there were no answers.

He pushed open the main doors and walked in.

Three or four young boys were gathered around the noticeboard to the left, checking the names of the school under-15 football team. They seemed oblivious to his presence as he passed them, their attention riveted to the team-sheet.

Reed passed through another set of double doors and was about to turn right into the staff room when a familiar figure appeared ahead of him.

Noel Hardy looked at Reed, his face expressionless. 'Could I have a word with you in my office, please?' he said, stepping back, ushering Reed in.

Reed followed, accepting the chair which Hardy offered once they were both inside.

The Headmaster's office was slightly larger than his own, perhaps to reflect the older man's authority.

It had a profusion of houseplants, all of which looked remarkably healthy – due, Reed was sure, to the high temperature inside the office. It was always warm in the room. Even in summer Hardy kept the radiators on, Reed had noticed. The older man either didn't mind the heat or didn't feel it. Despite the fact that the morning air was a little crisp, the office was uncomfortably warm. The air smelled stale.

Beside each plant pot was a small bottle of Baby-Bio. On one windowsill he noticed a pair of secateurs. There was also a small fish tank to the left of the Head-master's desk: a variety of tropical fish swam back and forth. Watching them was supposed to relieve stress, Reed recalled. He wondered if he should get one for himself.

'I wanted a quick word,' Hardy said, officiously.

'Fire away.'

'This isn't easy for me.'

Reed frowned.

'The incident with the police yesterday,' the Headmaster continued. 'I saw it. I'm sure a number of other people did too. I'd like to know what it was about.'

'It's private.'

'Not if it happened on school property it isn't. I want to know what happened.'

'There was a misunderstanding. I went to the police station to help clear it up.'

Hardy stood by one of his houseplants and rubbed a leaf between his thumb and index finer.

'It's bad for the school,' he said. 'Teachers involved with the police. God knows there's been enough trouble at St Michael's lately. Brought about, I might add, by you.'

'If you're referring to the children, then—'

Hardy cut him short. 'It's been all over the newspapers,' he snapped. 'What do you imagine people will think of the school?'

'And what would you have done? Let those kids suffer? The police *had* to be called in.'

'The damage done to the reputation of this school could be irreparable and it's because of you.'

'To hell with the school's reputation. What about those kids?'

'First you bring the police here and then you yourself become involved with them. God alone knows why. What have you done?'

'I haven't *done* anything.'

'That's not what I heard.'

'What are you talking about?'

'You were taken to Theobald's Road Police Station yesterday, questioned about assault charges against your own daughter.'

'How do you know that?' Reed demanded.

'I know. That's all that matters.'

310

'Who told you?'

'So you don't deny it?'

'I don't deny I was questioned. But, as I told you, there'd been a misunderstanding.'

'It sounds like more than a misunderstanding. But then you always did have a talent for understatement, didn't you?'

'I want to know how you know.'

'I'm asking the questions here, Reed,' Hardy said, defiantly.

'Was it my wife?'

'I have no choice but to suspend you indefinitely, effective immediately. I'd appreciate it if you left now.'

'This is what you've been waiting for, isn't it?'

'I don't know what you're talking about,' the Headmaster said, dismissively.

'You never wanted to help those kids, did you? You were always more concerned about the reputation of your bloody school,' Reed snarled.

'Leave now, please.'

'Or what? Are you going to call the police?'

'If necessary.'

The two men locked stares, then Reed got to his feet and headed for the door.

'You'll be notified if any further disciplinary action is to be taken against you,' Hardy told him.

'Fuck you. And your school.'

'Now you know how the parents of those children felt. The ones you accused. Not pleasant, is it?'

Reed had no answer.

Seventy-six

Detective Inspector James Talbot dropped the file onto his desk and sat back in his seat, eyes closed.

For a long time he remained like that, watched by DS Rafferty and Phillip Barclay.

The coroner had a file of his own perched on his knee and he flicked distractedly through it while waiting for some kind of response from Talbot.

Rafferty lit up a cigarette, blowing out a stream of smoke, watching it dissipate in the air.

'It's not much to go on is it?' Talbot said finally, eyes snapping open. He looked at each of his companions in turn. 'We know someone was in that warehouse: that much is obvious, but who and why?' He shrugged, allowing the sentence to trail off. 'What have you got, Phil?'

'A rather mixed bag, you could say,' Barclay answered, smiling.

The smile faded rapidly when he saw the expression on Talbot's face. 'A few prints, mostly footprints,' he continued quickly. 'Corroboration of what you already know. Someone has been inside that warehouse.'

'How recently?' Talbot asked.

'A week, ten days, certainly not more recently,' the coroner replied.

'What about the blood?' Rafferty enquired.

'I'm coming to that,' Barclay told him. 'We found traces of blood *and* semen.'

'And?' Talbot persisted.

'The semen wasn't much help,' Barclay said. 'It's only possible to divide it into three systems anyway. Secretor and non-secretor, ABO and a PGM sub-group. Not very specific compared to the serology.'

Talbot sighed.

'Do you want to give me that in English, Phil?' he said, wearily.

'You can ascertain blood groups from semen samples, right, just as you can from sweat or urine, but it's obviously not as accurate as a blood sample itself for DNA profiling, unless you're talking about something like a rape. The semen samples found in that warehouse were almost useless.'

'Why?' Rafferty wanted to know.

'Because they were too old.'

'Older than the bloodstains?' the DS continued.

'In most cases. The spermatocytes were dead, decayed: it makes the typing virtually impossible,' Barclay explained.

'Fingerprints?' Talbot asked.

'There were about twenty-seven identifiable, the rest were partial prints, or whoever left them had been wearing gloves.'

'What about the footprints?' Talbot continued.

'Again, difficult to pick out. I'd say fifteen or sixteen different sets but very few complete ones. The dust in the warehouse *should* have made it easy to pick out imprints but unfortunately it didn't work like that.'

'Some of the ones I saw were clear enough,' Talbot argued.

313

'*Some* were. Most were made by bare feet.'

'Male or female?' asked Rafferty.

'Both.'

'And kids?' Talbot enquired.

'None that I could find.'

'Shit!' hissed Talbot.

'With the fingerprints, Phil, are they clear enough to secure a conviction if we can match them with a suspect?' Rafferty asked.

Barclay nodded.

'What about the blood?' Talbot added.

Barclay sucked in a deep breath. 'We did peroxidase tests first, just to confirm that the stains *were* blood. Then we ran precipitin tests on them.'

'Keep it simple, will you, Phil?' said Talbot.

'Precipitin tests can identify the nature of the blood. Human or animal.'

'And?'

'There were thirty-two identifiable blood samples in the warehouse. Six of them were A, three were O.'

'And the rest?'

'Animal.'

Talbot frowned and sat forward in his chair. 'What kind of animal?'

'Dog and cat accounted for twenty-one of the other samples,' Barclay told him.

'That still leaves two unaccounted for,' Talbot persisted.

'That's because we don't know *what* they are,' the coroner said, irritably. 'We keep anti-serums for most domestic and farmyard animals.'

'So what are you telling me?' Talbot demanded. 'That you don't know which animals the other two blood samples came from? How many possible are there, Phil?

314

I mean, once you've eliminated fucking giraffes and rhinos, what's left? Logically, what kind of animal could have been in that warehouse?'

'Logically, I would have said it had to be a domestic animal of some kind, a sheep or goat at a stretch. It had to be some kind of animal that was fairly easily obtainable, perhaps from a pet shop.'

'Some kind of exotic pet?' Rafferty offered, looking at Talbot.

'Any ideas?' the DI said.

'It depends what was going on in that warehouse. If they were carving up dogs and cats, Christ knows what else they might have used,' the DS said.

'The bloodstains were all concentrated in one main area of the warehouse, that's why it was difficult to identify them all at first,' Barclay explained.

'What other physical evidence did you find?' Rafferty asked.

'Hair and fibres,' said Barclay. 'Do you want the list?'

The policemen nodded his head in affirmation.

'Head hair, eyebrows, axillary hair and pubic hair,' the pathologist said.

'How the hell can you tell the difference?' Rafferty wanted to know.

'Head hair is circular in cross-section, pubic hair is triangular in cross section, eyebrows—'

Talbot held up a hand to silence him. 'Yeah, OK, Phil, we get the picture. What about fibres?'

'Cotton, wool, nylon. I've got another list,' Barclay informed them.

Talbot shook his head. 'So, the only mystery is where those two unidentified blood samples came from, right?' the DI said.

Barclay nodded.

'There was enough physical evidence in that ware-house to secure a conviction, should we find a suspect,' the pathologist said.

'The parents of the abused kids. We don't need to look any further.'

'How can you be so sure, Jim?' Rafferty asked.

'I can't. That's the whole point,' Talbot told him. 'The *media* has already convicted these people. Not us.'

'And this satanism angle?' Rafferty continued.

'That's bollocks, you know it is,' Talbot snapped.

'What if it isn't?' the DS persisted. 'Those symbols we saw, the statements given by the kids . . .'

'For Christ's sake, Bill,' Talbot responded angrily.

'What makes *you* such a bloody expert, Jim?' Rafferty hissed.

Talbot avoided his colleague's gaze.

Trust me.

'This wasn't even *our* case,' the DS continued. 'Why the interest?'

'Because the case we *were* working on is linked to this one, remember?' the DI said, acidly.

A heavy silence descended, broken finally by Barclay. 'Look, I've got some more work to do,' he said, getting to his feet.

'Find out what you can about those unidentified blood samples, Phil,' Talbot said.

Rafferty also followed the pathologist towards the door.

'I've got some stuff to do as well,' he muttered.

'Trust me on this one, Bill,' Talbot called to his colleague.

Rafferty closed the door as he left.

Talbot sat forward in his chair, head bowed.

Trust me. I know what I'm talking about.

He brought his fist down hard on the table top. So hard it hurt.

Christ, he needed a drink.

Seventy-seven

'There must be something you can do,' Catherine Reed said, exasperatedly.

Her brother sat motionless on the sofa in his flat, a cup of coffee gripped in his hand. He barely seemed to notice the heat which was searing his palm, so deep in thought was he.

'Frank,' she said and her voice seemed to shock him from his trance and make him aware of the heat he cradled.

He put down the cup and rubbed his hands together slowly.

'The police think I molested Becky,' he said, softly.

'They haven't charged you.'

'It's just a matter of time,' he told her. 'Ellen will press charges.' He began rubbing the nail of his right middle finger up and down the leg of his jeans. 'I was a fool. I should never have trusted her. It was too easy. She wouldn't let me see Becky for months, then suddenly, out of the blue, she rings up and says I can have her for the weekend. And all the time she was planning *this*. They were planning this. She and that bastard, Ward.'

317

Cath sat beside him and slid one arm around his shoulder. 'Frank, if you didn't do anything then they haven't got a case against you,' she tried to assure him.

He glared at her. 'What do you mean *if*? I *didn't* do anything. Do *you* think I touched Becky? My God, Cath.'

'I didn't say that. I know you'd never hurt her. What did the police say?'

'They said I touched her when I was drying her after she had a bath.'

'Did you?'

'How can you even ask me that?'

When she looked into his eyes she saw tears there.

'They can twist things, Frank,' she said, touching his cheek. 'Have you spoken to Becky?'

'I'm not allowed anywhere near her until this . . . enquiry is over. If Ellen has her way, I'll never see her again. That's what she wanted from the beginning and it looks as if she's going to achieve it.'

'When can you go back to the school?'

He shook his head. 'The suspension is indefinite. Hardy was waiting for *his* chance too.'

'Come on, Frank. You'll be saying they're in it together next. You know why Hardy had it in for you. You made him and his school look bad.'

'By telling the truth?'

'Like they say, "the truth hurts".'

Reed got to his feet and crossed to the window.

'If I *had* touched Becky,' he said, quietly. 'They'd be able to prove it, wouldn't they?'

Cath swallowed hard.

What was he saying?

She kept her gaze fixed on her brother.

318

'There'd be physical signs,' he continued.

Cath felt the hairs at the back of her neck rise.

'Frank,' she said, softly. '*Did* you touch her?'

'I held her in the towel after she had a bath. She dried herself, she dressed *herself*.'

Cath regarded him intently.

'I love her, Cath,' he said, his eyes misting over again. 'I'd never hurt her. But how am I going to convince people of that?'

She had no answer for him.

Only helpless silence.

She felt it kick.

Shanine Connor winced and clapped a hand to her belly. It was heavily swollen now.

Her breasts too felt uncomfortably large and conspicuous, straining against the threadbare material of the jumper she wore. It scarcely stretched over the lump in her belly.

She stood still for a moment, wincing at a sudden stab of pain , ignoring the fleeting stares of passers-by.

The sensations passed, and Shanine walked on along the Strand, one hand clutching the hold-all close to her, the other gripping one of the bars of chocolate she'd stolen less than fifteen minutes ago from a small tobacconists' at Charing Cross station.

The man had shouted at her.

She couldn't understand his words. He was foreign – Pakistani or something.

She'd run as best she could and no one had tried to stop her.

Out into Craven Street, into the throng of people in the Strand.

Gone.

She took a bite of the chocolate and continued walking until the Strand merged, narrowed and became Fleet Street.

She slowed her pace now, eyes alert, despite the fact they had not closed for longer than six hours during the past two days.

Her condition and the sudden change in the weather had conspired to deprive her of the sleep she needed so badly.

Shanine passed a shop window and caught a glimpse of her own haggard reflection.

Another young woman, perhaps a year older, also chose that moment to inspect her own image in the polished glass.

For fleeting seconds Shanine saw how *she* might have been.

The other woman was smartly dressed in a charcoal grey jacket and skirt, her hair freshly washed, blowing in the breeze.

Shanine blinked and the image was gone, the woman swallowed by the crowd.

Only her own tortured features peered back.

She stuffed what was left of the chocolate into her mouth and kept walking.

The building she sought was just ahead.

She stood gazing at it, at its tinted windows and the figures she could see moving about inside the reception area: a huge, cavernous arena of concrete and marble.

Above the main entrance was a sign: THE EXPRESS.

She reached into the hold-all and pulled out a rumpled piece of paper, unfolding it until she was looking at the face of Catherine Reed.

She knew every line and contour of that face now.

As she slid the paper back into the bag her hand brushed against the handle of the kitchen knife.

She waited.

Seventy-eight

Frank Reed was drunk.

Despite the amount he'd consumed, however, he found himself denied the stupor he sought.

Reed had never been a big drinker and he'd thought that the consumption of three quarters of a bottle of Bacardi would at least bring him the numbness he wanted.

He'd been wrong.

Instead, the world swam before him and he had to steady himself against the furniture every time he stood up. But, as for oblivion, it was probably another six or seven glasses away.

He sat on the floor in the hallway, the phone by his feet, the receiver pressed to his ear as he dialled.

He could hear the ringing tone.

His head was spinning and he closed his eyes for a second, but that only made things worse.

The phone was still ringing at the other end.

Reed reached for his glass and took a sip of the last drop of liquor he'd been able to find in the house.

He hated the taste of Bacardi but it was all he'd been able to find.

It should do the job.

The phone was picked up at the other end.

'Hello.'

Reed recognised the voice.

'I want to speak to Ellen,' he slurred, then belched, tasting a bitter mixture of alcohol and bile in his throat.

'I don't think she wants to speak to you,' Jonathan Ward told him.

Reed closed his eyes for a second.

'Look, let me speak to her,' he said, trying to remain calm.

Silence at the other end.

He heard muted voices briefly then Ellen's voice.

'You've got a bloody nerve,' she said, angrily.

'Just hear me out. About what happened the other day at your work: I'm sorry I caused a scene but—'

'I could have lost my job because of you.'

'And I could lose my daughter because of *you*!'

'Just leave me alone.'

'Don't hang up, Ellen,' he pleaded.

Silence.

'Ellen?'

'I'm still here. Make it quick.'

'Why did you make Becky say those things about me? Do you hate me that much?'

'I didn't *make* her say them.'

'I would never hurt her, you know that.'

'Why did you call?'

'Don't go ahead with this. Don't take it to court. Think about Becky.'

'Why didn't *you* think about her? Before you did what you did to her.'

'I didn't touch her,' he snarled, desperation now

colouring his tone. 'You know I didn't. You planned this whole thing, didn't you? You and *him*.'

'You're drunk, Frank, now leave us alone.'

'I want to speak to Becky.'

'Don't be ridiculous, it's after eleven. Besides she's got nothing to say to you.'

'She'd tell me what you made her say. Why you made her say I'd touched her.'

'Goodnight, Frank. Don't call again.'

'Don't do this, Ellen,' he rasped.

'If you call again I'll tell the police you've been harassing us,' she snapped.

'Just let me talk to her, please.'

'It's over, Frank. You won't see her again.'

'Please,' he shouted.

It took him a second to realise that he was listening to the monotonous drone of a dial tone.

'Fucking cunt!' he screamed at the receiver, slamming it down onto the cradle.

Frank Reed wept.

'It's stalled on me, Phil. I don't know what the hell to do next. Where to go.'

Catherine Reed stared at the array of daily newspapers laid out on the carpet before her and she sighed wearily, leaning back against the sofa where Phillip Cross was lying, one hand gently massaging her shoulder.

She was wearing just a long shirt, unbuttoned to the second fastening, her long slender legs curled beneath her.

Cross was wearing T-shirt and jeans.

The jeans were unbuttoned at the waist, the T-shirt, bearing the legend SAME SHIT DIFFERENT DAY, was untidily tucked into them.

323

'What about the rest?' Cross enquired, nodding towards the other papers.

'They've all got their angles,' she told him. 'The ones who are bothering to carry stories anyway.' Cath ran a hand through her long dark hair. 'I sometimes wonder if we're the only paper taking this child abuse thing seriously.' She picked up one of the papers, another tabloid. 'Two columns on page four. That's it in the *Mirror*. The *Sport* ran a double-page centre spread with colour pictures of women dressed as witches, but now nothing.'

'What do you expect? You know how they work. No tits, no story,' Cross shrugged, still gently kneading the flesh of her shoulder.

'Three columns in the *Sun*, one in *Today* and the broadsheets haven't even touched it.'

'Passing fad,' offered Cross.

'Jesus, Phil, we're talking about sexual abuse of at least nine children, a possible paedophile ring, parents suspected of molesting their own kids and, to top it all, the probability there's a ritual element to the whole thing, and still nobody gives a toss. They'd rather read how much Princess Diana spends on a sodding manicure.'

They sat in silence for a moment, just the sound of the TV in the background, the volume lowered so it was barely audible.

'So, what do you do now?' Cross asked.

'No one's talking any more,' she told him, reaching back to touch his hand. 'Not the police, not the Social Services, and certainly not the families. It's like it's all over. Pushed into some drawer out of sight. This is a bigger case than Cleveland or Nottingham, and no one wants to know.'

He continued massaging her as she went on. 'One

324

paper ran something about the video nasties that were found in a few of the houses. But they hardly mentioned the abuse. They were more concerned that the kids might have been watching violent movies. Instead of investigating the whole case they concentrated on the video angle. Some self-righteous MP stands up and calls for a ban on all 18 certificate videos. Jesus Christ, don't they get it?'

'You're talking about politicians, Cath, they don't live in the real world. Any of them.'

'What do you think?' she asked, turning to face him.

'About politicians? They're all a bunch of hypocritical, arse-licking, vote-catching, back-stabbing—'

She smiled and pressed her finger to his lips.

'About this story?' she corrected him, removing her finger.

'I think there's something going on, but don't ask me what. Kids abused, cats nailed to church doors, graves dug up, dawn raids. It makes no sense to me, Cath. I'm just a humble photographer.'

'But what do you believe?'

He could only shrug.

'Do you believe my story?' she asked. 'Do you believe that the abuse could be ritualistic?'

'Cath, I . . .'

'I need to know, Phil.'

'I think it's possible,' he said, quietly, stroking her hair. 'Why is *my* opinion so important?'

'It just is.'

She kissed him lightly on the lips.

'What are the police doing about the case?' he asked, sliding one hand inside her shirt, cupping one breast.

She made no move to resist.

325

'They start interviewing the parents of the children tomorrow,' Cath told him, sighing as she felt his thumb brush across her nipple, the fleshy bud stiffening and rising.

'All you can do is wait, Cath,' he told her, quietly, his hand still gently squeezing her breast.

She bent forward and kissed him hard on the lips, his mouth opening to welcome her probing tongue, his hand squeezing her breast.

She climbed onto the sofa with him, grinding her pubic mound against the bulge she could feel in his jeans, helping him to free his erection.

As he felt her hand grip his shaft he grunted with pleasure, fingers undoing her shirt, tongue snaking forward to flick her swollen nipples. With his free hand he traced a pattern across the inside of first one of her spread thighs then the other, feeling her shiver at his touch.

As she moved forward he felt the slippery softness of her cleft brush against the tip of his penis.

Cath sighed, wanting him inside her.

She glanced to one side, at the papers spread out across the carpet.

Then, as she felt the first glorious sensations between her legs, felt his stiffness slide into her, she turned her head away.

The phone was ringing when Talbot walked in.

He glanced at his watch.

11.27 p.m.

Who the fuck was calling now?

He snatched up the receiver.

'Hello.'

326

'Mr Talbot, this is Maurice Hodges,' said the voice at the other end.

The DI felt the colour drain from his cheeks.

Hodges sounded almost apologetic. 'I'm sorry to disturb you at this time, but it is important,' he said. 'It's your mother. It's bad news.'

Seventy-nine

That smell.

Hospitals always had that smell. Talbot didn't know what it was but it always made him feel sick.

If he'd been in the mood he would probably have found that particular irony amusing.

As it was he had other things on his mind.

He had no idea how long it had taken him to drive to St Ann's hospital in Harringay. The journey had been a blur, as if he'd been travelling through some drug-induced trance, not really seeing or hearing properly. He drove instinctively, amazed he hadn't killed anyone, such had been his haste to reach this place.

This place that smelled so strong it made him feel sick.

The room in which he sat was about twelve feet square.

It reminded him of a cell but for the leaflets on the wall.

Multiple sclerosis.

Rabies.

Cancer.

Always fucking cancer.

That particular leaflet was pinned just above the red and white sign which proclaimed: NO SMOKING.

Talbot felt more like a cigarette than he'd ever done in his life.

A nurse had brought him a cup of tea when he'd first arrived.

That same cup now stood untouched and cold on the table before him.

The room was lit by a small table lamp fitted with a forty-watt bulb. It was barely adequate and the room was filled with long shadows. Thick and black, they seemed to move of their own accord.

The door of the room opened and two men entered, one of whom Talbot recognised as Dr Hodges from Litton Vale. The other man was also, he assumed, a doctor, his features pinched, his hair swept back so severely it looked as though his scalp had been stretched.

But, for all that, he had sad eyes. Great saucer-like orbs which homed in on Talbot like searchlights on a fleeing man.

'How is she?' the DI asked, rising to his feet.

The man with sad eyes kept him fixed in that watery gaze.

'I won't lie to you,' he said softly. 'I'll be surprised if she lasts the night. I'm very sorry.'

Talbot stood motionless. 'What was it?' he said, looking at Hodges.

'A massive heart attack,' the doctor told him. 'One of the night staff called me: I live close to Litton Vale, I don't know if you know. I drove there, I called the ambulance immediately, then I called you.'

'Can I see her?' Talbot asked.

'She's in a coma,' the sad-eyed man told him.

'I didn't ask you that. I asked if I could see her,' the DI persisted.

'I'd advise against it, Mr Talbot—'

'I don't want your advice, I want to see my mother.'

The sad-eyed doctor glanced at Hodges then back at Talbot. 'She's in ICU. I can show you—'

'I'll find it,' said Talbot, pushing past him.

As he stepped out of the room he saw several signs on the blue-painted hospital wall.

One pointed the way to Intensive Care.

Talbot stalked off down the corridor and jabbed the lift call button, waiting as the car bumped to a halt before him.

As the doors slid open he saw an old man in a dressing gown inside, who shot him a questioning look. The man was using a frame to walk and even that didn't seem to be of much help.

Talbot wondered what he was doing up and about at such a late hour.

The policeman stepped into the lift, watched by the old man, pressed the required button and the doors slid shut.

He leaned against the rear wall as the lift rose to its appointed floor.

The smell here seemed even stronger, but Talbot ignored it and headed towards the nurses' station, his footsteps echoing through the stillness.

The nurse who looked up at him was in her early twenties.

'I'm looking for Dorothy Talbot,' he said. 'I'm her son.'

The nurse stared at him, pity filling her eyes, then she rose.

Talbot followed her along a short corridor towards a room, the door of which she pushed open, ushering Talbot inside.

'Oh Christ!' he whispered.

The only sound in the room was the steady blip of an oscilloscope.

'You can't stay long,' the nurse said, apologetically, stepping aside as Talbot moved closer to the bed where his mother lay.

There was a plastic chair close to the bed and he pulled it over, seating himself beside her, gazing into her face.

Her skin was the colour of old newspaper, her eyes sunken so deep into her face she looked skeletal.

The nurse paused a moment then stepped out of the room.

Talbot sat gazing at his mother, at the tubes running from both arms to drips near by. At the catheter, half full of dark liquid.

'Mum,' he said, softly, reaching for her hand.

It was so cold.

Her skin felt waxen to his touch.

And so cold.

He could see her chest rising and falling almost imperceptibly but he couldn't hear her breathing.

All that was covering her was a sheet, and that was only pulled up as far as her waist. Talbot muttered something under his breath and noticed a blanket carefully folded on the bottom of the bed. He unrolled it then pulled both it and the sheet up to his mother's chest.

330

Carefully he tucked one of her hands beneath the covers, gripping it gently.

'Don't die.'

She looked so frail, so drained of life. So different from the last time he'd seen her.

Well, at least you won't have to worry about bringing her home, will you? You bastard.

He squeezed her hand more tightly, as if the action might rouse her from the coma.

Heart attack.

Jesus Christ, wasn't fucking cancer enough?

Talbot noticed that there was a small wooden cross hanging above the bed.

He eyed it malevolently.

She didn't deserve to suffer. Her least of all.

Allowing his mother's hand to slip from his grip, he got to his feet and plucked the cross from the wall placing it on the bedside table.

'Satisfied now?' he said, his words directed at empty air.

At a God he didn't believe in.

He reached for her hand again.

So cold.

'You sleep, Mum,' he whispered, barely realising there were tears rolling down his cheeks. The oscilloscope continued its slow rhythm.

Everything else was silent.

The nurse came to the door, peeked through the glass panel and saw Talbot sitting holding his mother's hand.

She hesitated a moment, then walked quietly away.

Eighty

The note had been on the pillow beside her when she'd woken that morning.

Cath had rolled over sleepily, slapping a hand in the general direction of the alarm clock, expecting also to feel the warmth of Phillip Cross's body but the photographer wasn't there.

She'd found the note moments later, sliding across her large bed and shutting off the alarm, glancing down to see the scribbled note: *'Some of us have to work for a living. See you later. Love Phil.'*

Cath remembered dimly that he'd said something to her the night before about having an assignment in Paddington early that morning.

Very early.

She glanced across at the alarm.

7.30 a.m.

Then she looked back at the note.

Love Phil.

Love?

Now, as she parked her Fiat in the car park at the back of the Express building, she looked down at the note once again. At first she wondered why she'd even kept it with her, stuffing it into the back pocket of her jeans.

She glanced at it and smiled.

Love?

Perhaps he did love her.

Perhaps she loved *him*.

Cath folded the note and slid it into the pocket again, picking up her briefcase from the back seat.

She usually entered by the door at the rear of the building. A security guard was posted there too, but he didn't ask to see her pass as she approached him. She smiled broadly at him and mentioned the previous night's football results. The security man smiled back and called something to her about Liverpool in a broad scouse accent.

She waved dismissively at him as she got into the lift. When she reached her floor, she stepped out and was enveloped by sound: raised voices, chattering keyboards, electronic printers, even the clacking of a typewriter. Some of the older journalists on the paper still typed their copy before transferring it to their word processors. Cath wondered if they saw it as a last desperate attempt to cling onto a now archaic way of working. One of the sports writers completed *all* his features on an old Elite machine.

The office was open plan, desks separated from each other only by movable partitions. They didn't offer much privacy and it sometimes made taking phone calls difficult, but Cath enjoyed the organised chaos of the newsroom. She had done ever since she joined the paper.

A number of her colleagues nodded greetings at her as she headed towards her desk. Others were either out of the office or engrossed in their own work.

She spotted the young lad who was in the office on work experience struggling with a cardboard tray filled with coffee cups from the vending machine.

Cath smiled. It seemed to be all the poor little sod did. Fetch coffee. By the time his week was up he'd probably have learned more about being a waiter than a journalist. He passed from desk to desk distributing beverages.

Cath reached her own desk and set down her briefcase. She sat down and was about to check her messages when she heard a familiar voice call her name.

Terry Nicholls stood in the doorway of his office.

'Have you got a minute, Cath?' he said, his face expressionless.

She smiled at the Editor and got to her feet.

'What's wrong?' she asked as he ushered her inside.

She saw the other occupant of the room immediately.

Cath frowned.

'This is who you want,' Nicholls addressed the seated figure, gesturing in Cath's direction.

As the journalist entered, the person in the swivel chair turned and looked into her eyes.

Cath looked back and met Shanine Connor's haunted stare.

Cath saw the pale skin, the lank brown hair, the hold-all which lay at the girl's feet and she noticed the large bulge of Shanine's belly.

'Why don't you tell Miss Reed why you're here?' Nicholls said, taking a seat behind his desk.

He motioned for Cath to take a seat, which she did, perching on the edge of the black leather sofa backed onto one wall.

She ran appraising eyes over Shanine, guessing she was in her early thirties. It might have surprised Cath to know she was only in her early twenties. The ravages of sleeping rough had taken their toll over the past few

334

days. There was a slightly acrid smell in the office, which Cath realised was coming from the visitor.

'My name's Shanine Connor,' she said, falteringly.

'I'm Catherine Reed.'

'I know who you are. I've read your articles,' said Shanine, fumbling in her jeans and pulling out the crumpled photo. 'I took this from one of them.' She held up the picture for inspection.

'She's been here nearly an hour,' said Nicholls. 'Security were going to throw her out. She kept insisting she had to see you. I brought her in with me.'

'What can I do for you, Ms Connor?' Cath asked, puzzled.

'Like I said, I read your articles, you know, about the cemetery desecrations, the things that have been going on with those children. It's terrible,' Shanine said, lowering her gaze.

Cath looked at Nicholls, who shrugged. 'What's your reason for wanting to see me, Ms Connor?'

'Shanine.'

'Shanine,' Cath repeated.

'I came to tell you you're right about what's going on,' the younger woman told her. 'You said it was satanism.'

'I said that it was *possible* it could be satanism,' Cath corrected her.

'It is.'

'How can you be sure? Are you involved in it?' Cath asked, excitedly.

Shanine looked unblinkingly at her. 'I'm the High Priestess of a Coven,' she said, softly. 'I'm a witch.'

Eighty-one

Cath sat motionless, her eyes trained on the scruffy, pregnant young woman before her.

Nicholls was the first to move.

He got to his feet and headed towards the office door. 'I think I'll leave you to it: I've heard Ms Connor's story once,' he said, smiling wanly.

As he passed Cath he bent and whispered in her ear: 'Good luck. Enjoy yourself.'

And he was gone.

'I know he doesn't believe me,' Shanine said as the office door closed behind the Editor. 'He thinks I'm mad.'

'Why should he?'

Shanine tried to smile but didn't manage it.

'Why don't you tell *me* what you told him?' Cath said.

'You'll probably think I'm mad as well.'

'Try me.'

'I don't know where to start,' the younger woman said, wearily.

Cath saw tears in her eyes.

'Would you like a drink? A coffee or something?' she asked.

Shanine shook her head. 'I think I need something stronger,' she said, again trying to force a smile, again failing.

'Listen, Ms . . . Shanine. What you said, about being a

High Priestess, a witch, it's not that I don't believe you, but walking in here and saying something like that,' Cath shrugged, 'it's like a scene from a bad horror film.'

'What do you want me to say? It's the truth. I came here because I need help, because I wanted to get away from them. They'll kill me if they find me. They were going to kill my baby, that's why I ran away in the first place. They would have killed my baby.'

'Who are *they*?'

'The other members of the group.'

'The Coven?'

Shanine nodded.

'How did you get involved with them in the first place?' Cath asked.

'My boyfriend,' the younger woman said, wearily. 'He was in the Navy when I met him. He was twenty-two, I was seventeen. He was gorgeous.' A slight smile flickered on her lips. 'About six foot, blond and muscly. Really fit. We spent nearly all our time in bed.' The smile faded slowly. 'I told him about my family. I was brought up Catholic but I got fed up with it. He said to me that I should come to a meeting with him, a meeting of his own church. I said yes. And it was fine. There were about fifteen other people there, about five or six of Stuart's friends from the Navy and some others.'

'Men *and* women?'

'Yes. They just sat around and discussed their religion, saying how happy they were and how much they got from their faith. I just assumed they were talking about Christianity and I enjoyed it. It was really relaxed, you know, a happy atmosphere. The only strange thing was I never saw a Bible, but I didn't think anything of it at the time.'

337

'Where did these meetings take place?'

'In Manchester. The room was like an office but with no furniture, nothing on the walls either. It didn't seem weird though. They had meetings every week and Stuart just said that as I'd enjoyed myself so much I should keep going.' She lowered her eyes momentarily. 'We were still sleeping together and I think I was in love with him by then. I just wanted to be with him.'

'What about your family? Did you tell them?'

'My mum left home when I was six, my dad was always out on the piss. I went to live with my gran when I was eight. I didn't see my parents again after that. My gran was good to me but it's not like having your mum and dad there, is it?'

Cath saw the despair in the younger woman's eyes and shook her head gently.

'What happened with the group?' she asked finally.

'Well, the next week another person, a man, joined. He'd been invited by one of Stuart's friends. All contacts were made face to face. I found out that the group was called The Open Church.' She began picking at the skin at the side of one nail. 'The meetings went on for about six weeks, then they started talking about weird things – the cult, ceremonies. They gave me books and pamphlets on it to read. I thought they were trying to show me the dangers of it.' She smiled bitterly. 'If only I'd known.'

Cath kept her gaze fixed on Shanine.

'They asked me and this bloke if we wanted to find out more – they called it "going deeper". They asked us if we wanted to stay. I said yes, but it was mainly so I could be close to Stuart. The only way I could keep his attention was to go further.'

338

'What about the man who joined?'

'He left,' Shanine told her. 'And, as soon as he did, they changed the meeting place. If anyone left, they always changed the meeting place. We must have moved six or seven times in the first ten weeks. Then they asked me if I wanted to come to a different kind of meeting. Stuart said it would be all right and I trusted him so I went. It was in a big place, a big building.'

'What kind of building?'

'Like one of those MFI places but it was empty.'

'A warehouse?'

Shanine nodded.

Warehouse.

Cath sucked in a deep breath. She reached for her cigarettes and lit one.

'Can I have one of those?' Shanine asked.

Cath lit a cigarette for the younger woman; she noticed that her fingers were trembling.

'What happened in the warehouse?' Cath asked.

'We all had a drink – just wine, but I think mine must have been drugged. They started praying and I just seemed to fall asleep, but my eyes were open. I was out of it for about the first half-hour. I mean, I've done drugs before but this was something else. I was smashed. Then, when I came round they were all sitting in a circle around me. There was just one candle lit and they were all praying in some language I couldn't understand. It sounded like Arabic or something. I felt calm though – I think that must have been the drugs – but the rest of them were going ape. They started off excited but then they got really aggressive, shouting. And there was always one man who led them, every time.'

'The same man?'

339

Shanine nodded, took a drag on the cigarette.

'It was always the same man and he never took his eyes off me the whole time they were praying. Stuart told me they were praying I was the right person for the group because they wanted me in their church. *They* wanted *me*.'

A solitary tear trickled down her cheek.

'That was the first time anyone had wanted me,' she said, softly. 'I was flattered. I wanted to be there because they *wanted* me.'

She took a long drag, blowing the smoke out in a bluish-grey stream.

'At the next meeting, they told me the truth,' she said, flatly.

Cath sat forward in her seat, watching as Shanine wiped the now freely flowing tears away with one grubby hand. 'The truth about what?' she asked.

'About the church, about who they were worshipping, who they expected me to serve.' Cath looked on in fascination.

'That was the thing, when they prayed, it was never to God, it was always to someone they called the Protector,' Shanine continued. 'They said I was to help them serve the Protector. I knew I'd gone too far then, that there was something wrong, but it was too late.'

'What did they call themselves, Shanine?'

'The Satanic Church, but they told me never to say that in front of others.' She ground out the cigarette in a nearby ashtray. 'After that they said I was ready.'

'For what?'

'Initiation.'

Eighty-two

Cath watched as the younger woman pulled another cigarette from the packet and pushed it between her thin lips.

The journalist again obliged with a light.

She watched intently as Shanine drew on the cigarette, brushing her hair from her eyes, shifting in her seat to try and ease the weight in her belly.

'Who decided to initiate you,' Cath continued.

'The other members of the group,' said Shanine, watching as Cath fumbled in her handbag and pulled out a microcassette recorder, which she set down close to the younger woman.

'You don't mind, do you?' Cath asked, pressing the Record switch.

Shanine looked at the machine, its twin spools turning silently.

'How many of the other members did you know by name?' the journalist asked.

'Apart from Stuart, none of them, but he told me that they were important people. He reckoned a couple of them were social workers. One was a businessman. There was a doctor, too. If any of the group were sick, they had to see him. We weren't allowed to see outsiders.' Shanine gave a hollow laugh. 'Stuart even reckoned one of the group was a journalist.' She looked at Cath and held her gaze.

'What happened when you were initiated?' Cath said.

'They did it inside the warehouse, turned it into our place, a sort of makeshift temple. All the fittings were removable. Curtains, shrouds, altar, and there was a block. Like a big piece of stone. That was where they did the sacrifices. There was water and herbs, too, but I don't know what they were. I can remember the smells though.' She paused, lowered her gaze. 'The altar was covered with a white cloth with black edging. They put a big cup on it, a chalice. That's what they collected the blood in.' She closed her eyes tightly, as if the effort of reliving the memory was causing her physical pain.

'The altar cloth was covered in symbols, penta-grams, upturned crosses – that kind of thing. And there was writing on it but I couldn't understand it. It looked foreign.'

Cath sat silently, her eyes never leaving the younger woman.

'We were all dressed in white robes, nothing under-neath. The High Priest wore a gold chain around his neck but it was really thick, like a padlock chain, and it had a gold circle on it with a smaller pentagram inside. He used to read the services from a big book on the altar. He was the only one allowed to touch it. He read the service in Latin.'

'How can you be sure it was Latin?' Cath asked.

'I told you, I was brought up a Catholic,' said Shanine. 'I've had Latin rammed down my throat since I was three.' She took a drag on her cigarette. 'Sometimes they'd say the Lord's Prayer backwards.'

Cath swallowed hard.

The image of the graffiti in the crypt at Croydon Cemetery flashed into her mind.

'What happened during your initiation?' the journalist persisted.

'I was washed, then anointed with oil. Another woman did it, a woman in her mid-twenties, then she rubbed oil on my boobs and here,' she motioned to her thighs. 'She held my arms above my head while the High Priest had sex with me. The others just watched. Even Stuart was watching.' She lowered her eyes again, as if ashamed. 'I had sex with another man later that night, too, with everyone watching. They said he was Satan and that I was one of his brides now.'

'Did you get a good look at his face?'

'No. He was wearing a mask. Like a goat's head.'

'Oh Christ,' murmured Cath.

'He was the one who cut me. Here.'

She held out her right hand and Cath saw a deep scar which ran from the bottom of her index finger to the base of her thumb.

'The blood was collected in the chalice along with the blood from the animal they killed,' Shanine continued. 'A cat, I think. I had to drink some of it. I thought I was going to be sick but they'd given me drugs before and after the ceremony – I hardly knew what was happening. From then on I was a Priestess. I took part in ceremonies all the time. I had sex with men *and* women. I helped initiate other people into the group.'

'Did you bring people to them?'

'No. That was done by Stuart and his friends. I helped once the new members were there though.' She paused, the knot of muscles at the side of her jaw pulsing. 'I found out three months later that I was pregnant. I knew it was Stuart's because I'd had only oral sex with the other men during that period, but they said I couldn't tell him. They let me go full term. They wanted the baby.'

'What for?'

'Sacrifice.'

There was a long silence.

Tears trickled down Shanine's cheeks.

'They killed it a week after it was born,' she said, sniffing, but not attempting to wipe away the tears. 'They did it in front of me. They even made *me* cut her. When the High priest was making the incisions he made me hold the knife as well and when they were finished they said the baby had been offered to Satan.'

'Did you try to stop them?'

Shanine could only shake her head, tears now pouring down her cheeks.

'They said it was either the baby or me,' she sobbed, finally. 'I said I didn't want it to happen but they said I had to let her go or Satan would be angry, and they told me if I told anyone they would kill me. No matter where I went, how far I ran. They said they would always know. That someone would always bring me back to them.' She looked imploringly at Cath who felt helpless to comfort her.

'Was yours the only baby killed?'

Shanine shook her head, her eyes now tightly closed as if she could shut out the visions in her mind, too.

'They used young children. Three or four years old,' she said, her voice cracking. 'They got them from people, I don't know who. Not group members. They paid them. Poor people. People who couldn't afford to feed themselves, let alone their kids. They killed them or they abused them and they warned the kids that if they said anything they'd kill their parents. Those kids were

344

terrified. They drugged them, too, so they wouldn't struggle while they were abusing them.'

Cath listened intently, her mouth slightly open, her eyes wide.

She wanted to cry.

She could almost feel the pain Shanine felt.

So *much* pain.

'Stuart told me he never knew they'd kill children,' Shanine continued. 'He said he was leaving the group. So they killed him. They murdered him and made it look like suicide.'

Cath sat forward. 'How did they do it?' she asked urgently.

'They worked a Death Hex on him, they forced him to kill himself. They were powerful.'

'I don't understand. How could they make him commit suicide?'

'They used something of his.'

'A lock of hair or something?'

Shanine managed a thin smile. 'No. It doesn't work like that,' she said. 'They didn't need his hair or his finger or anything he wore. The Death Hex works without all that. All they needed was a photograph of him.'

Cath felt the colour draining from her cheeks, her flesh rising in goosebumps.

'They stole a photograph of him,' Shanine continued. 'Three days later, he was dead.'

Cath, her hand shaking, reached frantically for the phone.

Eighty-three

The nurse had entered the room twice during the night. That much Talbot could remember.

Each time she'd found him sitting in the same position, holding his mother's hand, leaning forward slightly gazing at her face as if expecting his presence to drag her into consciousness.

The nurse had fiddled with the drips and the machinery and then left him in silence again.

In the dark.

He hated the night and the stillness.

There was only the ever-present sound of the oscilloscope to accompany his own breathing.

More than once he had pressed the first two fingers of his right hand hard into her wrist, searching for a pulse, terrified that she might have slipped away from him.

Each time he'd found the almost imperceptible rhythm of her weakened heart pumping blood so pathetically around her body.

He remembered that.

What he didn't remember was when he'd fallen asleep.

It had crept up on him like a hunter in the gloom, stalking him, then claiming him, drawing him into the blackness that surrounded him.

He woke with a start, found his head on the bed close to his mother's chest.

He still gripped her hand.

Even in sleep he hadn't released it, perhaps thinking that to cling onto her would retain his hold on her life.

As he stirred he looked intently at her. At the slow rise and fall of her chest.

Behind him, the oscilloscope still continued its high-pitched signals.

Talbot exhaled deeply and rubbed both hands across his face.

He glanced at his watch.

8.17 a.m.

Shit.

He had to phone Rafferty, tell him what had happened, tell him he couldn't leave his mother just yet.

Rafferty could handle things. He was a very able man.

A *good* man.

Like you? Are you a good man?

He got to his feet, patting his mother's hand lightly, touching one of her cheeks with the back of his hand.

'I'll be back in a while, Mum,' he said softly, and turned towards the door.

There was a bathroom at the end of the corridor, for the use of patients, he assumed. Not that many of them in this unit would even be able to get to the toilet.

Talbot glanced around, saw that the nurses' station was unattended. He strode up the corridor and into the bathroom where he splashed his face with cold water. The clear fluid felt good against his skin and his flesh prickled, momentarily revitalised.

He rubbed a wet hand around the back of his neck soothingly, before running both hands through his hair, slicking it back until it looked as though his hair had been oiled.

He inspected his image in the mirror on the wall.

The face which stared back at him was that of a man who needed sleep badly. The whites of his eyes were criss-crossed with red veins, the lids puffy and swollen. As he ran a hand across his cheeks and chin he could hear the stubble rasp.

'Fuck it,' he grunted and dried his face on the roller-towel.

He felt a swelling in his bladder and urinated in the single cubicle; then, taking one last look in the mirror at his haggard reflection, he made his way back down the corridor towards his mother's room.

As he entered, he saw a dark figure standing beside the bed.

Talbot looked at the priest for a moment, his eye focusing on the cleric's white collar.

'Good morning,' said the priest.

'What do you want?' Talbot replied, warily.

'I was asked to call on one of the patients in this unit,' the priest answered. 'I usually look in on them all if I'm here.'

'Well, you're in the wrong room,' the DI snapped.

The priest looked at him with a slight smile on his face. He was only five or six years older than Talbot, his hair short but thick and lustrous on top.

'I know how you must feel,' the cleric soothed.

'Do you? I don't think so.'

'If there's anything I can do to help.'

'What, like give her the last rites or something? Why don't you just leave her alone? You can't do anything to help her.'

'Then perhaps I can help *you*. At a time like this I find that families need help.'

'From you?'

'From God.'

Talbot opened the door.

'Get out,' he said, irritably.

The priest hesitated.

'I don't need your help,' the policeman said. 'Yours or God's. If God wants to help, why doesn't he bring her out of that fucking coma? That'd help.'

'I'm sorry you feel that way,' the priest said, almost apologetically.

'How do you expect me to feel? Look what your God's done for my mother.' He jabbed a finger angrily in the direction of the bed. 'Go on, get out and take your God with you.'

The priest left without answering.

Talbot slammed the door behind him and exhaled deeply, eyes closed.

The sharp beeping noise startled him.

For one terrible second he thought it was the oscilloscope, then he realised it was his pager.

He snatched at it and checked the number, pushing out into the corridor again, glancing around for a phone, remembering there was one at the nurses' station.

It was manned when he reached it.

An older nurse looked up at him as he lowered over her.

'I need to use a phone,' he said, pulling his ID from his pocket.

The nurse glanced quickly at the card, then nodded and motioned to the white phone before him.

Talbot jabbed the digits and waited.

At the other end the receiver was picked up and he recognised Rafferty's voice immediately.

'Bill, it's me. What do you want?'

'Where are you, Jim?'

'At the hospital with my mother, she's very bad.'

'Christ, I'm sorry. Listen, Jim, I know this is difficult but something's happened here. You have to get back to the Yard as soon as you can.'

'Can't you deal with it?'

'You need to hear this yourself.'

Talbot hesitated.

What if he left now and she died?

Are you going to let her die alone?

'Jim?' Rafferty persisted.

Again Talbot hesitated.

'What we've got here is going to blow this abuse case wide open,' Rafferty told him. 'Maybe even prove links with the three suicides.'

Another long silence.

'I'll be there in an hour,' Talbot said.

Eighty-four

They sat in silence watching him.

The three of them, eyes fixed upon him as he sat back in his chair, hands entwined behind his head, his own gaze lowered.

Shanine Connor shifted uncomfortably in her seat and took a drag on the cigarette, glancing occasionally at Catherine Reed who touched her arm reassuringly.

DS William Rafferty was perched on the corner of the desk gazing at his superior.

Talbot loosened his hands and stretched, before cracking his knuckles, the sound reverberating around the silent office.

He glanced at his watch.

12.06 p.m.

He had sat silently for almost two hours.

Listening.

Shanine Connor had spoken for the duration of that time, faltering in tears on a number of occasions, getting through a packet and a half of cigarettes.

Talbot had hardly taken his eyes off her during that time.

Cigarette smoke hung like a filthy curtain across the office and the DI got to his feet and opened a window to try and clear it.

He chewed on a mint and returned to his seat.

'It's bullshit,' he said, finally. 'The whole fucking story is bollocks.' He looked at Shanine. 'The only bit you left out was where you keep your broomstick.'

'I'm not lying,' Shanine began, but Cath interjected.

'You think she made the story up, Talbot?' the journalist said, scathingly. 'Why should she?'

'Money. How much will your rag pay for shit like she's just come out with?'

'I don't want money,' Shanine said. 'I came here to stop them killing my baby.'

'Of course,' Talbot said, scornfully. 'You don't want it sacrificed like the other one, do you? Why come here in the first place? Why run from Manchester to London? They've got coppers in Manchester you know?'

'I wanted to get away from the group, I said that. I couldn't think of anywhere else to go,' Shanine protested, looking at Cath as if for support.

'According to you there are groups everywhere, aren't there?' Talbot snapped. 'At least three in Manchester, didn't you say? Christ knows how many there must be in a city this size. You took a chance coming down here. Why not go somewhere nice and quiet like Devon, or are there witches down there too?'

Shanine opened her mouth to say something but the DI continued before she had the chance.

'If what you say about murdering your own kid is true, then you're bloody lucky we're not charging you with manslaughter instead of wasting police time.'

'So you don't believe any of it?' Cath asked.

'What do *you* think?' Talbot snapped.

'So you're going to ignore all the facts she's given you?' the journalist persisted. 'The similarities don't strike you as odd, Talbot? The mentions of a warehouse, the use of children, graveyard desecrations, killing animals. And what about this Death Hex? You've been investigating three suicides and the only thing stolen from each victim was a photo. Two days ago a photo was stolen from *my* flat, nothing else. Maybe I'm next.'

Talbot raised his eyebrows and smiled.

Cath turned away from him angrily, lighting a cigarette.

'What about you, Bill?' Talbot said, looking at Rafferty. 'What do *you* think?'

Rafferty shrugged. 'I think she could be telling the truth.'

'Jesus,' Talbot grunted. 'I don't believe this. Am I the only one who hasn't lost his fucking mind around here?'

'There's a lot of coincidences, Jim, a lot of similarities

with these cases we've been investigating,' Rafferty insisted.

Cath smiled to herself.

'All right,' the DI said, irritably, turning his gaze upon Shanine. 'Tell me again about this "Death Hex".' He spoke the last two words with contempt.

'They steal a photograph of the person they want dead,' Shanine said, sucking on her cigarette. 'It's put into a box with three thorns, some cemetery earth and a dead insect, then it's buried close to the victim's home.'

'And what's this thing called?'

'A Misfortune Box.'

'And this is what was done to your boyfriend,' the DI proclaimed. 'There's no possibility he could have just topped himself? Was he depressed? Suicidal?'

'*They* killed him,' Shanine blurted. 'And they used the Death Hex to do it, to make it look like suicide.'

'And we're supposed to believe that Parriam, Hyde and Jeffrey were killed the same way? Forced to commit suicide because of this "Misfortune Box"?'

'It *does* tie in, Jim,' Rafferty said. 'The stolen photos start to make sense if this is true.'

'*And* the graveyard desecrations in Croydon,' Cath added.

'So, who's responsible? The parents of the abused kids?' Talbot wanted to know.

'That's what *you're* supposed to find out, isn't it?' Cath said, challengingly.

'Don't tell me my fucking job, Reed,' Talbot snapped. He glared at her for a second then turned his attention back to Shanine. 'This box, how big is it?'

She held her hands about six inches apart.

'They seal it with black wax,' she told him.

Talbot eyed her suspiciously.

'What do you get out of this?' he said, quietly. 'What difference does it make to you what happened to those three men? Or what happens to *her*?' He nodded in Cath's direction.

'I just want my child to be safe.'

'You said that the members of the group were frightened of what would happen to them if they rebelled, if they spoke out against the others. Aren't *you* scared?'

'I told you I was. That's why I ran,' Shanine insisted. 'But I'm more frightened for my child. I won't let them take this one, too.'

'What if they've worked this Death Hex on you?' the DI said.

'They might have. But they're more likely to come looking for me.'

'Why?'

'To punish me.'

'Why not just kill you?' the DI demanded. 'If they're that powerful it should be easy.'

'They'd want to make me suffer for betraying them, and they'd want my baby,' Shanine told him. 'They wouldn't kill me.'

'How can you be so sure?' Talbot said.

'Because I ran away once before, not long after my boyfriend was killed,' she told him. 'They found me. They'll probably find me this time, too.'

'What did they do to you last time?' Talbot asked.

Shanine looked at Cath and the journalist saw tears in her eyes.

'Well, come on, tell me,' the DI persisted. 'Make me believe that all this isn't just bullshit.'

Shanine stood up, tugging at the buttons of her shirt, dragging it open.

Talbot gritted his teeth, his eyes fixed on her torso, her breasts.

'Jesus Christ,' murmured Rafferty, his gaze also riveted on the young woman.

'Is that enough for you?' said Shanine, defiantly, a solitary tear rolling down her cheek.

The flesh from her collar bone as far down as her navel was criss-crossed by scars.

There were several darker marks around her breasts, which Talbot recognised as burns.

Shanine shrugged off her shirt and turned around slowly, and Talbot saw that her back was in an even worse condition.

There was a mark between her shoulder blades, visible through the maze of weals and scars. Darker.

It looked like an A enclosed in a circle. The sign usually associated with Anarchy.

It took him only a second to realise it was a brand.

'There're others if you want to look,' she said, undoing her jeans.

Talbot shook his head, reached for the young woman's top and handed it back to her.

'Don't you want to know which ones were done with knives and which ones were done with whips?' she said, angrily.

The marks on her belly were even more prominent, great red welts which seemed to glisten on the swollen flesh.

'Get dressed,' Talbot said, quietly.

She pulled the top back on.

Rafferty looked across at his superior, who met his

355

gaze and held it for a moment before leaning back in his chair.

'Just assuming this shit about these Misfortune Boxes is true,' he said, finally. 'How long would it take this . . . *spell* to work?'

'Two or three days, maybe longer,' Shanine informed him. 'Not more than a week.'

'Parriam, Hyde and Jeffrey all died within a week of their photos being stolen,' Rafferty offered.

'So that leaves you two days to find this box, Reed,' the DI murmured. 'Otherwise it looks like you might be joining them.'

'Where do we start looking?' Cath responded.

'It'll be hidden somewhere near your house,' Shanine told her.

'Get men round to the houses of the three dead men, search the gardens of their places and the houses close by. Use fucking JCBs if you have to. But find those boxes,' Talbot said to his colleague.

'What about me?' Cath asked, her face pale.

'You'd better hope that all this *is* shit,' he said, flatly.

'They usually try to work the Hex to coincide with one of the important days in the satanic calendar,' Shanine offered.

'Like what?' Cath asked.

'Candlemas, that's February the second,' Shanine told her. 'Or the summer or winter solstice. Some groups even use the High Priest's birthday as a festival.'

'Are there any dates coming up?' Rafferty asked.

'Beltaine. Walpurgis night. April the thirtieth,' Shanine informed him.

'That's two days from now,' the DS said, looking at his colleague.

Talbot was looking intently at Shanine.

'How do we stop the Hex?' Cath asked.

'It'll come into force at midnight on the thirtieth,' Shanine told her. 'You've got to find the Misfortune Box before then. You *must* find that box and destroy it.'

Eighty-five

Frank Reed held the piece of paper before him.

Just a simple piece of paper.

A4 size.

The envelope which he'd taken it from moments earlier lay on the kitchen table close to his elbow, close to the mug of lukewarm coffee.

He'd read and re-read the words on the paper.

Tears were running steadily down his cheeks.

Throw it away.

He put it down on the table, smoothing out the creases.

Burn it. Burn the envelope too.

Two other envelopes were in front of him, the single sheets of paper they contained also laid out for inspection.

All the notes were handwritten but the graphology was different. Three different hands had penned these notes.

One of the envelopes bore a Hackney postmark, the others nothing at all. Not even a stamp. They had obviously been pushed through his letterbox by hand.

But from where? From whom?

It didn't seem to matter that much. All that mattered was that they were here.

One was written on pink notepaper bearing a printed rose in one corner. The type of notepaper usually used for 'Thank you' notes. The type friends would use to correspond. The sort women might use.

Perhaps this note had been written by a woman.

Maybe they *all* had.

The only thing missing was the scent of perfume, Reed mused, wiping the tears from his cheeks.

All the notes were short, one of them only a few words, but what mattered was that someone had taken the time to write them and, more importantly, to deliver them.

He looked at each in turn.

At the pink notepaper with its rose in one corner.

At the words it bore.

I can scarcely disguise my disgust for your actions. A man in your position should be ashamed.

You are a disgrace to your profession and to your kind. I will pray for your daughter.

The second letter was written on plain paper, but the words were remarkably straight. Reed could only imagine that the writer had used a lined sheet, placed beneath the plain one in order to keep the spaces between the lines uniform.

You deserve to die for what you've done.
You sick bastard. If I see you in the street
I'll spit in your filthy face.
You scum.
If you go near my lad I'll kill you.
That's a promise.

The last letter (two words . . . it hardly constituted a letter, did it?) was written on a single piece of bonded typing paper.

He could see the watermark in the paper, even the make.

Conqueror paper.

Reed looked at the words.

He felt warm tears flowing down his cheeks once again and this time he made no attempt to stem the flood. Instead, through misted eyes he fixed his gaze on the two words which stood out so starkly from the almost blinding whiteness of the paper.

CHILD
MOLESTER

Frank Reed wept as he'd never wept in his life.

Eighty-six

'We can't do that, Mr Talbot,' said the voice on the other end of the phone. 'Without the necessary care your mother could die within hours of leaving the hospital.'

'You said she wasn't going to make it through last night, but she did,' Talbot snapped. 'I want her home with me.'

There, it's said.

'I can't authorise that.'

'She's my mother,' the DI rasped.

'She's my patient at St Ann's, I won't take responsibility for her once she leaves the hospital.'

'No one's asking you to. If she wants to die at home, then let her. At least give her that much dignity.'

'I can't authorise it.'

Talbot gripped the phone tightly, trying to control his temper.

If she comes home she dies. End of story.

'I realise how painful this is for you, Mr Talbot, but if you insist on taking your mother home then she'll die.'

'She'll die anyway,' Talbot said, quietly.

He could think of nothing else to say.

'Can't you do it for her sake?' he asked, finally.

For *her* sake? Or for *yours*?

Guilt pricking a little too sharply this time, is it?

'Perhaps we should talk about this when you come in later,' the doctor offered.

Talbot didn't answer. He merely put down the phone.

The DI ran a hand through his hair and sat back in his chair.

You gave up too easily. You should have insisted.

'Jesus,' he murmured, exhaling deeply, wearily.

What next? Wait for the phone call telling him it was all over.

His thoughts were interrupted by a knock on the door, then Rafferty walked in without waiting for an invitation.

Talbot looked up at him, gaze momentarily blank, then he seemed to collect his thoughts.

'Is the girl OK?' he asked.

'I've got her downstairs in protective custody,' Rafferty told him. 'She's got a TV set, a bed and plenty of food, one of the WPCs is with her. She's fine.'

Talbot nodded and got to his feet.

'Did you order searches of the houses and grounds around Parriam's, Hyde's and Jeffrey's places?'

'Sorted,' said the DS, nodding. 'Where do you want to start?'

'Let's see what Macpherson turned up when he interviewed the parents of those kids.'

As the two men made their way down the corridor, Rafferty looked at his colleague. 'What if it does turn out to be true, Jim?' he said.

'Witchcraft?' The DI shook his head. 'It's bullshit,' he murmured.

Rafferty noticed that some of the conviction had gone from his voice.

*

'Frank!'

He heard her call his name, but he didn't answer.

Even when she banged on the door, Frank Reed didn't stir. He continued to sit at the kitchen table, the three letters still laid out before him, the whiskey bottle close by.

She called again, then there was silence.

The phone rang. He managed a wan smile.

She was calling him on her mobile.

Standing outside his front door, she was holding her phone and calling his number.

The phone continued to ring.

Catherine Reed listened to the tone impatiently.

He *had* to be inside.

Where else would he be?

She pressed the End button on the phone and bent down, peering through the letterbox into the hall beyond.

'Frank,' she called again through the small aperture. Still no answer.

Frank Reed got to his feet and stole into the sitting room, where he slumped onto the sofa and closed his eyes.

A second later he heard the letterbox clang shut, closely followed by the sound of Cath's receding footsteps.

He was alone again.

God, it felt so good.

As the warm water splashed her body, spurting from the shower head, Shanine Connor turned her face towards the spray. Water ran in rivulets across her skin, her hair.

Her scars.

The WPC sat outside the room while she washed away the accumulated filth of her time on the streets of London.

What would happen to her when all this was over she had no idea.

If it ever *was* over.

But, for now, she was safe. As safe as she was likely to be, anyway, and warmer than she'd been for a while.

She glanced down at her feet, at the soap suds and grime which were flowing down the plughole.

It was as if some outer skin was being washed away.

Shanine felt the swell of her belly, running both hands across the skin.

As she looked down she saw more scars on the insides of her thighs and knees. There were some on her buttocks too.

The ones she had not shown to Talbot.

Reminders.

She knew that if they found her now there would be fresh ones to join those which already covered her skin.

Shanine had told Talbot that they would not kill her but, as she stood beneath that cleansing spray, she realised that the child was their only concern.

Her betrayal had left them no choice.

She would have to die.

And they would still take the child.

With her finger, she traced a path from her pubic hair to just above her navel.

That was how they would cut her to reach the child, rip her open if necessary.

What they would do before that she could only imagine.

Even beneath the warm shower spray, she shuddered.

Eighty-seven

Talbot got to his feet, pacing the room slowly, one hand rubbing his stubbled cheek.

'No physical evidence at all,' he said, incredulously. 'Are you fucking serious, Mac?'

DI Gordon Macpherson shrugged.

'Twenty-three houses raided, seventeen kids taken into care, every single one of them examined and interviewed. Seven, no, sorry, *nine* of them. Nine. Nine of those kids exhibiting signs of physical abuse, enough porn and dodgy videos seized to start a fucking mail order business, and you're telling me you haven't got enough physical evidence for one single conviction?' Talbot raged. 'What did the parents say? What did you ask them for Christ's sake "Did you molest your kids?" "No." "OK, then off you go." What the fuck were you doing?'

'Don't come down here throwing your fucking weight around, Jim,' snapped Macpherson. 'What's wrong, do you reckon you could have done better?'

'On the amount of evidence we had piled up it had occurred to me.'

'We had medical reports on those injured kids: there was nothing to suggest that any of the physical damage was inflicted by the parents,' Macpherson told him. 'Call the medical examiner if you don't believe me. What did you want me to do, change the geezer's report because it doesn't fit in with what *you* want?'

'So *who* abused them, if the parents didn't?' Talbot challenged. 'How did they get to that warehouse? How come all the kids' statements were virtually the same?'

'A week ago you were the one saying it was all because of the videos they'd been watching, that they all had overactive imaginations. Make up your fucking mind.'

'They're going to walk,' said Talbot. 'Every fucking one of them. They'll let this die down, then in six months' or a year's time, the same thing will happen again. More kids will be hurt, maybe even killed.'

'There was nothing we could do, Jim,' Macpherson told him. 'I wanted someone nailed for this abuse business as much as you did, but we can't prove anything against the parents. I interviewed most of them myself: some of them were as frightened as the kids.'

'Frightened of what?'

'That their kids were going to be taken away from them when they hadn't even done anything.'

'You told me yourself that there was a child abuse ring in operation,' Talbot reminded his colleague.

'I was wrong.'

'No you weren't.'

'Then where's the fucking evidence?' Macpherson shouted.

'Nine physically injured kids, seventeen statements. Jesus Christ, even Hackney Council believed there was something going on. Something bad enough to take seventeen kids into care.'

'They're releasing the kids back to their parents tomorrow,' said Macpherson.

Talbot stared at him. 'I don't believe this,' he said, quietly.

'The whole case has collapsed around our fucking ears, Jim,' Macpherson said, irritably. 'There's nothing left.'

'Somewhere out there are the real abusers,' said Talbot. 'If those parents didn't commit the acts themselves, they know who did.'

'And what do you propose we do? Pull them all back in for questioning?'

'If necessary.'

'Get real, Jim,' Macpherson said, dismissively. 'It's over. Face it.'

'It's not over for those kids.'

A heavy silence descended.

DS Rafferty glanced at the other two men in the room.

Talbot was still pacing agitatedly back and forth.

Macpherson reached for a cigarette and lit up, blowing out a long stream of smoke.

'The girl told us that kids are sometimes bought by these abusers, bought from the parents,' Rafferty offered, finally.

'What girl?' Macpherson wanted to know.

Talbot explained briefly about Shanine Connor.

'That might be the case with *these* kids,' Rafferty continued. 'The parents might not have inflicted the damage themselves but they might know who did.'

Macpherson sat forward in his seat.

'Let me get this straight,' he said. 'You've got some bird in protective custody who reckons she's a witch?'

Talbot nodded.

'And you're taking the piss out of *me*?' Macpherson snapped.

'I was more sceptical than you, Mac,' Talbot told him. 'She's very convincing.'

'She must be. What else did she tell you? Your fortune? What's going to win the three-thirty at Haydock?'

'She told us how these abuse groups operate,' said Talbot.

'The other witches?' Macpherson chuckled.

'Fuck you, Mac,' Talbot snapped. 'I want those parents brought in and questioned again.'

'No,' Macpherson said, defiantly.

'Mac, I'm *telling* you.'

'You're telling me nothing, Jim,' the older man exploded. 'This isn't even your fucking case. It never was. Why the hell does it mean so much to you, eh? It's over. We tried, there's nothing more we can do. End of story. I'm as sorry about it as you are, but we're fucked. No evidence, no case.'

Talbot glared at his companion.

'You let them slip through, Mac,' the DI said quietly.

'Fuck off, Jim. Just go, will you?'

Talbot headed towards the door, Rafferty close behind him.

The DI paused, prepared to say something else, then wrenched open the office door and walked out.

In the corridor beyond, Rafferty had to quicken his pace to keep up with his colleague.

'Where to now?' he asked.

'Hackney Social Services.'

Eighty-eight

Every shred of common sense told Catherine Reed that what she was doing was insane.

And yet, common sense seemed to have deserted her.

She had been through her flat slowly and carefully, through every drawer, cupboard and container.

Searching.

She had removed books from their shelves and checked behind them. She had even checked inside shoe boxes in her wardrobe. The Misfortune Box was nowhere to be found.

Not that she even knew what she was looking for.

Shanine Connor had described it as being about six inches long, rectangular and more than likely made of hardwood.

Like a small coffin, she'd said. The similarity seemed appallingly apt.

It would be placed near the victim's home.

Cath looked around her, satisfied after her exhaustive search that the box wasn't hidden within the flat itself.

But where else?

How far away could it be?

In one of the other flats perhaps?

What was she to do, knock on each door, request entry and permission to search the dwellings of the other residents?

And when they asked her reasons?

'A Death Hex has been placed upon me by some practitioners of Black Magic.'

Great.

'Come in,' they would say. 'Make yourself at home while we phone the nearest asylum.'

Cath locked her flat door behind her and stood in the corridor for a moment, then headed down towards the lift.

She rode the car to the ground floor and the doors slid open.

She hesitated a moment, then glanced at the panel of buttons inside the lift.

There were the numbers designating floors. A G for ground, and then another button.

She pressed the last button and the lift descended once again.

When it bumped to a halt in the basement there was a moment's hesitation before the doors opened. When they did Cath was surprised that the smell which swept into the lift wasn't that of damp and decay but of wet paint.

She stepped out of the lift, the smell strong in her nostrils. So strong in fact it made her wince.

The doors closed behind her and she looked up at the lighted panel to see that the lift was rising again, back towards the first floor.

The basement was huge and surprisingly well lit.

She couldn't remember having been down here more than twice since she had moved in.

The residents were allowed to use the cavernous area for storage if necessary, but Cath had forgone that option. Others she noticed, had not.

The basement wasn't crowded, but there were over a dozen large chests, some marked with the numbers of the flats upstairs, dotted around gathering dust. There were cupboards on the walls too, also for storage.

In the centre of the room was a boiler, a massive metallic monolith which, she reasoned, at one time had perhaps provided heat for the entire building. It was no longer functional, the pipes leading from it along the ceiling now cold. It stood like some lifeless heart, the thick pipes that had once carried heat from it resembling wasted useless, arteries.

As Cath moved deeper into the basement the smell of paint grew stronger, closing around her.

She realised it was the wall closest to her that had been re-covered in a dark, iron-grey coat of emulsion.

The basement was lit by two large banks of fluorescents and, as Cath moved through it, she could hear them fizzing and buzzing above her like predatory insects. One flickered and she glanced up at it, seeing the long white tube flash quickly on and off, then glow brightly once again.

She crossed to the cupboards closest to her and began pulling them open.

The first two were empty.

As she opened the third a large, bloated spider scuttled across one of the shelves.

Cath gasped as the hairy creature disappeared into a funnelled web at the back of the wooden storage unit.

She checked several others and found little inside except a few old newspapers and magazines. One or two contained some yellowing paperbacks. There was even a set of copper pans in one, unusable because the handles were missing.

Cath moved towards the boxes, the tea-chests stacked in places like huge wooden housebricks.

She peered inside the first and saw that it was half full of children's clothes.

The journalist reached inside, fumbling around, trying to find the box she sought.

About six inches long, wooden. Rectangular.

Nothing.

She moved to the next.

And the next.

There were several board games inside. Monopoly. Cluedo. Others she hadn't seen before, the boxes of most were yellowed and ripped.

At the very bottom was a small wooden box.

About six inches long.

Rectangular.

Cath swallowed hard and reached for it.

She could feel her heart thudding hard against her ribs as she inspected the box.

It was sealed with black masking tape.

She tugged at it with her nails, cursing when one broke but she continued to pull at the tape until she finally freed the lid.

It slid back easily.

There was a number of chess pieces inside.

'Jesus,' breathed Cath, dropping the box.

As she raised a hand to push back a strand of hair she noticed that her hand was shaking.

She looked around relieved.

The furnace stared back at her, its rusty door closed.

Cath sucked in a deep breath then took a step towards it.

*

Talbot had sat in virtual silence since he and Rafferty had left Theobald's Road Police Station.

The traffic was heavy, their progress slow.

There'd been an accident in Old Street.

Talbot tapped agitatedly on the side window, glancing across irritably as Rafferty lit up another cigarette.

'At least wind down the fucking window,' hissed the DI, waving his hand in the air to dissipate the smoke.

Rafferty was in the process of doing so when the two-way burst into life. 'Puma Three, come in. Over.'

Rafferty reached for the radio.

'Puma Three receiving. What is it? Over.'

'Bill, this is Penhallow. We've found something. Over,' the DC informed him.

Talbot looked across.

'Where are you, Colin? Over,' Rafferty replied.

'In the garden of Neil Parriam's place. If I were you I'd get here as quick as you can. Over.'

Talbot took the radio from him.

'This is Talbot. What have you found? Over.'

'It's easier if you come and look, guv. Just one thing. Do you want us to open this now or wait until you get here? Over.'

'Open what? Over.'

'We've found the box.'

Eighty-nine

Cath tugged at the furnace door, finding, as she had expected, that it was wedged shut.

372

A latch sealed it and, by the look of it, whoever had been painting down in the basement had given the furnace a coat of emulsion too. It looked as if they'd painted over the latch, making it impossible to move by hand.

Cath pressed the tip of her finger tentatively to the metal, ensuring that it wasn't wet. Seeing that it wasn't, she tried to release the catch, but her efforts proved useless.

She glanced around and saw another large box close by. It was filled with tins of paint, rags, brushes and a bottle of clear liquid which she guessed was turps.

Cath rummaged in the box and found a thick piece of wood, which she guessed had been used to stir the paint.

It might just do the job.

She slid the thick wood between the latch and furnace door and levered the catch upwards.

For a long time it resisted her efforts then, finally, paint flaked off and the latch gave way.

Cath tossed the piece of wood aside and pulled at the furnace door.

It opened with a loud creak, which echoed around the large basement.

A chill breeze seemed to blow from the open mouth of the furnace, like cold air from some yawning set of metal jaws.

The furnace was clean inside. No ashes left over from the days when it had been fully functional. Cath reached for her lighter and flicked it on, squinting into the darkness beyond.

It was huge. Large enough to allow her passage if she wished.

The door might be a tight squeeze but, once inside, she could see that the furnace was large enough to allow her to stand upright. She could see the outlet pipes leading off from the centre.

Could the box be hidden in one of those?

She paused for a moment.

Who would bother to clamber through a furnace door four feet square to secrete the Misfortune Box inside?

Someone who wanted her dead.

She paused a moment, flicked off the lighter. It was growing hot in her hand.

Inside the furnace?

Cath sucked in a deep breath. A breath tinged with the smell of paint. Then, cautiously, she ducked through the furnace door into the blackness beyond.

She flicked on the lighter once more and checked the pipe closest to her.

Nothing.

And the next.

Empty but for a few ashes at the bottom.

The air inside was stale, acrid.

She coughed, the sound reverberating around her.

The open door offered her a little extra light but she still needed to use the lighter to peer into the darker recesses of the pipes leading off in so many directions from this central point.

Cath checked a couple more.

Both were empty.

The lighter grew hot in her hand again and she flicked it off for a second.

The furnace door swung shut with a dull clang.

She was plunged into darkness so impenetrable it was almost palpable.

Cath couldn't see a hand in front of her.

She flicked wildly at the lighter.

All she saw in the thick gloom were sparks.

It wouldn't light.

She pushed it back into her pocket and pushed at the door.

It was stuck fast.

Cath felt sudden uncontrollable fear grip her. It raced through her veins like iced water. She pushed harder against the door.

Jesus, what if the catch had dropped back into place?

She banged on the door, but still it wouldn't budge.

The dank smell inside the furnace was beginning to clog in her nostrils now. She was finding it difficult to breathe.

She took a step back and aimed a kick at the door but, in the blackness she overbalanced and went sprawling.

Cath felt something hard and gritty beneath her hands, something which dug into her palms.

Cinders?

She kicked out at the door again, frantic now.

Her second blow sent the door flying open.

She was on her haunches in seconds, pulling herself from the maw like a child desperate to escape the steel womb.

She scrambled out of the cold furnace and dropped to her knees outside, sucking in deep breaths, not caring that the air was thick with the acrid smell of paint. She could even taste it at the back of her throat.

She slammed the furnace door shut and dropped the catch.

Her jeans and shirt were covered in black smudges, soot deposits which also stained her palms.

Cath got to her feet slowly, her breath still coming in gasps, her gaze fixed on the furnace door.

How had it closed?

A gust of wind perhaps.

From where?

She ran a dirty hand through her hair.

Come on, get a grip of yourself. Your imagination's running riot.

She looked at the furnace door, then around the basement.

Cath was shaking.

Where was that fucking box?

She knew there was only one person who could help her now.

Ninety

Her clothes had been washed, her hair shampooed and blow-dried. She smelled of soap.

She smelled clean.

Talbot glanced at Shanine Connor and thought what a pretty girl she was.

Aware of his gaze upon her she looked at him and managed a small smile but the DI merely nodded towards the three objects on the worktop before them.

Three boxes.

Each one about six inches long, half that in width.

Hardwood.

The lids had been removed, the contents placed beside them, each separate piece tagged by the pathology department.

The head of that department now stood beside the DI, his eyes also fixed on the boxes and their contents.

Phillip Barclay rubbed his chin thoughtfully.

DS William Rafferty prepared to light up a cigarette but remembered the large NO SMOKING sign opposite him. He popped the cigarette into his mouth and flicked at the filter with his tongue.

'Those are the Misfortune Boxes,' Shanine said, softly.

'Each one was found in the garden of each of the dead men,' Talbot said. 'Any prints off any of them, Phil?'

'None,' Barclay told him. 'Whoever put them there wore smooth gloves.' The pathologist picked up a pair of tweezers and, using them with great care he touched the contents of each box, one object at a time.

Three thorns, possibly from a rose bush. Some earth, now dried. A cranefly which looked as dry as the earth itself and a small photo of Neil Parriam.

The other boxes contained exactly the same, apart from the second which had held a picture of Peter Hyde and the third which had borne a photo of Craig Jeffrey.

'It's hard to believe,' said Barclay, softly.

Talbot looked at the pathologist, then at Shanine.

'Why bury them in the gardens?' he asked.

'They're always buried close to the victim's home.'

'Anything else, Phil?' Talbot wanted to know.

'A strand of hair in the second box, possibly left by whoever put it there. A speck of dried blood on the third, but not enough to type.'

'Were they well hidden?' Talbot enquired.

'No more than six inches below the surface in all three cases,' said Rafferty. 'But who the hell would think to look for something like this, anyway? Unless the three men knew these boxes were hidden in their gardens, why the hell would they go looking?'

'That's their strength,' said Shanine. 'No one believes.'

All eyes turned towards her.

'Ignorance is the greatest ally,' she continued. 'They said that to me once. No one believed in what they did, no one understood. As long as they're treated as a joke they're safe.'

'Do you think the group *you* ran from could have anything to do with the ones who killed Parriam and the others?' asked Talbot.

'They might be linked,' Shanine said. 'Lots of the groups are. Some of them exchange things.' Her voice faded.

'Like what?' Talbot demanded.

'During some of the orgies or when kids were being used, the ceremonies were videotaped or pictures of the kids were taken,' she told him. 'They were sometimes passed around between groups and the kids were told that if they let anyone know what they'd seen then their families would be shown the films or pictures. Some of the tapes were sold too.'

'To whom?' Rafferty asked.

'Paedophiles. Porn merchants,' she said, eyes fixed on the boxes.

'I still think it's crazy,' Talbot muttered. 'We're supposed to believe that three blokes topped themselves because of these things?' He jabbed a finger in the direction of the boxes.

'I don't think we've got much choice other than to believe now, Jim,' Rafferty echoed, still chewing the unlit cigarette filter.

'And if you don't find the next box before midnight

tonight there'll be another death – that journalist,' Shanine offered.

A heavy silence descended.

It was broken by the ringing of the phone.

Barclay ambled over and picked it up.

'Jesus Christ,' hissed Talbot. 'So many fucking leads but nothing to link them, not one concrete piece of evidence.' He exhaled deeply. Angrily. 'Three suicides that could be witchcraft murders; all three men are involved on a building project which just happens to involve a warehouse supposedly used as a meeting place for a ring of child abusers and satanists. Seventeen kids taken into care, some showing signs of physical abuse, some saying they were raped by the Devil. Those same kids are now being released back to the families we suspect did the damage to them because we can't prove otherwise. Cemetery desecrations in Croydon and a pregnant tart who thinks she's a witch who's running to stop her kid being sacrificed.' He looked at Shanine and Rafferty. 'Would one of *you* like to tell me what the fuck is going on because I've just about given up.' He held out a hand to Rafferty. 'Give me a fucking cigarette.'

The DS handed his boss the packet of cigarettes and the lighter, watching as he lit up and inhaled deeply. He looked at the NO SMOKING sign and blew out a stream of smoke in that direction. 'Fuck it,' he muttered.

Barclay turned towards him, one hand over the mouthpiece of the phone.

'Jim, it's for you,' said the pathologist.

Talbot looked puzzled.

'She says it's urgent,' Barclay continued, holding out the phone towards the DI. 'She insists she's a journalist. Catherine Reed. She sounds frightened.'

Talbot took the receiver from him.

'Talbot,' he said.

'I can't find it,' Cath told him. 'I can't find the box.'

'We've been luckier. We found boxes at the homes of all three dead men.'

'So it *is* true? They were witchcraft killings?'

Talbot didn't answer.

'Talbot, if they killed those other three men then they're going to kill me,' Cath said anxiously.

'Unless you find that box,' he reminded her.

'Let me help her,' Shanine Connor offered.

Talbot looked at the young woman, then at Rafferty, who nodded almost imperceptibly.

'Where are you?' Talbot asked.

Cath told him.

'Just sit tight,' the DI said. 'There'll be someone there as quickly as possible.'

Cath sat on the edge of her chair looking down at the phone. Should she call Phil?

He was in Glasgow. A light aircraft carrying sixteen passengers including the French Ambassador had gone down just outside the city, killing all those on board. Terrorism was suspected.

Cross wasn't expected back until the following day.

He didn't even know what was going on.

Didn't even know her life was in danger.

If it was.

She hesitated a second, then dialled her brother's number. There was no answer. Cath put down the receiver and waited.

Ninety-one

The summons had arrived in an official-looking brown envelope.

Summons.

Frank Reed looked at the headed notepaper and read the word over and over again.

So, at last, the waiting was over.

He was to appear at Hackney Magistrates Court in three days time for a preliminary hearing. After that a decision would be made on whether or not his case went to trial.

What fucking case?

The alleged abuse of his own daughter?

He wanted to shout and scream at the top of his voice, to give vent to the rage and frustration he felt building inside him. A pain which had grown steadily over the last few days, swelling and expanding until he thought the pressure would erupt within him, would destroy him.

Thoughts and emotions whirled around inside his head, too numerous to focus on, too jumbled to consider.

He felt dizzy.

Was there one single word to describe how he felt? One solitary exhortation to express his desolation at the enormity of this situation he faced.

He sat at the kitchen table, staring at the summons, his fingers curled into fists.

At least at the hearing they would be forced to consider *his* feelings, *his* views.

There shouldn't even be a hearing.

They would hear what he had to say and they would understand.

And if they didn't?

Reed found a vision forcing itself into his already confused mind. A man standing in the dock, in court, facing a jury.

Him.

Jesus, the thought was too much to bear and he tried to push it aside, but it persisted.

He swallowed hard, fear now creeping in amongst his other emotions. It glided easily in beside the anger and the pain.

He got to his feet and wandered through into the sitting room, snatching up the summons as he went.

As he reached for the phone he sucked in a couple of deep breaths, trying to control his rage then, satisfied it was under control, he dialled.

And waited.

The voice at the other end wasn't the one he'd expected to hear.

'Can I speak to Ellen Reed, please?' he said, falteringly.

The voice on the other end told him she wasn't in that morning.

'Thank you, I'll try later . . .'

The voice told him that Ellen had taken a couple of days off work.

He put down the phone and dialled another number.

It rang for what seemed like an eternity but the answering machine didn't kick in so he assumed some-one was there.

382

A second later he was proved right.

He recognised Ellen's voice and, overcome with conflicting emotions, he found it impossible to speak.

When she spoke again it seemed to break the spell.

'Ellen. It's me,' he said, trying to keep his voice low.

'I've got nothing to say to you,' she snapped.

'It didn't have to come to this. Court. What are you trying to do to me?'

'I'm doing this for Becky, not you.'

'You're doing it for yourself,' he snarled.

'Goodbye, Frank,' Ellen said, flatly.

'No wait,' he said, imploringly. 'Listen to me, Ellen. All we had to do was talk. It didn't have to go this far. It's not too late. You can stop these court proceedings: you started them.'

'Afraid of what they'll find out, Frank? Frightened they might uncover the truth?'

He gripped the receiver tightly, his jaw clenched.

He wanted to bellow at her and the effort of restraining himself was almost too much.

'I don't want you near our daughter again,' Ellen told him. 'This court case will make sure she's kept away from you.'

'You don't have the right—'

'I have every right after what you did to her,' Ellen snapped.

'I did nothing to her,' he roared, desperately. 'Speak to her. Ask her. She'll tell you nothing happened.'

'*She* says it did.'

'She's saying what you tell her to say, you and that bastard Ward.'

'Don't bring Jonathan into this.'

'He's a part of it, he has been since the beginning.'

'I love him, Frank, and I love Becky, that's why I'm protecting her from you.'

'You bitch!' he bellowed.

'See you in court,' she said, calmly, and hung up.

'No!' He screamed the word, his rage uncontrollable now.

Reed snatched up the phone and hurled it across the room with such force that it cracked in three places, the wire torn from the wall.

'Fucking bitch!' he yelled, then the anger seemed to drain from him. 'Fucking bitch.' It was replaced by that growing sense of desolation.

He was fighting back tears now, but he sucked in a deep breath.

She wasn't going to get away with this.

If only he could see her, speak to her.

Reason with her.

No, it was too late for that. Reed looked across at the shattered remains of the phone, the lead hanging from the wall like some ruptured umbilical cord.

There was to be no reasoning.

No talking.

He knew there was only one option left.

The time had come.

Ninety-two

There was a fairly large expanse of well-manicured grass at the rear of the flats in Biscay Road. The lawn was edged on three sides by flower beds and shrubs, all of which were in bloom. The entire colourful display was enclosed by high privet hedges. At two corners there were strategically placed weeping willows. Here and there leaves tumbled across the grass like green confetti.

It looked delightful, but the seven individuals who stood in the centre of the lawn seemed unconcerned by the array of colour before them, unimpressed by the peacefulness of the scene.

Three uniformed constables stood stiffly alongside the other four visitors.

'The box is here somewhere,' said Shanine Connor, glancing around.

Talbot shook his head almost imperceptibly. 'You're sure it's not inside the building?' he asked Cath.

'I looked.'

'In every room, in every flat?' the DI asked.

'The other three boxes were found in the victims' gardens, Jim,' Rafferty offered.

Cath shuddered involuntarily at the word victim.

'All right,' Talbot said. 'Get on with it.'

The three uniformed men split up, one moving to each side of the garden.

Each was equipped with a spade.

Talbot looked on as they began to dig, turning the earth as carefully as questing archaeologists anxious not to disturb some priceless hidden relic.

The spades went no deeper than eight or nine inches each time.

Rafferty wandered towards the bottom of the garden, standing close to one of the uniformed men as he dug.

The constable worked his way along the border,

turning earth, gazing down to inspect anything he may have unearthed.

Rafferty saw worms writhing in the wet soil, one of them sliced in two by the blade of the shovel.

Shanine Connor moved towards the closest hedge and kneeled beside the privet perimeter, occasionally lifting the leaves of plants to look for any signs of disturbed earth.

Cath did the same thing at the base of one tree, urging the constable there to dig around the willow. He nodded and turned more of the damp soil, muttering to himself as it clung defiantly to the spade.

He stopped for a moment, banging the blade against the small tree, clods falling from the implement.

When he dug again he struck something hard.

He kneeled, using his hands to pull away the remaining soil.

Whatever he'd hit was close to the surface.

Cath moved nearer, her heart pounding.

It was a tree root.

She sighed.

The constable continued with his task, moving a few more inches to his right.

'What if it's buried deeper than the others were?' Rafferty said, rejoining Talbot who was still standing in the centre of the lawn looking around him as helplessly as a lost child in a supermarket.

'Then *we* dig deeper,' the DI replied.

'It still might not be here,' Cath said, agitatedly.

'Then where do *you* suggest we look?' the DI snapped. 'This is for your benefit, try being grateful.'

Cath was about to say something when she heard Shanine Connor's voice behind her.

Distracted.

'What's that?' said the younger woman.

Cath, Talbot and Rafferty turned to see her pointing through a gap in the hedge.

She was motioning across the road towards a small children's playground.

It was protected by a line of low conifers and a black-painted iron fence. Shanine could see a small girl clambering to the top of a slide. Another smaller boy was hauling himself over a climbing frame. On a bench near by, a woman watched them vigilantly, calling to them every now and then.

Sounds of laughter could be heard drifting on the air.

'We should look there too,' Shanine said, her eyes still fixed on the children. As she watched she touched her own swollen belly.

Soon.

'You said the box would be buried in the garden,' Talbot snapped.

'I said it would be close to the victim's home,' Shanine repeated.

Cath shuddered.

That word again.

'That's close,' Shanine continued, jabbing a finger towards the playground.

'You three stay here,' Talbot said to the uniformed men. 'Keep digging. If you find anything, come and get me.'

Cath and Shanine were already heading out of the garden, then hurrying across the street towards the playground.

Talbot and Rafferty followed.

The woman with the two children looked around in

bewilderment as Cath and Shanine entered the play-ground, the plain-clothes policemen only moments behind them.

Talbot saw the concern on her face and smiled what he hoped was a reassuring smile.

The children seemed uninterested in these new-comers: they played happily while the others wandered around them.

Cath crossed to a litter bin and peered in.

Empty.

Talbot sat on a swing and watched disinterestedly.

One of the children smiled at him and he smiled back.

Shanine pushed the leaves of a bush aside and dug at the earth with the toe of one trainer, disturbing the soil there.

Rafferty was doing something similar next to a newly planted tree.

The playground surface was woodchips, but the pathway surrounding it was concrete flagstones.

As he was taking in the scene around him, Talbot noticed that one of the flags was slightly raised, dark earth spilling from beneath it.

He stepped off the swing and crossed to the paving stone.

The rest of the path was flat, the stones flush.

The one he was peering down at looked as if it had been prised up.

He hooked his two hands beneath it and lifted, sur-prised at how easily the stone came free.

Watched by the woman on the bench, he flipped it over, gazing down at the dark earth beneath.

With his bare hands he began to scratch at the dirt like a dog in search of a bone.

It was a matter of seconds before his fingertips touched something cold.

Something wooden.

The others had seen what he was doing and wandered over to join him. Shanine kneeled beside him, pulling more of the earth away.

Rafferty moved closer to Cath as if to reassure her.

Talbot and Shanine pulled the final clods away.

The woman on the bench looked on in bewilderment.

The box was about four inches below the surface.

'Is that it?' Talbot asked.

Shanine Connor nodded slowly. 'Burn it,' she said, flatly. 'It's the only way to break the Hex.'

Talbot hesitated.

'Do it, for Christ's sake,' Cath urged.

The DI gripped the box in one powerful hand then brought it crashing down onto one of the paving stones.

The wood split, the lid came free.

The contents spilled out into view.

Three thorns. Some dried earth and a dead beetle.

The photo fluttered out, twisted right side up.

Half a photo.

The picture had been ripped in two down the middle.

'Oh my God,' murmured Cath.

She was staring at an image of her brother.

Frank Reed smiled back from the torn photograph.

'Why is Frank's picture in there?' she gasped.

'Is that part of the photo that was stolen from your flat?' Talbot asked.

Cath nodded. 'But why Frank?' she whispered, eyes riveted to the torn image.

'There's something else,' Talbot said, a note of

urgency in his voice. 'If your brother's half of that photo is in the box, who's got the part with *you* on it?'

Ninety-three

Frank Reed drew the razor slowly across his foamy cheek then rinsed it in the sink.

He splashed his face with water and gazed at the image that peered back from the bathroom mirror.

With the dark shadow of two days' accumulated stubble removed he looked better. Fresher.

Ready.

If you look like shit, you feel like shit.

He leaned closer to the mirror and stared into his bloodshot eyes. The lids were puffy through lack of sleep.

He splashed his face again, perhaps hoping he could wash away his tired, haggard features.

Reed towelled his face dry and wandered into the bedroom where his navy blue jacket and trousers were already laid out on the bed.

He'd pressed them before showering and shaving.

He wanted to look smart.

He wanted to prove to those who saw him that he was master of this situation.

You can fool them, but you can't fool yourself.

Standing before the full-length mirror, he slipped on a white shirt, pulled on his trousers, and stepped into a pair of shoes. Then he reached into the wardrobe for his tie. As he did so, he glanced to the other side of the cabinet, and his eyes narrowed.

When she'd walked out on him, Ellen had left a few things: only the odd item of clothing pushed into the back of the wardrobe, but a reminder.

A single white blouse hung there; beneath it a tattered pair of suede high heels, the toes scuffed and dirty.

He bent down and picked up the shoes, pulled the blouse from its hanger.

He dropped all three items into the wastebin in one corner of the room, then returned to the wardrobe to fasten his tie.

He checked himself in the mirror and was satisfied with what he saw.

Reed glanced at his watch.

He had time.

The drive would take him less than twenty minutes.

Becky didn't leave school for another thirty.

He would be there when she walked out of the front gate.

Waiting.

He walked back into the bathroom and ran a comb through his hair, then he strode back through the bedroom, where he gathered his car keys.

He wondered if Ellen was intending to pick up Becky from school.

Perhaps she'd send Ward to do it.

Fucking bastard.

He gritted his teeth at the thought of *his* daughter with another man. A man who dared to call himself her father now.

'I love him.'

Ellen's words echoed in Reed's mind. Discordant syllables.

He wondered when she had stopped loving *him*. What he'd done to drive her away.

It's not your fault. She chose to go. You're not to blame.

He went into the kitchen, glancing down at the summons which still lay on the table. Reed picked it up and slipped it into the inside pocket of his jacket.

He felt curiously calm. A serenity he'd not experienced for some time had settled over him. Even his anger seemed momentarily quelled.

Again he looked at his watch.

Becky would be leaving school soon. He must be there to see her.

Must be there when she walked from those gates.

Before Ellen or Ward.

He slid open one of the kitchen drawers and looked down at the contents.

He selected a knife with a three-inch blade, razor sharp.

Reed slid it into the pocket of his jacket, then pushed a handkerchief in on top of it.

Time to go.

Twenty-five minutes and Becky would be leaving school.

His timing should be perfect.

He headed for the front door.

Ninety-four

'There's no answer,' said Cath anxiously, the mobile phone gripped in her hand.

'We've got to warn him,' Shanine repeated.

Cath was already turning, hurrying towards the road. She had to go to Frank.

'Who would want to kill your brother?' Talbot asked.

'I haven't got a clue,' she gasped, pulling the keys of the Fiat from her pocket.

'What's his address?' Talbot snapped.

Cath told him.

'And a car? Make, registration?' he added.

She stopped in her tracks, flustered.

'Come on, for Christ's sake. Think,' the DI urged.

'Dark blue . . .' she faltered. 'Honda Civic.'

'The reg?' Talbot pressed.

'Jesus Christ, Talbot, how can I remember?'

'If you want him to stay alive you'd better remember,' the policeman snapped.

She held his stare for a moment, her mind spinning.

'F,' she said, chewing a nail, desperate to remember. 'F720 PPX. That's it. I'm sure. F720 PPX.'

The DI turned to Rafferty.

'Put out a call to any units near that address,' he instructed. 'And tell them I want that car traced, too.'

The DS nodded and hurried off to relay the information.

'You get to him now,' Talbot said to Cath. 'We can have men at his flat within ten minutes. Fuck knows what they're going to say to him when they get there, though.'

Cath managed a smile.

'Thanks, Talbot,' she said.

'Just doing my job.'

She nodded. Then she was gone.

Frank Reed sat behind the wheel of the Civic gazing into empty air.

Across the street two women were standing talking, one of them gently pushing a baby-buggy back and forth, occasionally looking down at its occupant.

A little girl about a year old, Reed guessed.

A beautiful child.

Like Becky was at that age.

As she *still* was.

He pulled the summons from his inside pocket and scanned it for the hundredth time that day.

The words and letters didn't miraculously change.

Things didn't get any better.

Summons.

He tossed it onto the passenger seat then started the engine, stepping on the accelerator a little too hard so the roar of the Civic caused the two women to look round at him.

He was aware of their stares but ignored it.

Reed stuck the car in gear and pulled away.

As he did he patted the pocket of his jacket and felt the knife there.

'There could be another box for you,' said Shanine, glancing across at Cath, who seemed more concerned with the car which was blocking her passage ahead.

She hit her hooter and swerved around the vehicle.

'There might be another Misfortune Box with—'

'I know that,' Cath snapped. 'All that matters now is that I get to Frank in time.'

She drove on.

Frank Reed parked the Civic across the road from the main entrance of the school and waited.

He shifted in his seat, rolling his neck gently.

There was pain beginning to nag at the base of his skull.

He looked at his watch, checked it against the dashboard clock.

Not long now.

Other cars were parked across the street, some close to his own. More parents preparing to meet their offspring, he assumed.

He scanned some of the faces seated in the stationary vehicles.

No sign of Ward or Ellen.

Again he felt the knife in his pocket.

Again he glanced down at the summons, still lying discarded on the passenger seat.

He paid no attention to the police car which cruised slowly past.

'Puma Three, come in. Over.'

Talbot snatched up the two-way as he heard the metallic voice crackle over the airwaves. 'Puma Three here. Over,' he responded.

'That dark blue Honda Civic you wanted traced,' the metallic voice said. 'One of the mobile units has clocked it.'

'Where?' Talbot demanded.

'Outside a school in Macklin Street, Camden. Over.'

Rafferty glanced across at his companion.

'Tell the officers on the scene to approach the driver. Over,' Talbot said. 'Do it now.'

Ninety-five

Frank Reed saw the first few children scurrying through the school gates and sat up excitedly in the driver's seat.

He turned slightly, eyes scanning the ever-increasing flow of children in blue uniforms, who were now flooding from the gates, some in groups, some in twos or singly.

There was still no sign of either Ellen or Ward.

He would be able to get to Becky first.

If only he could see her.

A number of the other children had already climbed into waiting cars, ushered in by their parents. Some of the vehicles were pulling away.

Heading home.

Home.

He looked across at the summons, the knot of muscles at the side of his jaw throbbing angrily.

He didn't even see the police car parked twenty or thirty yards behind him. Didn't notice the two uniformed men climb out and begin walking towards his car.

Becky emerged from the school gates with two of her friends, all three of them chattering and laughing.

God, she was so beautiful when she laughed.

His little girl.

The advancing policemen were less than fifteen yards from the car now.

Reed swallowed hard and gazed raptly at his daughter.

She was standing close to the school gates looking around.

Perhaps she expected someone to be there to pick her up.

The two constables were only ten yards away now.

Becky waved goodbye to one of her friends and stood chatting to the other who glanced at her watch, then looked up and spotted her mother. The woman had just pulled up close to the school entrance and Reed watched as the other girl hurried off and climbed into the car, waving to Becky as the vehicle pulled away.

She was alone now.

Waiting.

The two constables were within touching distance of Reed's car.

He spotted one in his wing mirror but he thought nothing of it.

His mind was focused on Becky.

He pulled the knife from his pocket.

She was alone there.

He took one final glance at the summons.

Did Becky understand what they were saying about him? he wondered. Did she understand the shame the accusations had brought? Could she ever realise the pain he was suffering?

He felt tears brimming in his eyes.

'I'm sorry, Becky,' he whispered.

The first constable reached the Civic in time to see the knife glinting in Reed's hand.

397

He was about to shout something to his companion when Reed lifted it higher.

His eyes never left Becky.

'I'm sorry,' he said again.

Then he pulled the blade hard across his throat.

'No!' roared one of the constables, making a dive for the driver's-side door but, as he tugged on the handle, he found it was locked.

Inside the car Reed felt fleeting moments of pain, barely noticeable, as the knife sliced effortlessly through the flesh and muscles of his neck, severing carotid and jugular vessels.

Blood exploded from the gaping wound, spattering both the windscreen and the side windows. Great crimson gouts ejaculated from the torn veins and arteries.

Reed dropped the knife.

He was dimly aware of a battering on the side window, of glass suddenly flying inwards, of hands grabbing for him.

It slipped away very quickly.

Blood was still spurting wildly from his gashed throat, but he sat upright in his seat, his body now jerking uncontrollably as the muscles contracted.

His vision dimmed, fuzzed, then cleared slightly.

When he looked slightly to one side, Becky was gone, glancing across at the commotion around a car she could not see into, wondering what those two policemen were doing.

He tasted blood in his mouth, felt it pouring over his lips.

His head lolled backwards against the top of the seat and the gaping laceration seemed to open further, yawning like some blood-choked mouth.

Reed was surprised how little pain he felt.

One of the constables had managed to open the driver's door by now and was reaching for him.

Through a haze he heard words like:

'. . . dying . . .'

'. . . Emergency. . .'

'. . . ambulance. . .'

One twitching hand touched the summons, now also spattered with blood.

He slumped back in his seat, his vision clouded red.

Reed felt as if he was going to vomit.

It never happened.

He was dead before his stomach managed the contraction.

Ninety-six

She wondered why she hadn't cried.

Catherine Reed sat on her sofa, legs drawn up beneath her, eyes staring blankly ahead.

Why?

It was nearly four hours now since she'd been informed of her brother's death, and yet still she found no tears filling her eyes. Where there should have been tears she felt only dazed bewilderment. Where there should have been pain she felt only a consuming emptiness.

Talbot himself had told her the news.

He hadn't been specific until she'd asked about the nature of the suicide.

399

Even then she'd felt merely a shudder, not the explosion of emotion she had expected.

She told herself she was in shock. The weeping would come. The realisation of loss.

For now she was numb.

Why had Frank been killed? Why had *his* picture been inside the Misfortune Box when it should have been hers?

Where *was* hers?

She glanced at her watch.

11.35 p.m.

Was her time yet to come?

Would she hurl herself from the window when the hands of her watch met at twelve?

Talbot had offered to leave men outside her flat.

To what purpose?

If she was going to die it would be by her own hand. No one could prevent it, short of tying her down. Even then, perhaps she could swallow her own tongue. When it came to taking life, the human mind was blessed with quite staggering powers of invention.

The phone had rung, the answering machine collecting messages of condolence.

She had not bothered to pick it up, not bothered to return any calls.

There would be plenty of time for that.

Wouldn't there?

What if at midnight . . .

She forced the thought from her mind.

Instead she got to her feet and crossed the room where she refilled her glass with Bacardi and Coke. A strong measure of the former.

'Frank,' she whispered under her breath.

Even mention of his name didn't bring the tears she expected. Tears she hoped for.

Shock.

She was heading back towards the sofa when the phone rang. Who the hell would call so late? she wondered.

The tone sounded unusually loud in the stillness of the room, then she heard a voice she knew only too well.

'Hello, Cath, it's me,' said Phillip Cross. 'I . . .'

She snatched up the phone.

'Phil,' she said, and suddenly the tears which she had thought locked away inside her broke free.

'What's wrong?' he said, worriedly.

'It's Frank,' she said. 'He's dead.'

'Oh Christ!' Cross murmured. 'Look, I'll be over in thirty minutes, let me get changed. I've just got back from that job in Glasgow.'

'I need you, Phil,' she said, her voice cracking.

'I'll be there,' he told her. 'Just take it easy. Thirty minutes.'

'I love you,' she said quietly.

He paused, unsure whether or not he'd heard the words correctly.

'I love you too, Cath,' he said, softly. 'See you soon.'

And he put down the phone.

So, Reed was dead, Cross thought as he pulled on his leather jacket.

He was out of her life. Out of *their* lives.

They'd always been close – too close. Cross had always felt feelings akin to jealousy for Cath's brother. He wondered if she'd have spoken those words had Frank still been alive.

'I love you.'

He smiled.

Now there was *only* him to love.

No competition.

Cross flipped open his wallet and pulled something from it.

A small piece of paper.

Shiny paper.

The torn half of a photo.

It showed Cath.

The other half had shown her brother.

That had been the half Cross had buried in the Misfortune Box.

Just as he'd learned.

Just as he had known that the photos of Neil Parriam, Craig Jeffrey and Peter Hyde had been buried close to their homes.

Cross had not buried those, but he had known who had.

They had worked.

Carrying the ripped photo of Cath, he wandered into the small room next to his bedroom. He'd been using it as a home dark-room for the last couple of years. Inside the smell of chemicals was strong.

There were photos in the developing trays. Some pinned to the thin wire which was stretched across the makeshift dark-room.

The ones which hung from the wire showed children.

Some as young as eighteen months.

Every child in every picture was naked.

Some were older, some bore bruises or scars.

There was a photograph of Shanine Connor pinned to the small cork noticeboard on one wall.

It had been sent to him three days earlier.

402

He knew what she looked like.

The network prided itself on its communications.

Her time was close.

He took down the photos from the wire, gathered them up and pushed them into one of the heavy metal drawers of a filing cabinet inside the dark-room. The ones in the tray of developer he rinsed, then clipped into position on the wire.

He would remove those when he returned from Cath's the next day.

They would be hidden with the others until they were needed.

Cath.

He locked the dark-room behind him, glancing at the tattered half of her picture.

Her image smiled back at him.

Cross carefully folded it and replaced it in his wallet, then he picked up his car keys and headed for the front door.

He had to hurry. She'd sounded upset.

She would have a lot to tell him.

Cross smiled.

She needed him.

When I fell from Grace,
I never realized,
How deep the flood was around me.

Queensrÿche

<u>CAPTIVES</u>

Shaun Hutson

The murders had been savage and apparently motiveless. Carbon copies of killings committed years earlier and by men currently incarcerated in one of Britain's top maximum security prisons. How could this be? Detective Inspector Frank Gregson must find the answers. Answers that will bring him into conflict with one of those prisoners, a man framed for a murder he didn't commit and determined to discover who framed him and why. These two obsessive men, on their private quests, will clash as they seek the truth that links Whitely Prison with London's seedy underworld of sex-shows and drug barons. One wants vengeance, the other wants the truth. What they discover threatens not only their lives but their sanity . . .

'The man who writes what others are afraid even to imagine'
Sunday Times

NEMESIS

Shaun Hutson

Sue and John Hackett are contemplating the ruins of their marriage. The brutal murder of their young daughter has brought an already strained relationship to breaking point, and to try to salvage their lives they retreat to the small peaceful town of Hinkston. But Hinkston isn't peaceful any more. It's being torn apart by a series of horrific, unexplained murders. And it holds a fateful, fifty-year-old secret – a secret with such appalling consequences that it was supposed to have died during the war. It didn't . . .

☐	Assassin	Shaun Hutson	£4.99
☐	Captives	Shaun Hutson	£4.99
☐	Deadhead	Shaun Hutson	£4.99
☐	Death Day	Shaun Hutson	£5.99
☐	Erebus	Shaun Hutson	£4.99
☐	Heathen	Shaun Hutson	£5.99
☐	Nemesis	Shaun Hutson	£4.99
☐	Relics	Shaun Hutson	£4.99
☐	Renegades	Shaun Hutson	£4.99
☐	White Ghost	Shaun Hutson	£5.99

Warner Books now offers an exciting range of quality titles by
both established and new authors. All of the books in this
series are available from:

Little, Brown and Company (UK),
P.O. Box 11,
Falmouth,
Cornwall TR10 9EN.
Telephone No: 01326 317200
Fax No: 01326 317444
E-mail: books@barni.avel.co.uk

Payments can be made as follows: cheque, postal order
(payable to Little, Brown and Company) or by credit cards,
Visa/Access. Do not send cash or currency. UK customers and
B.F.P.O. please allow £1.00 for postage and packing for the
first book, plus 50p for the second book, plus 30p for each
additional book up to a maximum charge of £3.00 (7 books
plus).

Overseas customers including Ireland, please allow £2.00 for
the first book plus £1.00 for the second book, plus 50p for each
additional book.

NAME (Block Letters) ....

....

ADDRESS ....

....

....

☐ I enclose my remittance for ....

☐ I wish to pay by Access/Visa Card

Number ☐☐☐☐☐☐☐☐☐☐☐☐☐☐☐☐

Card Expiry Date ☐☐☐☐